Once Upon a Crush

Kailee Barton

Contents

Chapter 1

4 Years Ago

"Macey!" I hear my mom call from downstairs. "The Chapmens are leaving, come say goodbye!"

Yeah sure. I'll come say goodbye to the soon-to-be famous actor/heartthrob.

It's bitter-sweet for me. Bitter because I have to lose my best friend, Adrian. Sweet because his dreams of becoming an actor is coming true and I'm happy for him.

"Coming!" I call back. I shut my laptop and head downstairs. The adults' laughter echoes throughout the whole house.

"Oh, Connie! I'm going to miss you so much!" I heard my mom say with a strained voice.

"Don't worry, Liz! We'll visit when we can!" Adrian's mom assured. At the end of the stairway I saw them clutching each other tightly with tears streaming down their face.

"Dave." My dad says holding out a hand.

"Scott." Adrian's dad says taking his hand and pulling him into a man hug.

I bite my lip hard to resist the tears. I don't want to see them go either, they're like my second parents. They took care of me when my dad and mom were late coming home. We spent many holidays with them too as well as many vactaions.

Connie and Dave turn towards my older sister, Emma, and give her a hug.

"Oh, Emma!" Connie cooed hugging her tight.

"Good lucky in college, Em!" Dave said patting her back.

"Thanks Connie, Thanks Dave. Tell Kelly I said hi! If she ever gets married soon you have to let us know!" Emma sniffed. Kelly is Adrian's sister and Emma's best friend in the whole world. Kelly's attending fashion school in NYC and will be moving to Hollywood once she graduates. She left a week ago so she could get settled in New York.

"Of course, sweetie!" Connie exclaimed bringing her into another hug and seeing me over her shoulder.

"Macey, dear!" Connie gasped motioning me over to her. I walked over to her as she pulled me into her arms, stroking my hair.

"We're going to miss you, Mace!" Connie sobbed.

"I'm going to miss you guys too." I squeaked. Now I couldn't hold the tears back. She pulled away and held my face in between her hands. "Don't you worry okay? We'll stay in touch and make sure our Adrian doesn't turn into a conceited snob!"

I had to laugh at her words. Those were some of the reasons I'm afraid is going to happen. Adrian's not that kind of guy to have a massive change like that but you never know. He was going to famous for God's sake.

I turn to Dave and give him a hug too. "Take care, kiddo. Do good in school, okay? And no drugs!" Dave said while ruffling my hair.

"Yes sir!" I laugh.

"Now, the girls and I baked something for you guys before you leave! Scott even helped." My mom said motioning to the kitchen. I laugh at the last part. All my dad did was take the cookies and cupcakes out of the oven.

Everyone went into the kitchen while I stayed in the living room. I felt something tackle me from behind, arms wrapping around my waist and lifting me into the air while spinning. I let out an embarrassing scream.

"Adrian! Put me down!" I shriek between laughs. Adrian spins me a few more times before setting me on my feet. I slap his hands away and turn to my laughing best friend.

"Ugh. I hate you." I groan rubbing my now soar sides.

"No, you don't. You love me." Adrian smirked wrapping his arms around my waist and pulling me towards him again.

I wrap my arms around his neck and hug him tightly.

"I'm gonna miss you." I mumble into his shoulder.

"I'm gonna miss you too, Mace." He said hugging me tighter. Adrian pulled back and took a small box out of his pocket, handing it to me. "Here."

I take the box from him, frowning. "You didn't have to get me anything." I tell him.

"I know. But I wanted to." Adrian shoved his hands into his pocket and smiled. The smile that made me fall for him in the first place ever since we met when we were little. Inside the box is a silver necklace with a heart pendant and my name engraved in it.

"Oh my god.." I gasped. Adrian smiles as he picks it up and goes around to put it around my neck. I hold it in my hand and observe it. I feel Adrian's arms wrap around my waist pulling me so my back was against his chest, his chin laying on my shoulder.

"Thanks Adrian.." I say looking at him from over my shoulder. I felt Adrian kiss my cheek lightly.

"You're my best friend Macey Daniels and I love you. Don't ever forget that." He said quitely. I turn around and gave him another hug.

"I love you too.."

Present Day

I groan as I type furiously on the keyboard of my laptop. A few weeks into the school year and I'm trying to figure out how to do my stupid math homework because our oh-so genius teacher didn't teach us how to do our homework. Not the sarcasm. I was about to click enter when a window pops up.

'Its_A_Secret_391 wants to chat with you'

I frown at the computer screen and hesitate for a second, debating if I should accept it or not. It's better than homework. Math homework. I click 'Accept' and the chat bar pops up.

Him: Hello :)

Me: Umm.. Hi?

Him: How are you?

Me: Good..

Ok.. Normal small talk.. Nothing creepy.

Him: I'm really excited :)

Me: Why?

Him: To see you.

I froze. Ah, damn it. Spoke to soon.

Me: Umm.. Excuse me?

Him: I can't wait to see you again.

Me: Wait.. Who is this..?

Him: Username says it all, babe ;)

Me: Oh great. You're a stalker?

Him: Not necessarily.

Me: Right.. I'm going to go now.

There. I'm not talking to this creep anymore. Could be a rapist for all I know.

I pick up my water and drink as I wait for his response.

Him: Ok. See you soon, my sweet Macey :)

And what did you think I did there, drinking water and finding out this person knows my name? Yup. I choked on my water and did a spit take. Luckily, I turned away from my laptop when I did. I pounded my chest while coughing severely as I typed back to him.

Me: Who the hell is this?!

Him: Goodnight, Mace :)

The chat disappeared and I stare at it for a few seconds. I close my laptop and fall onto my bed covering my face with my hands. Great. Just great. Now some stalker knows my name. Who the hell was that?! I sigh and go under my covers, turning off my lamp.

Sweet Macey. Only one person and one person only has called me that. It couldn't be him though, right? I let out another sigh and buried my face into my pillow.

This is going to bother me all night..

"Macey Daniels get up right now!" I heared my mom call from downstairs. I jolt awake before falling back onto my back.

I groan before yelling back, "Okay, mom!"

Lazily, I get up from bed and trudge towards my closet. After changing into a light purple hoodie and some shorts, I head downstairs, shaking out the braid I slept in.

"Morning, mom." I say as I enter the kitchen.

"Eat up, sweetie! I got to get to the hospital early today." My mom informs me as she kisses the top of my head. "Brynn's giving you a ride, right?"

"Yup. Oh and after school I'm helping out at that big animal adoption." I tell her in between mouthfuls of cereal.

"Oh.. Well, come home as soon as possible okay? After an hour or so. We're throwing a little welcome back party for some old friends." My mom mumbled into her coffee and avoiding my gaze. I frown at her as I roll up my sleeves.

"Which old friends?" I ask.

"Well.."

A car honking cuts her off.

"Woops got to go!" I say putting my bowl in the sink and grabbing my backpack. I kiss my mom on the cheek and made my way towards the front door. "Tell dad I said bye! See you later!" I called over my shoulder and rushing out of the door to find Brynn honking over and over.

"Brynn! Shut the hell up will you? We don't want the neighbors to complain again!" I hiss as I get in the car. Brynn flipped her medium long blonde hair behind her shoulder and glanced at me with her green piercing eyes. Being the crazy girl that she is last week, the Morenos from down the street called to complain on Brynn's continuous honking.

"Sorry!" Brynn laughs while driving out of my neighrborhood.

"No, you're not." I mumbled with a smile. No matter how many times I tell her to stop, the honking never ceases. It's our morning routine and Brynn's not a girl of change.

Brynn leaned forward and turned the radio on before flashing me a smile. "Yeah, you're right." Brynn's iPod was already hooked up to the radio. We listened to her playlist all the way to school which just so happens to be a lot of One Direction. Francis High comes into sight soon after. Teenagers were lingering outside and posters made by the student council are hung on the poles and walls.

Brynn gasps and turns down the volume. "Did you hear?" She asks in full excitement as she parks the car into the school parking lot. We get out and head towards the school.

"Hear about—"

"Macey! Brynn!" A voice calls out. We stopped in our tracks and turn to face Amber jogging towards us. "Hey guys!" Amber greets us. Amber is my other best friend. She has long brown hair that goes all the way down to her waist. She's also wicked smart and a bit of a dork, which is what we love about her. She's also the most peppy one of the group.

"Hey. Brynn and I say together. We walk into the school and I stop in my tracks. Everyone is running around in a rush, crowding the hallways and girls are jumping up and down with their eyes wide and goofy smiles plastered on their face. I grab Brynn and Amber's wrists and pull them through the crowd. Once we get past the crowd of excited teenagers I head towards my locker.

"What the hell is going on?" I ask in deep confusion as I open my locker. "Why's everyone freaking—"

"Ahh! He's here!" A girl shrieks. About the whole schools runs towards the door. From the giant window at the front of our school I see a limo pull up.

"What's with the limo? What's going on?" I shout through the screams.

"This is what I was asking you about!" Brynn shouts back.

"An actor is attending Francis High!" Amber squealed.

"And he's super cute!" Brynn adds.

"No way!" I gasp. It's cool that a star is attending our school but I wasn't going to be one of those people that drool and stalk him.

We watch the commotion outside from my locker. By now there was a humongous crowd outside and I could even see some paparazzi outside with their cameras. Some girls started screaming and jumping with glee and the cameras started to flash. After a few minutes later people start to run towards the door, starstruck teenagers entering the school.

"So, who is it?" I ask closing my locker and turning my back to the entrance.

The high pitched screams begin again and there's a lot flashes going off.

"It's..." Brynn shouts but I couldn't hear the last part.

"What?!"

"It's A..." Amber shouts, her voice getting lost in the multiple screams echoing through the school.

"Who?!"

Amber and Brynn exchange irritated looks and they both yell, "IT'S—"

"Woah!" I yell when someone rams into me. Somebody grabs me by the waist and keeps me from falling. I open my eyes and I freeze. My eyes widen, my mouth drops open, my breathing quickens, and my heart skips a beat as I lock eyes with a very familiar face. A face I haven't seen in 4 years other than through media, is standing right in front of me.

Oh Crap...

"Adrian?" I gasp.

"Macey?" Adrian asks, his mouth drifting open and his eyes widening.

A circle of people forms around us and the screams die down a bit. I feel their eyes staring at me. I, Macey Daniels, in the arms of the famous Adrian Chapmen. Adrian realizes that he's practically dipping me so he pulls me up so I'm on my feet again. The thing is, he didn't let go. Nope. He actually pulled me closer to him. Adrian kept his arms wrapped around my waist with my hands at his shoulders. I just stared back at him in utter shock and he stared back at me with total surprise.

"Mace.. Is that really you?" Adrian asked quietly.

"I.. I-I.. um.. well.." I stuttered, struggling to find my words. Just then, the bell rang.

Thank the Lord! Saved by the bell!

"Got to go!" I said nervously breaking away from him, grabbing Brynn's wrist, and pulling through the crowd of gawking teenagers to our next class: English. I rushed through the hallways and into Mrs. Fuller's class. I took my seat quickly and buried my head in my arms on the desk. Brynn places her things at her seat (which happens to be right next to me) and towers over me.

"Macey Daniels look at me right now." She ordered.

I look up at her.

"What. The. Hell. Was. That." Brynn said slowly.

"What do you mean?"

"What do I mean? I mean the famous Adrian Chapmen knowing your name and looking at you like the way he did!" She whisper-shouted.

"I.." My gaze focused to the door when Adrian coming through it. "Crap, crap, crap, crap!" I buried my head back down into my arms.

"Macey!" Brynn whined shaking my shoulder.

The bell rang signaling for everyone to scurry into the classroom and take their seats. Mrs. Fuller gets up from behind her desk and shook Adrian's hand. Mrs. Fuller was the best teacher ever. She taught us but still wasn't that strict nagging teacher that everyone hated. With Mrs. Fuller we could talk, eat, go on our phones and whatever else we wanted as long as we did our work.

"Okay, guys." Mrs. Fuller said going to the front of the class. "As you may know, this is Adrian." She said gesturing to Adrian. He smiled and waved to the class. Adrian's eyes landed on me and I quickly averted my gaze.

"I want you to treat him like a normal student okay?" The class nodded and agreed. "Yes? Great! Adrian just sit next to Andrew." Adrian nodded and went to sit next to Andrew. Luckily he was at the other side of the room. Mrs. Fuller told us the assignment for the day and it went on from there. I glanced at Adrian to see him working with some of the other guys in our class. I sighed and turned toward Brynn. She wrote something on her paper and then turned to face me.

"Spill." Brynn demanded.

I took a deep breathe and told her about Adrian and I when we were younger till the day he had to leave for Los Angeles.

"Wait. Is he the guy that gave you that necklace?" Brynn asked pointing to the pendant around my neck. I nodded.

"Aww!" Brynn cooed hugging me.

"No! Not 'Aww'. What if he's a total jerk. What if the fame got to his head and he's not the same Adrian?" I question pulling away from her and starting on the assignment. "Or what if he ends up hating me because I'm.. me? Normal me!"

"I don't know, Mace.." Brynn said smiling. "The way he was looking at you in the hall looked like he was really happy to see you. And him holding you in his arms. Holding you close." Brynn wiggled her eyebrows and poked me multiple times.

I narrowed my eyes at her before poking her in the side so she squealed loudly. It just so happened to catch Adrian's attention. He looked at Brynn and then at me. I looked away quickly, hiding behind my hair.

"Brynn!" I scold.

"You poked me!" She said in defense. "Tickle me and I am not responsible for you injuries!"

"And what about the fact that he's been checking you out all period?" She added, directing back to our previous conversation. Brynn can be so persistent when she wants to.

"Okay, look. He looked at me in suprise and held me in shock." I say getting up to turn in my assignment with Brynn after me.

"Oh, please! You should've seen him from another set of eyes. I also saw Cammie scowling at the fact that you were so close together." Brynn sang. I rolled my eyes and turned around to start walking, only to run into someone.

"Woah there!" The owner of the voice said grabbing me by the waist.

"Oh sorry! I'm so sorry I..." My voice trailed off as I saw it was Adrian. My face heated up when I realized how close we were.

I felt eyes land on us again and I could see Brynn smiling like an idiot from the corner of my eye.

"It's okay." Adrian whispered, smiling a little. I let out a nervous laugh as his gaze dropped down to the necklace. His necklace.

"Sorry again for running into you." I apologize, giving him a small smile.

"Don't worry about it." Adrian assures, slowly taking his hands off my waist. I give him a small nod and walk back to my seat. Once I'm sure he's not staring at me anymore I turn towards Brynn and bury my face into her shoulder.

"This is going to be a long day.." I mumble.

Chapter 2

Macey's POV

After avoiding Adrian from 3 of my classes that he just happened to be in, it's finally lunch.

"Tell me, tell me, tell me, tell me!" Amber begged.

"I've explained this already! To Brynn!" I groan putting my food down at our table.

"So you told Brynn but you won't tell me?!"

"I'd be happy to tell you, Ams!" Brynn insists with an evil smile.

"Ooo! I want to hear this too. Can I?" My other friend, Dylan, asks as she sits next to Brynn. Like Brynn, Dylan's hair is medium long but brown with blonde dyed at the ends. She's just as crazy, idiotic, and weird as the others. But nonetheless, you gotta love them.

"Gladly." Brynn says smiling sweetly at me.

I shoot her a glare. "Did I even say you can tell them?"

"Nope! Too bad!" Brynn sticks her tongue at me and then turns to explain my whole history with Adrian. Amber and Dylan nod, squeal, or awe at every thing Brynn has to say. I listen just to make sure Brynn doesn't exaggerate anything.

"Oh my God!" Dylan gasps turning to me. "He gave you that necklace?" She demands with a dramatic surprise face.

"So what? It's not the most shocking thing in the world! He got me a farewell present and I still wear it to this day. Nothing's going to happen while he's here, guys." I confirm.

"You wait and see." Amber sings. "He's going to fall for you and then you're going to have happy fun time and—" Amber jumps out of her seat as I choke on my drink at the phrase 'happy fun time'. I pound my chest feverishly while Brynn and Dylan laugh their asses off. Apparently me have a coughing fit caught many peoples' attention. I felt a hand on my back.

"You okay?" A voice asks. I turn around, startled to see Adrian standing in front of me with a worried smile.

"Yeah. I'm.. I'm fine" I say in between coughs pounding my chest. I give Amber a death glare and Brynn has finally stopped laughing but Dylan was still giggling.

Adrian pats me on the back before turning to my soon-to-be dead friends.

"Hi, I'm Adrian." he introduces himself.

"Brynn." Brynn tells with a smile.

"Amber." Amber adds doing a peace sign.

"Dylan." Dylan said once sober.

"Nice to meet you guys. What happened over here?" Adrian switches his gaze to me. I avoid his stare.

"I told Macey she was going to have happy fun time in the future and she choked." Amber explained holding back a laugh. Brynn however, burst out laughing.

"Amber!" I hiss.

"Oh, really?" Adrian chuckles.

"Nope! No, no she's very confused and an idiot." I object. I punch her shoulder

"Macey's going to have 'happy fun time with you'!" Dylan laughed, clutching her stomach. My mouth drops to the floor and I could feel my face burning.

Adrian raises an eyebrow at me. People are staring at us again, making me panic.

"I um.. Oh look at that, food's done! Got to go, bye!" I rush grabbing my laughing friends pulling them roughly outside. Once we're out of the cafeteria and I let go of their arms and turn to face them.

"You guys are so dead!" I yell while jabbing Brynn's side. Brynn starts shrieking and laughing while slapping my arms.

"Stop! Macey stop!" Brynn pleaded. I turn around and start tickling Dylan as well. Just then the ball rang. Dylan grabbed my arms saying

"Have fun in gym!" And ran away with Brynn. I whip around to face Amber. Her eyes widen before she darts towards the girls locker room. I roll my eyes and go after her.

"Let's go! It's a jog not a walk!" Our teacher, Mr. Powell, yells. We're running our daily laps around the blacktop under the beating sun.

"Macey! Wait!" I hear Amber yell after me. I walk a few steps and continue jogging once Amber is right next to me.

"You're still dead, you know." I point out.

"Okay fine but seriously, that was hilarious." Amanda replies with a smile.

"For you, Brynn, and Dylan! I'm glad my embarrassment entertains you." I say sarcastically getting a laugh from Amber.

"I'll probably tell James you like him even though you hate his guts." I smirk.

"No!" Amber gasps quickly. "No no no no! Please no!" I laugh at her quick plead.

"Alright, that's enough!" Mr. Powell yells. We all stop and walk towards him. "Walk, play basketball or something, do whatever." He orders. Today's our do whatever day. It's too hot to do anything.

"Adrian's in this class. You know that right?" Amber says as we sit down under a tree.

"He is?" I groan, looking around. I spot him shooting hoops with some guys. "That's the fourth period today!"

Amber gasps. "It's fate!" She exclaims dramatically.

"Yup. That's it. I'm telling James." I decided. Amber's face contorts into disgusted horror, making me laugh.

Adrian's POV

"Nice!" I clap my hands together as one of the guys makes a three pointer.

"Your turn, dude." The boy, Bradley, nods as he throws me the ball. I go to the three point line, shoot, and of course, make it. The guys yell and high five me. I could tell who's with me because of my fame and those who could care less. I look around observing the blacktop and field. I spot a fimilar figure leaning against a tree talking to someone.

Macey.

She's been avoiding me the whole day and I have no clue as to why. I could see now that she's talking to Amber, the one who mentioned the 'happy fun time' and made Macey choke at lunch. I laugh and shake my head. Macey's the way I left her 4 years ago but somethings are different.

For one thing, she's a lot hotter than I remember. Yeah sure, I always had a slight crush on Macey when we were children but now it's different. I can tell Macey's still that happy playful girl she was when we were younger. And of course, there's those other features that change as time flies by. Her brown hair's longer, she's taller, but she's maintained that model figure that me and her dad used to tease her about becoming a supermodel one day. Only difference is: Macey's no slut like some of the other girls strutting around here in their tights and very low tops since there is no gym uniform.

"You done checking Daniels out, bro?" a voice snaps me out of my daze. I suddenly felt embarrassed now that I realized I had been checking out Macey for a good 10 minutes. I turn around to see the owner of the voice and see another familiar fac with brown hair that fell down to his eyebrows and hazel eyes.

"Chase?" I ask with a smile.

"Yeah man! What you been up to?" Chase asks patting me on the back.

"Becoming a famous actor and one of the hottest dudes in the country, if I do say so myself. Nothing much." I say shrugging.

"Getting cocky, are we?" Chase smirked.

"It happens." I chuckle. "So how's your girl? Vanessa was it?" Chase hung out with Macey and I through middle school. Near the end of 8th grade he started dating a girl named Vanessa and spent all his time with her.

"Oh, her." Chase said picking up a ball and making a basket. "We broke up during sophomore year. Just wasn't the right girl."

"Ah," I nod stealing the ball from him and shooting it into the hoop.

"Speaking of the right girls.." Chase laid his arm on my shoulder and looked in Macey's direction. I feel the sudden embarrassment again as I remember how I just checked her out not too long ago. "You still haven't hooked up with Mace? After all those years?" Chase said in disbelief. Chase was one of the people that knew I had a crush on Macey.

"No. We grew apart when I left for Los Angeles and we never really considered going out before that." I explain looking over at Macey and Amber who seem to be laughing. Another thing that hasn't changed about Macey is how her face lights up when she laughs or smiles. It makes her look 10 times more beautiful.

"You're staring."

"I am not."

"Dude. You got to admit." Chase places his hands on my shoulder and turns my whole body to their direction. "She's gotten hotter."

We watch Macey and Amber for a few seconds. They seem to be fighting about something but they're laughing.

"Okay, so she's gotten hotter." I admit. So what?"

"So go talk to her!" Chase ordered giving me a shove.

"I can't just do that." I say turning around and throwing another ball into the hoop.

"And why not?"

"Because she's been avoiding me all day. Trying anyways. She's probably holding a grudge on me or something."

"Macey? Your sweet little Macey Daniels holding a grudge on you? Please." Chase rolled his eyes. "Grow some balls and get over there."

I open my mouth to object but Chase cuts me off.

"Macey!" Chase calls out loudly that half the people outside stop to look at us.

"Dude!" I snap. Chase wraps his arm around my neck and urges me forward. Macey steps away from the tree and Amber stares at us with a confused expression.

"Hello, ladies!" Chase once we're standing in front of them.

"Um.. Hi?" Amber greets awkwardly. "Can we help you?"

"Yes actually!" Chase walks over to Macey, still choking me forward, and puts his other arm around her. "Mace! Say hi to our old friend, Adrian?" He asks with a smile.

"Yes." Macey shifts uncomfortably and glares at Chase.

"Well you two should have some.." Chase pushes Macey forward so she stumbles closer me. "Catching up to do, am I right?" He finishes, wiggling his eyebrows at us.

"Ever heard of the rule 'Keep your hands to yourself'?" Amber asks in disgust.

"I don't follow the rules, babe." Chase winks.

"Ew!" Amber gags. Then she raises an eyebrow at Macey and pushes her against me. I catch her by instict.

"Amber!" Macey snaps.

"Who's not following the rules now, hmm?" Chase aks crossing his arms.

"Have some happy fun time!" Amber laughs.

Macey's mouth drops open before yelling, "JAMES! AMBER LI–" Amber clamps her hand over her mouth.

"Don't you dare tell– EW!" Amber screams jumping back, wiping her hand on her shirt. "You spit on my hand!" she whines.

"Well you put your filthy hands on my mouth."

A whistle goes off and we all look at Mr. Powell. "Put the balls away and line up!" He yells. Macey immediately backs away and grabs Amber's wrist. "Let's go." she ordered and stalked away.

Once they're farther away I turn to Chase. "See,"

"Okay maybe she's just shocked that you here. Being famous and all maybe she's starstruck." Chase suggested as we walked towards the boys locker room.

"That definitely does not sound like Macey." I mumble.

Macey's POV

"You guys are total idiots!" I scold as I walk ahead.

"Oh come on! We didn't do anything that bad!" Dylan objected while lightly pushing my shoulder.

"You told him I wanted to have happy fun time with him!" I throw my hands in the air.

All three of them start laughing hysterically as we approach the big adoption event. Their laughing died down as we entered the animal shelter.

"Hannah? We're here!" Amber called out. Brynn went up to the counter and took a sucker out of the bowl of candies.

"Girls?" A voice came from down the hallway. "Down here!"

We walk down the hallway and through the backdoor. "Oh, cool!" Dylan awed. The big backyard that the animals used to play in is now decorated. Balloons lined with paw prints are tied to the fence around the yard, tables are set up with food, water, and cages containing different animals. In the middle are small pens where different breeds of dogs were put. Down at the other end of the yard were kiddie pools filled with water so we can wash the animals before they were sent home to their new families.

"Girls! I'm glad you can make it!" A voice says behind us. I turn around to see a smiling Hannah with a t-shirt that says "We Love Animals" on the front. "Before I assign you your positions for the next hour, I have something for you!"

The four of us exchange looks as we walk toa table with a cardboard box sitting on top. Hannah opened it and handed me a jacket. I opened it up so I can see it better. It was a hoodie with my name on the front, on the back was the Animal Shelter's logo. She gave Brynn, Dylan, and Amber a hoodie with their names sewn on too.

"Aww thanks, Hannah!" I say giving her a hug.

"No problem, darlings! Now let me tell you where your stations are, people are arriving!"

From the last hour, I had helped families with picking out their dogs. So far 7 lucky pups went home with new families. Amber helped out with the bunnies and hamsters, Dylan was selling food and helped with customers' needs, and Brynn was giving the dogs a bath before sending them to their new homes.

"Macey, honey? Can you help Brynn wash some of the dogs? She could use a little help." Hannah asked pointing to Brynn who was struggling to get a Labrador into the kiddie pool.

"Sure thing." I chuckled, rolling up my sleeves and heading to Brynn. "Need some help?"

"Well no shit, Sherlock!" Brynn groaned grabbing the dog by the collar.

"You got it, Goldilocks!" I laugh. Brynn gives me a look before turning her attention to the dog. I help keep the Labrador in the pool while Brynn quickly shampoos him. Once we finish wrestling with the dog, we hand him over to his new owners.

Brynn and I wash the dogs, getting help from Dylan and Amber when we get some difficult dog. I start washing off the soap on a small poodle when I hear a high pitched scream. I turn and end up rolling on the floor laughing as I see a big German Shepherd pinning Brynn to the floor.

"Get it off!" Brynn shrieked. Dylan comes running over and tries to get the dog off but since she's laughing to hard, she fails. Amber and I come to her rescue and pull the dog off of her. Only for it to jump on to Amber, making Dylan and I laugh until tears come out.

"Guys! Get him off he's dripping on me!" Amber yelled. After pulling the giant dog off of our friend, I hold him firmly by his leash. I felt my phone vibrate in my pocket and I let go, only to have him pounce on Dylan.

"Really?!" Dylan screams.

"Karma!" I laugh getting up and taking my phone out of my pocket to see my mom calling.

"Hello?" I answer

"Macey? Macey where are you? I told you to be here quick! They're already here!" my mom said quickly.

They..? I think for a second before remembering the conversation with my mom before Brynn's annoying honking interrupted us.

"Oh! The welcome back party! I totally forgot mom I'll be home soon!"

"Okay but hurry. And bring Lulu!" She adds before hanging up.

I turn around to see Amber and Brynn hauling the dog off of Dylan. "Guys I got to go. I'll call you guys later!" I tell them before running off to find Hannah.

"Hannah! I got to go, can I take Lulu with me now?" I ask running up to Hannah.

"Yeah sure thing, hon." Hannah puts down a hamster before we walk into the animal shelter and into the kennel.

"She's all ready to go, her treatment's done." Hannah explained taking out my little golden retriever, Lulu, out of her cage.

"Thanks, Hannah." I say as hook a leash onto Lulu's collar.

"No problem, doll. Why do you have to leave suddenly?"

"Oh, we're having a welcome back party for some old friends." I tell her, walking to the front door.

"Really? Who is it?"

"I'm not sure." I chuckle. "Thanks for helping Lulu. Bye!" I rush out to the street and down the sidewalk.

As I approach my house 20 minutes later, Lulu starts getting a little jumpy and excited. I laugh as she pulls on her leash for me to hurry up.

"Alright, alright!" I chuckle picking up my pace. A car is parked in our drive way. At the front door, I reach into my backpack for the house keys, losing the grip on Lulu's leash. Lulu takes advantage of that and runs around in my front yard. I give up the scavenger hunt in my backpack and ring the doorbell. I turn around to see Lulu jumping in a mud puddle made from the broken sprinkler.

"Lulu no! You're getting dirty!" I scold walking up to her. She barks as the door opens and sprints toward it.

"Lulu!" I call after her as I start towards the house. When I get inside, I see muddy footprints heading down the hallway and Emma holding Lulu in her arms.

"Emma?" I ask confused.

"Macey!" Emma gasps bringing me into a small side hug.

"You're the 'old friend' we're throwing a welcome back part for?" I laugh. Emma grabs a towel from one of the closets and wipes the mud off of Lulu before setting her down again. Emma slings an arm around my shoulder and pulls me towards the living room. Laughter seems to fill the house.

"Not exactly." Emma sang with a wide smile. I raise an eyebrow at her and let her lead me down the hallway.

"Guess who's here!" Emma announced once we entered the living room. I froze in my spot and mentally slapped myself. Sitting in my living room with my parents is the entire Chapmen family. How did I not put this together?

Connie's wearing a sundress with pearl jewelry, Dave's in a button down shirt and khakis, and Adrian's leaning against the door frame of our kitchen wearing a muscle shirt and some jean shorts. Even Kelly, who turned out to be a successful fashion designer, was sitting next to a guy I have never seen before and wearing a pink floral lace dress.

Everyone stared at me, waiting for a response. Everyone was dressed up for the BBQ party and my clothes were a bit soggy from the dog baths I had to give. I'm almost positive I smell like animal. I saw Adrian hide a smile from the corner of my eye.

Act casual.

"Hey!" I greeted happily, throwing my hands in the air. Connie got up and ran to give me a tight hug.

"Oh Macey!" She cooed pulling back so she can take a closer look. "Look how much you've grown! You look so beautiful!"

"You too, Connie." I tell her honestly.

I turned to Dave and gave him a hug too.

"Look at you, kiddo!" Dave let out a hearty laugh while patting me on the back. "Doing good in school? No drugs?" He pointed a finger at me.

I put my hands up in defense. "I actually got straight A's last semester and still on a drug free life!"

"That's our girl!" Dave ruffled my hair.

"Kelly!" I exclaim when Kelly stands up to give me a hug.

"Aww Macey! I haven't seen you in so long!" She gushed. "Oh and this is my boyfriend, Oliver." Kelly introduced. Oliver was tall with a brown buzz hair cut and a friendly smile. "He's a photographer."

"Nice to meet you." I shook his hand before looking over at Adrian who is now smiling at me from the doorway. I've seen Adrian before on TV or magazines. Seeing him in person Adrian was taller. Other than everything else was the same. The same hair, the built body, hazel eyes, and every other feature that all the girls drooled over. One thing that was kept the same after 4 years is that smile.

I'm not going to lie, Adrian's really cute. We didn't say anything to each other but merely just stared.

"I was expecting a better reunion than a staring contest." My dad pointed out from the couch.

"Oh." I murmured looking away. "We kinda met at school already."

"That's great! Now you two can catch up and have study dates together." My mom decided. "In fact, why don't you two catch up right now?"

"No!" I said a bit too quickly. "I mean.. I can't. I have to.."

Think Macey!

I hear a bark come up from behind me. I turn around and see Lulu with dried mud stuck in her fur. "Clean Lulu." I confirmed, turning back to the others. "I have to give Lulu a bath."

"Adrian can help you," Kelly suggested with a sly smile.

"Oh no he doesn't have to-"

"Actually,"Adrian cut me off."I would love to help you bathe Lulu, Macey." Adrian said with a glint of amusement in his eyes.

"Macey. Let him help you." My mom said sternly.

"Alright fine." I mutter, turning on my heels.

This was going to be a long night.

Chapter 3

"Lulu! Stay still!" I scold as I push Lulu back into the bathtub for the hundredth time. Adrian laughs as she jumps on to the side again and splashes even more water on us. My clothes went from soggy to soaking in just a few minutes of bathing her and there's a mini flood in the bathroom. Adrian, on the other hand, seems to be enjoying getting splashed with dog water while kneeling in a small puddle.

Lulu jumps back on the side and shakes her fur out. "Lulu!" I groan.

Adrian laughs and points at Lulu. "Bad girl! Get back in the tub and stay!" Obediently, Lulu jumps back into the tub and stays put.

"Oh, okay. I'll just call Adrian over the next time you don't listen to me." I mumble as Adrian begins to scrub her fur. I take the shower head and wash the soap off.

"Didn't you hear? I became a dog whisperer in the last four years I've been gone." He teases. Lulu looks up and starts to slap the water, grunting.

"She's usually not like this, you know." I tell him.

"Oh yeah?"

"Yup."

"And why is that?"

"Hmm.." I raise the shower head higher as Lulu begins to get jumpy again. "Maybe it's because of the presence of a famous star." I gasp dramatically.

"So I steal the hearts of girls and dogs as well, huh?" Adrian chuckles splashing me with water.

I quickly flick the shower head in his direction so it wets him a little. "Gotten cocky, Adrian?"

Adrian stands up and looks at his wet shirt. "Hey! Easy on the water, Mace. I have people to woo later."

I roll my eyes as turn off the water before turning around to get a towel. "Adrian!" I exclaim. A shirtless Adrian was standing over the sink, wringing his damp shirt.

"What? Oh come on, Mace. You've seen me shirtless before." He tells me.

That's true, I've seen him shirtless before many times. Four years ago, that is. My eyes wonder down to his six pack and toned biceps that wasn't there back then. Adrian used to be just skinny now he's all built. Adrian leans back against the counter and smiles at me. "You done checking me out?"

I scoff and push him aside so I can get a towel out of the drawer. "How did you become so cocky and egotistic over four years?"

He holds my gaze for what seemed like forever, his brown eyes boring into mine. "It's a secret, babe." Adrian winked at me. I narrowed my eyes at him before realizing the username that I talked to last night. I gasped.

"You were that guy I was talking to last night, weren't you?"

"Well, haven't you gotten slower over the years." Adrian smirked. I rolled my eyes and whipped him with the towel.

"A big ego isn't good for a person, Adrian." I state coldly before walking past him.

"Mace, I–"

"Lulu!" I cried out when she jumped out of the tub. Lulu dashes out the door, tripping me in the process. I stumbled into Adrian's hard chest.

"You really need to stop falling for me." He snickered. I glared at him before tearing out of his arms and running out of the bathroom. I almost slipped over Lulu's wet trail a few times. I heard a few screams and hollers from the living room. I ran in and found Lulu sprinting around the room with people sitting on the couches and their feet up.

I ran after her but she started running like a madman. "Lulu!" I called out. "Lulu, what are you doing?!" Lulu ran into the kitchen and swerved between Kelly and Emma's legs. Adrian ran into the kitchen, still shirtless, and tried to catch her. Only to run right into me and almost making me fall if not for him clamping his hands on my waist.

"Maybe you should stop running into me." I scowled. I pushed past him and went after Lulu who had ran back to the living room. My dad and Dave stood up and tried to grab her but Lulu dodged their arms. Everyone began to call her name and tried to catch her. Somehow, Lulu escaped all nine of us.

I stopped and groaned, trying to think of how to get hold of my psycho dog. I suddenly remembered something and ran into the kitchen. I dug through 3 drawers before I found the old dog whistle that I used to train Lulu and some of the dogs in the shelter. I grabbed a dog biscuit on the way to the living room.

I blew into the whistle just as Lulu was about to enter the kitchen. She stopped and tilted her head at me.

"Sit." I ordered firmly, pointing to the floor. Lulu obeyed. I kneeled down and picked her up. I gave her the treat and sighed. "Good girl." Everyone started to laugh and sigh in relief. Dad came up to me and ruffled Lulu's soggy fur. "Well, isn't she energetic today? Wonder why."

I glanced at Adrian who was leaning against the door frame still without a shirt. Everyone switched their gaze to Adrian. "Sweetie, where's your shirt?" Connie asked, quirking an eyebrow.

Adrian scratched the back of his head nervously. "Uh.. Upstairs." He laughed shakily.

Kelly raised an eyebrow at her little brother. "What were you two doing up there?" she laughed. Adrian's face turned red and I snickered, clamping a hand over my mouth. Emma laughed, coming to my side to wrap an arm around my shoulder. I simply shrugged at Adrian's death glare.

"I think she likes it." Adrian points out as I dry Lulu with a blow dryer. Lulu laid on her stomach with her head rested in between her paws. Adrian and I sat on the floor of the living room while everyone prepared for the party later in the backyard. Our house is actually pretty big for just the three of us, even with Emma here. The backyard's one of the biggest places in the house.

I turned off the hair dryer and leaned back on my hands. Adrian took Lulu on his lap and stroked her gently. I watched him lightly stroke her fur all cool and collected. Nervousness started to prickle in my chest again. What if he really is a egotistic jerk. Not the Adrian I remembered? The one I had a crush on. Adrian looked up and noticed I was looking at him.

"What?" he asked softly.

"Nothing.." I reply a little too quickly. I stood up and put the blow dryer away before turning to him again. "I should go take a shower." I mumble, making my way out of the living room. I heard him call my name but I quickly walked down the hallway and up the stairs. I was nearly to my room when someone grabbed my hand and pulled me back.

"Adrian!" I gasp when he pins me to the wall. He keeps his hand on the wall next to my head, staring intently at me.

"Macey... What's really going on?" he asks me quietly.

"What do you mean?" I ask casually.

"I mean you giving me the cold shoulder ever since I bumped into you this morning." Adrian whispers. I don't know why he's whispering. It's not like anyone else could hear us.

I don't want to tell him. What? I say 'Oh I'm afraid that you became a total jerk and you're not the same Adrian you were four years ago"? I lean my head back on the wall and close my eyes.

"Adrian.." I sigh.

"Macey, please." he pleaded. I open my eyes and stare him straight in the eye. His eyes pleaded for me to tell him. I sighed.

"I was afraid."

"Afraid? Afraid of what?"

I hesitated before answering him. "I.. I was afraid you weren't the same Adrian." I said quietly. He gave me a confused look so I continued. "I was afraid that the fame had gotten to your head. That you.. you know.. turned into a.."

"An asshole?" He asked.

"I was going to say jerk, but that works too."

Adrian sighs and thankfully leans back. Him being that close still made me nervous, especially since he's gotten more good-looking over the last few years. He runs a hand through his chestnut hair and looks away for a few seconds.

Was it a mistake I told him that? Was he going to yell at me now? Ah, crap.

"You know, it kind of hurts that you think that." Adrian muttered so inaudible I could barely make out what he said.

Whoops.

I focus my stare on the floor, not knowing what to do next. I felt Adrian turn back to look at me again. His fingers wrapped around my chin, forcing me to look at him. His face was relaxed, a gentle smile plastered on his handsome face. I felt a blush creep up my face.

"Mace," he said softly. "I may have became famous and a bit cocky, but I'm still the same Adrian," He chuckled. "I'm not hooking up with every pretty girl, I'm not making dramatic scenes everywhere I go, I'm not blowing off my education so I'm supported by money and fame with no brain at all.. I'm still your Adrian."

His words made my heart leap, and I gave him a shy smile.

Adrian took his hand away and wrapped it around my waist instead, pulling me closer to him. "Your one of the main reasons I came back, Mace." he stated.

I raised an eyebrow at him. "What do you mean?"

He looked at me for a minute before embracing me. I stiffened at first but then relaxed. I buried my face into his shoulder. His light cologne filling my nose.

"When I'm ready to tell you, I'll tell you." He whispered into my ear. Even though I'm curious on why I'm one of the reasons he came back, I respect his decision. Plus, I feel the urge to shower badly. I've had enough dog baths to fill a month.

"Can I shower now?" I groan into his shoulder.

"Yeah, you smell like dog." He chuckled as he pulled away. I shove his shoulder and give him a look before continuing down the hallway and into my room. I went straight to my bathroom and stripped my clothes off. Quickly, I stepped into the shower and let the warm water relax my muscles. Once the dog stench was off my body, I hop out of the shower and wrap a towel around my body and hair. The sound of the doorbell echoed from downstairs when I stepped into my room, indicating people have arrived. I walked into my closet and put on a white sleeveless high low top and some shorts. I dried my wet hair with the small towel.

Just as I was almost done straightening my hair I heard a knock on my door. "Macey! Hurry up, will you?" Emma's muffled voice came through the door.

"Almost done!" I call back. I turn off my flat iron before running out of the bathroom. I stand in front of my full sized mirror as I put on converse and, of course, Adrian's necklace. A patch of skin shows when I raise my arm just a bit, making me a little skeptical of showing up downstairs wearing this shirt. I didn't need my father's delusional comments about me being a "future model."

A hot breeze greeted me when I walk out into the backyard. All of the dads are gathered around the grill, moms are under the patio, teenagers are lingering, and very familiar faces are running and screaming across the backyard.

"Macey!" A voice shrieked behind me. I whip around to find little Abby running towards me. She grabs my shirt and hides herself behind my tall body. I giggle as I pat her head.

"Abby!" Another voice called out. I look up and see her cousin, Melody, coming our way. Before she can get any closer, Abby grabs my arm and yells, "Macey's base!" I give her an offended look that makes her giggle.

Melody groans and turns to the other kids running around in my backyard. "I'm tired of being it!"

"Here," I say as I pry Abby's hands off of my shirt, "I'll be it." Abby immediately runs away with Melody close behind her.

"Stop making everything a base!" I complain loudly. I stop and hunch over to catch my breath. For the last half hour, I've been forced to be it while everyone else announces a new base when I get closer.

"You're tall and fast, you could've caught us already." Abby's sister, Caitlyn, rebuts.

"You slowpoke!" the only little boy, Jacob, yelled.

"Excuse me if everything you touch is now considered a base!" I object, putting my hands on top of my head with a sigh. "Someone else be it. I'm tired."

"I'll be it." A guy offers. I don't even open my eyes to see who it was.

"Yeah. Sure, whatever." I say. A few giggles later, and then I was tackled from behind. The kids burst out laughing at my loud shriek. Strong arms were wrapped around my waist signaled who was holding me hostage.

"Adrian!"

"How'd you know it was me?" he laughed in my ear.

I slap his arm and he lets go, still laughing. "Lucky guess."

"You.. You should've seen.. your face!" an 8 year old, Brooke, laughs as she gets on the ground while clutching her stomach.

Brooke was an easy girl to make laugh, she was always happy and crazy.

I shake my head at their dramatic reactions to Adrian attacking me from behind. I didn't find it that funny. Then again, I was the victim they were laughing at.

"Just go play." I say flatly. I turn my back on them as I start to walk back to the house.

"Aww, Mace. Come on!" Adrian whined. I smile and turn on my heels.

"I'm just going to get a drink." I told him.

Adrian gives me a wide smile and winks, making my stomach do a back flip. "Hurry back."

I wave my hand dismissively at him before going back into the house. I grab a drink from the cooler and go back outside. Adrian's chasing after Jacob and Caitlyn.

"You're even slower than Macey!" Brooke shouts mockingly. Adrian stops in his tracks and turns towards her.

"Oh, really?" he asks in a mysterious tone.

"Better run, Brooke!" I call out to her. Adrian takes a jump at her and Brooke immediately tries to sprint to the other side of the lawn. Unfortunately, she wasn't quick enough. Before her little mind could process what was happening, Brooke was staring down at the grass, hanging off his shoulder like a ragdoll.

"Put me down!" she screams, pounding her little fist on his back. The others laugh as they watch Brooke be carried around like a rag doll. My phone vibrates from my pocket. I take it out and notice it's Brynn.

Brynn ^.^

Hey! How's the party goin ;)? Thanks for letting Godzilla drool on us..

A smile spread across my face at the memory.

Me:

You guys deserved it. How'd you know there was a party today?

Brynn ^.^

Hannah told us. Party's for Adrian huh? ;)

Me:

Maybbee...

Brynn ^.^

Made out yet?

I choke on my drink as I read the text.

"Mace? You okay?" Adrian calls out. I give him a meek smile.

"Yeah, I'm fine."

Adrian narrows his eyes before turning back to the game. I scowl as I reply back.

Me:

You made me choke, nimrod. If you mean MAKE UP then yes!

Brynn ^.^

Woops ;) Honest typo.

Me:

Typo my ass, Brynn. -_-

Brynn ^.^

I shake my head disbelievingly. Revenge is coming towards that girl. I lock my phone again just as Adrian comes up and plucks it from my hand.

"Hey!" I pouted. Adrian gives me a disapproving look, slipping my phone into his back pocket. I refuse to dig my hand through there in order to retrieve my phone.

"My best friend is texting at my welcome back party. What kind of best friend are you?" He exclaims, feigning a hurt expression.

"The one with wack jobs she calls friends." I say flatly. "Now give me my phone!"

Adrian flicks my forehead with a grin. "Nope. You'll get it back at the end of the night." I open my mouth to protest when Adrian's dad announces it's time for dinner. Adrian gives me a sly smile and wraps an arm around my shoulder, pulling me inside.

Inside I help the kids get their food first. The adults and grandparents wait patiently for there turns while helping out those who are tilting their plates backwards so their food is in danger of being exposed to Lulu's hunger.

"Macey!" A voice gasps. "You look so beautiful!" I turn around to face Adrian's grandmother. We haven't seen her much as we used to since Adrian had left for Los Angeles. She's gotten more frail since the last time I've seen her but she still has that friendly smile.

"Oh Grandma Aida, hi!" I say, giving her a gentle hug. Once she pulls back, she scrutinizes my whole body. Her smile is wide and soft. "Look at you. You've grown to be so pretty!" She gushes. "Don't you think, Adrian?"

Adrian looks up from the tray he was getting food at. "Huh?"

"Don't you think Macey's pretty?" His grandmother asks with a twinkle in her eye.

Adrian's face turns a little red and looks away quickly. "Uh, yeah. Yeah grandma, she's pretty." he replies sheepishly.

Amused, I raise my eyebrows at him. "Why's your face red, Adrian?"

Kelly flashes a smile and wraps an arm around her brother. "Yeah, lil bro. Why are you blushing?" She quizzed.

"I am not blushing." He replies defiantly, shrugging Kelly's arm of his shoulder.

"Showing some skin there huh, Mace?" Abby and Caitlyn's dad asked. I groaned internally.

"I guess." Was my nonchalant response.

"You're still so skinny!" Aida points out, tapping my stomach with her bony fingers.

"I told you, she could be a model!" My dad cries out. From the corner of my eye, Adrian grins widely.

"You are very right, Scott!" Adrian agrees. I glare at him, and he smiles. "Should've came with me to LA, Mace."

Little, short Jacob quivers with the large soda in his hand, and I pour it for him before Lulu gets another trip to the veterinarian office. "Oh, please."

"You could be one of the models in my next fashion show!" Kelly gasps. At first, I thought she was kidding. But the deterimined glint in her eyes caused my mouth to drop in horror.

Oh, hell no!

The room bursts out into conversation about my fake future modeling career. In their freaking dreams! I take my plate and head towards the backyard but not without giving Adrian a you're-so-dead look.

Through the night I spent time with the kids. I am a child at heart, after all. Adrian joined as well, chasing after the kids and making them shriek so loud that neighbors would think someone was getting murdered if it wasn't for all the hysteric laughter that boomed through the warm air. Adrian even gave me my phone back earlier than he said. Not like it mattered, I barely checked my phone in the last few hours. I also knew that Adrian couldn't possibly figure out my password, which happens to be the day we got Lulu; not my birthday or some random sequence.

We got the Chapmens a cake that had 'WELCOME BACK' written in frosting. There was also the additional mango cake that the adults seemed to enjoy. Adrian helped build a campfire out in the backyard so we could roast marshmallows. The already built pit was meant for this exact purpose so it's not like we're setting my backyard on fire with some logs, paper, and a lighter.

Around 10 that evening, mostly everyone had gone home since a good night sleep was needed for school and work the next day. The Chapmens stayed of course to help clean up.

"I'm so tired," I yawned as I fell down onto the couch in the living room. Adrian chuckled as he sat down next to me, wrapping an arm around my shoulder and pulling me closer. I laid my head on his shoulder and sighed.

"It was really great do see everyone again." Adrian said after a while. It took all my will power to pry my eyes open and look at him.

"Yeah?"

"Yeah," he confirmed, giving me a smile. "For once, everyone didn't really care that I came back after 4 years to become an actor. They treated me like Adrian Chapmen and not the famous Adrian Chapmen." Adrian seemed lost in thought after his explanation. I had a feeling he was thinking about the reason he had came back in the first place. Smiling, I laid my head back on his shoulder. He let out a contented sigh and gave me shoulder a squeeze.

"That's because you're still the same Adrian and not some famous stranger." I tell him. "You're still our Adrian."

We settled in a comfortable silence while the adults spoke in the kitchen.

"I'm still your Adrian, Mace." He replied softly. His response made me feel warm inside. I'm glad the fame hadn't gone to his head. All the worry and nervousness I felt earlier, about him being a conceited jerk, was gone in an instant. He was still that sweet, kind, down to earth Adrian. Sure, he got a little cocky and what not, but I wouldn't change a thing.

"Okay, done cleaning up!" My mom's voice filled the room as everyone poured into the living room. Emma dropped down next to me, heaving a deep sigh.

"Kelly said she has something to tell us before they head out." Emma announced so everyone could hear. Kelly stood in the middle of the living room, wiping her palms nervously on her dress.

"Yeah. It's kind of important." she replied, her voice shaking. Connie sat down next to my mom.

"What's wrong, honey?" she urged, concern filling her voice. Dave sat down on the arm rest while my dad stood next to him. Oliver went to Kelly's side and took her hand. After a small nod and an assuring smile, Kelly took a deep breathe.

"I'm getting married." she announced.

We all stared at her in silence. My mouth dropped open a little and Adrian was staring at his sister in utter shock. There was a moment of silent as we stared at Kelly and her soon-to-be husband. Kelly's face contorted into extreme regret and nervousness once she didn't get a response. However, Emma was the one to break the silence.

"AHHHHHH!" She screamed as she ran up to Kelly and giving her a big hug. "Oh my gosh! That's so amazing!"

Everyone came back to planet Earth and started to cheer and congratulate Kelly.

"Sweetie!" Connie gasped. Tears were coming out of her eyes while she embraced her daughter. "Congratulations, Kelly!" She sobbed. Dave left his spot and walked over to Kelly, giving her a big hug.

"Congratulations, sweetheart." He told her, proudly.

"Thanks, dad!" Kelly replied, relief and happiness clear in her tone. Dave pulled away and hugged Oliver. "Welcome to the family, son!"

"Thank you, sir. And I promise I will take care of you daughter." Oliver told him, hoping not to get any threats if he screwed up. My mom stood up to give Kelly a big hug too, with my dad grinning happily. I got nervous again when Adrian's expression remained blank and unsmiling. It wouldn't be a great situation for Kelly to have her own brother disapprove of her future husband.

Adrian noticed my worried look and stood up. Everyone made an aisle for him when he approached Oliver. Nervousness flooded on to Kelly's face as she looked hopefully at her brother. Adrian crossed his arms, his eyes narrowing at Oliver. The man stood tall and looked back at Adrian. After having a staring contest, Adrian pointed a finger at him.

"She snores like a monster, you know."

Kelly's face turned a deep red. "Adrian!" She exclaimed. Oliver let out a bark of laughter.

"I'm kidding, Kell. I approve. Congrats, sis!" Adrian chuckled, giving his sister a hug.

"I think I can handle the snoring." Oliver chuckled, shaking Adrian's hand.

"Good luck with that." He laughed.

Kelly punched Adrian square in the shoulder but was clearly relieved that she got her brother's approval. "Can you be on of our groomsmen?" she asked.

Adrian faked a considering look before replying. "As long as there's awesome cake, then yes." he agreed.

I laughed and stood up to congratulate Kelly as well.

"Congrats, Kelly. I'm so happy for you!" I told her. Kelly pulled back and gave me a hopeful look. "Mace, can you be one of the bridesmaids? With Emma?"

I gave her a shocked look. "Oh.. Um.."

"She would love to be a bridesmaid, Kell!" Adrian interrupted, throwing an arm around my shoulder. I gave him a death glare, earning a sly smile.

"Really?" Kelly asked.

I hesitated for a second before saying, "Sure. I'd love to."

Emma squealed and clapped her hands. "Yay! This is so exciting! You two can walk down the isle togther!"

"What?" Adrian and I said together.

"Oh come on," Kelly smirked. "You were bound to walk down the isle with eachother one way or another." She said in a singsong voice. I felt Adrian's arm tense.

"But we're just friends. Nothing else." I confirmed.

"Mhmm.." Kelly smiled at Adrian.

"Okay, okay. Let's talk about this another time. You two have school tomorrow." My mom announced, looking at me and Adrian.

"See what you did!" I hiss once everyone is out of the living room. Adrian laughed and gave me a big hug.

"Good night, Mace." he said softly.

"Night, Adrian."

Adrian kissed me quickly on the cheek and ran out of the living room. I blushed a little at his action, but wasn't fazed by it. We're so close that we've done it before, just not on the lips. That would be akward for just friends.

I walked up to my room and changed into a tank top and shorts before going into the bathoom to brush my teeth. I got under the covers and turned off the light. Before I dozed off, my phone rang. I groaned and reached under my pillow, turning it on silent. This is why I never turn it on ringer.

It was a text from Adrian. Yet I don't remember putting his number in.. I'll ask him tomorrow. I unlock my phone and squint at the bright screen.

Adrian

Love you Mace.. :)

I smiled and replied:

Love you too Adrian, welcome home <3

I shoved my phone under my pillow and went back to sleep.

Chapter 4

"**W**AKE UP!" A voice booms. I jolt awake and hit my head on something hard. I raise my hand up to my forehead and groan. I pry my eyes open to a familiar figure that's rubbing his head with a scowl.

"Adrian?" I ask groggily.

"Ow, Mace. What the hell?" Adrian groans, confirming that it is him. I grab my pillow and throw it at him.

"What are you doing here?!" I hiss. Glancing over at the clock on my bedside table, it's early in the morning. Too early in the morning.

"Your mom opened the door for me before she left for her appointment." Adrian told me. "Thought I'd give you a ride."

I take my phone out from under my pillow to see a text from Brynn. "Usually Brynn does that,"

Brynn ^.^

Can't carpool today, got early bird :(See u at school!

"Just not today." I added.

Adrian stands up and claps his hands together. "Well then, get dressed! I'm going to make breakfast. What are you up for?"

I throw the blanket off my body and stand up as I run a hand through my hair, "I usually have cereal."

Adrian frowns at me before slapping my stomach. "No wonder you're so skinny."

I give him a flat look earning myself a laugh. He pulls me in for a hug and kisses the top of my head. "I'm cooking you something, okay?"

I bury my head in his shoulder and sigh. "Fine." I grumble. Adrian gives me a tight squeeze before pulling back to slap my cheeks repeatedly.

"Don't fall back asleep."

"Kay." I sigh wearily.

"And believe it or not but it's kinda of chilly outside so dress warm."

"Mhm."

He kisses my cheek and heads towards the door. "Don't burn the house down!" I call out to him.

"No promises!"

I roll my eyes and walk into the bathroom.

Adrian's POV

I bounce down the stairs and into the kitchen. Opening the fridge, I take out a few eggs while a few barks echoed through the house. I felt a slight scratching motion down on my ankles. I look down to find Lulu jumping on my legs. "Wait for your turn." I laugh.

Finishing the last of the eggs on the pan, Lulu begins to whimper impatiently as she waits to be fed. I sighed at the fact that she had been scratching at my ankles since the aroma of fresh breakfast drifted through the house.

"Macey!" I groaned loud enough so my best friend could at least take the hint to get her ass down here and feed her dog. Getting no reply, I sighed and focused my attention on the eggs. Truthfully, I'm surprised I hadn't burned the poor eggs since I had no experience of cooking my own food for a while now. The staff around our house used to take care of our every need back in LA. I would watch the chef cook once in a while, observing their techniques.

"Your two are so impatient."

Cracking a smile, I turn my attention away from the eggs and to the figure leaning against the counter with her signature smile. Macey's hair flew down in waves and she was wearing a white sweater with 'LOVE' written across. Lulu let out a sharp bark and continued her obnoxious whimpering.

"For God's sakes, Macey, feed your damn dog!" I order rudely, giving Lulu a death glare as if I'm trying to kill her with my stare. Macey rolls her eyes at me before heading to the pantry. Lulu's at her feet once Macey poured a cup of kibble into a bowl.

Lulu's whimpering became more yearning for her breakfast. However, the constant noises perished when Macey let out a strange whistle.

"Sit."

Lulu obeyed. Macey smiled and placed the bowl down before her. Lulu quickly got up on her feet and skidded towards the bowl.

"Now shut up before Adrian hurts you." Macey warned in a low voice. I let out a dramatic gasp and give her a hurt expression.

"I would never abuse a dog." I inform her.

"So you would abuse a cat?"

I give her a look as I placed the plates down on the counter. Macey giggles and makes her way around the table to sit on a stool. Taking a caution bite, she chews slowly as if I had poisoned it. I roll my eyes.

"This is actually not bad." Macey admits.

"Of course not. It was made by me." I tell her in a 'duh' tone.

We take our time eating the somewhat decent breakfast I had cooked up for us in a comfortable silence. The gloomy weather let off a calm feeling on the early morning. It was quite a change to not have the sun beating down on me everywhere I go. Don't get me wrong, I'm not goth or anything but I do like my cloudy days once in a while.

"So," Macey broke the silence, "Any reason why you had to desperately come so early in the morning?"

I shrugged. "Just wanted to see you."

Macey got up from her seat and went over to the sink. "You could've seen me at school." she pointed out as she started washing her plate. Finishing the last of my eggs, I went over to her side and placed my own dish in the sink. "Well, I wanted to see you earlier."

"So severely you couldn't wait an hour?"

I sigh and make my to the back of her. Just as Macey dries her hands, I wrap my arm around her waist and place my head on her shoulder. "Mace," I said softly. "I have four years to make up for. I want to be with you as much as possible." After a few moments of holding her close, Macey turns around and wraps her arms around my neck.

"I've really missed you, Adrian."

I hug her tightly as I breathe in her sweet scent. I really missed having Macey in my arms again. It always gave me a warm feeling when I did. I loved the fact that even though we grew apart for a while, she was still willing to take me back in her life again after leaving her for a new life. I just hoped she accepts the things that come with the new me.

"I've missed you too, my sweet little Macey."

She laughs at my corny nickname. I've always called her my 'Sweet Macey' since we were kids. Macey was always that quiet shy girl that people never really got to know better. But once they did, Macey was a really sweet girl to hang around. Getting older, she broke out of that shell a little bit; getting less shy and going for it more often. Through and through, Macey was still my sweet best friend. That's one of the many qualities that didn't change once I moved back to Florida.

Macey pulled back and glanced at the clock, groaning as she did. "We have an hour before I usually head out for school."

"Well then," I wrap an arm around her shoulder and walk into the living room. I sit down on the couch with her right next to me. Remembering something we used to love as kids, I grabbed the remote and flicked the TV on. "Let's watch something, shall we?"

Macey laid her head on my shoulder as I scrolled through the channels in search of one in particular. Since it was so early in the morning, I'm pretty sure what show would be on. Just as I predicted, a yellow sponge was running down a street repeating a phrase we know so well. His shoes squeaking with every step he took and a goofy smile morphed onto his face.

I'm ready! I'm ready! I'm ready!

"Oh my god!" Macey laughed once she saw the famous Spongebob Squarepants.

"Up for a little Spongebob?" I chuckle, planting a kiss on the side of her head.

"That's our guy, Adrian!" Macey exclaimed. Back when we were little, Macey and I used to wake up early in the morning to watch

Spongebob when I was over. The Daniels's house was like my second home. It still is.

After an hour of watching Spongebob, we finally headed to school in my new Porsche. Macey gave me an impressed look when she saw it.

The smell of rain drifted in the morning air and a frigid ocean breeze nipped at my body. Sliding my hands into my pocket, I followed Macey down to her locker. Two familiar girls were already standing in front of it.

"Hey guys!' Macey chirped. The two girls that I recall as Amber and Dylan looked at me and then to Macey with a confused look.

"Uh.. Macey?" Amber asked in a hushed tone.

Macey, who was currently putting her things into her locker, turned to look at her two looking anxious friends. "What?" Macey asked. "He's not going to bite. Right, Adrian?"

Macey turned to look at me with a raised eyebrow. I smile. "Not at the moment." I tease. Macey rolls her eyes at me and grabs her binder before closing her locker and turning to face her friends.

"We're cool, guys. Talked it over last night at the party." She informed them. Their confused faces turned into realization.

"Oh right, the party you left for when the world's most smelly dog was soaking us." Dylan said with a glare towards Macey. "Thanks for that."

"I felt violated." Amber stated in a way too serious tone that made us laugh.

Macey gave them a sly smile before we heard a voice calling someone from down the hallway. I turned my head and saw Brynn running in our direction. "Hide me!" she pleaded once she had reached us. Brynn quickly hid behind Macey and Dylan while peeking over their shoulders to make sure the coast is clear.

"What's wrong with you?" Dylan laughed.

"The big bad wolf coming to eat you?" Amber teased in a childish tone.

"No, that big bad wolf was adopted yesterday by a man that looked like a scary biker." Brynn informed us.

"It was a German Sheperd!" Macey exclaimed with a satisfied smirk. She gave me a look and mouthed 'I'll tell you later'. Nodding in understanding, I leaned against the row of lockers and gave Brynn a confused look.

"So why are you hiding?" I ask.

Brynn returns the confused look, wondering why I'm standing near them in the first place.

"Macey..?" She asked.

"I'll tell you later." she sighed.

"Okay. Thing is there's this total idiot in my early bird class who's been bothering the crap out of me all morning. Such a retard! Moved into our class today!" Brynn cried out in disbelief. Assuming the coast was clear, Brynn came out from her horrible hiding spot to stand in front of us.

"Yo, Goldy!" a voice echoed through the hallway. Brynn let out a loud groan and turned to face a boy coming towards us. The boy was short and scrawny with blonde hair that was spiked up in different directions. "Think you can get away that easily?" His voice asked stupidly. I hid a smile at his strangely high pitched voice for a senior.

"What do you want, Josh?" Brynn spat.

"Came to annoy the hell out of you because it amuses me so much." The boy, Josh, replied. His eyes switched over to Dylan, then to Amber, and lingered on Macey. "Who's your friends?"

In an instant, I didn't like this guy already. He'd been here for less than 30 seconds and he was already checking people out. I didn't like the way he was looking at Macey either. It made me want to push the guy outside so he could get struck by lightning. I was about to say something but Macey beat me to it.

"Ew." she said, giving Josh a disgusted look. Amber let out a laugh.

"This the retarded idiot?" Dylan asked with a smirk.

"For your information, you wish you could have some of this." Josh said, gesturing to his stick-like body. It was my turn to laugh.

"Really? I've seen girls with more muscle than you." I chuckle.

"And what makes you so special?" Josh shot back. The four girls bursted out laughing at his stupid comment.

"Are you blind?" Amber laughed.

"You're so stupid! You don't know who this is?" Dylan asked, still laughing. Brynn didn't say anything for she was too busy laughing herself. Macey sobered up and came to my side.

"Adrian Chapmen? The famous Adrian Chapmen? The guy with so many awards that it could fill a janitor's closet and considered one of the hottest guys in the country according to several high read magazines. Not to mention almost every girl falling head over heels for him." Macey stated simply with a mischievously sweet smile and her head tilted to the side.

Josh's mouth dropped to the floor and his eyes widened to the size of soccer balls, making the girls laugh again. Loving the way

Macey had set things straight, I crossed my arms and smiled at him. "Anything you want to say?"

A moment later of him gawking at me, the bell rang and he quickly retreated.

"SUCKER!" Brynn called after him, still laughing. I let out a small chuckle myself and wrapped an arm around Macey's shoulder.

"I like the way you explained my utmost importance." I praised, kissing the top of her head quickly. The three other girls widened their eyes at my action. I realized they didn't know how the relationship between me and Macey worked. It was completely normal for me to show affection like this. I simply shrugged as Macey said she'd explain everything later and that we should head to class.

I proceeded to mess around with my pencil throughout World History. This class was the only class that doesn't have someone I actually knew. I did, however, try to interact with the rest of the people in the class. Unfortunately, they didn't treat me like a normal student like I wanted. Nerds offered to do my homework. Pretty much all the girls in the class would stare and drool at me which, I merely ignored. And the jocks would agree with everything I had to say. Even when I threw out a straight up false statement of watching reruns of Barney on DVD while wearing my Spongebob PJ's in my race car bed for hours.

To summarize: They saw the famous Adrian Chapmen instead of regular high school student, Adrian Chapmen who simply wants to graduate with an education.

Sighing at the thought, I redirected them to Macey. Unlike the other starstruck teenagers that currently filled the room, Macey treats me the way she always does. Moving back here, I was afraid she was going to shut me out of her life or try to change herself as if she wasn't good enough to be seen around me. Which for one thing, is totally wrong.

The Macey I found yesterday was the Macey I was hoping for. And I'm glad that her friends didn't treat me like a king. I had also maintained the same joke filled, childish relationship with Chase. Just earlier in science, we were making the frog that was suppose to be dissected, dance on it's tray before cutting it open.

"Mr. Chapmen?"

I jump out of my thoughts and look up to the front to find my teacher, Mr. Schultz, giving me an expectant look.

"Um.. Sir?"

"I asked you a question." he replies with a raised eyebrow.

"Right, Uh.."

The boy next to me clears his throat while tapping on his notebook. I discreetly glance over at the white paper and notice a circle around a date written in big numbers.

"1927." I said. Mr. Schultz keeps his stare on me before replying.

"Very good. Just making sure you're paying attention."

I nod and give him a smile. Mr. Schultz faces his back to us and continues his lesson. I let out a sigh of relief and turn to the guy next to me. He has short blonde hair with piercing green eyes and a wide smirk glued to his face.

"Save you daydreaming for Math class, dude." he told me in a quiet voice. I could hear the amusement in his tone.

I chuckle as I lean back into my chair. "Thanks, man"

"Name's Brandon." Brandon introduced himself.

"Adrian."

The smirk returned to his face. "I know. Pretty much all the girls are gushing over you. Let's not forget the small amount of guys."

"There are gay guys here?" I laughed silently, inspecting the guys around me.

"Well, not for sure. But I have my guesses." he replied smoothly, leaning back on his own chair. "So, you're Daniels's best friend, am I right or am I right?"

I chuckle at my options. "Right. Do you know her?"

"Nah. I see her hanging around Brynn Tucker and a few others."

I scrutinize his face. "You do look a little like Brynn. You two related?"

Brandon laughed. "No, but we get that a lot. Brynn's in my 5th period with Dylan too."

I couldn't help but notice the faint color that filled his cheeks at the thought of Brynn. I give him a sly smile. "Somebody's got a crush, doesn't he?"

Brandon stared at me blankly but the flourishing blush gave him away. I laughed. "Don't worry. I won't announce it to the whole world."

"Better not mention it to MTV or your little reality show or whatever." Brandon warned.

"I don't know about everyone else, but I don't want a camera stalking me everywhere I go, filming every single moment of my life for creepy people to watch later on."

Brandon's loud laughs drowns in the loud ringing of the bell, signaling us for lunch. Brandon and I grab out stuff before heading out into the hallway. Girls wave at me in a flirting manner as they leave the hallway. I ignore their demand of attention and turn to face Brandon instead. "Want to get some lunch?"

"Sure. That okay if I join you?" he asks as we head towards the cafeteria.

"Yeah. I'm sure Brynn will be there with Macey." I wiggle my eyebrows at him. Brandon scowls at me while shoving my shoulder.

"Yo, guys!" a voice calls out. I turn and find Chase running towards us. He bows down once he's close enough. "May I have the pleasure of joining you two fine gentleman for an unhealthy school lunch that is most likely making us fatter by the day?" he asks in a British accent.

"Sure, Chase." Brandon laughs. Assuming the both of them have met already, we head to lunch.

Macey's POV

"That was disgusting!" Amber complains, setting our tray down at a table.

"Dissecting things is a part of High School, Amber." Dylan says coolly.

Brynn shivers in her seat. "It was kinda gross, either way."

I let out a shiver of my own once the memory of cutting the frog open and digging around inside it's deceased body invades me head.

I felt a sudden presence behind me as I take a sip of my drink. "Hey, guys." A voice says. The voice takes a second to register into my mind.

"Hey, Adrian." I say with a smile, not even turning to look at him. Sure enough, Adrian takes a seat beside me while Chase makes his way over to a seat next to Dylan. Another body stands awkwardly to the side.

"Oh hey, Brandon." Brynn greets the boy. I raise my eyebrows at Brynn's sudden red cheeks.

"Hi, Brynn." Brandon said. There's a short silence before Adrian speaks up.

"Guys, meet Brandon. Brandon meet the guys. I'm pretty sure you know their names already."

"Oh, right! You're in my English class." Amber exclaims dramatically, pointing at him.

"Sit down, Brandon. Don't stand there." Dylan laughs.

"I must warn you though," I said as he takes a seat across from Brynn. "Adrian might choose this moment to bite."

Amber and Dylan laugh once they remember what Adrian told us that morning. Brandon puts his hands up in a defenensive way.

"Woah, Adrian! We're not that close. I prefer not to get your dentures in my skin."

Brandon's comment suceeded to get the whole table laughing. Adrian glared at Brandon before sending him an evil smile.

"Now now, Brandon. Let's not forget what I know, shall we?"

Brandon's smile drops as his face turns into a deep shade of red. "Aww!" Brynn cooes. "Brandon's got a dirty little secret!"

"Did you cheat?"

"Did you ditch school?"

"What are you hiding in your locker?"

Everyone threw questions at Brandon, naming everything possible. Except one.

"Who's the girl?" I ask loud enough to cut through everyone's questions. Brandon's face turns red again.

"W-what do you mean?" Brandon stuttered, looking flustered. I saw him glance at Brynn before quickly averting his eyes. I smiled.

"Ah, I understand now." I say, continuing my lunch. Brynn looks at me with a confused look and I send her a wink. Dylan seems to catch on because she sends Brynn a playful glare. Amber, however, still had a confused look. I wave my hand dismissively at her, signaling I'd explain it later. I have a lot of things to explain..

The day went by pretty fast for I was now gathering my stuff to head home. It was now raining outside, giving me a happy feeling. Living in the sun for so long, I loved the rain when it did came. Rain started pouring from the gray sky during PE so we ran back to the doors. We got pretty drenched since Mr. Powell took his sweet ole' time to open the door. I closed my locker and was half way scared to death when I found Adrian leaning on the row of lockers next to me.

"Adrian!" I half shouted at him, putting a hand over my hear, "Don't do that!"

He simply smirked before kissing the side of my forehead. "Well get used to it. Ready to go?"

"Yup." I affirmed. Walking down the hallway, a shrieking high pitched voice stopped us in our tracks.

"ADRIAN!"

Chapter 5

"ADRIAN!"

Adrian and I stopped in our tracks. I cringed at the familiar feminine voice. The queen that all idiots and retards alike look up to. I heard her high heels click on the floor in a fast pace, her jewelry clinking together with each step.

Cammie Brooks.

I heard Adrian mutter something under his breath before turning around to face the witch herself. "Hey, Cammie! Nice to–"

Cammie cut him off when she threw herself at him. Wrapping her bony arms around Adrian's neck and pressing her lip against his. I guessed Adrian was caught off guard since he stood there awkwardly while Cammie kissed him passionately. I crossed my arms and waited patiently for her to stop eating Adrian's face. Adrian glanced over at me. I smiled and put a finger in my mouth, gagging silently. Adrian laughed against Cammie's lips and pulled away. Cammie gave him a questioning look before whipping around and giving me an icy glare.

I gave her a dumbfounded look and smiled innocently "Hi, Cammie."

"Macey." She replied distastefully.

We continued at stare at each other for a moment until she turned back to Adrian, flipping her curly blonde hair in my face. A wave of strong perfume hit my nose and I didn't bother to make my gag silent but Cammie simply ignored my disgust.

"Adrian, it's so great to see you again, babe!" Cammie exclaimed.

"Uh.. You too, Cammie but-" Adrian said.

"We should totally catch up right now. I'dr really want to talk about us." Cammie interrupted, looping a protective arm through Adrian's.

"Cammie, I-"

"Because I was really thinking we should get back together since you're-"

"Cammie!" Adrian demanded, ripping away from Cammie's grasp.

Cammie stopped. "What?"

"We broke up, remember? I'm not.." Adrian paused to find the right words, "Interested anymore."

I stifled a laugh, pressing a hand to my mouth. Adrian caught my reaction and held back a smile. "Now, if you'll excuse me," Adrian walked to my side and grabbed my hand. My eyes widened as I stared down at our hands. I look back up at Adrian to see him giving me a cheeky smile. "I have to take Macey home." he told her, not tearing his gaze away from me.

I dared to catch a look at Cammie's reation, which was a mistake. She was shooting daggers at me, her jaw clenched and her mouth pursed into a straight line. I cleared my throat and focused my attention to the floor. Tension filled the hallway for it was now almost empty. Luckily, there isn't enough people to make a scene in front of.

Adrian pulled me towards the door, giving my hand a reassuring squeeze. I slung my backpack back onto my shoulder and followed Adrian's lead. I could practically feel Cammie's cold eyes boring into mine like a drill into the ground. Giving me a death glare as if that will make me drop dead on the floor.

Adrian pushed the front doors open and we walked out together. The rain was a constant pour with lightning flashing through the sky. I rubbed my arm with my free hand, trying to warm myself against the cold front that caressed my skin. Adrian let go of my hand and wrapped it around my shoulder, pulling me closer.

"Ready to run?" Adrian asked loudly over the loud patter. I gave him a confident smile. We sprinted down the parking lot towards Adrian's new car. He unlocked it quickly and we scrambled into the car. Adrian shook the droplets off his hair while I ran my fingers through my hair.

"Don't you just love the rain?" Adrian chuckled.

"Yeah. It's nice to have this kind of weather once in a while." I reply with a smile. Adrian nods and starts the engine.

A short while of driving, waiting, and thinking, a question and a memory makes its way into my mind. I turn to Adrian. He's focused on the road while tapping to the beat of the song currently playing on the radio. The windshield is continuously wiping the rain away from the window.

"Adrian?"

"Hmm?"

"Why'd you act that way with Cammie?"

I saw Adrian tense up at my question but discreetly relax again. The thing between Adrian and Cammie was that they dated back in middle school. They dated for all of 8th grade until a few months after Adrian found out he got the role in the movie that launched his career, Adrian suddenly broke up with Cammie. She was furious and made a scene in one of their classes. The news spread throughout the school like an epidemic. Cammie was so embarassed and staged that their wholebreak up was my fault since she never like me for the fact that I was Adrian's best friend. She accused Adrian for having 'stronger feelings' than our friendship. She couldn't be more wrong.

Adrian was my best friend and that's all that's to it. He looked at me like a sister at the most, nothing more.

Adrian came over to study for our Geography test one day and told me the news. I remember that day vividly; I was shocked. They had a somewhat good relationship and I supported him even though I didn't approve of her.

I heard the door close from downstairs.

"Macey!" his voice called out.

"In my room!" I yelled back. A moment later, Adrian strolled into my room. He threw his bag onto the floor and collapsed at the edge of my bed, covering his face with his hands.

"Something wrong?" I asked, not even looking up from my math homework. He stayed silent. I sighed. Finishing the problem I was on, I closed my book and plopped down next to him.

"Adrian," I said. "What's going on?"

Adrian let out a long sigh before sitting up and facing me. "I broke up with Cammie."

"What?" I cried out, standing up. "Why? What happened? I thought you really liked her!"

"Thought, Mace." Adrian replied. "She's just not the girl for me, you know? Not the one."

I frowned. "How come? What'd she do?"

Adrian looked at me intently before shrugging. "She got this new attitude after she realized she was dating a soon-to-be star. Began to brag about him than the real me. Tried to make the others jealous."

I rolled my eyes at him. "Adrian, she always has an attitude. She's a.." Not wanting to insult his girlfriend. Correction: Ex-girlfriend. I walked over to my desk and picked up my Geography notebook before sitting beside him again.

"It's not a big deal, Mace." Adrian told me. He picked up his backpack and took out his own notebook. "Besides," he paused and looked at me with a look in his eye, a look I didn't recognize, "I've got a thing for someone else."

"Really?" I asked, nudging his shoulder playfully. "Do I know this mystery girl?"

Adrian chuckled. "More than you think."

I narrowed my eyes at him before letting it go. "Well," I said while I flipped through pages in my notebook. "As much as I would love to pry it out of you, I'll do it another time."

The corner of his mouth turned up a little, giving me a slight smile, starting on our first topic.

"No reason." Adrian's voice made me jump a little, coming back to reality. I looked at him as we stopped at a red light. "You were thinking about that day before our Geography test, weren't you?"

"Yes." I admit. I'm surprised he remembered such a small memory. Of course he would; it was a breakup with one of the most prettiest girls in the school. Let's just say, Cammie isn't one to take things lightly.

"Look, I just don't want to get involved with her anymore. She's obviously in for the fame instead of actually hanging out with the 'without a label until graduation' guy." Adrian told me casually.

"How do you know if people are in it for the fame or if they're in it for you?" I asked, curiously.

The light turned green again and Adrian moved forward. "You just learn to tell. I don't know how to explain it."

I nodded even though I didn't understand. The rain started to lighten up as we closed in on my neighborhood. We sat there with the radio playing and the rain falling onto the car. After a few minutes, Adrian filled the silence.

"Like you, for example."

I looked at him. "What about me?"

"I could tell you're in it for me and not the famous me" Adrian pointed out with a smile. "Right?"

"Well..." I teased.

Adrian gave me a short semi-glare before turning his attention back to the road. We approached my house soon after. Adrian parked his car in front of my house and turned the ignition off. "Your destination, my lady." He said in a medieval accent, gesturing to my house.

I laughed. "Thank you for your time, kind sir." I said intimidating the same accent. I was about to open the door but stopped. I turned to Adrian who was now furrowing his eyebrows in confusion.

"What's wrong?" he asked.

I leaned back into my seat while crossing my arms and shooting a smirk his way. "Who was that mystery girl that I never pried out of you that day?" I quizzed.

Adrian's eyes widened but quickly averted his eyes. "Nobody."

I rolled my eyes at him. "Oh come on, Adrian." I said, nudging his shoulder. "It's been four years, you probably don't even know this girl anymore."

Adrian laughed silently to himself before turning to me again. The corners of his mouth turned up, his eyes twinkling. "I can't say that's true, Mace."

"So she's still here?"

"Yup." he told me, popping the 'p'.

"Do you still know her?"

"Yes."

I narrowed my eyes at him. "Well, with that in mind; now I have to know." I urged him stubbornly.

"No."

"Yes."

"No."

"Yes."

"No."

I groaned. "Do you even still have feelings for her?"

Adrian paused for a moment before answering. "I'm still debating on that. Are we done with the interrogation session?"

"Hmm, let me think about that... No." I said.

Adrian sighed dramatically as he laid his head back on the seat. "Macey, listen to me," Adrian reached over and took my hand. I looked up and studied his expression which was calm and serious. "It was just a childhood crush, okay? That's all. Nothing to harass me for."

Still unconvinced, I sighed in defeat. "Fine. But if you ever develop a crush, I'm going to rip it out of you if it's the last thing I do." I stated seriously.

Adrian laughed and kissed my hand. "Alright, fine. Now get out."

I retracted my hand and stuck my tongue out at him in a childish manner.

"Out." he chuckled, shoving my shoulder.

I put my hands up in surrender. "Pushy!" I exclaimed, opening the door.

Adrian snorted. "Right. I'm the pushy one." he said sarcastically as I got out the car.

"Bye!" I chirped before slamming the door shut. I gripped my backpack tighter as I ran up my driveway with the rain lightly pelting my body. Once in the safety of shelter, I gave Adrian one last wave before heading inside. I slid down the closed door and sighed. I keep pondering the thought of this girl that Adrian fell for.

It probably wasn't important who this 'childhood crush' was. But I couldn't help but wonder who made him dump one the most popular girl in our school. Cammie – who could make poor suckers do anything she desired with just a snap of her fingers because she was worshipped – was dumped by Adrian for this amazing mystery girl.

I wonder who that girl is.

Chapter 6

"Ow! Lulu!" I yelped putting down my straighter and clutching my ankle. Lulu looked up at me impatiently with her head cocked to the side. "We need to cut your nails or something." I grumbled. Lulu let out another impatient bark as I stepped over her and walked back into my room in search of my backpack.

"Emma! Are you home?" I yelled aloud. Emma has disappeared every morning since Kelly informed us about her wedding. They've been making plans for the last week but giving us only vague information.

"Yeah, I'm heading out soon! What do you need?" Emma's voiced called out. Finally finding my backpack under my bed, I swung it over my shoulder before heading towards the door. I clicked my tongue to call Lulu out of my room before shutting the door behind me.

"Feed Lulu, she's being annoyingly impatient!" I called back slightly agitated over Lulu's constant demand for food. I bounded down the stairs while running a hand through my hair while Lulu sprinted into the kitchen. I followed her quickly to find Emma pouring kibble into Lulu's bowl.

"Eat up, girl." Emma told Lulu once she placed the bowl onto the floor. We let a small laugh when Lulu raced towards her bowl and buried her face into the kibble. I muttered a curse at the time. I only had about 10 minutes before Brynn showed up for school. Emma watched me as I treated myself to a bowl of cereal.

"Off to discuss wedding plans with Kelly again, Em?" I asked through a mouthful of cereal.

"Don't talk with your mouth full," Emma scolded with a chuckle. "But yes, we're deciding on the center pieces today."

Making sure to swallow first before talking, I asked, "When's the wedding anyways?"

"May," Emma replied as she grabbed a banana off the counter. "A few weeks before your graduation."

I slightly choked on my cereal. "Why are you planning so soon? It's September right now."

"Kelly's excited and wants to make it extravagant since she's big in the fashion biz." Emma explained with a hint of amusement. "Even wants to make each bridesmaid dress represent the person who's wearing it with a few choreographed dances here and there. Plus her fashion show is still close behind and she doesn't want to stress."

"It's a wedding, not a ball." I retorted, dumping my bowl into the sink. Emma rolled her eyes and gave me a light shove.

"It's her big day, leave her be!"

I stuck my tongue at her just as a loud blaring noise cut through the air. I titled my head up and groaned loudly.

"Your ride's here," Emma laughed. "We're going to get more complaints if Brynn continues that."

"Yeah, yeah. I know, I'll strangle her." I snorted. I gave my sister a quick hug and ran out the door. The hot air blew against my body as I walked down the driveway towards Brynn's car. The honking sounded more urgent and continuous this morning making me want to rip the steering wheel off and throw it down a cliff.

"Brynn! Enough! People will think someone's getting mugged!" I hissed once I was in the car. Brynn had a huge smile on her face as she looked at me with wide eyes, a glint of excitement in those green orbs of hers.

I leaned back into my seat and gave her a sly smile. "This is about Brandon, isn't it?" As if on cue, Brynn squealed in excitement and started shaking my shoulders harshly.

"You'll never believe what I heard!" She shrieked. I pried her hands off my shoulder with an eye roll.

"Tell me once all the girls are here, I don't want to hear the same story all day. We need to pick up Dylan but Amber went early to take a test." I told her. Brynn let out a dramatic sigh but pressed hard against the gas pedal putting the car in drive.

"Can I tell you now?!" Brynn exclaimed. Brynn, Dylan, Amber, and I are standing in front of my locker with a few minutes to kill before the bell. Brynn was practically hopping from one foot to another, trying to control her excitement.

"Okay, fine, Brynn. What's this oh-so amazing story that you've been harassing us to know?" I asked with an exaggerated sigh.

Brynn started babbling about a flirtatious moment between her and Brandon and Chase's opinion on Brandon's 'true feelings' for her.

"Dude, can you be anymore oblivious?" Dylan scoffed with a smile.

"What do you mean?" Brynn asked.

"It's obvious that you like each other, Brynn." Amber told her.

"You don't know that!" Brynn objected defensively.

"It's very suspicious about your true feelings, our little love puppy friend." I exclaimed in a dramatic tone. Brynn pursed her lips together and smacked me in the face.

"Shut it." She ordered.

"What about you, Mace?" Amber asked with a smirk.

"What are you talking about?"

"What's going on between you and your smoking hot 'best friend'?" She asked wiggling her eyebrows at me. Dylan and Brynn gave me a similar mocking expectant look. I rolled my eyes at them.

"Oh, please. There is nothing going on between me and Adrian." I snorted.

"That's what she said." Brynn sang. I gave her a flat look before slapping her in the side of the head.

"Cammie seemed pissed between you two, though Especially after school yesterday." Dylan pointed out.

"Cammie's never liked me since Middle School, big whoop." I told them in a monotone voice.

"Well, what happened?" Amber asked.

"Adrian and Cammie used to date back in middle school and me, being the best friend who's a girl, was accused of trying to steal Adrian from her. When they broke up a while after Adrian landed the movie roll, Cammie thought it was my fault and, therefore, hates me with a burning passion." I informed them. I raised an eyebrow when they looked past me rather than commenting on Adrian and Cammie's middle school relationship.

"Well, I wouldn't blame her since my best friend is so amazingly awesome." A voice said behind me as strong arms snaked around my waist and pulled me closer to their owner.

"Hi, Adrian." I chirped without looking back at him.

"Talking about me again?" Adrian asked next to my ear, his breathe tickling my neck and making me shiver.

"Nope." I said, popping he 'p'. "What makes you think that?"

Adrian chuckled and kissed my cheek lightly. My friends raised an eyebrow at me earning themselves an eye roll.

"And you say nothing's going on between you two." Dylan scoffed.

"There isn't!" I cried out defiantly. "This is totally normal."

"Maybe not to Adrian, it isn't." A new voice joined. Brandon came from behind and stood next to Brynn. Brandon's presence was enough to make Brynn blush lightly. I smirked.

"Well, if it isn't Brynn's Prince Charming!" I said cheerily. The others laughed at Brynn's gawking expression and Brandon's embarrassed face. The bell rang before Brynn got to shoot me down.

"That's the bell!" I said quickly tearing away from Adrian's arms and grabbing his hand instead. "Say your goodbyes, lovebirds." I told the embarrassed duo before waving a quick goodbye to the others and rushing to first period with Adrian.

"You know she's in our next class and that she's going to kill you right?" Adrian chuckled while slinging an arm around my shoulder.

"Yes, but embarrassment is going to be the death of me caused by that group so I might as well embarrass them when I get the chance."

"Embarrassment for what?" Adrian asked faking a curious tone. Unfortunately for him, I've know him long enough to catch any other meanings behind his tone. Amusement is quiet clear in his question.

"Nothing." I mumbled.

I could practically feel his smirk playing on his sculpted face before he kissed the top of my head and entered English class.

Chapter 7

It's been weeks since Adrian made his victorious return back to Florida and wrenched himself back into my life. And may I say, I couldn't be happier. Adrian felt like the other half of one of those broken heart necklaces that were given to another as a promise to stay together no matter what. He completes the other half.

Corny, right?

Just another one of his changes to my life; not a good thing. But because of him, Chase and I replenished that bond we had back in our middle school days while Brandon continues to amaze us with his impeccable wit. Sometimes though, it's more like flirt techniques for our little blond headed friend. My girls seem to enjoy—well, at least less hate— coming to school. I could safely say that school has been more enjoyable this year with all the upsides Adrian brought with his new label. For the down sides...

"Move, you tramp!" Cammie screeched. I cringed at the freakishly high pitch of her voice. Cammie dug her long nails into my shoulder and roughly pushed me into a row of lockers.

"Jesus Christ, Cammie." I mumbled. "Trim down those witch nails of yours."

Cammie has somehow raised the 'Hate Macey Daniels' bar by several notches since Adrian arrived. As if she couldn't hate me anymore with her constant insults, pranks, and scenes before Adrian came back.

Cammie turned sharply on her heels to face me. I gagged as her dyed blond hair flicked me in the face sending a wave of suffocating perfume into my lungs.

"It's called fashion." She stated with her head held high.

"It's called an excuse for you to freak out like breaking a nail is more important than losing your virginity." I snorted before gasping and pouting my lips. "Oh, wait. That's the truth, my bad."

Cammie glared at me with her piercing blue eyes before whipping around and strutting down to lunch. A triumphant smile crept up my face as I watched her furiously snap at a couple freshman to get out of her way.

"Aw, Macey!" A voice called out. I looked to my left and found the whole crew walking towards me with different expressions glued to their faces. Brandon had his hands up in a disbelieving way and gave me a what-the-hell look.

I stepped away from the lockers and made my way over to them. "Problem?"

"We're gone for five minutes and you almost start a cat fight?" Dylan quizzes.

Chase grasps my shoulders and shakes them. "You know how much we love when you guys fight!"

I slapped his arms away from my shoulders and roll my eyes at them. "We did not almost start a fight." I said. The hall was completely empty by the time we started walking towards the cafeteria. Several heads turned in our direction when we walked in. A few whispered and pointed at me when I started towards our usual table.

Another down side was that part of the school population stared or whispered about the famous Adrian Chapmen's best friend. Some drooled and awed over our close relationship. Most girls envied it. Some liked to gossip about it and twist the words like the whole school joined in a game of telephone. Rumors were spread about Adrian and I being an item and becoming the next 'it couple'.

Oh, please.

Me and Adrian? Yeah, sure. Come back to me when all mythological creatures are proved to be real and not figures of a whack job's imagination. You don't see Big Foot dancing on stage with Lady Gaga or Johnny Depp riding the streets of Hollywood on a magical unicorn now, do you?

Everyone but me and Amber fled to scavenge some food. Being the non-fan of the mysterious substances that they put in the food here, I bring my own for lunch from home when I'm in the mood to eat. Adrian's been forcing me to bring food instead of 'starving my stick figure down to twigs' as he put it. Dramatic much?

"So, Adrian still off doing interviews?" Amber asked after taking a bite from her usual PB & J sandwich.

I swallowed the chip I was currently chewing before answering, "Yup. That and other various ways of keeping that heartthrob image of his."

Amber laughed loudly and slightly choked on her sandwich. I rolled my eyes at her with a amused smile. Amber is Amber. The others returned shortly with their hands filled with different drinks, chips, and other food. Chase unwrapped his chicken sandwich and bit at least half of it off. I cringed at the uncooked meat.

"Gross, Chase!" Brynn exclaimed with a disgusted look. "That's not even cooked!"

Chase shrugged as Brandon unwrapped his own sandwich and took a giant bite. Dylan tore a piece off of her sandwich and passed it to me. I gave her a questioning look.

"Don't worry, it's fine. Try it."

I stared at it for a second before taking it from her hand and popping it into my mouth. My eyes widened as my tongue began to burn like hell. The others began to laugh uncontrollably at my reaction. Dylan knew all too well that my tongue was sensitive to spicy things. I could eat some basic spicy foods but the terrible burning sensation from this sandwich was torturing my poor tongue. I hurried to swallow it and grabbed my water bottle.

"Holy, crap! That's freaking spicy!" I shrieked once my mouth was empty. I fumbled with the cap before chugging the water down my throat. The others continued to laugh at me; Chase with his mouth full and Amber choking once again.

I was just about done finishing up my water bottle when two hands clamped over my eyes with the word "BOO!" yelled right next to my ear. Being me, I choked, did a spit take and started coughing like a maniac. I managed to spray water at all my friends that Brynn and Dylan shot out of their seats, Amber's face was turning red from her laughing fit, and Brandon and Chase fell out of their seats because they were cracking up.

Another laugh– an all too familiar laugh– joined them from right behind me. I was well aware that probably the whole cafeteria was watching me die of embrassment. I was going to kill the guy behind me.

"Damn it, Adrian!" I yelled between coughs. I reached behind me and punched what I assumed was his stomach. Still laughing, he parked himself right next to me and gave high fives to Brandon and Chase from across the table. Once everyone was sober I punched Adrian again with a groan.

"Ow!" He yelled with a fake hurt tone; his amused face said otherwise.

"What the hell, Adrian!" I huffed angrily, burying my face into my hands. The whole cafeteria just witnessed my embarrassment. I could feel my face burning up. Luckily, the bell rang signaling for fifth period. I shot up from my seat and glared at Adrian. "Hello to you too." I hissed before grabbing Amber's arm and tugging her to our next class.

"I'm in your next class you know!" Adrian called out to me. I ignored him and headed straight to the girls locker room while pounding my chest and coughing a little.

"Macey!" Adrian called from the down the hall. It was the end of the day and I managed to ignore Adrian through the whole day

Ignoring him for the billionth time, I shut my locker and headed towards the exit. I could hear his frustrated groan as he ran after me. Adrian caught up with me just as I opened the door of the school's entrance.

"Mace, you can't ignore me forever."

Ignored.

"Macey."

Nothing.

"Macey Daniels!" Adrian grabbed my shoulder and whirled me around to face him.

"What?" I snapped.

"Mace," Adrian began. He took my hand and looked me straight in the eye. "I'm sorry, okay? It was just a joke. I didn't mean to embarrass you."

"You do that too much, you know that?"

Adrian dropped my hand and crossed his arms across his chest. I looked down at what he was wearing. Adrian looked pretty laid back today with his shorts and muscle shirt. He probably did a photo shoot today... Yeah, that's what he said he was doing today. I shook my head and pulled myself back to reality to look at his face. His usual smirk was there as he looked at me.

"Yeah, I know." he replied.

"Well stop."

"Where's the fun in that?"

I rolled my eyes at him and walked off. Adrian was by my side within a few steps. "You know you have to come home with me, remember?"

I stopped and mentally slapped myself. High class clients were coming over for dinner and my parents didn't want their 17 year old daughter there to embarrass them. Right, like I'm the embarrassing one. I've lost count on how many times they've embarrassed me over the years.

I let out a defeated sigh while running a hand through my hair to control it from whip lashing someone in the face because of the wind. "Are you sure it's okay if I come home with you?"

"You're always welcome, Mace. You're like their third child of course it's okay. We've finished packing anyways."

Strangely unconvinced, I took out my phone to call my mom only to find already had a text from her.

Mom:

'Go home with Adrian. We'll call you when you can come home. Don't be a nuisance, have fun :)'

I rolled my eyes and locked my phone. Seeing that I have no choice, I sighed. "Fine. But you're not forgiven."

Adrian smiled and slung his arm around my shoulder. "You can't stay mad at me for that long." He said as he towed me deeper into the parking lot.

"Yes, I can."

Lie.

"No, you can't. Because you love me that much."

True.

"You just can't stand the fact of me being mad at you for that long." I retorted.

"Very true. I can't have my Sweet Macey mad at me for more than a half hour." Adrian confessed with a smile. I rolled my eyes at his nickname for me and gave him a small nudge. Adrian simply chuckled and planted a kiss on my temple.

"How are we getting to your house anyways? You said you lived several miles from here." I asked.

As if on cue, Adrian took out his car keys and stopped in front of a red Ferrari. My mouth dropped to the floor as I gaped at it. A few distant people were admiring it from a far but not being so discreet about it.

"The hell, Adrian?!" I exclaimed. "When did you get this?"

"Ah, this thing?" Adrian gestured to his luxurious car as if it was an old jeep. "Got it a few days ago."

A few freshman and sophomores were gawking at Adrian's car as well. Adrian laughed and pushed my chin up so my mouth was closed. "I mean, I know it's as hot as me but," Adrian smirked at me from the corner of his eye. "No need to drool over my car."

I rolled my eyes at his ego with a small shove.

All the single ladies

All the single ladies

All the single ladies

Now put your hands up!

I burst out laughing as Adrian scrambled for his phone. He scowled at the device mumbling a curse under his breathe.

"Aww," I cooed pinching his cheeks. "Is little Adrian a fan of Beyonce?"

Adrian gave me an annoyed look. "Kelly must've messed with my phone again," he grumbled.

"Yeah, sure."

Adrian rolled his eyes before answering his phone a few feet away. I tried to ignore the scrutinizing looks from the younger class men while Adrian took his call. I resisted the urge to do something I shouldn't if they continued.

"Hey, babe!" One of them called out, I turned to their direction to find 4 sophomores looking at me with smirks. They eyed me from head to toe. Before they could say another word, I put my hand up to stop them.

"Piss off, will you?" I scoffed not bothering to hide the clear disgust in my tone. Unfortunately, my words went through one ear and came out the other; not bothering to register through the thick skulls of theirs. They made cat calls and let out hollers. Just as I was about to cuss them out an arm wrapped protectively around my shoulders. I sighed in relief as I was pulled against a hard chest.

"You heard the lady," Adrian's husky voice rang in my ears. "Piss off." He warned them slowly. The guys were shorter than me. While I'm pretty tall for my age, Adrian managed to tower over me by a few inches more. To clarify, Adrian was intimidatingly tall which made these sophomores look like trembling trolls. Their eyes widened at Adrian before mumbling a quick sorry and scurrying off.

"Idiots. Least they pissed off." He grumbled.

I looked up at him. "Didn't need to make them piss their pants." I pointed out with a smile. Adrian looked down at me and returned the smile.

"Yes, I did." He sighed. I giggled and bumped him with my hip.

"Come on, I wanna see your new place!" I chirped. With a laugh, Adrian made his way to the drivers seat while I got shotgun.

"Another up side of having me back, don't you think?" He asked as he slid into his seat.

"It has its advantages," I told him. I glanced over at him and smiled. "I'm just glad to have you back." I told him sincerely.

Adrian kept his gaze on me before leaning over and kissing my cheek, leaving small tingles. Even though he's done it before, I blushed slightly.

"Thanks, Mace." He said softly. "It's great to be back."

"You know," I sighed turning back to the front. "I'm starting to see why people think we're dating." When he didn't respond I returned my gaze to him and saw a small smile playing on his face as he stared at the steering wheel.

"What?"

"Nothing." He said as he started the ignition. He took out a pair if sunglasses and slid them on. A small scoff left my mouth. I assumed

Adrian was giving me a look as he glanced back at me. He then leaned over and opened the compartment in front of me. Adrian pulled out another pair of sunglasses and handed it to me. I eyed it for a moment before taking it from him.

"What's this?"

"Sunglasses."

I rolled my eyes. "Well no shit, Sherlock."

"Wear them. They're my moms but she doesn't wear them any-more." He said as he turned the engine on as well as the radio. I smiled when Thrift Shop started playing. Adrian let out a sound of approval and turned the volume up louder anyone within a mile radius could be able to hear. I put the sunglasses on and turned to Adrian for his opinion.

"Supermodel, much?" He smirked. I rolled my eyes him even though I was well aware he couldn't see it.

"Just drive, Mr. Heartthrob."

Chapter 8

"You live here?" I all but shrieked.

After taking a rather long drive around Miami for Adrian's amusement, we were finally parked in the driveway of his new house. The word 'house' would be an understatement. A mansion—beach mansion to be exact–, now that's just the word. I shifted the sunglasses to the top of my head and stared.

The inviting looking mansion was a gigantic 3 story home with palm trees aligning the drive way. A few balconies stuck out on the 2nd and 3rd floor. A beautiful fountain with a naked angel was positioned in the middle of the circular drive way. The beach was no more than a 5-10 minute walk from here since it was just around the block. I was too busy gawking that I didn't realize Adrian get out if the car and make his way to my side to open the door. Shaking out of my daze, I stepped out of the car.

"I didn't realize you've taken up foster care, Adrian." I half teased, half serious. Even with Kelly and Oliver, that makes five people living in the Chapmen residence. Adrian gave me a small shove before grabbing my hand and towing me inside.

"We've got money, Macey. We're gonna use it." Adrian gloated.

No shit he's got money! I swear the Angel's wings were real gold. GOLD!

"Yeah, yeah, Superstar." I mumbled under my breathe. Too bad Adrian has a freaky high sense of hearing. He held the door open for me, sending me a look as I walked in. I switched my gaze to my feet as I proceeded inside. I could've walked straight into a wall if the faint echo of my footsteps hadn't made me look up. I stopped in my tracks.

"No. Freaking. Way." I breathed out. The floor was shiny white marble. Sunlight flooded in from the several panes of windows of the house. A spiral staircase spun so high I had to crane my neck to see where it ended. I felt Adrian's arm wrap around my shoulder.

"How 'bout a tour?"

"Do you want me wandering around like a lost puppy?"

"I wouldn't mind." He shrugged. "It'd be cute."

I elbowed his stomach so he doubled over a little. "Just show me around."

"I promise you that I'm going to get lost if you leave me alone to wonder in your home, Adrian." I huffed while making my way down the spiral staircase. After taking a quest throughout the whole Chapmen house, there's about 15 rooms in the entire place with a man cave in the attic– courtesy of Adrian and his dad– and their own private pool in the backyard. I didn't understand the pool since there was a boardwalk leading to the beach from their backyard.

"Well then I shouldn't let you wander now, should I?" Adrian chuckled. Adrian took my hand and pulled me towards an archway that lead to the living room. Our footsteps echoed lightly throughout the house and faded within an instant. I took in all the riches around me and tried to get used to that this is what Adrian's life is now. Luxurious, grand, extravagant. Being around all these fancy furniture is starting to make me feel small and unworthy.

"Hey," Adrian's voice cut through my thoughts. "You okay?" He was staring down at me with a confused expression that made him look absolutley adorable.

Stop it, Macey! That's your best friend! I snapped to myself. Shaking my head a little I gave him a smile.

"Yeah!" I chirped. "Just zoned out."

"You're weird." Adrian snorted. He positioned me in front of the couch and then pushed me so I stumbled backwards. He pointed a finger at me. "Stay."

"Yes, Sir." I pouted my bottom lip and gave him a look. Adrian rolled his eyes before strutting into the kitchen. I giggled and clutched one of the couch pillows to my chest. The living room was probably one of the most cozy rooms in the mansion. There was a flat screen above a fireplace, a coffee table in the middle of the room with a couch and two smaller couches to the side. There was a small glass table at both ends of the couch I was sitting. A lamp and some books were at the other end while another lamp and a picture frame was on my side.

I cocked my head to the side and picked up the picture from the table. A small smile crept it's way up my face as I looked down at the picture. It was a portrait of me and Adrian at the boardwalk down by the beach. The sun had already set and the different color lights from the booths and rides twinkled in the summer night. Adrian had his arms wrapped around my waist from behind me, a huge smile etched to his face. I was laughing and my wavy hair was flying to the side. I remember Kelly took this picture the night before she left for New York.

"That's my favorite picture of us."

I continued to gaze down at the picture. I had the same picture on my bedside table at home. "Me too." I said quietly. Adrian's head suddenly appeared next to me with his signature dazzling smile.

"You still like grapes, right?" he asked. Adrian held out a bowl filled with my favorite fruit.

I gasped and snatched the bowl from him. "You remember!"

"Of course I remember. You eat so much fruit because you hate vegetables with all your heart."

"Aww!" I cooed, kissing his cheek. "I can't believe you remember."

Adrian chuckled and made his way around the couch to where I was seated. The couch bounced a little when he collapsed next to me. "Let's play a game."

I tore a grape off a branch and popped it in my mouth. "What game?"

"Well, since I want to know what's been up with you these past few years, let's play a game. Question for a question. I ask you a question exchange for one in return."

I took another grape and tossed it into my mouth. "Alright, let's do it."

"Okay," Adrian sighed while grabbing a grape and throwing it in his mouth. His eyes furrowed as he tried to brainstorm a question.

"Any day now.."

"Okay, okay." Adrian mumbled. "When did you start volunteering at the Animal Shelter?"

"Umm..Junior year. Since I've always loved animals, I thought it would be pretty fun to help out."

"Okay, your turn." Adrian said, laying his arm across the sofa behind me.

"What's it like being famous?" I ask a minute later.

"Good and bad, I guess."

"What do you mean?"

Adrian held up a finger and wiggled it in my face. "Ah, one question only."

I swatted his finger away from my face. "Fine, shoot."

Adrian laid his head back onto the couch and stared up at the ceiling. "Umm.. When did you meet Brynn, Dylan, and Amber?"

"Brynn and Amber I met in freshman year. Dylan I met as a Sophomore."

Adrian nodded in response and picked up another grape. A smile found it's way up my face when a question popped into my mind.

"How many times have you stupidly gotten your ass drunk?" I asked with a sick innocent tone. Adrian stopped mid-chew to look at me with an incredulous look on his face.

I suddenly remembered the time where the famous Adrian Chapmen was found walking through the streets of Los Angeles holding up a 'I'm a Hobo and begging for a banana!" cardboard sign. Not to mention he was wearing My Little Pony boxers and was drunk out of his mind. The whole scandal was plastered on every gossip media out there. I couldn't imagine the level of embarrassment if that ever happened to me.

Adrian leaned closer with an annoying smirk and whispered, "Too many to count."

"Ever get that banana?" I added.

"Don't push it."

"I bet every girl loved your My Little Pony boxers." I gushed while fanning myself with my hand for exaggeration. Adrian glowered at me. A killer look flared in his eyes. I would've been worried if amusement didn't wash over his face.

"You're asking for it."

For the last hour, Adrian and I traded a question for a question. I got up 3 times to refill my bowl of grapes. After my 'drunk stupidity' question, Adrian has been asking me total awkward and uncomfortable questions here and there. The rest of the time were real questions that came with an answer or a story.

"Wait.." I said in between laughs. "How'd his pants end up on the chandelier that was 30 feet up in the air?"

Adrian put his hands up in a defensive way. "Beats me. I didn't grab a ladder and hang it up there, Macey!"

"You would if you could."

Adrian pursed his lips and shrugged. "True."

I laughed and threw a grape at him. I caught sight of the grandfather clock ticking in the corner of the room. It was a quarter till 8. Emma's sure to be home soon. I'm suppose to meet her at our driveway so we could go eat dinner elsewhere while my parents wrap up things with their clients. My parents are crazy.

Heaving a sigh, I slumped back against the couch and stared up at the ceiling. "I need to head home. Besides, I've ran out of questions for now."

I felt Adrian's eyes lingering on me for too long and a sudden urge of self-consciousness kicked in. He was drumming his fingers against the fabric of the couch behind me. I vaguely remember this being a habit of his when he's trying to figure something out.

I looked at him from the corner of my eye. I reached out and tapped the side of his head. "I could hear the gears in your mind cranking." Cracking a smile, Adrian scooted closer and laced his fingers with mine. "What's wrong?"

"One more question and then I'll drive you home."

I shrugged. "Okay." I assumed he was trying to find the right words since Adrian opened and closed his mouth a few times like a fish in water. If he was trying to think on how to phrase his question then it was probably a personal or awkward question. The thought made me nervous. Adrian suddenly found a cup of water sitting on the coffee table much more interesting than asking me his question.

I nudged him with my elbow. "Just say it, Adrian. You're scaring me." After a moment, Adrian flicked his eyes to mine and asked:

"Did you start dating when I left?"

I blinked. "What?"

He started rambling. "Well, I-I mean like.. Did you start dating when you reached high school? You know, go out with a dude, flirt, become official. I mean, I was always protective of you back then and I want to know if some douche bag broke your heart then you ate ice cream and bawled your eyes out while watching The Notebook or something. Because if bastard did break your heart I would've–"

I laughed. And I mean a throw-your-head-back-clutching-your-stomach kind of laugh. That's what he wanted to ask me about? I thought he was going to ask some complete absurd question like how many one nights stands I've had – which for the record is 0– or something along those lines.

"What's so funny?" Adrian cried out in an annoyed tone. His bewildered expression made it all the more funny. After 5 minutes of uncontrollable laughter I found myself with a mouthful of fabric. Adrian's strong arm was holding me face down against the pillow on his lap. "Are you done?"

I muffled out a yes. Once I was out of his grasp, I turned around so I was laying on my back with my head rested on the pillow. Adrian was staring down at me like I just celebrated a relative's death. "What the hell was that?"

"Sorry." I giggled. "Out of all the perverted questions you could've asked me, you asked me if I went out with anyone since you've been gone."

Adrian raised a challanged eyebrow. "Do you want me to ask you a perverted question?"

"No!"

"Well answer my question. I still have to get you home, idiot."

"No." I said.

"No? No you won't tell me or no you haven't dated?"

I rolled my eyes. "No, Adrian. I did not start dating the 4 years you've been gone therefore, I've never had a boyfriend."

Kind of embarassing for a 17 year old girl, I know. But I've never been into the whole dating thing. Sure, I've had a few crushes on guys and some guys have had a thing for me but everyone knew I didn't date. Not to mention my parents were sensitive on the whole topic. They made it specfically clear that I date if and only if he was 'the one'. If he wasn't then I'd have to wait till after college. To this day, I fid it completey stupid. I mean, how am I suppose to know the guy's 'the one' if I can't get to know him on a romantic level? Something tells me they set the bar the way they did because of a certain someone.

"Good."

My mouth dropped open. "Wha– Good?!" I exclaim in disbelief. "Adrian, it's sad! I'm 17 and never went on a date before!"

All I got was a shrug before I was pushed rather rudely off the couch. I landed on the rug with a thud and a bruised arm. I propped up on my elbows and shot him a glare.

"Asshole." I muttered. Adrian was drumming his fingers against his thigh as he stared down at me. He's thinking. Analyzing. If I still know my best friend, Adrian waits a few seconds before changing the subject.

"What now?" I ask.

1.. 2... 3.... "Let's get you home."

Score for Macey!

I stood up and rubbed my injured arm. Normally I would pry out what he was thinking about but I had to get home or Emma will give me one of her 'I'm the oldest, you have to listen to me!' lectures.

"Lead the way."

Chapter 9

M acey's POV

"Macey!"

I looked away from my locker and saw Dylan running down the hall. Her curly hair was flying behind her and she had a huge smile plastered onto her face.

"Hey, Dyl." I chirped once she was closer.

"You ready to go?" She asked while leaning against the lockers.

I shoved the rest of my binders inside of my locker. "What do you mean?"

"You didn't forget, did you?" Dylan sneered. She looked around the hall before leaning closer like she was about to gossip a deep dark secret. "We have that thing.. After school.."

Everything seemed to click. Dylan had her duffel bag today. I slapped a hand to my mouth with a loud gasp. It's been a week and it's time to go back. More importantly, the girls are the only ones who know. "Oh, crap! I forgot to tell–"

"Hey girls," A pair of strong arms wrapped around my waist. I looked over my shoulder at a smiling Adrian. Brandon and Chase were behind him wearing similar smirks. "Driving you home today, right?" Adrian asked. I turned my head back to Dylan who had her mouth slightly parted. I shook my head a little. Adrian doesn't know where we're going and I don't plan on telling him. I couldn't tell anyone else. Not after what happened a few years ago.

"Actually.." I walked over to Dylan's side to face the three boys with my best fake smile. Adrian can read me so easily; hopefully I can hoax him this once. "I have to go somewhere with the girls."

As if on cue, Amber came running down the hallway yelling our names. "Dylan! Macey! Hurry up, Brynn's waiting!" Once Amber was by our side, she bent over to catch her breathe but sadly continued to talk. "I brought my stuff for later. Did you guys bring your–" Amber abruptly stopped as she stared at the floor. I followed her gaze to the guys' shoes that were standing right in front of us. Amber slowly straightened herself to look at the guys.

"Oh.. Hi guys." Amber greeted them in a timid voice.

Adrian folded his arms across his chest with a raised eyebrow. Chase came to his side doing the same. "Where you girls off to?" Chase quizzed.

Brandon stepped forward and looked at the three of us.

Crap.

"Uh.." I glanced over at the girls. We all looked like a dear caught in headlights. An excuse finally popped in my head a second later. Much to my dismay, so did Dylan and Amber since we all blurted out our lies at the same time.

"Work on a project."

"Library."

"Waffle house!"

Dylan and I snapped our head in Amber's direction.

Waffle house? What?!

Amber Olsen everybody. Leave it to her to hand us over right handed. Amber's face blushed deeply as she said 'Sorry' with her eyes.

"Well, which is it?" Brandon asked in a teasing voice. Chase was smiling like he broke us and Adrian was drumming his fingers against his forearm with a smirk. Amber looked at Dylan, who looked at me; causing the guys to do the same. I took a deep breathe and refrained from biting my lip. I wasn't bad at lying but Adrian could read me like an open book. Biting my lip was a habit of mine when I was nervous. Looping my arms with Amber and Dylan, I gave them the best poker face I could muster.

"We are going to the library to work on a project and then heading to the Waffle house downtown." I told them in a calm voice. I shifted my weight to one foot and flashed them a smile. Amber's arm tensed but I focused on the guys; not breaking eye contact. Dylan seemed to be taking this seemingly well. She kept her gaze leveled on the guys with a blank expression.

After a forever-lasting stare down, Chase was the first to break. He shrugged. "Okay."

"Yeah, alright." Brandon said. I exhaled the breathe I didn't realize I was holding. Amber let out a nervous chuckle and her arm relaxed. I looked at Adrian. He was looking straight at me. Right there, I thought he could see right through me. His fingers were still drumming against his forearm. Brandon and Chase looked at him too, followed by Dylan and Amber.

1..

2..

3..

4..

5…"Okay. Be safe, alright?"

A smile broke onto my face and I completely relaxed. I walked up to him and planted a kiss on his cheek. "I'll call you later when I get home."

After getting a nod, I grabbed Dylan and Amber's hand. Together we made our way down the hallway towards the front of the school. Once we turned a corner and were out of sight, Dylan and I both slapped Amber's arm.

"Ow!" Amber complained, rubbing her arm.

"Waffle house?! Really, Ams?" Dylan hissed.

"I panicked!"

"You think those apes wouldn't come with us to a freaking Waffle House?"

"I'm sorry! I just—"

I thew my hands in the air. "Enough!" I snapped. They both stopped their little argument and looked at me. "We're off the hook so let's just go before Brynn has our heads hanging on a cabin wall in Utah with the rest of the animals she's killed!"

Dylan shook her head in amusement and began to drag us down the hall. "That girl needs to take us hunting next time."

The strong smell of rain greeted us when we stepped out into the cool air. The sun decided to take a berak on Miami today. Brynn's Ford Explorer was parked at the other end of the parking lot. The light pater of rain was like music to my ears since I adored the rain. Amber, however, cursed at the rain and sprinted towards Brynn's car. Dylan and I laughed and jogged after her. Amber quickly popped open the trunk of the car, threw her bag inside, and pushed past us to get to the front seat.

"Slow down, hot stuff." Dylan teased when Amber scrambled into the car. Dylan proceeded to toss her own bag inside before we got into the back seat. My bag was always kept in Brynn's car for personal reasons. Once we were inside, Brynn glared at us through the rear view mirror. If looks could kill, Dylan and I would have been slaughtered on the spot. Amber avoided Brynn's death look by looking out the window.

"Where were you guys?" Brynn asked.

"Being interrogated." I mumbled. Deciding not to be shot daggers at with Brynn's piercing eyes, I switched to focusing on the water droplets racing each other down the window.

"If anyone asks, we're going to the library to work on a project and then to a Waffle House." Dylan exaggerated the last part and shot Amber a look. Amber suddenly took interest in the row of bikes parked at the bike rack, very interesting.

Brynn laughed and switched the engine on. "Oh, Amber." She sighed. Using a Waffle House as a cover up was a sure Amber Olsen thing. "You will be the death of us one day."

"Shut up you guys." Amber grumbled as she crossed her arms tightly across her chest while sliding deeper into her seat. The rest of us laughed at Amber's behaviour. Just as we were turning out of the school parking lot, I spotted Adrian's Ferrari parked near the front of the school. I sighed. We may have gotten off the hook but I am sure as hell he was not convinced.

"Guys! Take this seriously!"

I clutched my aching stomach and doubled over. Brynn falling to the floor because of her laughing only made me crack up even more. Dylan pranced around the room with the most pedophile smile ever. Her hair was put into a messy side ponytail and giant nerd glasses were covering half her face. Her purple baggy shirt was tucked into her shorts and she was wearing a green sweat band with knee high socks. Dylan often came to practice looking like a freaky hipster to piss Amber off.

Dylan started to shimmy towards Amber with a goofy look on her face. Amber pushed her roughly back, causing Dylan to stop her act and join us in our uncontrollable hysteria. "You're suck a dork, Dyl!" Amber shrieked. She could've passed off as annoyed if the smile on her face didn't give her away.

"Alright..Alright, I'm done." Dylan gasped between laughs. Amber turned to Brynn and I, who were still trying to stop.

"That's enough, girls."

We all froze in place. The urge to laugh was gone. Brynn slowly got up from the floor while I straightened myself. At the doorway was the women in charge of the studio– AKA Amber's mother– giving us a disapproving look. Dylan pulled the band from her hair so it cascaded down in her regular curls.

"Hi, Mrs. Olsen." We greeted.

"Hey, mom" Amber said shyly, nudging Dylan. Dylan immediately fixed herself back to a normal human by removing her ridiculous items.

"This is dance practice, girls." Mrs. Olsen sighed. Then she waved dismissively at us. "And I've told you a hundred times! Call me Lucile. 'Mrs. Olsen' sounds so old."

We all let out a chuckle. I let myself slouch a little instead of my frigid state. Lucile would always scold but quickly let it go. Dylan tossed her nerd glasses, socks, and sweat band into her duffel bag and walked to the middle of the room. Brynn patted down her hair and followed Dylan with Amber right behind her. I sat down on one of the chairs that were pushed up against the walls.

Lucile made her way to the front of the room. "Alright, ladies! I'm assuming you did some kind of practice while you were here?"

Lucile sighed and Dylan shrugged. "Not many people know that we dance anyways, Lucile. It's not like we're going to have a recital or something."

"Yes, that may be true. But I would like for you girls to continue and flourish–" Lucile began to flail her arms dramatically for em-phasis. "– In the world of dance." She stepped closer and continued her little speech while gesturing in the girls' faces. "Dance is a way for you to express yourself! A way for you to let loose and have fun! Dance is a way–"

"Uh, Miss?"

Lucile's arms fell back down to her sides. She tilted her head up in aggravation instead of looking at the man poking his head at the corner of the studio room. "Yes, Curtis?" she sighed.

"There are some gentleman at the front desk." Curtis informed us.

"Yes, yes. I'll be there in a minute." Lucile dismissed. When Curtis disappeared back to his post at the front desk, Lucile turned to us. She put her hands on her hips and gave us a stern look. "You girls better have done one dance routine by the time I get back, understood?"

We nodded and Lucile left the studio. Amber clapped her hands together. "Alright, let's do this." Being the daughter of the studio owner, Amber learned how to dance at a very young age. She may be a smart girl and a bit of ageek but Amber is a phenomenal dancer.

"That is if you can focus." she added

Brynn snorted. "You think we can't focus?"

Amber gave Dylan a look and then turned back to Brynn. "Yes."

"Well, Miss. Perfect. We'll show you we can focus." Brynn replied while stretching her arms.

"Besides, I'm in the mood for those waffles." Dylan said with a smirk. Amber shot them a glare before jogging over to the stereo that sat on a table in the corner of the room. A smile slowly crept up her face when she found a song. Amber pressed play and ran back to Dylan and Brynn. The tune of Party in the USA by Miley Cyrus started booming from the stereo.

Dylan folded her arms and raised her eyebrows. "Really?"

"Yes! Let loose, will you?" Amber shot back.

Jumped in the cab, here I am for the first time.

Look to my right and I see the Hollywood Sign.

This is all so crazy, Everybody seems so famous.

Brynn pretended to rub her chin and started tapping her foot. "I wonder who that reminds us of." Dylan winked at me from across the room.

"Oh, shut up." I glared playfully at them from where I was seated. Dylan laughed and jogged over to me.

"Come on!" Dylan grabbed my hand and pulled me towards the others. "Nobody else is here, Mace. You can do this."

Glancing at the empty door frame, I sighed and faced the front of the studio. The whole wall was a mirror so we could see ourselves. I ran a hand through my long hair and stared at my reflection.

There's nobody else here.. I assured myself.

Just as the chorus came up, I heaved a sigh. "Let's do this." I told them. Amber and Dylan cheered in response as Dylan fist pumped the air.

So I put my hands up

They're playing my song, and the butterflies fly away.

I'm noddin' my head like 'Yeah'

Movin' my hips like 'Yeah'

I got my hands up, they're playin' my song

I know I'm gonna be okay.

Yeah, it's a party in the USA

Yeah, it's a party in the USA

The choreography for the song was done by the 4 of us with the help of Lucile. We often did this song when we wanted to have fun. Dylan ran back to her bag and took out her nerd glasses. We switched from messing around to the regular choreography, like we usually do. Throughout the song, I forgot about the horrible past that came when I first started to dance. The reason why I was so skeptical about dancing in front of anybody else than the ones who already knew dissappeared. Dancing with the girls was the most fun I could ask for. It gave me an opportunity to not give a damn about anything and just let go.

At the end of the song, we froze in our finishing pose. Then we started laughing. It was one of those carefree laughs that I always shared with the girls during dance practice. It would've been a great way to end the day if multiple loud clapping didn't echo through the room. We all froze and snapped our heads in the direction of the clapping.

Oh, Shit...

I let out a shrill scream and whirled around so my back was facing them. Standing under the door frame were three clapping idiots. All three wearing self-satisfied smirks.

Adrian.

Brandon.

Chase.

"This is what you get for lying to me, Macey." Adrian said aloud.

Damn it.

Chapter 10

Adrian's POV

It all started when the girls disappeared around the corner..

"Do you really think they're going to do a project in a library and then go to a waffle house?" Brandon asked, earning himself a smack in the head from Chase.

"Really, dude?" Chase snorted.

"What? It seemed pretty legit to me."

"You believe they're going to waffle house?" Chase deadpanned.

"Well.." Brandon replied sheepishly, scratching the back of his neck.

Chase rolled his eyes and turned to me with his arms crossed. "What do you think, Adrian?"

I was still staring at the spot where Macey and the girls disappeared. I could tell Macey was putting up a good fight to lie to me but even after disappearing from her life for four years, I could still tell when she was lying. Their lie would've worked if Amber didn't mention going to waffle house. Leave it to her to ruin a secret..

"Adrian," Chase repeated. I looked to him with a pointed look on my face.

"Of course I don't believe them." I scoffed. As much as I do respect Macey's privacy, I hated the fact that she was lying to me about it. I mean, how bad could this secret really be? It's not like they're breaking into a bank or robbing a jewelry shop or some shit like that. If she was willing to hide this from me, then I'm damned determined to figure out why.

The corner of my lip pulled upwards into an evil smirk. I turned to the guys. As if reading my mind, they produced a smirk of their own and shot me a smug look.

"Up for a drive, boys?"

I ended up falling last in line while following the girls to their secret destination. A red Ferrari tends to gain attention, especially when a star is riding in it. But of course, the top was on and my windows were tinted a bit, but that wouldn't stop the girls from noticing that they're being followed.

Brandon had borrowed his grandpa's old car so the girls have no idea who the driver is. Hopefully they don't notice the trash on wheels trailing behind them. Chase was next in his Ford Explorer with me behind him. More and more rain droplets were pounding against the window, blocking my vision. I turned the windshield on just as Brandon changed lanes.

Only when we were driving deeper and deeper into down town did my thoughts start to swirl in my head. Obviously, they weren't going to the library since the nearest public library was only a ten minute drive from our school. Where the hell are they doing?

I got my answer about ten minutes later when I mimicked Chase's actions of parking next to the sidewalk a few feet away from a building. Trying to see through the drops of water stuck to the window, I saw Brynn's blond hair jumping out of the drivers seat and making her way to the back of the car. Amber was next, scrambling quickly to the trunk and grabbing a purple backpack before making a mad dash for the front entrance. Two brunettes exited the back seats and walked casually to the trunk.

The only difference between the two was one of them had blond ends, meaning it was Dylan. She took out a duffel bag and passed a black backpack to who I assumed was Macey before making their way inside with Brynn. Once they were inside, I waited a few minutes before opening the door and stepping out into the rain.

I made my way towards Chase and waited for Brandon to come out of his crappy car. I shouldn't be one to judge but even he called it a shitty car.

"What the hell is he doing?" Chase scowled when Brandon didn't emerge from his car. We made our way towards his car to see Brandon still sitting in his car. Chase knocked loudly on the window with an annoyed expression.

Brandon opened the window a peak. "What the hell are you doing, man? Come on." I told him. Brandon shook his head.

"Do you see what's happening out there?" He asked. I felt my eyebrows furrow in confusion. What did he mean? The rain?

I smirked.

"You mean the water falling from the sky? Yeah, that's called rain." I told him slowly as if I was trying to teach a 5 year old.

Brandon rolled his eyes "I know what rain is, asshole. I'm not going to get my hair wet."

Chase and I hollered in laughed. Seriously? It was understandable that Amber sprinted to the entrance instead of taking a walk in the rain but she was a girl. Girls worry about this kind of stuff.

Last time I checked, Brandon wasn't gay. Was he?

"You're not gay are you?" I asked for confirmation, amusement lacing through my tone. Chase chuckled next to me.

"Of course not!" Brandon snapped.

"Well then grow some balls, stop being a wuss, and let's go." Chase ordered. He nodded towards the entrance and together we made our way over. It wasn't long when Brandon pushed past us and dashed for shelter.

There wasn't any sign on the building whatsoever so we had absolutely no clue to what this mysterious building was and why the girls had disappeared into it. I then realized that we were pretty much stalking them but my curiosity got the best of me. I had to know what Macey was hiding from me. The girls seemed to know about it, why would she keep it to from me?

A small part of me was hurt that my best friend was keeping secrets from me, especially since I didn't want to keep anymore things from each other since I started being a part of her life again. I mean, she lied to me about it! What could she possibly be hiding from me that she couldn't tell me?

A rush of warm air greeted us when we pushed the doors open. Not much was in the building from what I could see, only a front counter and a hallway at either side of us. A guy – probably no more than 25 – was playing with a ball of rubber bands, tossing it in the air with the whole get-me-out-of-this-hell-hole look on his face.

"Excuse us?" Brandon said to the receptionist. He barely acknowledged our presence but grunted at us like we were a nuisance.

"Yes?" He asked in a monotone voice. I pulled a face at the man.

"What is this place exactly?" Brandon asked him.

"This is a private studio. If you have do not know this then you are not allowed in this building. Please exit." He informed us still with his dull voice. He didn't even look up from the damn rubber band ball.

Clearly annoyed, Chase slammed both hands on the counter. Curtis jumped twenty feet in the air and looked up at us in bewilderment. I pushed between the boys so Curtis could see me. One advantage to being famous – even when you're on a break – is they usually do anything they can to satisfy you. And what I want right now, is to know what the hell this building is and why the girls are in here.

His eyes widened when they landed on me and I felt my mouth pull up into a sly smile.

"Listen.." My eyes flicked down to his name tag. "Curtis," I continued. "A couple our friends came in here and they lied to us about it. So what is this place, exactly?"

"M-Mr. Chapmen," he stuttered. "This is a studio owned by Mrs. Olsen. Your friends – I'm assuming – are Miss. Tucker, Miss. Castro, and Miss. Daniels. As well as Mrs. Olsen's daughter, of course. They come here every other week."

I raised an eyebrow. Chase and Brandon mimicking my actions as well. Why are they at a studio every other week? And since when did Amber's mom own a studio? I probably didn't notice since I was flying from state to state for interviews and photo shoots before I can really go on break. I guess that's why I didn't notice Macey disappear with the girls to this place.

"Uh.. What do you mean studio?" Brandon asked. "Why would they come here?"

Curtis hesitated before answering. "This is not my information to give."

"And why not?" I questioned with a challenged eyebrow.

"I-I was t-told not give out a-any information."

"By who?"

"By Mrs. Olsen."

I sighed. I need answers and I'm going to get them. "Is Mrs. Olsen here?" I asked.

"Yes, Mr. Chapmen."

"May we speak to her?" Chase asked, feigning innocence when we were actually stalking the girls and prying for answers. Call it creepy or whatever but I was curious.

Then again, Curiosity did kill the cat... An inner voice snarked.

"Yes," Curtis shot to his feet. "One moment." And he headed towards the right wing. Not even five minutes later, a short bubbly women came bounding towards us. She shared the same eyes and hair color as her daughter but I was pretty sure Amber had a few inches over her mother.

"May I help you, boys?" She asked, scrutinizing our appearance. "This is a private studio."

We all squirmed uncomfortable under her gaze. When none of replied, Amber's mom sighed and held out a hand. "I'm Lucile, by the way."

Knowing Brandon wouldn't make the first move and Chase was busy looking uncomfortable, I stepped forward and shook Lucile's hand. "Hi, Lucile. I'm Adrian Chapmen, sorry if we're interrupting something."

Lucile let out a light laugh and waved her hand dismissively. "Oh I know who you are, sweetie. You're the famous Adrian that also has my daughter and her friends constantly picking on pour Macey." She said with a wink.

I flashed an uncomfortable smile. A lot of people thought we had something going on but in all honesty, I don't know if there is. Sometimes I wonder would would've happened if I stayed with Macey all those years I was living my dream. What would've came out of us..

I shook my head, ridding of the thoughts and gestured to the guys. "And this is Brandon and Chase."

"Brandon and Chase.. Brandon and Chase..." She repeated distantly. Suddenly, she snapped a finger at realization. "Ah, yes. Brandon Lockwood, supposedly flirting up a storm with dear Brynn and Chase Porcelli."

Brandon's cheeks flushed red, causing everyone to laugh at his embarrassment.

"So, boys," Lucile clapped her hands together. "How may I help you?"

"Well, we're here to see the girls. They were supposedly 'Going to the library to work on a project and then to a waffle house'." Brandon used air quotes around the her daughter's lie.

Lucile laughed. "That last part sounds like my daughter."

Check mate!

"She was the one who ruined the secret."

Lucile laughed before clasping her hands together. She gave us a serious look. "I see the girls still are keeping this whole thing a secret."

"What do you mean?" Chase asked.

"Well, this is a dance studio." I could've sworn my mouth dropped to the floor.

Dance studio?! Macey's a dancer and she didn't tell me??

The guys were giving Lucile a surprised look as well which she returned with a small smile. "Yes, all four of them are dancers. Brynn and Macey have been doing it for a few years now followed closely by Dylan. They've been hiding for Macey's expense but I do think it's time for them to come out from the shadows."

With that she beckoned us down the hallway. I trailed after her still in my shocked daze. How could Macey not tell me this? Why would they be keeping it a secret because of her?

I was so damn confused, it wasn't even funny.

But what we saw next made it clear as day.

Macey's POV

Present Time

I can't believe they followed us here. My hands were shaking and I could see my skin paler than usual.

"What the hell are you guys doing here?!" Amber shrieked. Through the mirror, I could see the girls staring at the guys. Adrian, Brandon, and Chase smirking at them. Adrian seemed so proud of himself for finding out our secret which only pissed me off even more.

Brynn went hand on hip. "How'd you guys get in here?" she demanded. I could hear the scowl in her tone.

"Amber's mom so kindly let us watch." Chase told us slyly. My whole body tensed. That means they saw the whole number. Awful memories started flooding my head, making my breath quicken. I shut my eyes tightly and clutched my head while the girls continued to yell.

"WHAT?" They all screamed. Every one of their heads snapped towards Lucile.

"Mom! How could you?!" Amber yelled at her mother in disbelief. Lucile put her hands up in defense.

"Girls, it's been years. You can't keep your talent a secret for so long."

"Damn well we can!" Dylan shot back.

"What the hell is your guys' problem?" Brandon interjected with an annoyed look.

"It's none of your business, Brandon! You guys shouldn't have stalked us here!" Brynn shouted, stepping closer. She looked like she was going to slap him right across the face. Not like I wouldn't mind..

Chase stepped in front of Brandon and held his hands up to stop Brynn. "Well then maybe you guys shouldn't have lied to us."

"You know what happened years ago, Mom!" Amber yelled at her mother again.

I whirled around to give my best friend a death glare. "This was your idea wasn't, Adrian?"

Adrian rolled his eyes at me and crossed his arms. "I don't get what the big deal is."

"Because you don't understand, Adrian!" I shouted loudly.

Adrian looked taken aback from my answer but pulled himself together quickly. "Well then make me understand, Macey!"

"No!" The girls and I yelled back. I was starting to shake in my shoes and tears were blurring my vision. I didn't want to tell anyone what happened. Especially not Adrian.

"Girls!" Lucile interrupted. "You have to tell somebody about this."

"Mom, you know exactly what Cammie did to Ma—"

"Amber!" I yelled in horror.

Dylan slapped a hand over Amber's mouth before she could finish her sentence, but it was too late. They know it was Cammie and they knew she did something to me.

"What?" Adrian breathed in exasperation. "Cammie's the reason you're keeping this a secret?" Everyone turned to look at me. I knew Amber was sending me an apologetic look and the others were sending me either shocked or worried expressions but I couldn't look away from Adrian. He had this hurt look plastered on his face that made my heart clench for not telling him, but there was a flicker of rage in his eyes when he heard that Cammie was the reason we're hiding our dancing a secret.

I cupped my right elbow with my left hand and stared at the floor. My lip was close to bleeding since I was biting on it too hard and the tears were falling freely now. I hated anything that involved what happened during freshman year. Whether it was thinking about it or talking about it. Now I have a whole lot to explain.

Brynn noticed my breakdown first and ran over to me. She tightly grasped my shoulders, telling me to calm down. From the corner of my eye, I saw Adrian take a step forward but Dylan stopped him. Amber left the room with Lucile, probably to yell at her mother for releasing our secret.

"You guys are assholes," Dylan growled at the three – now guilty looking – guys. "Say anything about our dancing or say a word to anybody, I will cut off your balls and shove them down your throat. Clear?"

They all nodded.

Ever since Dylan joined us in Junior year she became very serious about the whole secret. If anyone found out anything, Dylan would threaten them like she was their worst nightmare or beat the crap out of them until they forgot. Growing up with 5 older brothers had it's perks..

Amber came back a few minutes later in her regular clothes. "Okay," She announced to everyone in the whole room. "Since our secrets out, might as well tell them." Amber looked my way for approval. I gave her a small nod. "Alright, let's go get waffles while we're at it."

"Least not everything's a lie." Chase mumbled loudly, gaining a murderous look from Dylan. Brandon stayed dead silent after her little threat and Adrian was too far gone in his own thoughts. Brynn and I grabbed our bags and went to change, pushing the guys roughly to the side.

Kill me now..

Adrian's POV

I was leaning up against a wall near the exit of the dance studio. Brandon, Chase, and I were waiting for the girls to come back. They were taking extra long to come back. Curtis had left an hour ago and the rain had slimmed down to a very light drizzle.

"I can't believe Queen Bitch did something so bad to Macey that they'd actually hide the fact that they danced." Chase mumbled.

Brandon shook his head. "From what we saw, I thought their dancing was really good."

"You were probably just staring at Brynn's ass the whole time." Chase snorted, getting a scowl from his friend. I drummed my fingers against my forearm with my jaw clenched.

Cammie. That jealous bitch. What did I ever see in her?! God, I was so blind and stupid back then. How could she scar Macey like that? She looked so carefree and happy when she was dancing.

That full blown smile and laugh I've never heard before. Yet when they found out we were watching she had a panic attack.. The one thought that I was trying to ignore drifted into my head again.

What would've happened between me and Macey if I hadn't gone to LA? I don't have feelings like that for her like I did back then. Well, I don't think I did..

Before I could go any further the girls came down the hallway. A scowl found it's way on Dylan's face when she saw us. Brandon was such a wuss at her threat even though we all knew she wouldn't do it. But she did grow up with five brothers, who knows what she could do. Brynn gave us a glare but Amber came bounding towards us with a nervous smile. Macey was staring at the floor with puffy eyes and a frown that made my heart clench. I hate when she's sad.

"Waffles for dinner!" Brandon whooped, obviously trying to lighten the mood. The tension was unbearably suffocating when nobody said anything and the 2 out of the 4 girls were sending us such deadly stares. If looks could kill..

"Let's go!" Amber chirped. Everything around us was soaking wet and the smell of rain was still strong when we stepped outside. Before everyone could head to their separate cars, I reached out to grab Macey's hand and pulled her towards me.

"Uh, guys?"

They all turned towards me expectantly. "Go ahead. We'll catch up in a few." I told them. Ignoring the daggers being shot at me from Brynn and Dylan, I looked at Amber. She looked a little worried but then turned to Macey.

"That okay, Mace?" she asked. After a moment, Macey nodded slightly. Once they all disappeared into their own cars and started towards their destination, I towed Macey to my car. I positioned her in front of the hood and placed her on top. She finally looked at me when I wriggled in between her legs and placed both hands at the side of her so she was trapped.

"Adrian, not in public." Macey told me quietly, referring to the position we were in. There was just an inch between us but I didn't really care if any press caught us. I wanted answers.

"I don't care, Macey." I said firmly, leaning even closer. Macey placed her hands on my chest to keep my from moving any closer and avoided my eyes. I felt myself leaning into her touch instead of pulling away.

"Mace, look at me." When she didn't move at all, I wrapped my fingers around her chin and tilted it up. There were tears brimming her eyelids when she finally met my eyes. God damn, I was going to kill Cammie..

Not knowing what possessed me to do what I did next, I leaned forward and planted soft kisses down her neck. Macey tensed under my touch before relaxing. I felt her arms wound around my neck hesitantly before I snaked my arms around her waist confidently, pulling her closer.

What the hell am I doing?? This is Macey Daniels, dumbass. AKA, BEST FRIEND! Why are you kissing her neck continuously?!

Besides the snarky inner voice, I didn't stop. I continued trailing kisses up and down her neck. I don't know what would've happened if Macey didn't snap me out of it.

"Adrian.." She whispered shakily. Am I making her nervous?

Her best friend in the world is kissing her, why wouldn't she?

Oh, shut up..

"What happened, Macey?" I whispered next to her ear. "Please tell me what happened."

Macey let out a shaky breathe. "Freshman year wasn't all that easy without you." she admitted. I pulled away just enough so I could see her. She was looking over my shoulder with glassy eyes.

"What do you mean?"

"I mean I was still that shy nerdy girl that I was back in elementary and middle school." She admit. "But I didn't want to be that girl anymore.." Macey's eyes flickered to mine before continuing. "I told you I met Brynn and Amber during freshman year. One day after school, Amber told us she was going to dance practice and asked if we wanted to come. After a few times of going with her, Brynn and I both decided to take up dancing.

"Cammie still blamed me for your breakup back then, she was still out for revenge. The night of our first recital, I was really nervous, like I usually am before presenting in front of class. Cammie showed up backstage and started throwing insults and telling me I was going to fail. She told the whole grade about it and the almost the whole freshman grade showed up!" Macey's voice was rising and tears were brimming in her eyes again. "One step on stage and I was being booed out. She told them how I was about to fail. That nerd girl couldn't do this. She told them I was going to fail and when I went up there I did!

"I ended up throwing up on stage, Adrian. I freaking threw up on stage. It wasn't bad enough I embarrassed myself in front of almost the whole grade but the next day pictures were posted everywhere."

My jaw tightened but I didn't say anything.

"Pictures were posted all over the school. On lockers, in class-rooms. But that wasn't even the worst part!" Macey suddenly shot up on her feet, making me jump back a little. "We had an assembly that day for drug resistance. But instead of the video they were suppose to show us, Cammie charmed her way through a bunch of nerds and the video of me throwing up on stage was plastered on a wall for the whole damn school to see!" There were tears streaming down her cheeks now.

"Mace.."

"And she didn't even get in trouble!" Macey continued. She was yelling now with her hands tightly clenched into a fist. "I was made fun of until the end of the year, getting made fun of every chance they got. That was Cammie's revenge. She practically ruined my freshman year, she pretty much scarred me from telling anyone about dancing. And you know what? I didn't have anyone else but Brynn and Amber. Emma was in college, my parents were on business trips all the time, and all the 'friends' I had abandoned me because they were too embarrassed to be seen with me. And sometimes, Brynn and Amber were embarrassed of me too but they refused to show it.

"They still don't know about it." She continued, leaning against the car hood. I pulled a confused face. "Emma and my parents. They don't know about what happened and they don't know that I sneak away to come to dance practice. They think I'm with the girls doing homework or going to the library or something." I found it suprising that Emma didn't know. Those two were the most close sisters I've ever seen even if they do fight.

"How does Dylan know about it?" I asked, stepping in front of her. The corner of Macey's lips pulled up into a small smile.

"That's the only good thing that came out of this whole thing. Everything kind of blew over during the following school year. We met Dylan that year and Amber continued her dancing. When we were hanging out at the beach one day, Dylan brought an old stereo with her. We were in a secluded part of the beach when we were dancing to the all songs that came on. I realised I really did enjoy dancing and that I didn't want to give it up. We told Dylan the story and she suggested that we kept everything a secret so history wouldn't repeat itself. And that's what we did."

I stared at her for a while, not knowing what to say. Macey had calmed down but she was biting her lip nervously, waiting for me to say something. She was probably expecting me to laugh at her for throwing up on stage or back my ex-girlfriend on this. Instead, I smiled and pulled her into my arms.

"Damn, Macey." I laughed lightly in her ear. Macey's arms wrapped around my neck and I tightened my grip around her. "You're really strong you know. For pulling through."

Macey buried her head onto my shoulder."I'm sorry for not telling you." she said after a moment.

"I'm sorry for stalking you." I chuckled, stroking her hair. Macey pulled back a little and gave me an annoyed look.

She slapped my shoulder. "Yeah! What the hell, Adrian?! I can't believe you actually stalked us!"

"Well you lied to me."

"That doesn't mean you have to invade my privacy."

"But you lied."

"Stalking is a form of sexual assault, Adrian." She replied stubbornly. "Remember that from health class in 8th grade? So technically you assaulted me. Sexually."

I sighed, feigning defeat and tugging her closer. "Okay, fine. I'm sorry. But promise me something."

Macey gave me a skeptical look but nodded anyways.

"No more secrets." I told her. Macey's features softened. I knew she was guilty about lying to me since we were always honest with each other. A smile graced upon her face before Macey took one hand away from my shoulder and grabbing my right hand from her waist. She wrapped her pinky around mine and held it up to my face.

"Pinky promise, Adrian."

I smiled remembering how making a pinky promise was like offering each other your kidney to us. We never broke our pink promises.

"Good," I l said before pulling her into another hug. "But you know I'm probably going to push you to dance in front of a some kind of crowd, right?"

"I kinda figured."

"And that I'm going to make you tell your family?"

"Yes, Adrian."

"And since I love you, if any dumbass hurts my Sweet Macey I'm going to beat their face in?"

A surge of satisfaction ran through me when Macey let out a loud laugh. "I forgot how protective you are."

"Well don't forget, sweetheart." I teased.

Macey pulled away and kissed my cheek softly. "I love you too, Adrian."

Those words were impossible for me not to smile at. I planted my own kiss on her cheek and nodded towards the car.

"Let's get some waffles."

Chapter 11

Adrian's POV

"Waffles for dinner is the best fucking idea ever."Those were the first words to come out of Chase's mouth this morning. Not like it wasn't true though. After having that talk with Macey, we had went downtown to the Waffle House downtown. And may I say, it was freaking fantastic. The women who owned the place had even thrown in some on the house waffles for coming in. Apparently, the press had caught me going inside which gave Aunt Karen's Waffle House some big publicity. Luckily, Macey had gone in way before I had so the press couldn't twist some rumor up and spread it faster than a wildfire. Thank god they didn't get pictures of me.. Uh. Showing friendly affection to Macey. My manager would probably blow a gasket and I'd rather not drag Macey into my 'Hollywood life'.

Brandon scowled. "Are you kidding me? I couldn't sleep until 3 AM because I was on a sugar high.""Not our fault you soaked your waffles in syrup."

"Not my fault you put salt in mine."

I rolled my eyes and tuned out their bickering. Besides the giant argument I had with my mangager the minute I walked through the door about more interviews, Brandon wasn't the only one tossing and turning that night. There was only one thing – or rather person – on my mind all night.

"MACEY GIVE IT BACK!"

Speaking of that person..

Brandon and Chase's argument came to a halt when Amber's annoyed voice rang through the hall. Macey came running down the hall clutching a copy of The Fault In our Stars to her chest. Brynn and Dylan came trailing behind her with Amber hot on their heels.

"Guys give it back!" Amber whined.

"Get your head out of the book for more than an hour and maybe we will." Brynn called back. Amber stopped to catch her breathe, letting out a groan of frustration.

Chase came to her side and ruffled her hair. "Poor Amber." He cooed.

Amber slapped his hand away and gave us a pleading look. "Please help me."

Contemplating over the idea, we gave in to Amber's pleads. Brandon went after Brynn by gripping her tightly by her arms, Chase grabbed hold of Dylan and made sure she couldn't kick his insides in while I took Macey hostage inside my arms. She let out a squeal when my arms wrapped around her waist, pulling her towards my chest.

"Give it back." I whispered next to her ear. She shook her head stubbornly but she was laughing lightly. My mouth turned up in a smile. "Unless you want me to make a scene to up peoples' thoughts of us going out, I suggest you give Amber her book back."

Macey groaned and repressed the urge to struggle. After muttering something along the lines of 'traitor', she chucked the book in

Amber's direction who caught it oh-so swiftly by letting it hit her arm and fall to the ground. Note the sarcasm.

"I hate you." Macey huffed.

I chuckled and loosened the death grip I had around her waist, pecking her on the cheek. "Love you too, sweetheart."

Once Amber had possession of her dear book, Dylan took the opportunity to elbow Chase hard in the ribs. "Don't touch me." she spat as she stalked over to Amber. Brandon released Brynn's wrist but proceeded to drape an arm around her shoulder.

"So why the game of monkey in the middle?" he asked.

The girls sent a blushing Amber a pointed look. "A guy –" Dylan started.

"A really hot guy." Macey and Brynn added together.

"– A freaking sex god was flirting with our dear friend this morning but somebody was too busy shoving her nose into a book that she didn't even blink an eyelash at the sexy beast."

Amber stomped her foot on the ground with her arms crossed insecurely across her chest. "Why do you guys have to put it like that?" She whined.

"Because he was hot!" The girls chorused. It's like they've rehearsed this whole argument before it even started.

Chase rolled his eyes. "Oh, please. You guys hang with sex gods –" he gestured to himself, me, and Brandon, "– all the time."

Amber, Dylan, and Brynn turned to look at the girl in my arms with the same smirk plastered on each of their faces. "Macey even said he was hotter than Adrian." Brynn said in a sing-song voice.

Uh, Please. There is no way in hell this guy was hotter than Adrian Chapmen. I mean come on, who in their right mind would...

Wait.

It took a few seconds for Brynn's words to register in my mind. It was one thing to have a random fan think I'm the sexiest guy in the world but to have my beautiful best friend think I'm hot, that's something different in my book. Chase let out a wolf whistle while Brandon waggled his eyebrows at me suggestively.

Pfft. Like he's one to talk. This is the guy Lucile said was, and I quote, 'flirting up a storm' with Brynn.

I leveled my head down so I could see Macey's face better. Her lips were in a tight line but she was sending her friends a playful glare. I raised an eyebrow at her. "You think I'm hot?" I teased.

Macey rolled her eyes and thumped her head onto my shoulder so she could look up at me. "Adrian, our Math teacher thinks you're hot. Must you ask your best friend if she think's you're hot?" She deadpanned.

I smiled and kissed her temple. "Oh, no. I already know you think I'm hot. I just wanted you to admit it aloud."

Truth is deep down inside, I liked the fact that Macey thought I was hot. If it was anybody else but my girl, it would be a simple average compliment that I've heard a thousand times before. But for Macey, it was different and I have no idea why. Only you, Macey.. Only you could confuse me like you do.

Macey snorted and pulled away from my arms just as the bell rang. "Don't let it get to your head, Superstar. Your head's big enough as it is." She stopped in front of Amber and gave her a look. Brynn came to her side and pointed at finger at her nose. Amber's eyes went cross when she looked at it.

"And don't think we haven't forgotten about you, Missy. We're going to talk about this." And with that, I made my way towards 1st period with Macey and Brynn.

Macey's POV

"Alright guys." Mrs. Fuller clapped her hands together and made her way towards the front of the class. "Since it's Friday, the English department decided to do something fun. So get up and push the desks into a circle."

Since we were first period, we would always prepare things for the future periods. Usually it was going over answers with her for a key on a worksheet or just numbering papers on a class set. But this? I remember doing this in elementary school so the teacher could stand in the middle and hand out the candy award that resembled us the most. It was like taking a Grammy back in those days. It was how Adrian first got his 'Sweet Macey' nickname. I was awarded sweet tarts for being the sweetest girl in the class. How flattering.

Ah, the good ole' days. Where cooties was like catching the plague and the homework was simply finding words that rhymed together. Grade school now was probably filled with snobby brats who learned bad habits from their older siblings.

"What do you think we're doing?" Brynn asked as we pushed our desks up against the wall and slid in.

I shrugged at her question and placed my stuff on the floor. Adrian caught my eye from across the room, goofing off with some of the other guys in the class. He had managed to clarify who was truly interested in just him rather than the famous side of him, which I was glad for.

I must've been staring for longer than I intended because Adrian sent me a very obvious wink causing Brynn to nudge me playfully. I rolled my eyes at him and continued to get out a piece of paper just as Mrs. Fuller instructed. Adrian's loud chuckle rumbled through the whole room. I shook my head in amusement.

Soon enough everyone had gotten their own piece of paper and were waiting calmly for Mrs. Fuller's next directions. A calm high school classroom? Pfft.

It took a few moments for the noise to die down once Mrs. Fuller was in the middle of the circle of desks. "I want you guys to pass your paper to the right until I say 'Pass'. Write something down about that person whether its a feeling, compliment, a memory, and so on. But it must remain anonymous. Then you pass that paper to the person to your right. You keep going until you get your own paper back, got it?"

The class made a sound of approval filled with cheers. "Keep in mind that I'm just going to scan through them and take it as a completion grade so think about that while you write down something about that person."

"This is cool." Brynn squealed from next to me. "Means I can write something about you." she teased mischievously.

"Choose your words carefully, Blondie."

The whole assignment was actually quiet fun. We got to see what other people had put on each others papers and most of the time, it was pretty funny. I had went up the grades with these people so pretty much the whole grade knew each other. Most of my peers in this class I've known since elementary, middle, or just up to the recent years of high school. Suffice to say, there were whole lot of great memories.

For Brynn, I had poorly drawn an image of Goldilocks holding a pumpkin trick-or-treat basket. She dressed this way last Halloween and it was probably the best Halloween of my entire life. Never mind the fact that we were Juniors in High School because we loved trick-or-treating and we weren't just going to stop for the lame excuse of ageing. We ended up tee-peeing her ex-boyfriends house for dumping her for some skanky senior. We pigged out on candy behind a couple of bushes and waited for him to come home. He was absolutely pissed when he drove into his drive way. Brynn had stopped right in front of his car and threw a bucketful of green goo at his car window. Dylan, Amber, and I ambushed him with silly string when he got out of his car and ran out of there like maniacs. He was furious, sure, but we chose the trick part in trick-or-treat. It was all part of our Halloween spirit.

A couple of girls I had done a puppet show in drama class in 3rd grade were also in this class. Our theme was under the sea so we got the privilege of being crazy sea creatures. The whole skit was about a poor claustrophobic starfish that was stuck in an Atlantis elevator while the rest of us had to try and get help. My dolphin character had used her 'sea-cell' to call for help.

Rodger and Ben had made quiet an amusing 2nd period for me back in 8th grade. Everyone was concentrating on a lesson about Mythology when all of a sudden Rodger jumped out of his seat yelling 'EW' because Ben had been licking his elbow for the last ten minutes and he didn't have a clue. Ben claimed it was because a person wouldn't feel if somebody was licking their elbow so he decided to give it a go. That elbow licking myth was approved that day.

Let's not forget the group of boys who started Francis High's first and last food fight ever back in Sophomore Year. It started with a simple throw of a pizza crust which lead to all kinds of food flying through the air. Even the girls and I were involved in it instead of joining half of the female Sophomores hiding under the table for refuge or sprinting out of the cafeteria like their life depended on it. That was only because Dylan had smashed a pudding cup against Jerald's head, earning herself a face full of Jello. Being the awesome friends that we happened to be, we were eachother's backup. The whole grade ended up staying after school to clean the whole mess. The face that my mother had pulled the minute I got home was absolutely priceless.

I glanced at Adrian from under my eyelashes. I had his paper and it was quiet amusing to read. Someone even kissed the top right corner with their sparkling pink lip gloss. The stuff on his paper was pretty predictable.

I love you!

Marry me!

Back off, he's mine!

Handsome.

Smoking Hot!

Awesome dude

I couldn't help but laugh at some them. Someone – and I bet I know who – had put down my name with his inside a heart. I looked to my side and gave Brynn a look. She simply smirked and continued to write on her current paper. With a smile, I wrote down and waited to pass.

"Who put Beautiful Blondie on yours?" I giggled, placing my stuff down at our regular table. The whole cafeteria was buzzing over the little assignment in English. Some were gushing over the full page of comment, laughing at the faded memories, or pissed at the sheet of insults.

"How am I suppose to know? It's anonymous, silly."

"I'm pretty sure what you put on mine and Adrian's paper wasn't so anonymous, Blondie."

Brynn put her hands up in defense. "I couldn't help myself." I laughed and gave her a small shove. She had put the same thing she had put on Adrian's paper but instead of 'Macey', Brynn oh so anonymously put my sexy beast of a best friend. You didn't have to be a mind reader to know it was her.

"Everyone loves me. All compliments, babe, not one insult." A voice commented from behind us. Brynn and I rolled our eyes at the cockiness.

"You probably threatened them to put decent comments on there." Dylan's voice snorted. We were soon joined by the whole group who were also going over there paper from English. I stole Adrian's apple from his tray and gave him a thank you kiss on the cheek. He knows for a fact that I skipped breakfast and forgot to bring my lunch because I was running late. If it wasn't for Lulu's constant barking for breakfast, I probably wouldn't have woken until noon.

"Oh my God, let me see your guys' paper." Amber squealed, snatching Brynn's paper from her grasp. Everyone's papers got passed around the table. The predictable things were on their papers. Brandon and Chase got compliments from girls and usual reminders of their past pranks while the girls got compliments as well and jealous insults. One comment just about made my eyes pop out of their sockets while choking on my apple.

"Wait..." I coughed. "Amber who wrote this comment?" I laid her paper in the middle of the table for everyone to see and pointed to the bottom of the page. The words 'Will you go out with me?'

were scrabbled onto the paper. Our heads snapped to a blushing Amber's direction. She's blushing! Just like this morning!

"About that.. Uh. Remember that 'sex god' from this morning?" She asked sheepishly. We nodded. "Well.. He kinda.. asked me out?" The statement came out like a question but it was indeed a fact. That's when the squealing came. Brandon slammed his head onto the table while Chase groaned rather loudly. Adrian chuckled from next to me but the girls and I shot up from our seats to tackle Amber into a group hug. It wasn't the best idea since she ended up on the floor from the impact.

"It's not that big of a deal." Amber complained, getting back onto her seat with a huff. "Spencer seems like a great guy and this time I actually said yes rather than hiding behind my book."

We let out another squeal and round 2 of hugs begun. Amber was a beautiful smart person who deserved a great guy. This Spencer person better not hurt Amber or he'll have to face the wrath of her friends. Most likely because Dylan will flip a shit if he does anything to hurt her and you would not want to get on her bad side.

"That's amazing, Ams." I congratulated.

"He's a great guy so don't worry about it." Brynn added.

"He's a dead man if he doesn't treat you right, darling, so let us know." Dylan stated seriously. Chase cringed slightly from beside her.

Amber chuckled nervously and steered the direction of the conversation. "What was on your paper, Mace?"

I stopped mid-bite. Somehow it didn't occur to me to look at what people had put on my paper. Brynn had pulled me out of there so fast it didn't hit me until just now. "Uh.. I didn't check, let me –"

My binder was quickly snatched before my eyes before I could object. I let out a scoff and leaned into Adrian's side. "Well then.." I muttered.

Adrian laughed and wrapped an arm around my shoulder. He's been awfully quiet.. I nudged him slightly with my elbow. "You've been so silent. Everything okay?"

"Yeah, just tired."

Uh huh.

Before I could further interrogate, my eardrums just about burst at the high pitched squeals coming from my best friends. Brandon had actually managed to fall off his seat while Chase looked at the girls with bewilderment, lettuce from his sandwich hanging from his mouth.

My eyes narrowed at them. "What?"

Dylan took the paper from Brynn and literally shoved it in my face. "Explain this!"

"I can't see."

"Oh."

Dylan hastily took it from my sight of vision and placed it in front of me. The girls' presence was behind me in an instant. Amber pointed a finger to a spot on the paper. "This." My eyes widened and a smile lifted my lips slightly at the comment.

My Childhood Crush.

Aww! That's actually pretty sweet.. Though of course, I'd never find out who it was. Plenty of the guys in my class I have known since elementary so the answer wasn't just going to jump right out at me. I explained just this as the girls squealed into my ear.

"But that's still really cute." Brynn teased, going back to her seat. "A little kid liked little Macey."

"Who do you think it is? David? Shawn?" Amber gasped dramatically, "Xander?!"

I groaned, "Oh my God." From that point on, the girls started shooting out every boy name known to man. Not like I would admit this out loud but there was that burning question far far in my mind as to who this person was. But the girls were on a roll and I really don't want to add more fuel for them to feed off of.

"Julie?"

"That's a girl."

"Your point?"

"Dylan!" I screeched in horror. Where's the duct tape when you need one?

"What? It's possible!"

Letting out what was probably the millionth groan of the day, I buried my face into Adrian's shoulder. His cologne filled my nose calming my senses. I frowned. He hasn't spoken at all after I asked him if he was okay. Not like I bought his half-assed answer from eariler. Might as well get him to talk then. Lacing my fingers with his under the table, I looked up at him.

"Adrian?"

He looked down at me and gave my hand a squeeze. "Hmm?"

"Who do you think it was?"

There was a glint in his eyes at my question. At the corner of my eyes, I saw Chase smile slightly as he stared at the two of us. Adrian glanced away to look at him and then back to me with a small heart-stopping smile.

Okay.. What was that?

"No idea, sweetheart."

Chapter 12

Macey's POV

"WHAT?!"

"Guys please calm down.."

It's October 31st, Halloween Day, and all 4 of us girls are in the bathroom trying not to storm out and strangle a certain cheating sex god. Amber and Spencer's date had gone seemingly well the night before. That is, until Amber caught her date sucking another girl's face from behind the restaurant they were having dinner at. Then he blew her off and rode away with his new arm candy right in front of her eyes. Amber was stuck without a ride until Brynn came to get her.

"Who was the slut?" Dylan asked through gritted teeth. The anger was clear on all of our faces, but Dylan was ready to break this guy's nose. Her lips were puckered and her fists were balled up tightly by her side. The rapid tap of the black boots she was wearing was a habit when she was trying to control the anger bubbling inside.

Amber sniffed from her position on the top of the bathroom counter, the three of us in front of her. "I'd rather not say." she said quietly.

"Why not?" Brynn exasperated, her arms flailing as she spoke. "That dumbass has no right to screw another girl when he's on a date!"

Amber hesitated. Her eyes flicking between Brynn, Dylan, and landed on me for a split second before staring at her folded hands that rested on her lap. I winced at the sudden pain from the inside of my cheek. Apparently I was biting it out of habit. It happens when I'm waiting in anger.

"Amber," I said firmly. Amber slowly tilted her face up. "Who was it?" The fact that this Spencer guy had some nerve to cheat on someone as sweet as Amber is absolutely unbelievable. And this girl better have some sort of bodyguard if she doesn't want to end up bald and bruised.

After a moment's hesitation, Amber incoherently mumbled the witch's name. "Who?" Brynn pushed.

"... Mie,"

"Who?!" We all demanded.

"Cammie!" Amber cried out before burying her face in her hands. My blood went cold. The bathroom was deadly silent besides Amber's quite sobbing. Brynn patted her back lightly but Dylan and I remained stiff.

Cammie? That little...

I stormed out of the bathroom without another thought. The door slammed open a second time followed by the loud steps of Dylan's boots. If they think they're getting away with hurting our best friend they have another thing coming. Spencer, I was pissed at. But Cammie, this is something I would expect. It's what she does, and I should know.

All the things she did back to me in middle school just for Adrian's love. Ha, I could handle that. But hurt my best friend? Bitch better prepare to run in those 10 inch high heels of hers because when I get my hands on her –

"Guys, don't!" Amber called out from behind us. Dylan had fallen into step with me as we stomped down the hall. The Halloween decorations were all hung up around me. My eyes landed on a giant pumpkin down the hall, and for a split second, I was ready to pick it up and bash it through Cammie's head.

I probably would've if strong arms didn't wrap around my waist. As far as I know, Amber or Brynn didn't have strong arms and a rock hard six pack.

"Adrian, let me go!" I shoted, thrashing in his arms. Across from me, Dylan was being held down by Chase as well as Brandon.

"I swear to God, if you don't let me go you won't have any kids in the near future." Dylan threatened menacingly. Brandon immediately let go but rethought his decision and took hold of her again. Amber jogged down to the hall where we were with Brynn besides her.

"Guys, calm down." Brynn's attempt to calm us only pissed me off more. All I could see was red. Cammie. Cammie did it, of course she did!

"Mace, calm down." Adrian said softly next to my ear. Calm down? Calm down?! How could I calm down after seeing Amber's heart-broken reaction? To have Cammie ruin Amber's first ever date? To hell if she thinks she's going to get away with this!

"Brynn! How could you be so calm after what those twats did to Amber?" Dylan shouted in disbelief.

"You guys don't underst –" Amber started but I cut her off.

"I understand!" I shouted. "I've been through this! Do you know how many times Cammie has ruined my life because she had a thing for Adrian? She only ruined Amber's date because she knew it would get to me. Cammie's at it again because Adrian's back and she wants to – "

Adrian's wincing made me stop and bite my lip. There was a pain expression on his face when I glanced up at him. All the girls were giving me a pitying look. They knew what Cammie did to me because they were with me when she did it. Now she was targeting my friends just go to get to me just because Adrian is back in my life.

I folded my hands on top of Adrian's and shook my head. "They can't get away with this." Dylan pulled herself away from Chase and Brandon to give Amber a small hug. Tears were brimming in her eyes again.

"They're not going to get away with it." Brynn told us.

"What do you mean?" Dylan asked.

"Last night when I picked Amber up, I told Brandon and he told the guys. Being the evil mastermind that Chase is –"

Chase smirked triumphantly. "I came up with a plan to embarrass them for life," He finished, rubbing his hands evily. I know that look. It's the look he pulled before Chase rigged our 8th grade Geography teacher's computer so that a creepy picture popped up when she clicked on the grade book.

"There is another option in 'Trick-or-Treat'."

"Dressing as a sexy angel for Halloween, Sweetheart?"

My scream as well as the clank from the can I dropped echoed through my room. My wings hit the culprit as I whirled on my heels and came face to face with an assassin. The fact that there was some assassin in my room didn't surprise me but the fact that I indeed did not hear him sneak into my room was another story. Even the big white hood couldn't hide the fact that the person in my room wasn't here to attack me physically but rather to put me into cardiac arrest.

"How'd you get in here? I didn't hear you come in."

A condescending smirk appeared, "I climbed through your window so I could see your reaction."

"Adrian," I pouted. The smirk was the only thing visible on Adrian's face until I stepped forward and pushed the hood back.

"Are you trying to make me mess up my costume?"

Adrian pretended to ponder my question as he wrapped his arms around my waist and pulled me to him. "Only if your backup costume makes you look just as hot as you do in this one." He muttered before pecking my cheek and slowly pressed his lips to my neck, leaving tingles in every spot.

I have to admit that this costume was really cute. It was more of an avenging angel than an innocent guardian kind of angel. With the dark blue corset, vest, and sky blue skirt. My black leggings stuck to me like a second skin and was tucked in my knee high length boots. My dark brown flowed down in curls and Brynn came over to do my makeup before heading to the Halloween store to get supplies for our big plan.

The thirst of revenge grew inside of me at the thought of the plan. Spencer was throwing a Halloween party at his house. Those two were pretty cozy at school today meaning they were still together, much to our disgust. The whole scheme was a hundred times better than our prank last year. Future boyfriends should be warned not to mess with us when Halloween is just around the corner.

After all, revenge is a dish best served cold. And what better time to do it than the great season of pranks and scaring people shitless, right? Cammie had done it during my 8th grade Halloween..

"I'm really looking forward to tonight, you know," I said a little breathlessly. No response came from Adrian as he continued trailing up and down my neck. My heart pounded harder and harder on my chest but I continued anyways. "Cammie could really get a taste of her own medicine after all the wrongs she done with Amber and myself. Remember 8th grade year?"

That halted Adrian's actions quickly, tensing at my question. He knew exactly what I was talking about because he had helped his girlfriend do it. I came home from trick-or-treating with the kids when they were much younger. Opening my bathroom and being so tired to notice the 5 tarantulas crawling around the walls, I screamed so loud it wouldn't be surprising if the neighbors thought someone was being murdered. My heart was threatening to burst through my chest with the painful beating it was doing. Cammie and Adrian laughing their asses off was my first sight. Adrian had let themselves in with the spare key that he already had so they could pull the prank off.

The worst part? Adrian knew of my intense arachnophobia yet still did it because his girlfriend coaxed him into terrorizing his best friend. Another reason for me to ruin her tonight. I had ignored Adrian for a while after that but Cammie kept him busy. Only when we went over to the Chapmen residence for Thanksgiving dinner did he apologize. Of course I was still mad at him but forgave him nonetheless because I loved him. He was my best friend and I couldn't stay mad at him. But that doesn't mean I forgave Cammie for turning my best friend on me.

Adrian gripped my face between his hands, skimming both thumbs on my cheeks. There were many things written on Adrian's face. Anger, regret, guiltiness, and something else I could put my finger on. When his mouth opened to say something, a familiar loud noise blared from outside. I made a beeline towards my window and pulled it open. An evil jester and a skeleton dressed in a shredded black and gray robe stood outside was gesturing to the trunk full of bags with the local Halloween logo printed on them. Sending a thumbs up, I shut my window and grabbed my things.

"They're outside, let's go." I said, my eyes scanning the room for anything else I forgotten. Once convinced that everything was in my bag, I was out the door before Adrian could pull me into a conversation about the past.

"You guys look great!" I complimented once outside. "Step up from the Goldilocks costume I see." Winking at Brynn dressed in an adorable Racy Robin Hood costume and earning myself a glare. Dylan came around the car wearing a skeleton cocktail dress paired with skeleton tights and heels.

"What are you, an avenging angel?" Amber teased, making her way around the car in a sassy candy corn dress.

The thought of Cammie crossing the line made my blood boil. My hair flicked over my should as I turned sharply on my heels and started towards the trunk. "Well this angel ain't no sweet one tonight, that's for sure." I mumbled.

"Well after Adrian takes his eyes off your ass then let's get this show on the road, shall we?" Chase, also known as the creepy skeleton, clapped his hands together and rubbed them together like the evil scientist would do before he puts his plan into action.

Amber giggled and wrapped an arm around my shoulder. She was just as excited as we were for this whole thing to go down. The way her eyes scanned the condiments in the trunks viciously. Her hands were just itching to put them into use. It was a side I've never seen before. Loose and free rather than couped up in her home with a book studying for hours. Another reason why I'm completely looking forward to tonight.

Gripping the top of the trunk, Amber and I pulled down it down with all our might and shut it close.

"Let's do this."

Adrian's POV

"Alright, pass the blood."

The tiny glow from my flashlight searched the remaining items. Halloween remix songs boomed through the ceilings of the house and muffled the sound to where we were. Downstairs was filled with all kids of creatures and characters. Spencer's Halloween party was in full swing. Nobody spared us a glance as we crossed the blocked off stairway and made our way into the dusty room that is Spencer's attic. Pitch blackness overcome us besides the small ray's coming from our handheld flashlights or phone screens. The fake blood earned a spotlight once the bottle filled with the dark red liquid came into sight.

"Here," My hand wavered in the air until Chase's hand grabbed it from my grasp. "That should be everything. The rest is for later."

Chase was standing on a step stool, pouring the liquid down one of the worn down walls. The liquid streamed all the way down and created a thick puddle on the creaky wooden floor below. Brandon then painted his whole hand with the remaining blood and trailed hand prints toward the streams of blood.

"Phase one complete," Brandon said triumphantly. "Hope you bought some ear buds, boys, because Cammie's screams are going to deafen you without them."

"Spencer's too." Chase chuckled, stepping back and admiring his handiwork. To finish it off, he painted the words 'Don't turn around' right where Brandon's hand prints had stopped. The letters dripped menacingly as if someone had actually wrote it with their own blood.

"Oh man, they're so going to shit themselves." Brandon breathed in excitement.

I hope they do. Mess with my friends and they have another thing coming. Cammie wasn't just going to waltz in and screw another guy right in front of Amber without getting away with it. And the fact that this jealous whore had the nerve to do it just to get under Macey's skin takes it to a whole new level. Nobody's going to mess with my Sweetheart. As corny and over protective as it sounds, it's without a doubt true. After Macey brought up that one Halloween memory from 8th grade, I was damned determined to turn the tables on Cammie.

I still can't believe I did that all those years ago. Macey has the biggest arachnophobia I've ever seen a person have and what do I do? Put 5 giant tarantulas in her bathroom with the help of Macey's arch enemy. What kind of dick head does that to his best friend? The screwed up 14 year old me didn't even apologize until Thanksgiving dinner. If I was in that situation as I am today, I'd go knocking on her door the minute she kicked me out of her house and refuse to leave until I was forgiven.

Cammie has terrorised my Sweet Macey for too long and after this night, she better not even look at her or any of my friends again.

A certain 5-2-3 patterned knock alerted us that it was the girls. I crawled around the barricade of boxes and pushed the door open. I flinched at the sudden stream of blinding light that flooded into the attic. Amber came scurrying up the ladder and just about pushed me out of the way.

"They're here, they're coming upstairs soon!" She whisper-shouted at me. Brynn quickly climbed up the ladder followed by Macey and Dylan. Macey stumbled into my chest when Dylan pushed her forward in a hurry to close the entryway. My arms found their way around Macey's waist when the light dimmed down to a dark void.

Quickly but quietly, everyone around us took our positions. I managed to peck Macey's cheek in the darkness before taking a cautious step towards my position, being extra careful not to set off any of the traps.

Our visions adjusted by the time muffled steps and giggles increased in volume. The entryway of the attic opened soon after and I made sure to close my eyes so my eyes could stay adjusted to the darkness.

"This is so creepy!" A feminine voice slurred. This was comedy gold. Cammie was drunk. Was Spencer as well?

"It's just the attic, babe," Spencer's deep voice slurred. This is going to be too easy. The light was once again cut off and that's when things got hot and heavy in the attic. It was literally all I could do not to burst into a hollering laugh when their desperate kisses filled the whole room. My fist ended up in my mouth in order to keep snicker that was desperate to calm out when Cammie moaned loudly.

5 minutes filled with every feature that came with a fiery make out session and the first step in our Revenge was put in order. A simple squeak was all it took to put a road block in Spencer and Cammie's verge of ending up naked right in this very room. I'd be scarred for life if that were to happen.

Cammie and Spencer froze in the awkward position of Spencer gripping onto Cammie's thighs and lifting her up to his level, his lips on her neck. Cammie's hands had slipped under Spencer's pirate shirt and the sleeve of her slutty cop costume was half way down her shoulder.

Squeak... Squeak, Squeak... The sound of small feet pattered on the floor was quiet loud in the dead silent room. Cammie raised her head and slowly looked around the room. "What was that..?" she whispered. Spencer placed Cammie back on the ground and stood in front of her in a protective manner. But the slight sway in his step was noticeable in the dark. Somebody's going to be getting more than just a hangover.

The number of squeaks tripled in a matter of seconds once Dylan released the remaining of her brother's pet mouses from her position. Why her brother has 5 mouses as pets is beyond me. Macey came up with this idea based on her own experience with the tarantulas and was eager to put it in tonight's plan for one reason only:

Cammie. Hates. Rodents.

When a mouse was found scurrying down the hall in 7th grade, Cammie had let out the shrillest scream that could've ruptured everyone's ears within a 10 mile radius. And that's exactly what

Cammie did. My hands clamped themselves over my ears in order to protect my hearing while Cammie made a deafening scream. Dylan's position was just to the left of our victims and I could vaguely see the silhouettes of the mouses scurrying across their feet. Even Spencer let out the most girly shout I have ever heard.

A snicker escaped from Chase who was hiding in a dark corner of the room but wasn't heard because of the two wusses screaming their heart out. Cammie jumped into Spencer's arms in fright. Spencer obviously wasn't ready for that and with the help of alcohol, he stumbled backward and into the wall.

Above them, I watched in satisfactory as a hidden Brynn pulled a thin string attached to the trap door the guys and I had planted to the top of the ceiling. The compartment swung open and let out the bucket full of pumpkin guts drop on top of their heads

Spencer swore loudly as Cammie shouted a "WHAT THE HELL IS THIS?!" By the time they finished swiping off the gunk off their heads, phase 3 was already under way. From a crack between the barrier of boxes, Macey let loose the creepy toy that Brandon was desperate to get.

It was a wind-up walking baby. Nearly bald and tattered clothing, it came with a recordable voice box where we could record something and have it come out in a creepy baby voice. The heavy steps of the toy came more and more closer to Spencer and Cammie.

"There's no escape.. There's no escape.. There's no escape..." It repeated over and over as it waddled towards them. Spencer didn't even have the guts to go kick it over nor did he not make a move to shine some light on this situation.

"Spencer, what the hell is that?!" Cammie shrieked.

"I don't know what's going on!" Spencer shouted back. The recording came to an end and the baby toppled over. "Come on, let's get out of here." Spencer's voice cracked as he pulled Cammie towards the entryway for escape.

That's not going to happen.

"It's locked." He hissed.

"What?!" Cammie shrieked, pushing him over and giving the handle a go herself. "Why is it locked, you idiot?!" She began to jump on the door as if that would help unlock what we have locked with the hidden stick in the hinge. It was too dark to notice but big enough that they could possibly see it if there was more light illuminating the room.

But there wasn't.

"How did it fucking lock from the time that we were up –" Her words were cut short when one of the mice came crawling across her foot. Letting out another ear blowing shriek, she jumped at Spencer. With the incapably to keep his ground for more than 5 minutes, Spencer fell backwards and into another wall once again. This time the wall wasn't that dry.

"What the –" The both of them backed away from the wall to face it. Spencer finally came to his senses and took out his phone. "Holy shitnuts..."

Cammie gave him a disgusted look for his choice of words before catching sight of the artwork in front of her. I smirked and slowly came out of my hiding spot, sword in hand. Fake sword I might add. Chase came from his little dark corner and stood beside me. Brandon slowly crept up behind them to stand stone still in place.

"Don't turn around..?" Cammie repeated. Before any of them could do the opposite of what was written, Brandon had his face right between their shoulders and whispered,

"Boo."

A strangled –a very high pitched – scream came from not Cammie, but from Spencer as they whirled around and spotted an evil jester, the ripped up skeleton dangerously close to their faces, and an assassin standing behind them. I pointed my sword towards them. My hood hung low on my face so they couldn't see who I was but that didn't stop them from screaming and falling backwards onto the blood covered wall.

"NOW!"

The girls sprung from their hiding spots holding different buckets and cans, throwing them at the frightened losers in front of us. All they could do was scream when they got covered in green goo, cobwebs, silly string, and the remaining blood and pumpkin guts.

"Who are you?!?" Spencer boomed while we all started laughing. Spencer's phone was destroyed by the different liquids but then someone removed the stick withholding the entryway and pushed it open.

We were out of the attic and down the ladder before Spencer go the chance to strangle one of us. "Guys, the kiddie pool!" Brynn whisper-shouted. Above us, Cammie was screaming our names. All of us helped position the kiddie pool right under the hole of the attic just as Spencer slipped coming down, dragging Cammie down with him.

We all jumped back as they fell into the kiddie pool filled of caramel. It was a sight to see indeed. Both Spencer and Cammie's backsides were covered head to toe with caramel. Spencer's pirate shirt that was once white was now green from the goo. Cobwebs, and pumpkin guts were stuck in his hair as well as Cammie's.

"You guys are so dead!" Cammie screamed.

"Need a napkin for your period stain, Hun? Or do you prefer a tampon?" Dylan teased sweetly.

Cammie looked like she was about to kill. Her face was just as red as the blood stain that really did make her look like she had an accident with her period. Her face was smeared with goo and caramel and some of the silly string was stuck to the end of her hair and chest.

To put it short; they looked horrible. And it was hilarious. To say we were just laughing was an understatement. All of us were literally bent over, leaning on a wall for a support, or just plain laughing on the floor.

But we weren't the only ones laughing. "Do you guys hear that?" Macey asked a little breathless from the laughing fit. I smiled at my friends' confused faces and smirked towards Cammie and Spencer.

"We weren't your only audience." I told them. With that, I took Macey's hand and pulled her down the stairs. Brandon, Chase, and the girls quickly followed while Spencer and Cammie thrashed in the pool of sticky goodness. When we got downstairs, everyone burst into cheers and hollers.

"What's going on?" Brynn shouted over the noise. When we got into the living room, a huge projector was screening the different angles of the attic in night vision as well as the kiddie pool. Just as I planned, a couple of nerds dressed as wizards were seated next to their beloved setup with a satisfied smile. I gave them a thumbs up and turned to the others.

Macey looked at me in disbelief. "You filmed the whole thing?"

"Dude, that's genius!" Chase appraised, slapping me on the back.

"Yeah but why'd you do it?" Macey questioned, looking at the projected view of our master plan.

"You said Cammie projected that embarrassing dancing moment in front of the whole school back in Freshman year. I know it isn't as big as the audience back then but I thought it'd be worth it to do it here." I shrugged. "I told you Cammie's not going to get away with hurting you anymore and that goes the same with my friends."

A wide smile graced Macey's face as she jumped into my arms with a laugh. Not remembering when I've ever had this much fun before, I wrapped my arms around Macey's waist and twirled her around like I did when we were younger. Cammie came storming into the living room as I placed a kiss on Macey's cheek.

The moment she took step in this room everyone started laughing and pointing. Some took out their phones to get this moment on video. Spencer followed soon after looking completely flustered. Some of his jock friends just shook their heads and laughed with the others.

"YOU!" Cammie shrieked, pointing a finger at Macey. "This is all your fault! "

I opened my mouth to say something but Macey beat me to it. "To hell I did!" Macey said like it was the most obvious thing in the world.

Then Cammie looked at me and pointed a finger, "Who do you think you are walking around like you own Adrian?" She shrieked.

Is this bitch serious? Total subject change here!

Dylan and Brynn were by Macey side in an instant. Chase with an arm wrapped around Amber to hold her together of Cammie ruining her first ever date and Brandon just stood there scowling at Cammie.

"Who do you think you are messing with my friends?" Macey shot back. "If you have a problem with me, then it's between you and me. Don't go pinning it on my friends because I'm sure as hell you aren't going to get away with it. You know the saying, Cammie. Payback's a bitch, just like you."

This time the whole room burst into hollers as Cammie's face fumed. This would be the part where the steam would be blowing out of her nose and ears. To push her over the edge, I wrapped my arms around Macey from behind and placed a long lingering kiss on her cheek.

Several 'Ooo' sounds were made around us. I rested my head on the top of Macey's head and gave Cammie a smug look. This did it. Because with one last frustrated groan, she was out the door screaming for people to move out of her way. Spencer glowered at us.

"Get the hell out of my house." He growled.

"With pleasure," Dylan stepped forward, grasped his shoulders, and kicked him in his crotch. Spencer doubled over in pain and Dylan hauled him towards the food and drinks table. He tripped over the foot of a couch and stumbled against the table. The punch and chips adding to the top coat of grime already glued to his body. Dylan twirled to face us and gave a bow. "Thank you very much. Now let's get out of here."

Brandon shoved his mask on and pounded his chest, giving everyone a peace sign. "Happy Halloween to all and to all a good night! Hope you enjoyed the show!" He shouted specifically to those who were still filming. Then we left the house. I wrapped an arm around Macey's waist and pulled her to me.

"Good job tonight, Sweetheart." I whispered for her ears only. Macey smiled in response but the still young night made the blush noticeable.

"That was freaking awesome!" Brynn exclaimed as we made our way towards the car.

"Thanks for helping me guys. It really means a lot to me. And this Halloween was the best by far." Amber said with a wide grin.

Chase wrapped an arm around her shoulder and ruffled her hair. "No problem, Sugar pop." Amber scrunched her nose in disgust but didn't push him away.

"Woah, woah, WOAH!" Brandon flailed his arms in front of us before anyone could get into the car. We all stopped to give him a look. "What are you doing?!" He shouted at us like we just kicked his grandma.

"Going home," Brynn replied in a 'duh' tone. Brandon waggled his finger in our faces.

"No, no, no. It's too early for that!"

"Well what are we suppose to do?"

Brandon smiled suggestively at us and opened the back of the trunk. A minute later he was chucking fabrics at each of us.

"Pillow cases?" I asked, holding mine out in front of me. "What are we suppose to do with this?"

Brandon gestured grandly to the sight around us. Monsters and characters of all kind were running house to house. They walked down the sidewalk with their baskets filled to the brim of a kid's joy and happiness in just one chocolaty treat but every dentist and parent's worst nightmare.

We all looked at each other.

"Well let's get our trick-or-treat on!" Chase exclaimed.

That night, I was careful not to fall out of the tree outside of Macey's window. My arm could've broken earlier if not for the trusty window sill that I was able to shoot out and grab before I earned myself a trip to the hospital. Macey was just coming out of her bathroom, making me remember our 8th grade Halloween. Damn my stupidity.

I knocked on the window pane. Macey jumped and looked at the window in bewilderment before narrowing her eyes at my smug look. "What are you doing here?" she whispered shouted for Emma's case. Hell breaks loose if you wake that girl up during her beauty sleep.

I quietly climbed through her window. "Can't a guy see her best friend?"

"At midnight?" She deadpanned. "What are you, Romeo?"

"Macey, please, I'm way more sexy than him."

Macey scoffed, "He's way more romantic than you."

I sent her back side a look as she kneeled over her bed to move some pillows and covers out of the way before wrapping an arm around her waist from behind and pulling her towards my chest. "Want me to show you how romantic I could be?" I whispered huskily next to her ear. A smug smile found its way to my face as well as a wave of satisfactory when Macey tensed under me and blushed.

Then she pushed me away and got into bed. "Perv." she muttered. I laughed and sat down next to her.

"Seriously though, I brought a movie. Thought we could pig out on our candy and watch it."

True to our word, we went trick-or-treating. For one night, I was a kid. Who says growing up meant you can't go knocking on peoples' doors for free candy at age 17? Never in years have I been so happy or laughed as much as I did tonight. And it was all thanks to the people here. My friends here in Miami; not LA. My home is here with my best friend. This whole break thing was the best idea I've ever had and I'm glad I took the opportunity.

Macey snatched the DVD from my hand and then threw it back at me. "I'm not watching Paranormal Activities, Adrian. You know how I am with scary movies."

Oh how could I not? One time when I dragged her to a movie theater to watch a scary movie, she ran out within the first 20 minutes and waited outside until it was done. For the next week she had nightmares which to this day I still didn't understand if she just watched the exposition.

"It's not scary." I told her.

"That's what they all say."

I sighed and jumped out of her bed to put the DVD in. After turning out the light, I crawled under the covers next to her. "Watch it with me until you fall asleep. I promise you won't have nightmares." I said. Macey eyed the TV wearily but reluctantly complied to my desires.

Macey lasted a lot longer than I thought she would. She was tucked to my side, my arm wrapped around her. Every time something 'scary' would come out, Macey would bury her face into my chest and wait until I told her that it was okay for her to look. An hour later, Macey's face stayed buried in my shoulder and was out like a light. Her arms were wrapped around my waist and my thumb was absetmindedly skimming the small skin above her waist band where her tank top had rose up a bit.

By the time the movie ended, the urge to sleep was calling me. I shut the TV off and turned on my side. Macey shifted in her sleep, burying her head in my chest and readjusting her arms around me. I kissed her hair and rested my chin on the top of her head.

"Good night, Sweetheart."

"Night, Adrian. Love you." She managed to mumble.

My mouth twitched upwards. "Love you too."

Chapter 13

A drian's POV

"Adrian Chapmen, how do you explain this?!"

I rolled my eyes from my slumping position on the chair. The minute I parked my car in the driveway, my manager comes out all red in the face. I swear if this was a cartoon, his face could've melted with all the heat in his head. Yes, I did expect the video from the Halloween Party to be posted on Youtube. With the generation today, you think they wouldn't?

My problem is that I don't find it a big deal. Thomas has been my manager for as long as I remember. He was the one that arranged my first audition that landed me my first movie career and later launched my career. One of many cons of having him is that he's strict. And I don't mean 'Come-home-before-curfew-or-you're-grounded' strict, I mean 'If-you-screw-one-detail-your-ass-is-dead' military strict.

My parents stand behind me in the office. They care about my career a lot, sometimes more than me. But the reason Thomas was flipping his shit at me was for the smallest, most ridiculous of reasons. An action that is so normal my parents couldn't give a damn that I did it. An action I've done only God knows how many times that it's been a part of my daily life, a routine of mine.

Now you may be wondering what meaningless action could have Thomas pulling his hair out but my family staring at him like he's a complete moron.

I stared at the monitor in front of me with a blank face. The paused scene in front of me completely didn't faze me even in the slightest.

It was a shot of me kissing Macey's cheek.

I kissed her cheek. Did I kiss her lips? No. Did I kiss her neck? No. Did I kiss anywhere else? No. Were we making out on the spot and sucking each other's face off? NO! I kissed my best friend's cheek! I didn't drag her into a bedroom and rip her clothes off while filming the whole thing for God's sake!

Kissing Macey to me was a part of life. She's my best friend, she means the world to me. Not that I've told her that… But I assume she knows it. Macey and I are like peanut better and jelly, she's the ping to my pong, the ying to my yang, the normal to my crazy. Telling me that I can't kiss my Sweet Macey is like forbidding Brynn from liking One Direction.

Never. Gonna. Happen.

"Well?!" Thomas hissed. My eyes flicked between him and the screen. Then I looked up at my parents with a 'Seriously?' look. Dad literally rolled his eyes at Thomas.

"Are you kidding?" He asked dryly. "You're freaking out because my son kissed his best friend on the cheek?"

"Yes!" Thomas shouted, enraged at the fact. "This video got 500,000 views so far! Do you know how many of his fans are gossiping over this.. this.. Macey character?!"

Moron. And quiet frankly, I didn't like the way he said Macey's name. Like it was cursed or like some creepy hobo walking around the streets and not the girl I care for dearly.

"Thomas," My mom started. Her voice was calm but I could tell the words 'You dragged us all the way over here for this?' was at the tip of her tongue. "Macey has been apart of Adrian's life since 1st grade. Those two are so unbelievably close that this," She gestured to the screen. "Is completely normal."

"This is trending everywhere, Mrs. Chapmen. Several of Adrian's fans think that there is some relationship going on between this girl and Adrian!"

"Her name," I snapped tersely. "Is Macey. She's been my best friend for as long as I can remember and I've done this a thousand times –"

"A thousand times?!" Thomas cut me off again. Dear God, seriously? I've gave fans kisses on the cheek before so why is it a big deal that I kissed my best friend.

"Thomas, you can't be serious." My dad exasperated. He was in the middle of watching a basketball game when Thomas demanded a meeting. Get in between my dad and his sports time, Dave Chapmen won't be very pleasant.

"I am serious because this –"

"Alright that's it!" A new voice cut in. I turned in my seat to see Kelly strutting her way into the office with a very annoyed expression on her face. It was an expression she always wore around Thomas because she thinks he is a, and I quote, 'Complete douche who thinks he owns you'. Whenever one of these 'meetings' are called she would storm out of the room claiming she wants nothing to do with Thomas's plans for me but would be standing right around the corner listening in just in case he did something she didn't like for me.

Which was pretty much all the time.

"Listen here, Tommy," She scowled, emphasizing the name that Thomas hates with all his heart. She slammed her hands on the desk and leaned towards him with the coldest of glares. "Macey isn't some slut on the street, alright? She's a great girl and Adrian's little 'Sweet Macey'. They've known each other since grade school and as close as best friends can get. You may be his manager but you can't order him around like he's a dog. My little bro can kiss whoever he freaking wants to kiss."

Big sister to the rescue! I rested back in the chair with a smug look on my face. Kelly may be some highly well known fashion designer, but she was my big sister and we still look out for each other. Emma is Kelly's best friend and they've known each other way before Macey and I were even brought into this world. Macey is like a sister to Kelly and she isn't going to let somebody rant on about her – let alone someone she despises with everything's she has.

"This Macey girl –" Can he not just say 'Macey'? Now I was starting to get pissed. "Could ruin Adrian's reputation, his career –"

"Adrian's career is on hold. He's on break." Kelly stretched the word as if Thomas was incapable of understanding simple English.

"That doesn't mean –"

"Um.." Another voice cut in. I know that voice.

Everyone snapped their heads towards the door of the office. A very pale faced Macey was standing under the door frame practically shaking in her shoes. I abruptly stood from my seat. Why was she here? Did something bad happen? Last time we spoke, Macey said she had dance practice after school.

"Hey kid, what're you doing here?" My dad asked, confusion dripping with every word.

Macey took another step into the office. My gaze dropped down to the hand that was playing with the pendant hanging around her neck. The pendant I gave her. Now that I think about it, I've never really seen her without it. It was always there hanging around her neck.

I smiled at the fact.

Macey looked at Thomas and then to me. "Two guys in black suits jumped me when I was walking and brought me here." She replied quietly.

Kelly rounded towards Thomas. "You sent Ross and Mauricio to drag Macey here against her own will?!" She shrieked. By the looks of it, Kelly was all but willing to jump across the desk and claw his eyes out.

"I think it would be best if Macey was here when we set the ground rules." Thomas replied.

"Ground rules?" I repeated incredulously.

"Yes we need to talk about what you can and can not do with Macey here."

"Thomas this really isn't necessary." Mom sighed, looking frazzled by this conversation. My dad threw his hands up in the air exasperatedly.

"Are you for real?" Kelly shouted at Thomas. Ground rules? Was he seriously going to tell me what I can and can not do with Macey?

The whole room burst into one big argument. Macey watched the scene unfold before her before she caught sight of the computer screen. Her hands clamped over her mouth completely horrified.

"Oh my God!" Macey's muffled shriek caused the argument to come to a halt. She was staring at the computer screen with a pain expression, like she just committed the crime of the century. "Is this because Adrian kissed me?" She asked Thomas. "You think it's going to ruin his reputation or something?"

"Precisely." Thomas said. Okay, it was my turn to be insanely pissed at my own manager. I don't want Macey acting like she just stabbed a bunny because I kissed her cheek. We've done it so many times before and I'm not going to let my manager demand that it stops.

"Oh no," Macey groaned. "I am so s–"

"NO!" Kelly shouted, slapping a hand over Macey's mouth before she could finish her sentence. "No." She repeated directly to Thomas. "She is not going to apologize over something as stupid as this!"

Thomas glared at Kelly. "I'm doing this on behalf of Adrian's career, Kelly. Fans don't want to see Adrian kissing just some random girl at a party. Not to mention that the other girl accuses Macey of being possessive over Adrian making his fans think the same. What happened at that party did not make Adrian look good nor did it for you Macey."

Macey flinched at Thomas's words.

Kelly slammed the desk once again and went around the desk to push Thomas roughly. "Macey isn't some random slut that you always set up with Adrian!"

"Enough!" My mom ordered loudly. I had almost forgotten she and dad were here. "It was a simple kiss, Thomas. Stop being so dramatic. Keep in mind that, Thomas, you work for us and that we can fire you when needed. We will not listen to your useless ranting about something as ordinary as our son kissing his best friend's cheek!"

"Adrian shouldn't be kissing some nobody at a party!" Thomas shouted in defense.

That's it.

"I'm not going to listen to your stupid rules about this, Thomas," I snapped. I walked over to Macey and wrapped an arm around her waist. She tensed under my hold. "If there's one thing you can't control it's who I get to be with, who I'm friends with, and what I may and may not do with them. Who I kiss is none of your concern and if I want to kiss Macey then hell I will. Macey's a great girl and you can't keep me from doing whatever the damn I want to do. So you could shove your orders up your ass and leave it at that."

I left after that, slamming the door closed and dragging Macey with me. My anger was still high by the time we started down the grand stair case. How could Thomas say that in front of Macey? Especially after he sent my old bodyguards to go and practically kidnap her. He called her a nobody! My fans may not know her but that doesn't lessen Macey's value to me. She wasn't a nobody in my book. Not even close.

When it comes to being with Macey, I become a whole different person compared to what the whole world thinks I am. Every time I'm with her, I can let go. I don't need to watch my actions just to impress the fans, I don't need be around some whore that I couldn't care less about just for the press, and I don't need to be some heartthrob for all the girls out there.

I can be me. Laid back, joking around, normal me. I can go out in public and do whatever the hell I want. Macey brings out the old me and I don't want Thomas shutting her out of my life. This is Adrian Chapmen's life not famous Adrian Chapmen's life. He can't control this side of me. So if he wants to boss me around and tell me I can't do simple things like kissing Macey then he should take my advice and shove his orders up his –

"Adrian, please slow down." Macey's soft voice made me loosen the death grip I had on her wrist and slow down my fast pace. She stumbled on the last step but I shot out and wrapped my arms around her.

"Macey," I started. She didn't look at me. Her eyes stayed on my plain white shirt, avoiding my gaze. "Mace, look at me." I tried again. When she didn't move whatsoever, I wrapped my fingers around her chin and tilted her face up so I could look into her eyes. My anger spiked again when her eyes turned out glossy.

"I got to go," She whispered. Macey tore out of my grip and started towards the door. I mentally punched Thomas in the face a billion times as I ran after her and whirled her around to face me.

"Macey," I cupped her face between mine but she flinched and shied away. I sighed. "Macey, listen to me. Don't let what Thomas said get to you, okay? They're not true and nothing is going to change between us. You mean so much more to me than what Thomas gives your credit for." I said.

She didn't believe me. I knew she didn't. Even after the smallest nod I've ever seen her give, I knew she was thinking about what he said. But I also knew that she needed time so I didn't push it.

I leaned in to kiss her cheek but Macey flinched once again and placed her hands on my chest to keep me away.

This is what I was afraid of. That Macey would think she wasn't worthy of hanging out with me because she was normal. And Thomas just about rubbed it in her face like the idiot he is. I don't know why I haven't fired him yet and got a better manager.

"I've got to get to dance practice or Lucile will get mad. I'll call you later." Macey told me quietly. She was out the door after that.

Kelly always suggested that I fire Thomas.

Maybe I should consider it.

Chapter 14

Adrian's POV

"I'd punch him 50 miles away, make Dylan cut off his balls, and then bury him alive."

"Thank you!"

It was the day after the whole meeting with Thomas and Macey has been avoiding me ever since. Hours filled with no contact with her in any way, shape, or form. And that was bothering me.

A lot.

Each time I would approach her, Macey eyes would widen and it was like someone hit the complete panic mode button. A simple locker visit had Macey closing her locker on her hair in a rush. As amusing as it was, this was no laughing matter.

Students lingered around at the front of the school. After the last bell, I ordered the whole gang to meet up so we could talk this through. The girls had noticed Macey's shaken behaviour when she arrived at dance practice the other day. Throughout the periods, each of them noticed that Macey was unusually quite than normal.

Brynn and Amber started to question Macey's motives when she distanced herself as far away as possible from me. Math class's seating chart didn't really give her an option to do that but she had completely ignored my attempts to talk to her then.

After the last bell, Macey was up and out the door faster than the quarterback on the last game. This gave me the perfect opportunity to tell the guys what happened and for their opinions. Brynn had obviously agreed to my comparison of me getting ordered to never kiss Macey again was like forbidding her love for One Direction. The consequences were slightly different from mine but the same concept was still implied.

Thomas was a dead man if he were to literally forbid me my privilege. The fact that Macey was now treating me like I'm a contagious disease was really pushing Thomas's funeral date closer than planned.

Dylan leaned against the tree and scowled. "Your manager's an ass."

"I know." I sighed. My fingers drummed repeatedly on the stair step I was sitting on. My knee bobbed up and down as I stared forward with a puckered mouth.

Chase laughed from next to me. "When was the last time you kissed Macey?"

My movements halted briefly as I sorted through my memories. When was the last time I kissed Macey? "Halloween night." I finally remembered.

Brandon clucked his tongue on the inside of his cheek. I glared at the smirk forming on his face. "Somebody suffering from kiss withdrawal, Aidy Wady?" He teased in a childish voice, pouting his bottom lip at me.

"Says the guy who hasn't kissed his girlfriend yet." I shot back.

That wiped the smirk right off of Brandon's face and caused Brynn to tense up beside him. Amber nudged me with her shoulder. "They're not official yet." She whispered to me.

Chase snorted from his spot on the railing. "Seriously?" He gave the two a deadpanned look. "It's been weeks, man. I expected you to have fu–"

"Chase!" Dylan hissed. Chase pulled an innocent face and shrugged. Brynn left her spot by Brandon and sat next to Amber, hiding her reddened face on her shoulder in embarrassment.

"This isn't about our relationship status," Brandon glowered. "This is about Adrian and his kissing issues with Macey."

It was my time to glower at him. "It's not just about the kissing!" I snapped.

Thomas made Macey sound like she was no more important than the guy who gives me coffee at Starbucks. Kelly was right when she said that Macey wasn't some slut that Thomas had always set me up with for the publicity. I was tired of the fake in it all. The plastic smiles, the uncomfortable closeness, the false headlines and news. Let's not forget the bitchiness that comes with each one.

It was like giving me a more famous Cammie. Need I remind you that Cammie disgusts me after all the harsh things she had done to Macey. That had me replaying the memory of that Halloween night years ago. When Macey had ignored me for almost a month and I had done nothing about it.

Well not this time. I'm not gonna wait weeks on end before making things right with my best friend. It was bad enough I made her feel like I cared about a fake blonde more than the girl that was willing to ruin her perfect attendance record just to take care of a sick 14 year old me, but I wasn't going to let Macey think that she's just some grain of sand in my life.

She deserves much more than that. She means more to me than that.

My thoughts were just adding fuel to my anger. Luckily, Amber slapped my arm and told me to calm down. I looked at her with a pleading expression. "What do I do?"

She put her hands up in the air. "Why are you asking me?"

"Because you're the most smart one out of all of us." I said, making everyone but Chase let out an offended 'HEY' in unison.

Chase merely shrugged again and said, "Girl's a shoo in for Valedictorian."

There was a slight pause of silence as the words sunk in before everyone nodded in agreement. He had a point there. Amber grimaced. "I'm not sure that's going to happen but if I were you, just try and talk to her."

"What do you think I've been trying to do all day?" I exasperated. Not only has Macey been ignoring me in person but she has also been ignoring my calls and texting back lame excuses like 'Oh sorry, my phone's dying and I need to take Lulu out for a walk.'

Pfft, walk my ass!

"I meant," Amber started. "Try getting her alone and refuse to let her leave until you talk about what happened."

"So.. Basically you want Adrian to trap Macey hostage some-where and refuse to let her free until they've talked things through?" Brandon asked.

Amber cringed at Chase's choice of words. "Well when you put it like that.."

"Perfect!" Chase smirked evilly. Of course he liked the idea of locking a girl in a room and not letting her go. Who knows what kind of sick plans he has on the weekends. "Need help with that, Adrian? I have a whole box of rope left over from past reasons."

Damn.

"No, I think I'm good.." I trailed, sending him a skeptical look. I shook off the feeling to call Chase some mental help or a room in a mental institution and turned my attention to the girls. "So, any idea where she decided to hide from me?" I asked.

"Mace said she was going to head down to the Animal Shelter for some extra hours." Brynn said. I nodded and jogged towards my car yelling a goodbye over my shoulder.

I'm not going to mess things up with Macey this time.

The first thing that hit me was the different animal noises filling my ears. I looked around the building, taking note of the different animal posters. The desk chair behind the receptionist desk remained empty and there were no sign of anyone else in here. My eyes landed on the shiny silver bell sitting at the end of the desk. Shrugging to myself, I rang it twice. The amount of barks tripled as the chime spread through the whole building.

"Just a minute!" A voice sang from one of the rooms at the bottom of the hall. I leaned against the desk with my eyes on the floor. Am I seriously going to trap Macey into a room and refuse to let her out? Isn't she working? Or volunteering. Anyways, I'd be pulling her away from her job. I could get her in trouble!

Then again, there's been an on going sick feeling in my stomach since Macey decided to ignore me. The way she flinched every time I tried to get close to her or the quick panic attack that hit her the second she saw me. It hurt, in a way.

I've already had 4 years without her. And before that, I've been a total ass here and there. What was I thinking? Now that I think about it, I've chosen Cammie over Macey more than one occasion. Standing Macey up on plans we've thought about for a while just to go on a stupid date with Cammie that came up an hour before I was scheduled to meet Macey.

IDIOT! I thought. Stupid, stupid idiot..

I sighed and ran an irritated hand through my hair. I want to do it right this time. Not have things change for the worst just because I came back famous and all. And let's not forget about Thomas. Kelly better help me kick his ass once I clean up his mess.

"Hi there." A voice greeted. I turned my head to see a short women with short blonde hair walking down the hall.

I smiled and offered a hand. "Hi, I'm Adrian."

The women shook my hand and gave me a small. "Well Adrian, I'm Hannah. How may I help you? Dog, cat, bunny? No judgment here, sir! If you want a bunny, I can get you a bunny."

"Actually," I dragged the word nervously. "By any chance, is a girl named Macey Daniels here? I kinda really need to talk to her."

Hannah perked up with realization before smirking. Of course. "Oh sure, she's here. Head down the hall and follow the sound of barking, Macey should be there." She winked. I nodded in appreciation and started towards the hall and using my hearing sense, found the kennel.

Macey was there, crouching in front of a cage with a small terrier in her hands. My lips tugged up into a small as Macey held a small bottle to the puppy's mouth and cooed it quietly. I shoved my hands in my pocket and leaned against the wall, waiting for her to finish nursing the cute animal cradling in her arms. If she saw me, I'm pretty sure she would've threw the dog in the air and sprinted out of the room or something.

For a few minutes, that's how the scene stayed. Macey kneeling on the floor, whispering and feeding the little dog in her arms while I leaned against the door frame and watched her gentle nature. I'd be lying if I didn't say that she looked totally hot just doing that. Her brown hair was draped down across her back, a strand tucked behind her ear. A small smile graced her features.

I was staring and I knew it.

But that didn't really last long, however, because after Macey was done feeding the little guy and was safely placed back in his cage, it was like a 6th sense went off. Her body went stiff and she squeezed her eyes shut with a small groan. She hasn't even turned to look at me yet and here she is, dreading my appearance. I didn't like that. At all.

Well here we go.

"You didn't really think I would wait till Thanksgiving dinner again to fix things between us, right?" I asked, still staring at the side of her body.

"I.. I don't know what you're talking about." She tried to be non-chalant. She stood on her feet and faced her back in my direction.

Avoiding my gaze, huh? Well we'll see about that.

Without a reply, I picked her up by the waist and hauled her out into the hallway and to what I hoped was a closet and not where the bunnies were kept. Then again, Kelly might want a bunny..

Focus, Adrian!

Right.

Luckily, I had pushed her into a supply closet. The room was dimly lit, filled with different materials and animal food.

"Adrian!" Macey gasped when I pushed her up against the wall next to the door and placed my arms by each side of her head. Macey sunk deeper against the wall on her own accord as I leaned closer to her face. She was freaking out of her mind, I could tell.

Chase would be so proud. Assaulting a girl into a conversation? Yeah, he'd be proud.

With that thought, I dropped my arms down to her waist and held them loosely, leaning back just a little bit. Yeah, I wasn't going to handle this like Chase would. Trapping her in a closet, fine, but that's it. I don't want Macey thinking that Thomas ordered me to kill her off because of what happened. That so wouldn't help my cause right now.

I kept my voice calm and quite. "Macey, we need to talk about this."

Macey didn't look as alarmed than she was just a minute ago. She looked more reluctant, if anything. Like a little kid when they're ordered a time out in a corner or when teenagers are about to have the sex talk with their parents.

Totally against the idea.

"There's nothing to talk about." She whispered. There was a mixture of despair, anger, and guiltiness in her eyes.

"You've been ignoring me since you left yesterday. All I got was lame excuses as to why you haven't answered my calls or texts and when I try to approach you, you run away. It's like you're trying to ignore me for as long as possible." I told her with the same quite tone.

The last thing I needed was to have that Hannah women come in here and think we were having an intense make out session or something. I bet that would be the first thing she would think of with the look she sent me when I said I needed to see Macey.

Macey didn't respond to my statement which only meant it was true. She wanted to ignore me, shut me out of her life over a stupid gesture and my bitchy manager.

Ouch.

I backed away a little, slightly hurt at Macey's intentions. The thought of her doing just that made my heart clench. 4 years without her and when I finally get her back she wanted to run away, just like that?

Well tough luck, that ain't happening. I'm not giving up without a fight.

I stepped closer to her again and leaned my forehead on hers. Macey didn't object this time. Instead, she wrapped her arms around my neck and buried her head my shoulder. My own arms found their way to her waist, pulling her tightly against me.

How did I last almost a month of not having her near before? I can't even last a night of not texting or calling her just for the heck of it. As girly as it sounds.. Her sweet smell calmed me down. She made everything okay.

"It's not true." I whispered next to her ear. A strand of hair tickled my nose when Macey shook her head slightly.

"I already knew."

Knew what? "What do you mean?"

"About how I wasn't –"

"Don't even finish that sentence." I cut her off, my arms tightning around her. I already knew what she was going to say. I don't blame her. It was just in Macey's character to think that little normal her wouldn't be able to meet the standards of my new life. But the thing is, those standards don't even exist here.

I'm on break. And even if I wasn't I'd let Macey in my life without a second thought.

"I don't care," I muttered., pulling back and taking her face in mine. I looked her straight in the eyes and said, "I don't care what

Thomas says. I don't care about what people think. I don't care if I kiss you in public. And I don't care if you think you're not good enough because that's not true. You honestly don't know how much you mean to me, Mace. The fact that I'm famous doesn't change anything. You will always be my best friend that I care for so much. I love my Sweet Macey more than anything in the world and you," I poked her head. "Need to get that through your thick skull."

Macey laughed before burying her head on my shoulder again. "Okay, fine. I'm sorry. It won't happen again."

"Good," I sighed. Then pulled a serious face. "Can I kiss you now?"

Macey slapped my arm and pulled back, laughing. "Seriously?" She asked. When I nodded eagerly like it was the most stupid question ever asked, Macey leaned up and kissed my cheek.

"There." She smiled.

"So not enough." I shook my head in disapproval and started trailing kisses down her neck. Macey snorted and I was pretty sure she was rolling her eyes at me but didn't object.

No more suffering from Kiss Withdrawal.

Chapter 15

Macey's POV

A few seconds after the music ended, I made a beeline towards my bag in desperate need of some water. I tugged open my bag and pulled out a bottle. I was in the middle of feverishly chugging the liquid down my dry throat before a hand rudely snatched out of my hands, spilling a couple drops on my shirt.

"Rude." I chastised my blonde headed friend as she drank my water. She crushed the empty bottle and sighed in content. It was one of those days Lucile actually treated us like we were going to perform for an actual crowd. With hours of practice and making sure each move was perfect, it really takes it's toll on us.

It was worth it at the end, though, to have the feeling of accomplishment and to stare at one another knowing we nailed the routine. The magical thirst quenching liquid – also known as water – is a much needed item after a day's work. But it apparently also brings the thief out of an exhausted dancer.

Brynn grinned at me, "Sharing is caring, Macey." She said in a teacher voice.

"Well then you wouldn't mind knowing that I stole $20 from you earlier this week?" I asked sweetly.

"I also took some money." Dylan added, coming to stand beside me. Brynn glared at the both us and turned towards our quiet friend who was standing innocently at the front of the room. Amber put her hands up in mock surrender, silently saying she didn't steal anything when in reality, she stole a few bucks in order to purchase a book at the library.

"Bitc-"

"Don't finish that sentence, young lady," Lucile interrupted, sauntering back into the room with three boys trailing behind her. I smiled at the sight of my three favorite guys. "A dirty mouth leads you to nowhere in life."

"I beg to differ." Chase smiled triumphantly, getting a horrified look from Amber's mother. Brandon snorted from next to him and shoved his shoulder.

"You're disgusting." He retorted.

"And you're such a girl." Chase shot back.

"And you two fight like an old married couple." Adrian countered. Laughs filled the room while the two scowled at my best friend. It was times like this why I really enjoy dance practice, especially if the guys are here to liven it up a bit.

"Kids these days," Lucile shook her head with a smile before turning towards us. "Great job today, girls. Maybe next time you could give the boys a performance one day."

"I'd rather not give the boys a lap dance." Dylan said smoothly. My mouth dropped just like everyone else in the room. Amber flushed a bright color, knowing that we just humiliated her in front of her mom. It's pretty much a miracle that Lucile allows her daughter to hang with us, let alone Amber's innocent mind isn't corrupted by now.

"Bye mom." Amber shooed quickly, literally pushing Lucile out by the shoulders. After the door shut closed, Amber looked at us in complete disbelief.

"You guys are unbelievable!" Amber hissed. Chase laughed and ruffled Amber's hair.

"You love us anyways." He said cheekily. Amber scowled slightly but didn't object. Adrian's arms slid around my waist and pulled me to his chest. I rested my head back against his shoulder's with a sigh. The drama involving Thomas had disappeared for the time being. I was touched that Adrian didn't wait until Thanksgiving dinner to come and fix things with me, even if I was being dramatic about the whole situation. But the thought of changing what Adrian's fans thought of him was something I really didn't want to do.

As a child he was always thinking about becoming an actor. There's probably dozens upon dozens of home made videos that Adrian has acted in, me being his trusty camera girl. He wouldn't admit this but I knew Adrian loves his career and would give anything up to continue what he loves doing for the rest of his life. I just didn't want to be the one person that ruins it for him.

"So when are you going to dance for me?" Adrian's voice interrupted my thoughts.

I peered up at him. "You've seen me dance." I told him.

"But you pretty much freaked out after. You all did, actually. My balls were threatened that day!"

I laughed as I recalled Dylan's words. The day we got caught had shaken me up a little. But that was only because I had to confess something I never wanted to mention again. It was a lucky shot that it was only the guys and not some random stalker from school.

"Why do you want to see me dance so bad?" I wondered.

"Because it's something you like to do." Adrian said simply. "You enjoy to dance and you should share that enjoyment with me."

"You'd enjoy seeing me dance?"

"Yes."

"Why?

Adrian flicked my forehead. "Stop questioning me." He ordered. "Can't I want to see my best friend dance?"

I sighed lightly. Normally I wouldn't be so reluctant on things like this, but dancing brought me a bad history that I'd rather not relive. It would be nice to give the boys a performance of some sort, yet I can't force myself enough to the point where I could push past those fears and just do it.

"I have an idea!" Chase gasped suddenly. Everyone groaned at his words. Mock offense took over Chase's face. "What?"

"All of your 'ideas' is something deceptive and evil, Chase." Brynn responded. "I highly doubt whatever you have planned in that twisted mind of yours is going to take away Macey's fear."

"It's not like I'm going to make you march across the streets half naked doing the running man or something." Chase said with an eye roll. He turned towards me. "You just got to ease into dancing in front of people instead of going straight to performing on stage. After you're comfortable dancing in general than you could move up a notch."

To say we were shocked would be an understatement. Everyone was completely dumbfounded at the fact that Chase is capable of giving advice– let alone good advice.

"Wow." Amber breathed. She looked the most shocked. I'm surprised Amber didn't come up with it first. "That's actually a good idea."

"Who knew you had a brain in that thick head of yours." Brandon said, knocking his fist on Chase's head. Chase scowled and pushed him roughly aside.

"So what do you say?" Chase asked.

All eyes flicked towards me. I cupped my elbow and switched my gaze to the floor. Easing into dancing in general, huh? It didn't seem too hard to do. But knowing Chase, 'easing' into something could be just sucking it up for the greater good and be locked in a room with people until I dance. It sounds like something he would do.

"Well?"

I sighed in defeat. "Fine. What do you have in mind?" Chase curled his mouth into an evil smirk.

I am so going to regret this..

"I regret this."

Brynn's focus remained on the road but I could tell she was rolling her eyes at me. "Don't be so dramatic. We look pretty sexy if you ask me."

"That's the point, Brynn. I'm not sure about this." I argued, looking at myself in the mirror. My top was a sea green racer back tank paired with black faux leather shorts and boots. Brynn was decked out in a white flare crop top and high waisted shorts. Chase's instructions were to dress how we would if we were going out to a party. Now from what I've heard, there were no parties going on a Wednesday night.

"Can't we look nice for once?"

"With Chase in charge of the plan? I think there's a reason to worry."

Brynn laughed. "Remember that time where he landed us all in detention for involving us in some scheme to embarrass that sophomore?"

"Waste of tampons and paper clips." I muttered with a smile.

"It was totally worth getting Amber her first detention." Brynn said, pulling up Dylan's drive way. The familiar blares of the horn rang through the dark night. A sharp bark came from one of the distant houses at the alerting noise. Minutes later, two brunettes came bounding out the front door dressed for the night.

"I'm not the only one nervous about Chase's idea, right?" Amber's voice said a second later the car door was open, not even bothering for a proper greeting.

"Well hello to you too." Brynn joked as she pulled out into the streets again. I looked at the girls through the rear view mirror just in time to see Amber rolling her eyes. She flattened out her skater skirt and leaned forward so her head was between the two seats.

"Where are we headed?"

"Chase's house." Brynn replied. "He told everyone to meet him there and he'll lead the way."

"We'll just have to wait and see how it turns out.." Dylan trailed. I slammed my head back against the seat with a groan. The thought of just putting myself out there was making me feel uneasy about the whole thing. I know Chase said to ease into it, but I don't know if I'm ready for that yet. And judging by the way we're dressed, I just hope this place wasn't over the top..

"Are you sure about this?" I questioned aloud.

Adrian and Brandon had already arrived when we got to Chase's house. They ended up carpooling in Brandon's car while we followed in Brynn's. A drive to downtown later and we were all standing outside some parking lot in front of a nameless building.

Brynn looked at the building skeptically while Dylan kept her composure completely at ease, as did Brandon and Adrian. Chase rolled his eyes. "Would you relax? This is perfectly fine, trust me." He said before walking towards the building.

Brynn, Brandon, and Dylan followed after him. Amber floundered around a bit, trying to decide what to do. Eventually she ended up trailing behind the others leaving me still on the spot. I wrapped my arms around my stomach and just stood there.

Chase said this building was like an everlasting party, but not as rowdy as an actual one. It was run by his uncle who played as the DJ. Basically, it was just a hang out/dance club combined for people our age to come out and have fun without having to worry about drunk perverts. A lot of regulars serve as customers since Chase's uncle only built the place in some kind of secrecy. You'd have to know someone to get in.

It may not be as bad as a wild party where someone from our school is most likely to be there, but there's people. Dancing in front of people brings back the memories from that day. I practically vowed I would never dance in front people even though this is more like dancing with people. Nevertheless, it's not just a group of friends anymore. And that makes me feel uncomfortable.

I had almost forgot Adrian was waiting behind me until his arms came to wrap around my waist, pulling me flush against him. I sighed and leaned my head back onto his shoulder. "I don't want to do this." I mumbled. His intoxicating smell filled my nose, calming my churning stomach.

"You don't have to do it right away." He told me, his finger rubbing patterns on my stomach. "After a few hours we'll see where you're at, okay? No pressure."

"Thanks, Adrian." I said softly. Adrian's arms tightened around me as he hugged me to his chest.

"No problem, Sweetheart. Now let's get in there." Just as I was about to step forward, Adrian held me back once more. "By the way," He whispered against my ear, "You look really sexy tonight."

I was suddenly thankful that it was dark outside so he couldn't see my blush. I'm sure he knew anyways, but at least he wouldn't tease the sight. I pulled out of his arms and allowed him to pull me towards the entrance.

The others were waiting there for us and we all entered at once. Bright colored lights were shined on my face and the current song boomed in my ear. No wonders only regulars knew about this place. I marveled at the scene. Compared to the drab outside cover, the inside seemed like a complete transformation.

The lights were dimmed by over head lights, multicolored lights flashing around the whole room. Red couches and booths were set up against the wall giving way for a huge dance floor in the middle of the room. Now that part was interesting.

The platform we were standing on gave us a perfect view of people aligned in a square, clapping and chanting a couple guys competing it out in the middle. A guy with brown hair and head-phones hanging off his neck – who I'm assuming is the DJ – was standing on a small stage at the other side of the room surrounded by speakers and equipment. But unlike other DJs I've seen in my life, this guy was actually talking into a microphone narrating the whole dance battle.

"Woah." Brynn shouted over the music and cheers. Besides Chase, who looked completely smug with himself, the rest of us were all awing at the place before us. We watched as the two guys finished up their battle and clapped each other on the back with a smile.

"Alright everyone," the DJ said energetically into the microphone. "Those were a couple of our regulars, Andrew and Kevin, give them a hand!" Hollers were let out from the crowd, as well as a couple of fists pumping in the air.

Suddenly the DJ looked up and saw the seven of us standing at the door. A huge smiled erupted on his face as he said, "Hey, looks like we got some newcomers joining the party tonight! Give them a warm welcome, everybody!" Heads turned in our directions as more yells came from the crowd of people.

"That's Dallas, my uncle." Chase said loud enough for us to hear.

"Alright, everyone enjoy the music and if you have any requests come on up. I'll be back in a sec!" A new song was played through the speakers and some of the people dispersed out of the crowd and towards the booths and couches. Dallas hopped off the stage and made his way over to us with his arms wide open.

"Chase, my man!" Dallas shouted, happy to see his nephew. Chase walked over to him and pulled him into a hug.

"Hey, Uncle Dallas. It's great to see you." Chase told him. Then he turned towards us. "These are my friends. Brandon, Amber, Dylan, Brynn, Macey, and Adrian. Guys, meet my Uncle Dallas."

"It's great to know that Chase still has friends." Dallas joked as he walked up and gave us each a handshake. He stopped in front of Adrian. "Aren't you –"

"Adrian Chapmen? Yeah, that's me." Adrian answered automatically, his hand squeezing my waist. I leaned into him more. It was still weird knowing that people we haven't met know Adrian just by looking at him. Dallas whirled around to Chase, shock clearly written on his face.

"Since when are you cool enough to hang with this guy?" He questioned, jerking a thumb behind him.

"Since before he became a pretty boy and left for LA. Remember when you came for a visit and the ceiling fan in my bedroom was gone? Guess who was the one that broke that." Chase hinted. I laughed, remembering the time when Chase and Adrian showed up at my place in order to hide from Mrs. Porcelli's wrath. 2 hours later and she came knocking at my door with Connie, both looking angry with their boys.

It was very amusing to see them working a lemonade stand. Not for the money, but for the embarrassment. Let's just say seeing 14 year olds running a lemonade stand with drinks that tasted like piss didn't earn you brownie points. At all.

Dallas's eyes widened in recognition. "That was him?"

"Yup." Adrian chuckled. "But I wasn't the one swinging the bat." He defended.

Dallas let out a bellowing laugh. "Well it's nice to meet you and the gang. Enjoy your time and the activities start soon. So get ready to dance." He informed us before waving goodbye and heading back to his post.

"Activities?" Brandon asked.

"Yeah, Uncle Dallas doesn't just play the music. He makes up some dance moves for everyone to follow and then some people come and perform, do dance battles. Things like that. It's the reason I brought you guys here."

"That sounds so awesome!" Amber squealed, running down the stairs and onto the dance floor. Brynn laughed and trailed after her with Brandon close behind. Dylan turned towards Chase with an impressed expression.

"This is pretty smart of you, Chase." She nodded to herself.

Chase smirked. "Damn straight." He said.

Rolling her eyes, Dylan grabbed Chase by the arm and pulled him towards the others. Excitement bubbled inside me, replacing the nervous butterflies I was feeling before. Amber was right; this sounded fun! Adrian pulled me closer and I looked up at him with a smile which he returned.

"Ready?" He asked, slipping his hand with mine. I breathed deeply and laced my fingers with his, glancing at my laughing friends.

I could do this..

"Let's go."

"1.. 2.. 3!"

On the count of three, Brandon and Chase both both bit down into their monster burgers. We watched in amazement as the two boys scarfed down even more food. The rest of us had finished 15 minutes ago, but those two were still going. It was like they had an endless pit in their stomach.

"How could you still be eating?" Amber wondered, her eyes wide.

Chase muffled out an incoherent sentence. "Gee that was help-ful." Dylan joked. Brynn looked at Brandon in disgust when he chomped down on his burger. I cringed slightly to the left and into

Adrian's side. His arm was draped onto the seat behind me and I laid my head on his shoulder.

It was nearing eleven in the evening and I've been sitting in our booth for two hours. Adrian had offered to stay with me, but I refused to let him stay with him instead of joining the others. He is a star – break or not – and I don't want to be a roadblock in his enjoyment. Especially in a place like this.

"Alright, alright," Dallas's enthusiastic voice rang through the speakers. "It's the top of the hours, folks, and you know what that means. It's time for another round of dancing so everybody – and I mean everybody – " I looked up from Adrian's shoulder and towards Dallas, who was giving me a pointed look. "To get on the dance floor because this next song is a fun one!"

Brynn and Dylan both went out towards the dance floor while Brandon and Chase finished off their burger, sliding out of the booth and going after them. Amber pulled on my hand. "Mace, come on! This one's going to be fun and all you've been doing is sitting there!" She insisted.

Now that may be true, but it was entertaining to watch what Dallas came up with. The last hour people had a rap battle and the next a local dancer made simple moves during a song so everyone could follow along. It was nice to see my friends smiling and having fun,which is enough to satisfy me for one night. I did not need be there and join in.

"I don't know, Ams." I protested weakly. Adrian nudged me out of the booth;

"Just one round, please!" Amber debated. She began to hop from one foot to another, pouting at me childishly. Normally that wouldn't have worked on me, but that was until I looked towards

Dallas and noticed he was waiting for me to join the crowd. The crowd that was staring at me right this moment. It was then I noticed that literally every single person in the building was on the dance floor.

Except me.

"Okay, fine!" I gave in, earning an encouraging cheer from everyone. It wasn't like I was going to say no. Having everyone wait for you to come and join them, even though you have no clue as to who they are in the first place is pretty awkward.

"Atta girl, Macey." Dallas said into the microphone. I ducked my head in embarrassment and allowed myself to be pulled by Amber towards the others.

"Don't worry, Mace," Brynn assured. "It's really fun."

"Oh I'm sure." I mumbled under my breathe. I cupped my elbow with my hand and watched Dallas choose a song.

"Okay so this is how it's going to be," Dallas started. "You all are going to dance to this song, okay? But every time the singer chants 'Down' I want you to lower yourself onto the floor and then jump back up. Got it?"

He wants us to what?

Then the familiar tune of "Down" by Jay Sean boomed through the speakers and realization dawned on me. Now I knew what he meant. Lucile had choreographed a routine for this a few months ago where we did have to lower ourselves slightly with each 'down'.

I stood there awkwardly at first while everyone started moving to the music. Some were swaying their hips and waving their hands in the air, some were jumping, and some were dancing like pros. When the chorus came, Dallas chanted the words and everyone lowered down to the floor before popping back up. Every time the cycle was repeated, I stiffly followed everyone for I didn't want to be the only one standing there like an idiot.

I jumped when hands rested on my hips and started swaying them slightly. I turned my head to see Adrian smiling at me. My face grew burned and my body tensed as Adrian continued to move me against him. He seemed to notice this as he bent down and said, "Relax Mace."

Just let it be,

Come on and bring your body next to me.

I'll take you away (Hey)

Turn this place into our private get away...

My body gradually grew less tense and Adrian no longer had to control me. My hands found their way behind me and wrapped themselves around Adrian's neck as I moved against him.

"Well look at you." Adrian appraised, his arms leaving my waist to take hold of my hand and twirl me around. I laughed. An excited squeal filled my ear and I turned to see Amber smiling at me grandly. Soon, Dylan and Brynn joined us so that we were forming a little square of just the four of us.

"Let's do this part of the routine." Dylan shouted over the music as Lil Wayne's part came out. Amber and Brynn nodded and surprisingly, I did too. Remembering the routine that we nailed months ago, we danced along to the lyrics to Lucile's choreography.

She cold overfreeze,I got that girl from overseasNow she's my MIss America Now can I be her soldier please

I'm fighting for this girl on a battlefield of loveDon't it look like baby cupid sendin' arrows from aboveDon't you ever leave this side of meIndefinitely, now probably and honestly I'm down like the economy.

I had completely forgotten that we were dancing in front of a bunch of people that made way for us and were now watching and cheering. We were in the middle of the square leading the dance to the end with a spotlight shining above us.

My heart was soaring when the song faded away and the whole crowd erupted into applause. I could've sworn my mouth dropped open as I realized what I just did. And apparently I wasn't the only one.

"OH MY GOD!" Amber squealed, trapping me into a hug and jumping up and down. I let out a small groan when Dylan and Brynn tackled us and joined into the group hug. And then there was Chase and Brandon, who decided that I needed to be suffocated even more as they wrapped their arms around us and squeezed tightly. I felt my lungs collapsing.

"Let go!" I wheezed. The five of them quickly let go, only to have me stumble into another pair of arms. Though instead of squeezing me to death, my feet were suddenly lifted off the ground and I felt myself being twirled.

"Sweetheart, that was amazing!" Adrian yelled happily, putting me on the floor once again. I can't believe I did that. I just danced in front of a bunch of people. Spotlight and everything!

And the best thing was I didn't care.

"Before we end the night, grab that special someone and bring them down for one last dance."

It was the strike of midnight when Dallas decided to put on a slow song as the last one of the night. Only a few people had decided to leave earlier than everyone else while everyone else remained here. A few couples made their way to the dance floor and slowly swayed to the music.

Amber had fallen asleep with her head resting on a worn out looking Dylan's lap and Chase decided to eat some late night desert. Brandon stood up from the booth with a tired sigh and held out a hand to Brynn.

"Care to dance?" He asked politely. We all smirked as Brynn placed her hand in his and followed Brandon towards the dance floor. My head rested against Adrian's shoulder, his thumb running circles on my waist. The adrenaline of dancing in front of a crowd had long ran out and I was just as exhausted as everybody else. We had agreed to wait until closing before leaving just to enjoy our night out. But what I really wanted now was to sleep.

And I probably would've if I didn't feel myself being prodded repeatedly.

"What?" I mumbled tiredly. Can't they see I was in need of some sleep?

"Macey," Adrian nudged me again. "Dance with me."

I pried my eyes open, raising my head from his shoulder to look at him. "What?"

"Dance with me, Sweetheart."

My eyes widened at his request. I shook my head sheepishly. "I don't slow dance, Adrian."

Rolling his eyes, Adrian pulled my out of the booth and towards the dance floor. "Says the girl who said she can't dance in front of a crowd." He challenged. Too tired to argue, I wrapped my arms around his neck as Adrian wrapped his around my waist. Exhaustion was slowly taking over me once again so I rested my head against his shoulder.

And that's how it stayed. The both of us wrapped up in each others arms, swaying side to side to the slow sweet music. The lights had dimmed down dramatically compared to the bright neon lights that were flashing just hours ago. It was calm and eerily romantic in a way.

I felt a kiss being placed on my shoulder. "You were really great today." He mumbled quietly.

I nuzzled against his neck. "Thanks for being patient, Adrian." I mumbled honestly. "It means a lot to me."

"You're lucky I love you. I'm not a very patient person." I laughed. Patience was never an option to him.

"I guess I'm just special." I teased.

Adrian stayed silent until the song was over before inaudibly saying:

"You have no idea."

Chapter 16

November has to be one of my favorite months of the year. Now don't get me wrong, I love almost every month that has a main holiday in it. But the reason why November is always at one of the top spots on my list is the constant off days we get. Especially when we get four days away from all the stress, work, and school drama.

The average two day weekend is never enough.

A cool breeze hit my back as I slammed my door behind me. My tired limbs let loose of my backpack filled with binders and notebooks, dropping to the floor with a low thud. There is nothing better than falling onto your bed after an exhausting day at school.

It seems the teachers are rather tenacious about cramming in a ton of work during a fifty five minute time period due to the time they're losing with the off days. There was still the share of math homework that we always get, no matter what the occasion was. Other than the bundles of numbers and equations that are needed to be solved, it was Friday with another four day weekend ahead of us.

Exhaustion slowly forced my eyes to flutter shut, dream land calling my name over and over. I never did get the chance to walk through the entryway of the magical dream that awaited me, for the alarming sound of my door swinging open and crashing against the wall made me jolt awake immediately.

Emma stood under my doorway, smirking widely at me. I glared at her. "Can I help you?" My voice groggier from my five minute nap. If only it was longer.

Emma's connecting foot sent my backpack sliding against the hardwood floor and stop at the other side of my bedroom. My bed bounced when Emma's bottom dropped on top. "We, dear sister of mine, are going out." She said.

"Out?" I repeated dumbly.

Emma nodded. "I need time with you too, you know. That Adrian's back in town, I never get to see my sister anymore." Her lip jutted out in a small pout. Her words both annoyed and surprised me. I was clearly irked that I couldn't curl up under my covers and catch up on my sleep, but the other part of me was shocked that both the Daniels sisters were going to go out. Together. Just the two of us.

"I'm sorry, Em. I guess we really don't see each other as often," I said with a frown. It just hit me that the only time I see Emma was generally during breakfast and at dinner. It's not often that I come directly home after school since I'm always with Adrian or the others. "In all fairness, you're always out with Kelly." I added.

"I know," Emma sighed. Her hands wove through her long brown waves. "That's why I want to go out with you. We can go to the mall!" She stated excitedly.

I chuckled. The mall is Emma's ideal hang out place, no matter what age she is. With a huge dramatic sigh, I let my body fall against the bed. "Fine. When are we going?"

"Now. Duh," My wrists were then tightly clasped between Emma's hands as she tried to pull me up and onto my feet. I pushed all my weight back onto the mattress. "Come on, Mace, I saw the cutest pair of heels the other day and they're on sale!" She urged.

The moment of restraint on her tugging caused Emma to get more and more annoyed by the second, especially with the smirk I was trying to suppress. My arms were practically ripped out of their sockets when Emma gave a sudden rough pull to both arms. My shoulders let out a popping sound.

I rolled my elbows in circular motions while glaring at my sister who was now sporting a smirk of her own. I've always called her an evil sister as a child. Now I knew why; she could be very abusive if she wants to. Emma then turned on her heels and began strutting out my room. "Five minutes before I tear your legs off!" She called out in a sing song voice.

Evil sister indeed.

"Walk down the isle."

I sighed and dragged my feet down the isle and back. The type of shoe I was wearing now was nothing compared to the previous ankle breakers Emma calls shoes. These were a simple pair of black combat boots.

After buying about a dozen pairs (not exaggerating), Emma insisted that I got at least one. It would make her, and I quote, 'a mean and horrible sister if she did not do the honor of buying her little sister a pair of shoes.'

I could just feel the love, really.

Emma pursed her lips, her eyes calculating. "How do they feel? Do you like it?"

I shrugged. "They feel alright," I collapsed down on a bench and wrenched the boots off my feet, fitting them snugly into their box. "I like them."

Emma clapped her hands together. "Yay! We'll get these." She told the clerk at the front desk. The women nodded and began to scan our items. Being the dotting sister that I happen to be, I grabbed two of Emma's bag, as well as mine, to even out the amount she would have to carry.

"So, how about lunch? I really don't want to follow the whole 'shop till you drop thing'."

Emma nodded in agreement and we both set off for the food court. "Alright, Fatburger, no… Johnny Rockets, no… McDonald's, hell no!" Emma counted off as she scanned our options. "Ugh, do they want us fat?" She complain while dropping the bags onto a seat.

I looked at the possibilities with a blank stare. "We live in a cruel, cruel world, Em." I said dramatically. Emma's rants about how unhealthy the choices are today was not something new. It's the reason we never really eat here in the mall unless she's craving.

"Amen to that." She mumbled.

"Screw these foods, we can grab dinner later. Want some Ben & Jerry's for now?" I suggested while placing the shopping bags down against one of the nearby tables.

"Sure. You go get.." Emma's voice trailed as she stared distantly in the direction of Ben & Jerry's. I craned my neck higher to get a better look at what was holding my sister's attention. It soon became clear that I wasn't going to be the one playing the little maid. The only employ running the store was an exceptionally handsome looking man cleaning down one of the nearby tables.

"Actually," Her eyes wandered down his body hungrily. "I'll go order. The usual, cookie dough, right?"

"Yup." I casually hid my smug smile behind my hand.

"Kay, be right back." I watched as she approached the cute boy behind the counter. I knew exactly what was going to happen. It made me sigh internally. Seconds later and the two were already putting their flirting techniques to the test, the task at hand forgotten.

I rolled my eyes. Typical. Normally, I would've been cool with my sister trying to get it on with a total stranger, but my stomach was begging me to feed it. Emma and her boy toy may be making out in the back room at this rate and leave me to starve.

Look at me, complaining about ice cream. What am I, an obese food addict? I slumped back against my chair with a sigh. The two kept up the conversation for a whole fifteen minutes before I began to get antsy. My knee bobbed up and down impatiently as I glared at the back of my sister's head. I was just about to go up and order my own damn food before my phone started to vibrate and my ringtone belted out of the small speaker.

I slid my finger across the screen, smiling at the caller id, and raised my phone up to my ear. "This is Macey Daniels speaking, on a scale of one to ten, how much do you miss me right now?" I asked, feigning the worst British accent I could muster.

Adrian's chuckle vibrated from the other line. "And you thought I was cocky?" I grinned a goofy smile to myself. "To answer your question though, I say eleven."

I clicked my tongue. "Ooo, an extra one point. I'm flattered, Adrian, really." I teased, checking on my sister's flirt status. The boy was giving Emma the most pedophile smile ever while my sister had the look of disgust written all over her face. Maybe I'll get to eat soon.

"Only for you, Mace," A smile evident through his tone. "So where are you?" He sighed, all traces of playfulness gone in an instant. My lips turned down in a frown.

"I'm at the mall with Emma. Sister bonding, I guess."

"Oh. Sounds fun." The slight disappointment made me frown even more.

"Everything okay? You sound kinda down."

"It's nothing."

I remained silent. If he could only see the flat look I was giving him. Adrian may be able to figure out if I'm lying most of the time, but that doesn't mean I can't tell when my own best friend has something going on. And just from the six minute conversation we were having, the signs are going off.

"Okay fine," He sighed in defeat. I grinned in victory. It's like we have a best friend telepathy or something. "Thomas is getting on my nerves"

The smile was wiped off my face at the sound of his manager's name. It was obvoius that Thomas didn't like my presence around Adrian because I'm not some Victoria Secret model or something. I am a normal high school student that just so happens to be the best friend of a star. The fact is not new nor weird to think about. But when Thomas only trashes on me and not the others, it makes me wonder why I, out of all people, happen to be on his 'She's-not-good-for-your-image' list for Adrian. AKA, my best friend. The guy I've known longest out of the group.

"You better not be questioning your value." Adrian spoke, catching me off guard. Maybe we really do have a best friend telepathy. The thought almost made me snicker.

"I was not," I protested. There is that one role in his life that I play, and I knew that. No matter what his stuck-up bitch of a manager has to say about it. "So what happened?" I asked, trying to steer the direction of the subject to a different route.

"He's just been really on my tail about what I've been doing lately. 'This meal is unhealthy. How many hours have you been working at the gym? You are not wearing that in public.' Honestly, and Kelly would murder me if she heard me say this, he's starting to sound like my sister."

I was able to listen and process Adrian's words while, at the same time, watching Emma get aggravated by the ice cream man and start gesturing wildly in the air. "Sounds like he's PMSing. Is he on his man period?" I mused jokingly.

"That's a nice assumption, Sweetheart." Adrian laughed.

"Oh, I know," I twisted a strand of my hair mindlessly. Emma was now pointing at the glass over the tubs, her lips pressed together in a tight impatient line. Looks like I'm going to eat after all. "How about you lock yourself in your room? Oh, you can do your homework! He can't PMS about your education, right?"

"But that's so boring, Mace," He groaned. I rolled my eyes at his childishness. "It's a Friday night, Sunday is a homework problem. Or a few days after the dead line problem." The last part came out as an almost inaudible mumble.

"Come on. It'll get Thomas off your back!" I urged.

"But –"

"Adrian? Can you come help me with some things for the fashion show? I need you to model a few of my designs!" I heard Kelly call. The thought of Adrian strutting back and forth in one of Kelly's designs with a scowl on his face made me laugh. Kelly was a great designer, don't get me wrong, but the styles that she makes up for men is definitely not something I would see Adrian walking around in. Let alone wear against his own will.

"Hmm, what would you rather do? Homework or be a five hour Ken doll?" I pondered aloud in a sweet voice.

"Shit," I heard him mutter before he yelled back a response: "I'm doing homework, Kel, maybe another time!"

Much to his disgust, Kelly wasn't done. "Well then come do your homework down here so I could spot check you! Oh, and tell Macey I said hi and thanks for getting your lazy ass to do homework!"

I laughed so loud that I had to slap a hand over my mouth in order to lower the volume. Emma seemed to finish off blowing off the ice cream man, for she came bearing our orders to the table. "I hate you both." He muttered after calling back an okay to Kelly.

"Please, you love me." I cooed, mouthing a 'thanks' when a carton filled with two scoops of my favorite ice cream was placed in front of me.

"Whatever. I got to go, talk to you later."

"Okay. Love you too, Superstar."

"Back at you, Sweetheart. Bye."

After hanging up, I slid my phone back into my pocket and took a big bite of my ice cream. The cold deliciousness melted onto my tongue, a single ball of cookie dough softly being crushed between my teeth. I moaned at the taste.

"What happened with the ice cream man?" I asked Emma.

"Total bastard, don't want to get into it."

"That bad?"

"That bad of an asshole."

"Ah," I nodded.

"Was that Adrian?" She questioned, eating another bite of her mint chocolate chip ice cream. I never really liked the flavor, it was like continually eating toothpaste with some chocolate in it, ruining the purpose of the cleaning material.

"Yeah. Thomas was getting on his case again." I frowned. If Thomas was that much of a pain, I don't understand why they don't kick him to the curb. Kelly sure seems to hate him and the whole Chapmen family don't act like his biggest fan either.

"I hate that guy. He's such a control freak." Emma snorted. "He doesn't really like you, does he?"

"He doesn't really approve of me being in Adrian's life, no." I put more pressure onto a hard piece of cookie dough.

"Well he's going to have to suck it up since Adrian's got the hots for you and all." Emma said so bluntly that I choked on the ball of sweetness.

"W-What?" I coughed, grabbing a napkin and wiping my face off.

Emma stared at me blankly. "Mace, it's obvious Adrian still has feelings for you."

"Still?" I choked out. Since when did Adrian like me in the past? It wasn't physically possible!

"Omigosh, I thought you two have already talked about your little childhood crushes for each other. It was so obvious you'd have to be blind not to see the chemistry between you two."

I shook my head violently. "There's no.. I-I mean it can't... But we.. What?" Adrian and I have always been friends and strictly just friends. I mean, sure we're a little more.. intimate with one another, but there was absolutely no way Adrian would develop that kind of feelings for me. Right?

"You mean the way he looks at you, holds you, talks about you, kisses –"

"I get it!' I cut her off, dropping my spoon to hold my hands up in a stop position. "There's nothing special about the way he does all those things." I argued.

"He kisses you."

"Not on the lips! It's something normal like the cheek or my forehead."

Emma quirked an eyebrow. "You mean he doesn't kiss your neck a lot?"

"I.." How did she know that? We're usually in private if Adrian decided to do that. A blush made it's way up to my face.

"Best friends don't kiss their best friend's neck, Mace. Especially not the way he –"

"Don't!" I shrieked, clamping a hand over my ears. "No, no, no! Ugh, why do you have put things in my head?"

Emma laughed, taking another bite out of her ice cream with a satisfied smirk on her face. "It's in the job description, Sis. Face the music, Adrian likes you."

"No, he doesn't." I sighed in irritation.

Adrian does not like me. I thought confidently. We are best friends, nothing more nothing less. Even back all those years ago, it wouldn't be possible. And I knew exactly why that thought was nothing but some figure of Emma's imagination.

Cammie.

Cammie had been Adrian's whole world in our younger teenage years. Ever since 6th grade when Cammie's 'hard to get' attitude had turned Adrian on in the first place. After he had gotten her, it was like he was blind by love. Everything he would do, Cammie had to be in the center of it. The way he dressed up just to impress his girlfriend, the reason he tried out for the football team even if it was the sport he despised the most. Cammie was eighty five percent of the time why Adrian and I would always end up in a big fight.

Always.

The pranks, the rain-checks for hanging out, the misunderstandings. The tarantula incident was just the beginning of what things she coaxed Adrian to do, all to my disadvantage. And each time he would screw up and fall for that witch's spell, I would forgive him anyway. It would be an ignore-come back situation with the two of us. And every time he would come to apologize, I would forgive him anyways.

Adrian had spent the rest of his time here dating Cammie, leaving absolutely no room whatsoever to have any 'feelings' for me. Especially since he was my childhood crush. It was not the other way around. I was over the moon, though, when I found out those two had broken up since she was definitely not the girl for him, but Cammie loved to pin me as the culprit that destroyed their relationship.

"They dated until Adrian got his big break and then left for LA for four years. He was so infatuated with Cammie, Em. There's just no way."

Emma watched me intently as I finished up the remains of my treat. I was in the middle of savoring the last bite before she spoke again. "What did you say was the reason that those two broke up?"

"Cammie saw Adrian as the soon-to-be famous guy and not for what he really was." I answered easily. It was a simple question. Ever since word spread, Cammie clung to him like a second skin. She was always attached to his hip before, but this was different. She was just always there. For the fact that she could be dating a star.

"Yeah and what about after that?" Emma pushed. "When you told him that you thought he assured you it was no big deal?"

My eyes furrowed in concentration as I thought back to that day Adrian told me the news.

'Besides, I've got a thing for someone else.'

'Really?" I asked, nudging his shoulder playfully. "Do I know this mystery girl?'

Adrian chuckled. "More than you think."

The memory made me gasp. Was it really possible? Did Adrian really like me? A single possibility that Adrian returned my feelings back then?

No. No, he didn't. Just because he said he had a thing for some-one else doesn't mean that that girl was me. It could've been one of my close friends.

"Em, that doesn't prove anything. If Adrian liked me, I think I would've noticed. And as of the present time, I am absolutely positive that Adrian doesn't like me. Especially with what he could get." My tone upheld a high level of finality.

Emma seemed disappointed in my response as she sunk back into her seat with a sigh and a frown. "You're in such deep denial." She said quietly, more to herself than me.

It was true though. I was in denial. But it made perfect sense than the misinformation Emma was trying to feed me. Adrian could have any girl he wants, he's been exposed to much better girls out there. If he were to date someone, it wouldn't be an average girl from Miami, Florida.

Just as Thomas said: I'm just a normal girl.

Chapter 17

Adrian's POV

"Kelly, no."

"Please Adrian?"

"No."

"Just this last one and you'll be done, promise!"

A loud, dramatic sigh left my body as I trudged my way around the corner and into the open living room. I fidgeted with the fedora on my head and slouched begrudgingly in front of Kelly. Homework had been my excuse to not become a living manikin for Kelly's designs. But sooner or later, I had actually ran out of assignments to do, as well as studying for all of Wednesday's test.

It was a waste of a Saturday night, let me tell you. The outfits she created is definitely not something I would wear in public, but that's just me. The types of clothes Kelly creates should remain on the runway and the runway only.

They shouldn't even belong in the comfort of my precious living room.

Kelly stood under the doorway, her lips pursed and heels tapping on the hardwood floor. Her eyes analyzed the clothes on my body. "That color.."

"Kelly!" I groaned. I've been playing dress-up for a total of five hours now, and I'm ready to just up and leave this house. Unfortanetly for me, Macey's having some sister bonding time with Emma, Chase is still grounded (though he won't admit it), Amber refuses to stop studying for a test tomorrow, the two blonde headed love birds are out on a date, and Dylan's stuck in bed with the stomach flu.

There's nobody to save me from this fashion madness.

"Can you just try one one more shirt?

"Kell, I'm not – "

"Adrian Chapmen!" A voice I really didn't want to hear right now called my name, causing my eyes to widen. Not this again.

Thomas walked into the room with an annoyed expression. Only when his eyes landed on me that his face turned into shock before transforming to complete horror. I would've laughed at his face if it weren't for the fact that he has been a straight-up asshole this entire week. I could already hear what he has to say about my outfit.

In my defense, though, he's not the only one completely against what I'm currently wearing.

"What is–" His tone laced with disbelief. "That? It's absolutely –"

"Absolutely what, Tommy?"

I clicked my tongue against the roof of my mouth at Kelly's sneer. The hand on her hip and perfectly arched eyebrow was just the beginning amount of sass about to be done in this living room. Thomas' timing was just right but, at the same time, very off.

"He looks like a Ken doll!" Thomas flailed his arm at me.

"Excuse me?" Kelly yelled, offended. "Which one of us is the fashion designer here?"

"Obviously not you." Thomas' reply was very unprofessional, if you ask me. He's made it blantaly obvious of his hate towards my sister, and that's totally cool. But it's like the mere presence of her just pisses him off, making him release all negativity that he has stored in his body. And apparently it's a lot.

With arms crossed, Kelly rolled her eyes. "Such a childish excuse, Tommy."

"Says the women pouting and complaining like a little girl," Thomas snorted. "Add that to the fact that you're dressing my client like a play toy, it makes perfect sense."

Kelly gasped.

I sighed. This conversation isn't going anywhere. "Would you guys cut the shit," I droned. "Thomas, why the hell are you here?"

"I was here to talk to you about a few issues, but I see there are additional issues that must be discussed." Thomas referred to my clothes. The annoyance in me simmered. Kelly's designs wasn't something that needed to be talked about. The worst that I was doing was helping my sister see her own clothes on a person. Even if the fashion show is months away, I know how stressed Kelly is when she waits until it's closer before planning out the designs.

If I had to be a four hour human girly man doll, fine. But hearing Thomas rant on about what problems he has with my life, that's something I would rather get out of.

"You want to talk about it? Fine. I'm helping my sister with her designs. We're done talking." I could hear Kelly snicker as I walked away and towards the kitchen. The scowl on Thomas' face wasn't hard to conjure up.

I opened up the fridge and scanned it. The nearly empty shelves reminded me to tell my parents that we needed to restock. Thomas came in with Kelly behind him.

"We need to talk about the banquet Cara Pratt is holding next weekend, right here in Miami." He said.

The corner of my lips turned down at the sound of her name. Cara Pratt was my on-set love interest from the last movie I had done before moving back home. And that movie included several, and very close, intimate scenes. Cara and I had a few moments off scene as well, almost all of them strictly in the moment situations while the others were just to give the public a kick.

Did Macey see that movie? Or see the gossip news about us?

Damn. I really hope she didn't.

Why do you care?

My eyes widened in their own accord. Why do I care? It's my best friend we're talking about, not my girlfriend. This is the girl who knows pretty much everything about me. Who I've shared a bed with a billion times. The one person I've kissed more than my own mother.

Macey. My Macey.

So why does the thought of her knowing I had intense make out sessions many times, on and off set, with some model makes me sick to my stomach?

"Adrian."

It's like I got caught committing the crime of the century. Like having Cara's lips against mine was wrong, in a way. Or for some insane reason, it would Macey feel...Jealous?

"Adrian?"

It wouldn't be like that. It isn't even like that. It's been like it is now for as long as I can remember. She's never showed an ounce of interest in liking me. Macey doesn't have feelings for me, and I don't have feelings for her. Well, not anymore, that is.

Liar.

Not.

Liar.

Not.

Li—

"Adrian!"

The two voices yelling my name snapped me out of my thoughts. Both my parents had arrived home when I looked up from the counter top, both of them were looking at me questioningly. Emma stared at me with her eyebrows knitted together in confusion. I'm not one who gets lost in their thoughts.

"Sorry."

"Don't tell me you're thinking about that slut." Kelly's face scrunched up in disgust. She's never liked any girls that I acquainted back in LA. She's always thought they were the same Victoria's Secret model with fame invading their heads and taking all the humbleness and modesty that could've been there before.

Now she thought they were all just STD carriers.

"No, I wasn't thinking about that slut." I told her.

You were thinking about your false feelings for your hot best friend.

Since when did I have a nagging conscious?

Since you sunk into denial.

Oh, god.

I shook my head. No no no. I'm not going to have a battle with my inner conscious over something that isn't true. "I'm not going to the banquet." I said firmly. This whole break thing was for a reason and that reason was to get away from it all. Going to the banquet is just going to suck me back in once I'm in a room full stars and producers looking for their next hit.

Kelly looked like she was going to break into a happy dance before yelling 'HA' in Thomas' face. Thomas, however, looked like he was ready to bang his head against the wall because of the Chapmen stubbornness. It runs in the family.

"Why not?" He sighed.

"I don't want to."

Kelly grinned at me. My dad's lip even twitched upwards a bit.

Thomas touched his fingertips to his temple and pressed. "Adrian, please cooperate with me." He begged.

"No."

"No's a no, Tommy," Kelly clapped her hands together and smiled sweetly at Thomas. "Time to leave."

Thomas glared at Kelly before holding me at arm's length. "Adrian, this banquet is extremely important for your career," Kelly opened her mouth to remark but mom gave her a sharp look, shutting her up temporarily. "You've been on break for about two months, and your fans need to know that you're still willing to keep your career going. And right now, it seems unlikely."

"It's not like I've been on break for a year, Thomas." I said, rolling my eyes. It's been little under three months since I've taken a break from all the fame and glamour. There's still a few paparazzi catching me when I'm out, so it's not like I'm dead or anything. Thomas was just be dramatic.

And I surely do not have to go to whatever Cara's hosting for her image. The interviews and last minute photo shoots I had done a month ago should be able to spare me anything that relates to my Hollywood life.

"Why is Adrian attending Cara's banquet a necessity, Thomas. You specifically said that coming here would be Adrian's chance to take a time off from all things that involve his career." My mom said.

My dad had long left the kitchen to sit in the living room for some football. Coming home had renewed his love for sports, where as back in LA, he never got the chance to lay on the couch with a bag of Ruffles for hours until mom demands he gets up and do something else. He'll be having a six pack full of pudding cups if he keeps it up.

"It is still nice to show the fans that Adrian is still committed –"

"It's been two months!"

"Thomas, would you spit it out and tell my family why my son really has to go to that damn banquet?" My dad shouted from the living room. The snappy tone gave off his irritated attitude with Thomas.

Thomas sighed and crossed his arms together. "Cara wants you to be there."

I scowled immediately. Cara is more than capable to have her little banquet back in LA instead of Miami. I highly doubt that she's here just for the scenery. She always was clingy.

"Well, on that case, hell no." I said. I grabbed a water bottle from the fridge and joined my dad in the living room. Both of us let out a yell as the star quarterback dropped the ball. He could've caught that.

Kelly came in and plopped down beside me and stare at the screen with complete confusion. Even after all the football games our family sat down and watched, she never caught on to what was going on in the screen.

"I'm afraid you have no choice." Thomas voice made me groan out in the open. But then his words registered in my head and I snapped my attention to the blonde in the suit. What does he mean I have no choice? He can't make me go. Hell, he probably couldn't even drag me even if he wanted to.

"What is that suppose to mean?"

"I mean I've already confirmed this with Cara, and it's already been slipped to the public. They're expecting an appearance from you."

I shot up from my seat, "What?!" I shouted. There wasn't a choice left now. If I don't go, the media will conjure up some twisted up rumors to explain why. I've learned this through experience. And with Cara being the hostess, I could already imagine the gossip headlines now.

'Adrian Chapmen skips out on former love interest's banquet, Cara Pratt!'

Fuck.

"How could you agree to her offer without even talking to me about it?" I shouted. This guy has been pushing every one of my buttons lately, and I'm just about ready to pound his face in, manager or not.

"Because I knew you were going to refuse the offer. You've been spending too much time forgetting who you really are –"

"I'm a guy that happened to land some rolls in a few movies and commercials. I'm not some royal king who's in charge of running a whole country, for damn's sake!"

"Boys," My mom started, standing up from her seat at the perch of the couch's arm rest and lightly touching her hand onto my shoulder.

"You are a star with a reputation!"

"Not for the next seven months I'm not."

"Those friends of yours is transforming into a reckless, stubborn teenager," Thomas seethed. "Playing pranks, the slacking off, the stubbornness! Two months ago, your career would have been your first priority."

"No," I pointed a finger at him. "My friends and family will always be my first priority."

Thomas can't just walk in here and order me to do something that doesn't agree with what we decided to do months ago, and that was to take a time off. He told me that coming home and living the life of a normal teenage guy would be good for me. And when I'm doing just fine doing exactly what he said to do and believing that this, coming home and being with the people around me, was what I was suppose to do, Thomas comes in and tries to mix my Hollywood life with the life I'm enjoying now.

"Perhaps the only reason you don't want to go to Miss. Prat's banquet is because of that girl!"

I tensed. Macey?

"Who? My best friend?" My voice then rose dangerously loud as I realized what he was trying to say. "You're blaming Macey for the reason I don't want to go to that fucking banquet?"

"You and Cara had a rather close relationship before you flew over here and now you don't even want to see her. Maybe it's those feelings you're holding for Macey that has you against the idea."

"Cara and I were just a fling. Macey has nothing to do with this! And there is no," I quoted with my fingers, "Feelings for Macey other than that she is my best friend whom I care for more than anything in the world."

"I can see the chemistry, Adrian, don't deny it." Thomas said flatly.

Told you.

"I don't have feelings for her!" I shouted, more to myself than any. The crush I had on Macey is long over, and I don't feel anything special between us.

Yeah, keep telling yourself that. My inner voice snorted.

Feeling overwhelmed, I grabbed the keys off the coffee table and stormed out of the door. I could hear Thomas' voice calling after me, but I paid no attention to it.

Slamming the car door and jamming the key inside, I floored the pedal and took off with speed. There was only one person that could help me in my need for escape. Escape from this thing called my life.

Chapter 18

It was half past seven in the evening by the time Emma and I arrived home from the mall. We hadn't bothered to take a pit stop and buy some food on our way since halfway through our drive, Emma felt her time coming.

I'm positive that we went ten miles over the speed limit, turning our journey home into some joy ride, in order to save her favourite pair of jeans from being stained red.

We quickly skidded to a halt in front of our house before Emma began scrambling out the car.

"They're in the bathroom cabinet." I called after her. Emma's heels clicked rapidly up the driveway and disappeared into the house. Sighing, I climbed out of the car and slowly made my way to the trunk. I nearly groaned at the amount of bags in the trunk. I never knew how much Emma could shop until she dragged me along for the experience. Know I knew better to make up excuses if I didn't want to shop for hours.

Because my exhaustion didn't give me the will to take two trips, I piled all the bags onto my arms and dragged myself to the house. They immediately, however, gave way once I stepped foot inside. I looked down at the pile of bags dully.

I'll pick them up later. Or tomorrow. I was way too tired.

I kicked the bags to the side of the door and trudged up the stairs to my room. I shut the door and pressed my back to it, my eyes closing in their own accord. When was shopping so tiring? If I knew Emma was going to shop for as long as she did, I would've made up the homework excuse, just as Adrian had done.

With my eyes still closed, I hung my jacket on the back of my door. A sharp scream left my lips when I turned around to see a silhouette in the darkness. The shadow shot up from its seat on my bed and rushed in my direction.

I couldn't believe this. I leave for a few hours to do something simple as shopping and a random person was in my bedroom, ready to rape me.

If I'm not mentally scarred after this day, I will forever shop online.

Before my fist could connect with the stranger's face, it was caught and my lights turned on, revealing a startled Adrian staring back at me.

I let out a huge breathe of air. Thank god it wasn't some kind of murderer. I pulled back my fist and punched his shoulder instead, giving him an annoyed look. "You scared me!" I cried out.

Adrian chuckled at me. "I could tell."

I rolled my eyes and pushed past him, falling backwards onto my bed. "What are you doing here?"

"I'm happy to see you too." He said, collapsing next to me.

I turned my head to him. It was then that I noticed his stiffness. Something happened. And something tells me it was Thomas. "You okay?"

Adrian ran a hand through his hair and down his face, moving his head in a nodding and shaking manner, breathing deeply. I waited patiently for him to collect his thoughts and took the time to analyze him. It was obvious that he was upset. I could tell through the set jaw and clenched fists pressed against his eyes that were tightly closed.

The sudden uniqueness of his choice of clothes caught my attention next, and I knew he wouldn't have gone out in public if not for someone running him out due to annoyance, which brings me back to the whole Thomas thing.

Why they still kept him around if he was annoying as hell, I don't know, but I do know that I'll help Adrian give him the break he needed. And tonight was the perfect night to do it.

"Get up." I said suddenly, getting up from my bed and retrieving my jacket out of my closet once again. Adrian opened peeked through one of his eyes and raised an eyebrow at me.

"What?"

"I said get up." I repeated. When he made no attempt to get up, I latched onto his wrist and tried to pull him up, which I failed to do, of course. He's not the lightweight he was back in his puberty years.

Smirking at my attempt, he pulled himself up and allowed me to drag him out of my room and down the hall. Just then, Emma chose the perfect time to come out pantsless with only her long t-shirt covering just below her butt. It didn't help her at all when she had her stained panty in hand. I don't think I've ever laughed so hard at my sister's embarrassment.

"Oh my god!" She screamed once her eyes landed on me, and, more importantly, Adrian. "How did he get in here? Don't look!"

She shrieked, running back into the bathroom and slamming the door with a large thud.

Adrian looked completely flustered and uncomfortable, a tinge of red tinting his cheeks. I couldn't even imagine the level of embarrassment he must be feeling. Even if this whole stunt was highly amusing from my eyes.

Still laughing to myself, I pulled him along. "Enjoy the show of legs?" I teased.

"Why don't you take your pants off and ask me the same question?" He smirked back, wagging his eyebrows at me.

I mumbled out a 'Pervert' under my breathe and pulled away from him, leaving him laughing behind me as I went to grab my keys. "We're taking my car."

"Why?"

I narrowed my eyes at his outfit with my keys at hand. The shirt he was wearing was much too eye-catching. I ignored the soon-to-come awkwardness and began unbuttoning the top of his shirt. He stared at me with wide eyes, to which I rolled my own at him.

"I don't want you looking like you came out of a mens' magazine." I told him.

"And here I thought you just wanted to undress me." He teased.

"Keep dreaming, Superstar."

"If you wanted to see me naked you could've just asked, Sweetheart."

"Shut up." I muttered, sending him a harsh glare.

After pushing the top layer off, a plain navy shirt was left covering his upper body. Then I reached up and ran my fingers through his hair, messing it up as I did and taking away it's shape so it was back to his sexy, everyday look.

Sexy? I could imagine the smirk Emma would be giving me. The 'I told you so' at the tip of her tounge at the compliment that a best friend shouldn't be saying, even if it is normal in a relationship like mine and Adrian's.

During the time I was trying to make him look normal, the way Adrian was gazing down at me made a blush and squirm. The look he gave me was becoming more and more frequent these past few days. I didn't know why, and I don't think I want to know.

"Okay, we're done." I said quickly, pulling away and rushing outside, Adrian following from behind.

"So, where are we going?" He asked once we were on the road. Today wasn't the only day that Adrian has been on edge about the things Thomas has been trying to make him do. He hasn't said it yet, but I know he's the reason for his moody behaviour.

Adrian has lived the last four years of his life living the Hollywood life. His career was his main focus, every minute of the day. It's like it's trying to catch up with the normal life Adrian's trying to live for the year, and he doesn't want it to catch up just yet.

Tonight was the night to give him a free night. Where he could just relax and enjoy life as he was before he left for LA. And I knew exactly how to do it.

I gave him a sideways smile. "We're taking a route down memory lane."

"I can't believe you took me here." He breathed. I smiled and pulled my jacket tighter around my body. After a half hour drive and Adrian's endless guessing about where we're going, we finally arrived at the place I knew would allow Adrian to relax.

The boardwalk.

This boardwalk was not only our childhood place where we use to go to all the time, it's where the last place Adrian and I spent together before he moved. The picture sitting in his living room, as well as my bedside table, was set here. It also happens to be one of my favorite pictures of all time.

Adrian stared down the boardwalk with complete awe, as if he really couldn't believe I had taken him to the place we admired in our childhood days. The sound of crashing waves was nearly drowned out by the blend of conversation, screams, and laughing joy filling the early night sky. The twinkling stars came out to play tonight, making the whole scene perfect for my tonight's mission.

My eyes fluttered from the Mother Nature's twinkling night sky to the thriving activity a few feet down the boardwalk. Memories of coming down here with Adrian, as well as our family, flooded my mind, and I felt vastly satisfied with my choice of location.

Everything from the games we would compete for the bigger prize in and shrug off if we thought the game was rigged; the unhealthy yet immensely delicious food that we would scarf down in between booths and rides; the increasing thrill that came with each ride that became available to us as we grew older. This was my childhood. This was our childhood. Adrian and I was always at our closest when we came here, and it's here where my crush for my best friend was made clear to me.

Emma's words haunted my mind again and I internally shook my head. The romantic feelings I had for him faded when he left for four years. There wasn't anything in this world that could make Adrian like me when he could have somebody a hundred times better at his doorstep.

There wasn't a doubt in my mind that, one day, I will find someone whom I will love just as much as he loves me. And when Adrian finds his own half in the world, I will support him. And tonight, I'm going to give him the support he needs right now. The one night he desires to have it as it was back then, I'm going to make it a hell lot better.

"We use to come here every week," I smiled, still not looking at him, "I figured that if there's one place where you could be yourself for a few hours, it would be the place we use to have fun in since we were old enough to go on one of those baby rides."

When I did turn to look at Adrian, my heart skipped a beat. The intensity that was in his eyes back at the house seemed to triple with the way he stared down at me now. And the funny thing was, I didn't look away. I met his gaze and kept it, celebrating the fact that I managed to be looked at as someone that's capable of doing something wonderful, even if it is giving someone a chance to escape whatever is going on in their life.

Though it made my heart rate race beyond belief, I stared back into Adrian's eyes, a smile of my own erupting onto my face. My hand slowly found his and I intertwined our fingers together. He looked down at our hands and his smile widened more. As weird as it sounds, Adrian and I never hold hands. Usually, his arm was casually slung over my shoulder or around my waist when we would walk together. It wasn't strange or weird, the way his palm felt pressed against mine. It felt normal and comforting. I loved it.

Adrian suddenly caught me off guard by tugging me closer to him, colliding our bodies tightly as his free hand wrapped around my body and laid flat at the small of my back, lowering his face extremely close to me. My breathe caught in my throat and I suddenly turned into a dumb buffoon who doesn't know how to take oxygen into their lungs.

His forehead rested against mine and he sighed in content, making my own body relax and just enjoy the calm feeling that overtook my body.

We stayed like that for a while, time slipping my mind and the small piece of information of the boardwalk closing at midnight vanishing into oblivion. The familiar beach noises made up of the tides crashing onto the shore and seagulls squawking from the sky above mixed with the laughs and faraway music from the boardwalk. I closed my eyes and took in everything. Combined with the familiar noise and the warmth of being in Adrian's arms, the night was already the best I've ever had in months. And the night was still young.

My eyes cracked open just enough to see the boardwalk when Adrian's lips pressed softly against my cheek. My hand squeezed against his at the gesture. Although his breathe was warm against my bare skin, I shivered when he whispered in my ear.

"Thanks, Sweetheart."

I pulled away just enough so I could see his face. "Don't say thank you yet, we haven't even gotten to the fun part of the night." I said, grinning excitedly. The boardwalk never failed to give us a night to remember.

"Well then," Adrian leaned in closer again and brought his mouth to my ear, "Let the fun begin." He whispered.

The both of us paid for our tickets and entered the boardwalk. The inside was just as stunning as it was from far away. The different rides and booth illuminated the dock in all different colors. Bright signs from restaurants and rides flashed in different patterns, catching peoples' eyes and luring them to enjoy what they have to offer.

I think I was going to burst out of how excited I was to be back here again.

"Where to first?" Adrian asked, swinging our still joined hands back and forth.

"Food!" Was my immediate response. The sandwich I had during lunch combined with the ice cream I had a few hours ago was starting to dissolve, leaving my stomach to eat itself as replacement.

Adrian chuckled and pulled me towards a retro sit down diner. The whole interior design was filled with old pictures from the boardwalk's past, ranging from newspapers to old uniforms hanging on the walls. Adrian led us to a booth far into the corner.

"Why do you want to eat so far away?"

"I don't want anyone to recognize me. I just want this night to be the two of us. Hanging out like we use to."

Adrian's back faced the entire restaurant while his face was to me. It never seemed possible that Adrian would want to get away from what his life has turned into, considering this was his dream when we children. Now it seems like all he wants to do is hide away from all the cameras and people that might recognize him and sink back into his old life.

I patted his hand and gave him a smile. "I'll order the food, okay? You stay here and read that old newspaper that's right next to you on the wall."

With that, I stood up and left Adrian to read a framed article about the owner who opened this small diner in the 1900s. I returned with a tray full of only fries, chicken tenders, and two smoothies. We both know that if we wanted to eat all the other goods around the boardwalk, we should eat a light dinner.

"I learned that the guy who opened this diner died a few years before we were born." Adrian informed me when I set down the food. I settled back into my seat and snatched a fry from the basket.

"That's nice," I chuckled. I started to zone out while we ate our food, thinking about the main reason we were here. Why was Adrian so upset? I looked up to see he was absorbed reading the other articles framed onto the wall, a chicken tender in hand.

I shouldn't ask him. This was his night to forget about what he has to go back to next year. I didn't even want to think about that.

It's his free night, Macey. Give him one night before you shoot him down with questions.

"Why are you nodding?"

"Hmm?" Adrian had already finished eating his food and was looking at me curiously.

"You were nodding."

I was nodding to myself? Oops. "I was just.. nodding my head to the music." I said dumbly.

"Uh-huh.." Adrian leaned back in his chair and crossed his arms against his chest, smirking at me. Like he would've bought that excuse. Smooth is what I am, smooth as someone who has the worst case of acne. "There's no music."

At his words, I strained my ears to listen over the conversation flowing through the room and realized that he was right. There was absolutely no music.

"There's this tune I got stuck in my head." I shrugged, grabbing my smoothie and sucking the contents from the straw. Adrian's eyes went from my eyes down to my lips, watching me drink up the remaining liquid.

"What?"

"Nothing." He shook his head and got up from the booth. I followed suit and was pulled into him when his arm wrapped around my shoulders. "Come on, Pinocchio." He teased, making me laugh and relax under his arm. I won't question him tonight, but tomorrow he's in for an interrogation.

The time had only passed slightly, and the whole atmosphere was thriving. There was a higher number of people now. Teenagers goofing around with their friends, parents being pulled along by their eager children, and couples enjoying a date surrounded by the activities the place by seashore had to offer.

One couple in particular caught my eye. They were both teenagers, young, maybe no younger than fifteen. A tall, lanky guy with auburn hair strolled casually next to whom I assumed was his date. The girl was pretty, reaching up to the boy's shoulder in height with honey blonde hair that fell down her shoulders in curls. Her arms were wrapped tightly around her body and her eyes were content with staring straight down at her flats. She was nervous.

"It's their first date." I heard Adrian say softly, meant for my ears only. I smiled at the thought. First date, first love.

The boy bumped his shoulder against the girl's, finally getting his date's attention as she looked up at him. He said something that made her smile, and the two of them made their way to a nearby booth. It was one of those games where you had to three balls in which you had to roll hard enough to have them land on top of a colored cups. He had failed to get his date a prize while she appreciated the try, but he didn't give up. He placed three more dollars on the counter and tried again. This time, he was able to get two of the three balls on a colored cup. A smile and a blush appeared on the girl's face as he handed her a stuffed bunny.

"Adrian," I gasped, slapping his hard stomach frantically at what was happening before me. "Oh my gosh, look!"

The rumbling of his body indicated that he was chuckling at my reaction but watched the scene unfold. It was like a movie scene, where the main couple stare endlessly into eachother's eyes, like they could stay that way all night long. And then the guy slowly leans in closer, hovering just before their lips touch.

I rested my head against Adrian's shoulder before they advanced into their special little moment. Both of Adrian's arms snaked around my waist to pull me in a hug, and I felt him press his lips to the top of my head.

"It's cute," I said quietly, nuzzling my head against the crook of his neck.

"What is?"

"You know, first crush," I wrapped my arms around Adrian's neck and looked up at him. He was my first crush, even before I knew what feelings were. I wonder who his first crush was. "First date. First kiss. First love. A few of the best things in life."

Adrian tilted his head to the side. "How do you they're in love?"

I figured that their moment was over, so I directed my attention to see them smiling adoringly at each other. The boy looked like he just won the lottery and the prize was a million dollars. He was smiling an open mouthed smile, like he couldn't believe what he just did but was damn happy he did. And he had every right to react that way because the girl in his arms could be worth more than just a million dollars.

The girl looked like there was nothing on this Earth, big or small, that could ruin the perfect moment that she had with the boy that was looking at her like she was the only girl he would ever need in life. She was biting her lip gently to hold back the smile that was waiting to burst onto her face, her eyes never straying from the boy who was holding her close. You would have to be blind not to see the chemistry between them.

"The way they look at each other." I exhaled. A sudden tightness formed in my chest when I compared myself to that couple. I wanted to be the one that looked like that. I wanted someone to stare at me like I was worth something. To have someone who would take time out of their day just to spend their day with you because they wanted to. They want to be close to you, to hold you, and kiss you.

I wanted that.

I glanced up at Adrian through my eyelashes to see that same intense gaze he's been giving me this whole night, making a weird feeling erupt in my stomach.

Well he's going to have to suck it up since Adrian's got the hots for you and all.

It's obvious Adrian still has feelings for you...

you'd have to be blind not to see the chemistry between you two...

"You mean the way he looks at you, holds you, talks about you, kisses...

Face the music, Adrian likes you.

I sighed and let my head rest against Adrian's shoulder. No, no, no. I shouldn't even be dwelling about this. Not tonight, anyways. It's his night. One night, and I couldn't even give him that.

"Mace, are you okay?" Adrian's concerned tone made me snap my head back up. He was frowning, probably in confusion. One minute I'm gushing over a couple's first kiss and the next I'm sighing like someone just drained the life out of me. What is wrong with me?

"I'm fine." Moving on from the scene of young love, I towed Adrian farther down the boardwalk. "You know what's up next, right?" All our trips down here have been through the same routine, each and every time. This part just brought out how competitive he really is.

Adrian stopped and turned to me slowly. "You mean..?"

I smirked at him.

"Oh, you're so on."

Five minutes later, Adrian and I were competing at a booth called Casey at the Bat where we had to shoot 3 balls into the middle of the umpire's bat. Needless to say, It was rigged.

"I don't remember these games all being rigged back then." Adrian complained once we lost our eighth game tonight. I did, however, manage to win a Smurf from the balloon dart game that was purely out of luck. Adrian had refused to take my pity gift to him.

"You just suck at them, now that you've been gone so long." I laughed. With so much practice, Adrian had almost mastered all the games here. I guess the years he spent in LA had deprived him of his boardwalk mastery.

"I have not." He argued.

I rolled my eyes but couldn't keep the smile off my face. My phone read it was just past 9:30 at night, giving us enough time to play one more game before we direct ourselves to the end of our night trying to lose our voices.

Adrian switched to holding my hand while we scanned for our last game of the night. We were passing by a cotton candy stand when someone called out to us.

"Hey, hey, you two!"

We both turned around to see a short, energetic man with graying hair looking at us in front of a booth that I haven't seen before. He waved us over with his cane. Adrian tugged on my hand and brought us towards the man. I looked up at the fancy sign above of the booth.

Cupid's Arrow, it read. Ahead, there was several mini people, the ones you would see labeling which bathroom was which, hanging on the wall with a heart connecting between their hands. The old man smiled at us and held out three miniature arrows, or, in this case, darts.

"Win a rose for your lady, my friend. All you have to do is get one of these arrows into one of those hearts." He pointed, smiling at the two of us. His name tag said 'Harvey.' I would've objected to being Adrian's 'lady' if Adrian didn't take up his offer before I could say a word.

"Really?" I asked him as he placed three dollars on the counter and taking the darts from Harvey. So far this night, his aim has been beyond awful. If I didn't know him already, I would've thought he was blind when he accidentally knocked someone's hat off instead of the pyramid as it's original target.

"Sure, why not? Maybe I could win you something, for once."

I shrugged and sat up on the counter. If he wanted to try, I wasn't going to stop him. "Don't blow your money just to get me a single rose." I told him. Knowing what guys do for their lady friends, I didn't want him trying time and time again just to get me a single rose. Brynn's mother has been growing rose bushes since her daughter entered high school.

"I just want to try." With those words, he fired his first dart. It landed besides the man, landing in open space. The next one was a better aim, even if he managed to hit the women in the head.

"Head shot." He smirked.

"You're suppose to win a person's heart, not their head." I said sweetly making him stick his tongue out at me like a child.

A few people who suddenly took interest in the booth stood around us, watching Adrian. Twisting his last arrow between his fingers, he inhaled a breathe, drew back his arm, and threw it.

The arrow stuck perfectly in the middle of a heart. He had actually one something. Out of all the booths he could have won a prize at, he had won a rose for his 'lady.' Harvey grinned at the dart and reached under the counter, pulling out an actual red rose and handing it to Adrian. Smiling quite smugly, he plucked it out of his fingers with a thanks before making a big scene of strolling over to where I was sitting and grandly holding out the rose.

"Out of all the prizes you could've won tonight." I giggled, bringing the rose up to my nose and sniffing it. A glint flashed in Adrian's eyes as he lent over and placed a kiss on my cheek.

"Only the best for my lady." He said out loud, earning a positive response from the small crowd that happened to be watching. I even saw the young couple we had been watching earlier smile at us in which I returned.

"You are such a flirt." I told him low enough for only him to hear. A small, weird squeak left my mouth when he did something unsual. He just kissed my nose.

"Adrian!" I exclaimed, my mouth wide open and my cheeks heating up. He says he wants to be invisible to the public, yet he decides to make us look like a couple on a date. What if there's paparrazzi around? Does he want people to recognize him by drawing more attention?

Against my questioning thoughts, Adrian surprised me by grabbing me by the waist and pulling me off of the counter to twirl me around like he use to do when we were kids. I squealed and wrapped my arms around his neck. He hasn't done this in so long. And I never knew how much I missed it until spun me around in his arms so many times. I felt dizzy.

"Put me down!" I laughed. It took my a few moments until the world around me stopped spinning like a top. Once it did, I slapped Adrian's shoulder. "What are you doing? You said you didn't want to attract attention." The words came out soft and confused, not sharp and angry. He was practically hiding back in the diner, why would he come out like this now? Especially when Thomas thinks I would personally ruin his image.

"Mace, I want to be able to do things that I would have done if I wasn't famous. And right now, if my career didn't exist and I was nothing but an average teenager, I would've done what I did just now."

How do you breath again? I thought we went through this already. In, out, in, out. With Emma's words and how he's been acting today is really bringing up hopes that shouldn't even be in mind right now. I liked how he was teasing me and how he openly showed affection towards me. I wasn't suppose to, but I did. And I liked it so damn much.

"Let's go ride some rides."

The warm night air had suddenly dropped dramatically, leaving my thin jacket completely useless to my shivering body. We had just finished riding all the rides we were capable of, meaning whatever Adrian wanted to drag me onto. But now we were done, and I felt like I was going to throw up in the nearest trash bin.

Adrian came up to my spot on the bench with a bottle of water. I took it from him and began to drink it down when he spoke, "Remember when we were twelve and that ride was first installed? I told you that it didn't flip us upside down, and when we went on it, we flipped so many times."

I closed the bottle and laughed. "And I ended up loving it so much that we went three more times until we got sick and had to lay on the beach so we could calm down."

Hearing Adrian laugh with me finally made me satisfied with the night. Not only did he have fun, but I got to spend quality time with my best friend just like the good ole' days; none of his Hollywood life got in the way, just the way I liked it.

An immediate warmth was draped over my shoulders, and I noticed that Adrian had given me his jacket. I smiled in appreciation and wrapped it tighter around my body. "We should probably be heading home soon." I said, checking my phone. It was nearing midnight, which was my assigned curfew.

"I guess you're right." He sighed, leaning forward on his knees. "But first.." I was pulled to my feet and back down the boardwalk where the water was more close. "We have to end the night like we usually do."

Understanding dawned over me at the sight of the big Ferris Wheel in all it's circular, lighting glory. The Ferris Wheel was the last place where we would go to end our nighttime fun before leaving the boardwalk.

There wasn't a lot of people on, just a few couples and friends wanting to catch the scenery as the wheel rotated high up into the Miami air. The employee locked up our cart and nodded to his friend to start moving us up. I settled into Adrian's side as his arm came around my waist, my head resting against his shoulder. The exhaustion was slowly returning. By the time I hit the warmth of my comforting bed, I'd be out cold.

I closed my eyes and enjoyed the light cold breeze caressing my skin, but at the same time being warmed up by the arms of a certain guy next to me. I had no idea how many times we went around, but I had a feeling that we went around more than we were suppose to.

The once loud and energetic setting of the boardwalk and calmed down to a light hum of waves and left over conversation. A large groaning noise had told me that we stopped to let passengers below get off. The chilly breeze told me that we were high enough off the ground to see the whole beach.

"Hey, Mace?" It was the first time we spoke since we got on.

"Hmm?"

He didn't say anything at first. I could feel him hesitate. "Do you think that if I didn't leave for LA, that there could've been more between us?"

His words were slow and cautious, like I would freak out by what he asked. I didn't, but I wanted to. What I did do was freeze like my body all of a sudden locked in its position. Did I hear him right?

"W-What?"

Adrian breathed deeply as if this was a hard topic to bring up. "If I didn't move to LA. You know, leave you for all those years and stayed here, with you, instead of living the life I am now..." I rose my head from his shoulder to look at him. This couldn't be happening. "Was there a chance that we could have been more than just best friends? Even to this day."

And there it was. Like a bomb. A slap to the face. A plus on a pregnancy test. My mind could not simply fathom Adrian's words to know if he was joking or not. But his face said otherwise. It was straight and serious, a surge of hope gleaming in his eyes. It was real. What he said was real. And I already knew the answer.

I couldn't deny reality any longer. Adrian had just technically told me that he likes me. Kind of.

The crush I had for Adrian was there since I kept him company on 'The Wall' during fourth grade when he had gotten in trouble. Our parents knew one another before that, and Emma and Kelly were in middle school. We knew each other, but never exchanged more than a three minute conversation. Not until he was upset for getting a timeout during lunch with all the bad kids, and I stayed there beside him in the beating sun, sitting against hot concrete.

We were inseparable after that day. Always coming over to play in the backyard or make homemade videos of Adrian acting. I gave him advice whenever he wanted to get a girl's attention but didn't know how. He would skip school just to take care of me when I got sick, though it sometimes was just a simple flu. I supported him through all his relationships, even when one of them would bring me shit later on.

That crush stayed strong until Adrian left for LA to follow his dreams. He went off to be the person he always imagined to be, and he lived the life I knew he was destined to have. The loss of contact resulted into the loss of that crush that I've built over the years. I saw him on magazines, on the internet, through the TV, even on radio interviews. And somewhere deep down, I pushed away my feelings for him because I knew that our friendship was over. I would never see him again.

Obviously, fate had other plans by bringing him back home and into my life again, reminiscing in our memories and making new ones for the next year. And, of course, bringing back how I actually feel.

Adrian seemed nervous with my lack of response. All I could do was stare at him like a moron. Despite the millions of words and thoughts that I could say to him, I couldn't force out a single letter. It looked like he was going to say something instead if somebody didn't speak before him.

"Time to get off, kids."

The attendant looked at us with a flat expression, probably annoyed with the constant number of couples that are so immersed in each other realization that the ride is over doesn't come to them until he has to take it upon himself to tell them 'Get off.'

I said a quick sorry and clambered out of the cart, slipping my arms through Adrian's jacket sleeves and wrapping the fabric tighter around my body. Adrian caught up with me easily and the both of us absentmindedly made our way towards the car. We were so far into our own thoughts that none of us said a single word.

I had to repeat the process of squeezing my eyes shut and opening them just to keep myself awake long enough to drive ourselves home in my drowsy street. As much as I loved spending this night here with Adrian, I desperately wanted to go home and surrender myself to the art of sleep. Though, I don't know if I will be able to get a decent amount of sleep when I know Adrian's words will be on repeat in my mind until the early hours of morning.

Adrian must have noticed my exhaustion as he opted to be the driver instead of me. The drive home was silent. The radio wasn't even on to provide us something to fill the tension in the air. Adrian kept his focus on the road while I stared out the window. I didn't know where Adrian's question left the two of us. None of us could muster enough courage to talk about it, considering that I left his question unanswered. Suddenly, I was afraid that he mad at me for never giving him an answer. His whole nervous demeanour told me that it wasn't an easy thing to bring out.

I was relieved of my thoughts when Adrian reached over and laced his fingers with mine, sending me a soft smile that made my heart rate pick up. It hasn't done that for a guy in a long time.

The lights were off when we stopped in front of my house, indicating that everyone had already went to bed. I got out of the car and Adrian walked me up to the front door.

"Thanks for tonight, Macey. I had the most fun tonight than I've had in my last couple of months in LA." Adrian said genuinely, hooking an arm around my waist and pulling me into his chest for a hug.

I smiled and ruffled his hair playfully. "I'm glad I could give you a night. It was fun going back to the boardwalk with you."

The intense gaze was back, but a million times stronger. And in that moment, I knew that what I wanted was holding me in his arms right now.

I have someone who stared at me like I was worth something. I have someone who would take time out of their day just to spend their day with me because he wanted to. I have someone who constantly cares about me, holds me, and even kisses me. Even if it isn't in the same level as a real couple.

I have Adrian.

As if he could read my thoughts, Adrian decided to test how hard my heart could beat against my chest. He dipped his head low and pressed his lips gently on the crook of my neck, trailing upwards and leaving a trail of fire in every place his lips touched. He kissed up my collarbone, up my neck, my cheek, and even pecking my nose like he did at the Cupid's Arrow booth. But this isn't what got my heart almost ripping out of my chest. The part that caught my breathe, where the butterflies erupted and fluttered furiously inside my stomach, is when he kissed the corner of my lip for the longest time; I would have collapsed if he wasn't gripping my waist so tightly.

Kissing the corner of lip was enough not to cross the best friend boundary that we still have, but it's enough to cross it just to the point where we know things have changed for us.

And this night has changed everything.

He gave me one last kiss on the forehead before bidding good-night and walking to his car, leaving me still trying to calm my beating heart.

"Adrian?"

He turned around. "Yeah?"

I bit my lip. "I don't think those four years affected the way I feel about you back then... and now." My voice was so soft I'm not sure if he even heard me. It was the truth, though. I'm not going to lie to myself anymore. Those feelings were simply just put away until it flourished into a stronger sensation when I'm around him.

The wide smile on Adrian's face was something I wish I could snapshot and keep forever. I always loved when one of his famous wide smiles would spread across his face because it was impossible not to smile back at the sight. I always felt accomplished if I could make that smile appear but this one just meant something more.

He seemed highly satisfied with my answer and the smile never faltered. "Goodnight, Sweetheart."

Saving my inner organs from being trampled by the mob of butterflies attacking the inside of my body, I rushed inside and closed the door, leaning against it and sliding down until my butt hit the floor. Adrian was still standing outside, smiling at my house, when I peeked through the window beside the door. I saw him nod to himself before shoving his hands in his pocket and walking to his car. My inner fan girl, as crazy as it sound, was brought out when I rushed to the couch and squealed as quiet as I could into a couch pillow without waking anybody.

I felt like the 14 year old me as I sat there with a smile that could break my face in half and a heart beating like I ran a marathon. After all those times I felt like I was just his best friend, standing to the side as I watched him with Cammie or Reyna or whoever the hell he dated four years ago, there was still room for me in his heart.

I was startled when someone rammed into me by jumping onto the couch, giggling and squealing like a girl who just had her first kiss. Emma, dressed in her Tweety bird pajamas, stared down at me with a smile wide as mine, and I knew she had been watching.

"I. Told. You." She mouthed, shaking me by my shoulders and hopping up and down on the couch. I thought she was trying to be quiet for mom and dad but then she let out the loudest shriek that made our dad calm down with the emergency bat and mom almost running into him as she rushed down the stairs.

"What happened?!" He shouted. Still half asleep, dad immediately jumped to attack mode without accessing the situation properly before he swung the bat like a professional. The tip nicked the edge of a picture frame, but with the force he was using, the frame came flying and hit the couch Emma and I was sitting on.

"Dad!" We both yelled. Our mom let out a loud gasp as she stared down at the broken frame. Dad seemed to snap out of his sleep trance, dropping the bat and looking at our mom guiltily. His eyes switched to us, both safe and unharmed, and he huffed.

"What is going on down here?"

Emma and I shared similar deer-caught-in-headlights before we simultaneously said our answers.

"Nothing!"

Chapter 19

Macey's POV

I didn't sleep.

Okay, so maybe I did get some sleep, but it wasn't much. That seems far-fetched at the moment, but there are two reasons as to why I had only gotten about five hours of sleep.

1) My night with Adrian and the stupid butterflies having a raging party in my stomach.

2) My dear older sister.

My parents shortly left after the false scare that we gave them late into the night. I was lucky enough to get out of their interrogation since they had no clue about my night with Adrian, but that didn't mean I was free from Emma's continuous I-Told-You-So's. My parents headed off to bed, and Emma hauled me off to her room. Her suspicions about Adrian's feelings were as suspected, and she felt quite satisfied with that. The juicy details were a must, though, and Emma planned on getting all of it that very night.

Of course, I refused to tell her at first. That was until my gossip-starved sister tackled me roughly onto her bed and pinned me there with her knees on my arms, not letting me free until I spilled the details.

And spill I did.

I told her about the moment we had before we entered the boardwalk and about watching the couple outside the diner; about Cupid's Booth and the rose Adrian won for me (which is sitting in a slim vase on my bed side table). By the time I finished telling her about what happened on the Ferris wheel, Emma was practically jumping for joy. On my body, may I add.

Yeah, she was serious about not letting me go until I told her everything.

I went to bed with my stomach still churning and a smile that could not fade no matter how hard I tried to put it down. With a skip in my step, I went over to my closet to change into a new pair of pajamas before leaping not so gracefully into my warm bed. I wrapped the duvet tightly around my body and shoved my head into a pile of pillows, still grinning like a psycho.

My night at the boardwalk was on repeat. Every memory played through my mind as if I was reliving the whole thing over and over again. You think after a tiring day at school, an afternoon shopping with my sister, and having a very eventful day at the boardwalk rekindle my feelings for my old best friend, that I would be dead beat by now.

But I wasn't. Those hours were filled of me simply staring into darkness thinking about my day until exhaustion finally caught up, taking me into a deep, peaceful slumber that I desperately hoped to keep for more than just an average nap.

My phone, however, had different plans. My ring tone belted out of the small speaker, jolting me awake with an early morning heart attack. It turned out I forgot to close my curtains before going to bed since it was wide open. No sunshine came through the glass as grey clouds greeted my vision.

My eyes snapped over to my phone, and I glowered at it. Snatching it from my bedside table, I fell back into my mountain of pillows and pulled my duvet up to my chin. The morning air nipped at my skin.

"Hello?" I muttered, sleep lacing my voice.

"Anything interesting happen with you and Adrian?"

The familiar voice caused my eyes to open immediately, widening to the size of a doe. "Umm.. Excuse me?" I said hesitantly.

Brynn scoffed over the phone, her obvious eye roll being heard from this side of the phone. Then I heard another feminine voice yell out a "Put her on speaker!"

"Ow! Dylan, why'd you hit me?" Amber's voice complained through the line.

Dylan's voice came equally as loud, notifying me that I was on speaker. "Because it's too early for you to be yelling, and we're right next to you," She explained calmly.

Early? I raised from my bed high enough so I could crane my neck to the point where I could take a glance at the clock.

7:04 am. A groan left my lips at the sight. "Why are you three calling so early in the morning?" I whined, shoving my face into a pillow.

"A little birdy told us about your night with Adrian," I could imagine the smirk on Dylan's face.

Amber squealed excitedly through the other line. "I can't believe it! I told you guys that this was bound to happen. They're like soul mates."

I rolled my eyes at Amber's dreamy tone. "Emma called you up and spilled everything about what happened?" I questioned, a scowl appearing on my face.

"Are you kidding? She called me right when the sun was coming up. We spent the last two hours talking about it before I hung up and called the girls," Amber told me eagerly.

"I can't believe you guys told each other about your true feelings," Brynn teased.

"It isn't a big deal," I lied. A smile slipped onto my face at the rose still sitting in it's beautiful state. "It wasn't outrightly said, though. It was more hinted."

"Details, details. It's the same thing, Mace," Dylan dismissed. "The chemistry between you two was bound to reveal itself eventually."

I sighed, not up to arguing with three people early in the morning while I was battling through with only about five hours of sleep. "Whatever. Why are you all together? Isn't it a little early?"

"Oh!" Amber cried out, suddenly remembering something. "My mom woke me up before going to a doctor's appointment. She told me she wants us to go to the studio for some early morning practice. Says we've been slacking off lately."

Brynn scoffed in denial. "We have not."

"Well it wasn't my decision to wake you up so early." Amber countered.

"Maybe if you convinced her more that we weren't-"

"Anyways," Dylan said sharply, cutting the two girls off. "We're going out for breakfast. Expect us there in an hour."

"And prepare to tell us the whole story in your own words," Amber sang quickly before the line went dead. I took the phone away from my ear, huffing at it. I already retold the story once, I'd rather pass another opportunity, thank you very much.

Knowing that Brynn would be driving, and she referred driving faster then she should be, I reluctantly slid out of the bed with a sigh. The contact between my warm feet and the cold hardwood floor made me hop from one foot to another, trying to get use to it. My fingers lightly brushed the delicate petals of the rose as I walked by and made my way towards the bathroom for a shower.

My phone let out a muffled vibrate from under my pillow the second I stepped inside my room with a towel wrapped securely around my waist. My eyes furrowed in confusion. The girls couldn't have been here yet, considering I only took fifteen minutes in the shower.

I dug under my pillow in search for my phone, pulling out the device a moment later. The familiar fluttering feeling in my stomach reappeared at the text from the man whose been invading my mind since he stepped off my front porch.

Adrian

Good morning, Beautiful. Dream about me?

A small chuckle left my lips at the words. He couldn't slip the chance to be cocky, even if it is to send me an incredibly sweet morning text message. Most girls in my position would be ogling at the fact, but I simply let a warm feeling wash over me.

Macey

Sure did, Superstar. I had a dream that your head was too big for your shoulders. Maybe it's because of your big ego. Oh my mistake, it's true.

Adrian

Very funny, Sweetheart. I'll see you soon, don't miss me too much.

I rolled my eyes but let a wide smile slip onto my face without restraint. A quick glance at the time had me rushing to my closet to pull on some clothes. Lulu's sharp barking echoed through the whole house, making its way through my still closed door. Why I am the only one feeding the family dog, I don't know. It doesn't required a huge amount of effort, really.

The little Yorkie was at my feet in an instant, nearly tripping me as I descended down the stairs. Emma was awake, sitting at the door and shoving her favourite cereal into her mouth. I sent her a scowl when I entered the kitchen, Lulu barking rapidly at my feet.

"You can't feed the dog yourself?"

Emma rolled her eyes at me. She shoved the last of her cereal into cereal and walked around the island to wash her dishes. "Why should I do it? Lulu's more your dog as she is the family's." She said.

I huffed in reply and filled Lulu's dishes with her necessities. She was in the middle of digging into her own food when the doorbell made her ears perk up in curiosity. Once she made up her mind of her breakfast topping the importance than whoever was at the door, she returned her full attention to the food in front of her. I shook my head at the dog.

If we were ever in the face of danger, the thought of Lulu being there to protect us was sincerely comforting. That is, if we were in danger of a couple teddy bears out to get us with their cuteness as their highly lethal weapon.

"Such a great guard dog. I'll see you later, Em."

Emma made a farewell grunt at me as I jogged over to the door and opened it. I soon regretted that decision as Amber suddenly tackled me, her squeals filling my ears. "Tell us everything!" She said.

I struggled under her small frame. How could someone so small and thin be so heavy? "Amber, get off of me." I managed to choke out.

"Oops." Amber giggled, hopping to the ground. The smile on her face was wider than usual, which, quite frankly, scared me. I prodded the corner of her mouth.

"Loosen that smile, Ams. It looks as if it's going to freeze that way."

"I can't help it," She responded happily, looping her arms with mind and tugging me towards Brynn's car. I was thankful that Amber was at the door rather than Brynn using her usual way of announcing her arrival. The Monroes sure did get an early day Thanksgiving gift.

"Hey," Dylan greeted me from the passenger's seat. The sight of her smirk made me groan. "Ready to tell us your cheesy little date with Adrian?"

"It wasn't a date and it's not that big of a deal. Can we at least wait until my stomach has some food in it before you three force the story out of me?"

"Fine." Brynn let out a dramatic sigh and slammed her foot on the gas pedal and jerking us forward. I gasped and pulled the seat belt over me frantically. Unless Brynn learns to ease her ways with driving, someone else should be our designated driver. "But you better spill or you'll never have food again."

"Pushy."

The sounds of early morning breakfast sizzling on a hot pan and low chatter filled the room. We currently sat at the Wafflehouse. A mountain of pancakes sat in the middle of our tables while each of us had our own desired breakfast. I stabbed a piece of sausage and unattractively shoved the whole thing into my mouth. My puffed out cheeks gave a perfect replication of a chipmunk's cheeks filled with acorns.

When I looked up, Dylan and Amber were staring expectantly at me. I looked to my side and found Brynn giving me the same look.

"Time to keep your end of the deal, Mace," Brynn said cheekily. I gave her a semi glare and put my fork down. It was then that I launched into the full on detail of my night with Adrian, saying pretty much what I told Emma last night. Hanging to every word that came out of my mouth, the girls had my undivided attention.

It surprised me how interested they were in my relationship with Adrian. Their teasing and knowing glances were enough to acknowledge the fact that they all had a sneaky feeling on how we felt about each other. But I never knew they were, as Amber said, 'shipping' us wholeheartedly.

"Do you still have the flower?" Brynn asked, grinning.

"It's sitting on my bedside table."

Amber giggled excitedly, clapping her hands together. "Finally!" She celebrated.

"It's about time Adrian grew the balls to say something. Chase says he's been crushing on you since you were in middle school." Dylan commented.

"Well, I don't know about that..." I trailed off awkwardly. I knew I had a crush on Adrian back then, but I'm not sure if he returned those feelings. Chase use to tease us about it, and, from what I've heard, he use to push Adrian to make a move on me. Besides the usual acts of affection, he never went pass the friendship boundary.

"You're blind," Dylan sighed.

"And you're delusional."

"Denial," Amber and Brynn chorused. I groaned and shoved the last piece of my french toast into my mouth.

"Can we please not get into this?" I pleaded. "You already know the story, there's nothing else to talk about."

"Except if you two are going to take it to the next level."

I froze.

Would we take it to the next level? What does that even mean? Going on a date? Becoming a couple? Kissing? Getting married?

Woah, woah. Slow down there, Macey.

The thought of kissing Adrian made my insides squirm. We were so close last night too.

"I don't know, you guys," I sighed, running a hand through my hair. "It's complicated right now."

"What's there to be 'complicated'?" Brynn argued. "You two practically admitted that you liked each other; it's simple."

I knew that already. But what has me going over the thought of us being a couple over and over is Adrian's career. If we were to become a couple, what would Thomas think? Oh my gosh. What about his fans? His fans! Adrian's reputation is the number one thing that's keeping us from going beyond what we are now. Thomas says that I would ruin him, is that true?

Trying to figure out the answer made my head throb.

I shook my head and pressed my fingers against my temple, massaging it. "Can we just get to dance practice?" The girls nodded, knowing that I wasn't in the mood to talk about it.

"I need something peppy to dance to," Amber announced as we entered the dance studio in our gear.

"How 'bout a fun little warm up song?" I asked, stretching a bit.

Brynn grinned. "I got the perfect song." She said as a matter-of-factly. She took her phone from her duffel bag and placed it in the speakers a few feet away. The beginning words of "Dance With Me Tonight" by Olly Murs blasted through the speakers, causing a wide smile to spread across our faces. The song reminded me of Adrian the night we went to that dance club. And, of course, the song was indeed very perky.

"Oh my gosh," She cried out. "I love this song!"

My name is Olly. Nice to meet you, can I tell you, baby. Look around, there's a whole lot of pretty ladies. But none like you, you shine so bright. Woah, yeah.

I was wondering if you and me could spend a minute. On the floor up and close, getting lost in it. I won't give up without a fight.

This song is what Lucile likes to call a 'Spotlight' dance.

Spotlight is where we would all take turns dancing to the lyrics before the spotlight was passed, almost as if they were the one who had a spotlight on them while the rest of us were in the background. Once the chorus came on, the spotlight would spread to all of us and we would dance the actual choreography.

This routine was used only to perk us up when we're not in the mood to dance or just simply felt like celebrating a happy occasion. We wouldn't take the dance seriously, as it was created to loosen us up.

Laughs and funky moves were thrown around the place. Dylan and Brynn felt it necessary to emphasis some lyrics with their body movement or facial expression, causing Amber and I to crack up. This song is particularly fun to dance to with the whole vibe it gave off.

The song was ending, and I was in the middle of a laughing fit when arms came around my waist and under my legs, picking me up and twirling me around. I screamed in surprise and, admittedly, horror; clinging onto whoever was holding me captive in a middle of a dance routine.

The rooms were filled with laughs when the music died away, and I was getting dizzy. My culprit put me down but kept their arms wrapped around my waist; their chuckles next to my ear. Even in my dizzy state, I could identify who's arms I was in.

"Adrian," I whined, my head landing on his chest. I squeezed my eyes shut, letting the unbalanced sensation pass.

He chuckled again, his warm breathe tickling my neck. I raised my head from his chest to pout at him. I didn't mind being twirled around by him, but when it feels as if I went on one too many rollercoasters, then we have a problem.

"Sorry," He apologized sweetly, plastering an innocent smile on his face. "Forgot the spinning limits."

"Whatever," I huffed.

He laughed again, swooping in to give me a quick peck on my nose. "Hi to you too," He mumbled softly, gazing down at me affectionately. I smiled returned the smile, feeling the butterflies making their victorious return. Damn their insane flutters.

"The sexual tension!" Chase's voice cried out in mock agony.

"It's grown stronger now that they admitted their unrequited love!" Brandon said dramatically, raising a hand to his forehead.

"I think the roof is going to explode with the high level!" Brynn joined, pretending to faint into Brandon's arm. Their laughter erupted again, and I felt my cheeks heating up. I glared back at them hotly. Even Amber was laughing. The little traitor.

Annoyed with everyone's antics, Adrian grabbed my hand and pulled me towards the exit. As we were leaving, Dylan called out after us.

"Keep it PG!"

"Shut up!"

The cool fresh air outside warmed my cheeks down. I pressed my free handthe side of my faceg and looked down at the floor. Adrian let go of my hands only to grip my waist and plop me down onto the hood of his car. The warmness in my cheeks came back in an instant as he wiggled his way between my legs and leaned in close, planting his hands beside me. Trapped in his arms, huh? How many times has Adrian kept me imprisoned like this?

Not like I'm complaining. But that didn't mean I was nervous.

"W-What are you doing?"

Adrian didn't respond. Instead, he leaned in even closer. His lips hovered insanely close to mine, his warm breath brushing against my own. The beating of my heart was racing at an unhealthy rate, drumming so loudly I wouldn't be surprised if anyone within a few feet could hear it.

"Problem?" He asked in a bare whisper, closing the already small proximity between us. My hand shot out before he could move a millimeter more, laying itself flat against his hard chest. The lack of oxygen was making my brain go haywire.

The edge of his lip raised in a half smirk. My heart leaped to my throat and my eyes widened when he went against my hand's purpose of keeping a (small) distance and leaned in.

Only slight, slight, disappointment coursed through me when our lips didn't meet. However, I wasn't in the position to grieve over the loss as Adrian pressed his lips at the corner of my mouth instead, just as he did last night. Only this time, he seemed to be taking all the time in the world. A good thirty seconds later, he started to make his slow descent of kisses.

My eyes fluttered closed at his soft touch. As if by instinct, my neck automatically stretched to the side to which Adrian took advantage of. The quiet sound of my jacket zipper caught my attention. Soon, the fabric covering my right shoulder was gone, exposing my skin to the cool air so he could advance down to my shoulder and collar bone.

"Adrian," I breathed, my hands fisted tightly. "We're in public."

"Hasn't stopped me before," He responded smoothly.

He's going to be the end of me. With how hard my heart was beating against my chest, I'm going to die. And as if having a heart attack be the death of me, the moment his teeth grazed against my shoulder, I let out a moan.

It was a low, soft moan, but a moan nonetheless.

I never understood why a person would moan in appreciation for something. Not even for food. I guess I just needed to experience something that would make one small moan leave my mouth against my will.

The sound caused Adrian to smile against my skin. His arms suddenly wrapped around my waist and pulled me against his body, causing me to gasp in surprise. The smile seemed to take up his entire face.

"That was the sexiest sound ever." He chuckled breathlessly, resting his forehead against mine. "Just like you."

Yup. The death of me.

Chapter 20

Ah, Thanksgiving.

The holiday where we give thanks to everything we're grateful in life. Families reunite with loved ones and, best of all, kids get out of school. This is the one day where my dad has an excuse for the feverish amounts of turkey and pie sitting on the dinner table. If he were cooking, I'm positive that turkey would initiate our gag reflexes after we recover over a pie coma.

While as my dad would be sitting in a corner with apple pie sitting in his heads.

It's a good thing my mom voluntarily cooks our dinner on most nights.

"I'm off!" Brynn announced proudly as she hiked her backpack over her shoulder. I smiled and shut my locker door, coming to pull her into a hug. Brynn was off to California for the four day break from school and wouldn't be back until late Sunday evening. Her family was scheduled to leave straight after the bell, which is right now.

"Have fun," I told her with a smile, holding her at arms length.

Brynn tapped my cheek playfully. "Thanks, and don't get pregnant while I'm gone." She winked, effectively wiping the smile off my face and replacing it with a flat look.

"Just go."

Brynn let out a bark of laughter. We hugged once more before she jogged out the front doors and to her jeep. Turning
around, I saw Adrian and Brandon walking in my direction. Brandon
watched Brynn leave wistfully. Adrian's arm slipped around my
waist, pulling me into a hug and pecking my cheek.

"Hey," He greeted

"Hi," I said softly, giving him a smile. "Missing Brynn alright,
Brandon?" I asked the other boy, teasingly.

Brandon sighed deeply and leaned against the locker. "I can't
believe she's leaving for California for Thanksgiving break." He
pouted.

"Dude, she'll be back in four days. I think you'll live," Adrian
chuckled.

"Whatever," He huffed. And with that, he turned around without
so much as a goodbye. We watched him leave silently. Brandon
acts as if they're a long term couple, yet he hasn't officially asked
her to be his official girlfriend. I'm not even sure what they're status
is.

"He's confusing," I mused, turning to face Adrian.

"He is." He nodded in agreement. A look of discomfort crossed
over his face as he changed the subject. "I got to tell you something."

I quirked an eyebrow suddenly feeling uneasy about what could
come out of his mouth. With all the little bumps tripping things
between us that involve his career, I could never predict what's
going to happen next. For all I know, Adrian could be hopping onto
a plane and leaving the break as well, when the Chapmen family
are expected for dinner tonight at our house.

It's going be the first dinner our two families has had since they returned from LA. Emma is quite excited to catch up with Kelly about her upcoming events, and my parents are looking forward to having some time with their good friends.

Adrian tapped my nose with one finger. "Don't pull that face, you don't know what I'm going to say yet."

"Well you never know." I shrugged, leaning back on the row of lockers with his arms still wrapped around my waist. Adrian tilted his head to the side and leaned closer along with me.

"It's not world-ending news." He assured me.

"Well out with it then!"

Adrian clicked his tongue and said, "Thomas is coming with us to dinner at your house."

With that news, I abruptly ripped out of his arms. "What?" I shouted, refusing to believe the words. How is that even possible? Thanksgiving has always been just friends and family. And last time I checked, Thomas is not family nor is he certainly not a friend. His whole aura has the tendency to irk Emma off just with his mere presence in the same room. Not to mention Kelly's annoyance with his mere existence.

"He insisted on staying instead of heading home. My parents felt the need to invite him, so he isn't lonely for the holidays.'

"Doesn't he have a family to go home to? Parents? Wife? Kids?" Is that even possible?

Thomas with a wife or even kids is outrageous to think of. Thinking of it now, if he were to have a family, they would be left without him for times on end, seeing as he's practically glued to Adrian's side.

"Thomas is still hassling me into giving in to some things he wants me to do," He said in a gentle tone that was suppose to calm me down. His words didn't seem to help with Thomas still on Adrian's case about doing things that go against their terms of having a break from his career.

"That doesn't exactly help that he's coming over for dinner," I grumbled, crossing my arms over my chest. "I don't need any of his drama. It's Thanksgiving, Adrian."

"I know," He sighed, stepping towards me and grabbing hold of my arms. He leaned his head close to mine and promised quietly, "I'll make sure he doesn't ruin dinner, okay? It'll be just like old times."

His eyes begged me to agree instead of arguing here in the middle of the hallway. I knew that no matter how much I complained, Thomas is eating dinner no matter what I say. All I could do now was comply and see how it turns out.

"Fine," I muttered. I raised a finger and pointed sternly at him. "But if he so much as says one snarky comment, he's getting kicked out."

Adrian smiled, leaning forward and kissing my pointed finger. "Whatever you say, Sweetheart." He said sweetly before grabbing my hand and tugging us towards the exit. "Now let's go enjoy our weekend."

The next day, I woke up to a lot of shouting.

By shouting, I don't mean there's some hard core arguing going on down stairs. It's more last minute Thanksgiving actions that need to be done, and nobody has done it yet. My mind was only half awake and registering the muffled noises through the walls.

But I knew the routine.

5...

"Did you get the turkey?"

4...

"Sweetie, the pie is burning!"

3...

"Ugh! Why does this taste so bad?"

2...

"No, Lulu! Don't eat that!"

1...

My door slammed open.

"Macey!"

By then, my eyes were already open with old minimal drowsiness tugging them down. I stared at my sister, expressionless and silent, as she began to rant about the help she needed.

"You need to get up, shower, and change. After that you come with me to the store so we can buy ingredients. We need to make the..."

I tuned out Emma's words as I pushed the duvet off my body. Slowly, I got up and walked up to her to clamp my hand over her mouth.

Emma knew exactly how Thanksgiving morning turns out. It's the same every year. My dad forget's to buy the turkey, the pies in the oven are in danger of burning because of my mom's distracted state, and Emma is ordered around for two hours before she comes barging into my room, demanding that I wake up, so she doesn't have to endure mom and dad's chaos alone.

It's a Daniel's tradition, really.

The amusement shined in her eyes as I said, "I'll be down in a few."

"Don't you just love Thanksgiving morning?" She teased playfully over her shoulder.

"What's not to love?" I replied in the same tone, smiling at her leaving figure. Once she left, I swiftly began to get ready for the day.

My hair was still damp as I hopped down the stairs. A small part of my shoulder became wet with the damp spot on my T-shirt.

"Mace, let's go!" Emma called out impatiently. I quickened my speed, almost tripping over Lulu in the process, and entered the kitchen. A sweet smell filled the atmosphere and acted as my oxygen. Mmm, apple pie. As long as we don't eat it everyday, it's a nice treat to have.

"I'm here," I announced. The moment Emma laid her eyes on me, she started charging. Her hand latched onto my wrist in a painful grip as she pulled me forcefully to the door. I managed to save myself from tripping the first time, but the edge of carpet managed to surprise me this time.

I stumbled to the floor with a 'thud.' Sharp pain shot through my bottom for a split second before dulling down to an ache.

"Emma," I groaned, rubbing the injured spot.

My sister looked down at me apologetically. "Sorry," She giggled, helping me up on my feet and pulling me more gently to the door. "I'm a hair's width to throwing one of those pies at mom's face if she keeps bitching around like that."

"It's why I get some extra sleep in the morning," I said, getting into the car.

"It sucks that I'm able to make some dishes for Thanksgiving dinner, or I'd be lounging around in my pajamas for an extra two hours.

"What a shame that you're able to feed your family on this dear holiday." I put my hand over my heart and gave her a mock sympathetic look.

"Well this is why I drag you to the market," She replied moodily.

My smugness faded as I realized that my daily dose of Thanksgiving chaos is getting all the needed supplies in a limited amount of time while Emma trails behind me, drinking Starbucks and ordering which ingredients to get.

It's my part of the deal with a price of two extra hours of sleep.

"You better get me something from Starbucks," I muttered.

"Fine," She smiled at me. "Only because I'm thankful for an annoying little sister."

"Girls, the pies!" My mother shrieked from a few feet away. I jumped in surprise at the sudden loudness of her voice and dropped the bowl of gravy in my hands. The brown substance splattered across the floor and on both mine and Emma's sock-clad feet.

"Mom!" We both cried in exasperation and irritation. It seems that mom's even more on edge than past years. I'm not exactly sure why she would be even more picky about how everything is this year.

Before Adrian left, we always spent the holidays with them – including Thanksgiving. Was Thomas the reason why? Did she want to make a good impression.

Pfft.

I could care less about what the man thinks. I mean, he already has his judgments of me. But having judgments on my family is something completely different. And, quite frankly, it's something I'm not going to be happy about.

He can judge me, but not my family. He's lucky to be coming over here and having a traditional Thanksgiving dinner with company instead of microwavable dinner alone like a hermit.

I grabbed Lulu's and pulled her away from the mess of gravy while Emma cleaned it up. Our mom hovered over us with her hands planted on her hips. You could see the stress with one glance. From the messed up hair and wrinkles that won't seem to fade, she's aging extremely fast in an amount of seven hours.

"Girls," She scolded. "Look what you did."

"Maybe you shouldn't scream so loud when we're literally right across from you." Emma grumbled under her breathe as she mopped up the mess.

Lulu squirmed in my arms. I let her down but held her in place. I look up at my mom with a pleading look. "Can you relax? It's dinner with the Chapmens –" And Thomas. Sadly. "– not the President."

"I know," She let out a deep sigh and ran her hand through her hair, succeeding in creating an even messier look. "But I'm not very fond of Thomas, and I don't want him to think low of this family."

"Yeah, well I don't think the Chapmen's are very fond of him either," Emma pointed out. Kelly's snarky attitude when Thomas ordered two scary looking guys to take me in for an "I know what's best for my cliet, and you're not it" session, and began bashing on me directly to my face.

Complete jackass was my first impression of him.

"Whatever," She dismissed. "Just –"

"Ow!" My dad yelped. All three of us snapped our heads to our dad's direction. He stood hunched over, clenching his hand that was now colored a bright red, a look of pain contorting his face.

"Honey, what's wrong?" Mom asked, deep concern lacing his tone. She rushed to his side and laid a hand on his shoulder.

"Uh.." He trailed uneasily, caressing his red hand. "I forgot to use the oven mittens when I took the pie out."

Mom's head fell into the palm of her hand. "You are all hopeless," She groaned in surrender.

"Alright, girls." My dad turned on the faucet and ran his hand under the cold water. "Why don't you go get ready for dinner. Our company should be here soon."

Hallelujah!

"Gladly." Emma happily took the chance of breaking free of the kitchen madness. I followed quickly while trying to rip off my stained socks at the same time.

After taking another shower to wash off the day's gunk, I checked my phone to see at least five texts – each from the gang.

Brynn

Happy Thanksgiving, Cali's great Hope you're not pregnant yet ;)

Dylan

Happy Thanksgiving, bby!

Amber

Hey, girly! Happy Thanksgiving <3

Brandon

I'm taken a break from mourning over Brynn's absence. No need to mock me. Happy Thanksgiving though!

Chase

Childhood Lovers coming together for Thanksgiving dinner, eh? Don't make so much noise while you're going at it ;)

I blushed deeply at Chase's text. I was just finished replying to their texts when my phone vibrated once more. It was from Adrian.

Adrian

Happy Thanksgiving, Sweetheart. Can't wait to see you! Don't forget my promise, I'll take care of it.

I smiled and quickly responded.

Macey

Happy Thanksgiving, Superstar <3 I'm holding you to that promise.

After tapping send, I headed back inside my bathroom and unwrapped my towel from my hair. After blow-drying it, I took out my curling wand and left it to warm up while I went to change. The dress was something Emma bought for me during our last shopping spree. It was white and lacey that hugged my waist and flowed down above my knee, a thin tan belt and a scarf completing the look.

The doorbell rang twice, and Lulu's sharp barking echoed through the house. I shook my head of curls out and hurried to pull my boots on. Joyous greetings were heard from my open door.

I could see the whole Chapmen family as I walked down the stairs. I couldn't help but notice how sharp Adrian looked tonight.

His hair was slightly styled, but still holding that sexy mussed up hairstyle of his. The first two buttons of his white dress shirt were unbuttoned and his hands were stuffed in the pocket's of his dark washed jeans.

Having him look all hot with Thomas here sure isn't going to help my hormones.

When his eyes met mine, his smile immediately widened. I returned that smile, running down the remaining stairs to jump in his arms for a hug.

Adrian's laugh filled my ears as he wrapped his arms around my waist and twirled me around. "Happy Thanksgiving!" He greeted me.

"Happy Thanksgiving," I replied excitedly. I'd be lying if I said I wasn't happy to spend a holiday with Adrian. It's been so long since the excitement and happiness came so effortlessly with a special occasion bringing joy to the air.

It's great to be with him again like this.

I pulled away slightly just enough to look into his shining eyes. The look of admiration in his eyes awakened the butterflies, fluttering their wings in a complete frenzy.

We must have been staring at each other for longer than necessary, Adrian holding me in my arms in an extremely close proximity, because an awkward cough caused us to pull away immediately. Thomas stood looking at us, his facials arranged in a blank look.

What's that suppose to mean?

I nodded towards him in acknowledgment. "Thomas."

"Macey," He greeted in a leveled tone. What did Adrian do? Threaten him? Is he acting like this because of his promise?

"Macey!" A perky tone exclaimed. I looked to the left and saw Kelly raising her arms for a hug. My smiled returned, and I quickly walked over to wrap my arms around her. It's been a while since I've seen Kelly, and I missed her. "You look so beautiful, babe! Happy Thanksgiving!"

I pulled away with a laugh, seeing her fancy outfit. "You do too," I responded. Oliver stood next to her, looking at me with a smile. Oliver and I haven't exchanged much words. I don't even remember one full conversation we've had.

Well, that has to change.

"Hi, Oliver," I greeted politely.

"Hello, Macey."

Yeah, that's got to change.

After giving Connie and Dave hugs, we all began to make our way to the kitchen. I lagged behind everyone with Adrian, and before we entered the living room, Adrian pulled me to the side and pulled me into him.

I gasped, placing my hands on his shoulders to keep from stumbling once again. In an instant, I was wrapped securely in his arms and being pressed against the wall, Adrian's face about an inch away from mine.

Oh dear god.

"You look beautiful," He mumbled lowly, tilting his head to the side as he examined me.

I bit my lip. "You don't look half bad yourself."

Adrian's lips quirked up in a half smirk. "What do you expect from a sensational heartthrob and superstar?" He whispered.

My smile dimmed a little, and I placed my hands at both sides of his face. I locked my eyes with his and said, "Not tonight you aren't."

Confusion filled his features, so I continued. "You are not a famous super star. You do not have scary fan-girls that stare at your body like you're a piece of meat. And Thomas is not your manager," I whispered. "I haven't spent a holiday with you for so long, and I don't want it to be different because your dreams came true. No career talk, okay? No-no Hollywood tonight. Please."

Just for today, I want to forget the fact that Adrian's famous. I want to forget that he has vicious fan-girls that write fan fictions about him, or that he's plastered on every magazine. I want the only thought of Adrian is that he's my best friend who's having dinner with his family here on Thanksgiving.

That's all. Nothing else. Nope. Na-da. Zilch.

Adrian studied my expression for a second before nodding. "Okay. Hollywood is off," He responded softly. "Just Adrian."

"Just Adrian," I repeated, a smile tugging at my lips.

Slowly, Adrian pressed his lips against my cheek for a sweet kiss. My heart picked up pace as he traveled down to my neck, placing feather like kisses. One hand left my waist to tug at my scarf, leaving more skin available to him.

I let it go on for a few seconds, savoring the cluster of emotions that surround me with his touch. Then, I gently pushed him away.

"We have to go," I told him, smiling in amusement upon seeing his expression.

"Fine," He mumbled, intertwining our fingers together and tugging me towards the doorway. "I'm not done, though." He promised quietly, making me blush as we entered. Kelly and Emma looked our way and exchanged secretive glances with each other. Oliver, however, looked at the four of us, confused.

That's it, I'm making it my personal mission to get to know him tonight.

Kelly saw her fiance's befuddled face and giggled. She leaned up and planted an affectionate kiss on his cheek. "Don't worry, babe. I'll get you caught up later."

Without responding, he nodded and turned to help carry the food to the dining table.

"Is he always that quiet?" I questioned.

"Not for long," He answered. "You just have to give him a bit to adjust."

True to his word, Oliver had the whole table cracking up with his jokes and stories. Even Thomas was chuckling. Kelly placed her hand over his, doubling over in her seat with laughter.

"That must have been so embarrassing," She gasped between fits of laughter.

Oliver shrugged, smiling at all of us. "I didn't know it was a wig, okay? I was just going to ruffle his hair, and it fell off."

I shivered at the image of Oliver reaching up to mess up his coach's hair when it slides to the floor in a big black clump of fake strands. Admittedly, that would freak me out a bit.

"So, Thomas," My mom started conversationally. Uh oh. "Why is it that you stayed here for Thanksgiving instead of going back home. You have a family, don't you?"

I nearly face palmed myself with my mom's action. No! I knew why he stayed. It especially crossed the whole "forget Adrian's famous for a day" thing.

"I've been trying to convince Adrian into doing something that involves going back out in public as the famous figure that he is."

So much for that plan.

Adrian sent me an apologetic look. His warm hand enveloped mine under the table, and he squeezed it.

"Oh?" My dad raised an eyebrow. "And what's that?"

Thomas wiped the corner of his mouth with a napkin before folding his hands together and leaning forward, as if he was going to launch into a long, complicated story.

"Well, Cara Pratt is hosting a banquet right here in Miami. She requested that Adrian makes an appearance, and it's already been leaked to the public, but Adrian refuses to go. It would be great if he were to show up, seeing as it would show that Adrian is still committed to his career."

Here we go. Que the over controlling manager! If he doesn't want to go to Cara Pratt's...

Wait.

"Cara Pratt?" I piped in. "As in the girl who had an on-off relationship with Adrian?"

Why did that come out with a jealous edge? Stupid!

Thomas looked up at me innocently, though I could see the sinister glint in his eyes. "Why, yes. Adrian and Cara were quite close before he came here. Didn't you hear?"

Of course I heard. The breakup of the unofficial couple caused quite a rile up with both their fan bases. Some really looked up to them, thinking that they were the next 'it' couple and were made for each other. But then Adrian suddenly broke whatever it was between them around the time he came home.

I never knew that the cause was because Adrian decided to come back. I never kept tabs on everything in his life, even if he was my best friend. I would simply stumble across a random magazine article or segment on TV that stated what was the latest on the superstar.

Adrian and Cara were close. Very close. The girls and I went to see the movie that starred the two of them. Let's just say it was fairly awkward to see your former best friend and crush get really romantic with Greek goddess.

Something inside me stirred, and I slipped my hand away from Adrian's. I covered it up by running the hand through my hair before folding my hands together on top of the table. Without looking, I could feel Adrian's eyes weighing down on me.

I could see what Thomas was doing here. He was trying to get a reaction out of me by bringing up Adrian's old love interest. But I wasn't going to give him that satisfaction.

"They were very cute together," I commented unemotionally. Emma watched me carefully, gauging my reaction. Whereas Kelly began glaring daggers towards Thomas' slightly smug face.

"They were," He mused. "The fans loved them together. The chemistry between the two was really a sight to see. On set, they didn't even have to try when it came to the intimate scenes."

"Thomas –" Adrian warned lowly.

My heart clenched tightly at Thomas' words. Were they really that close? I racked my brain for anything I read about Cara and Adrian together. Magazines, gossip websites, social media. Now that I thought about it, they really were close.

Don't let him get to you.

"It would flow out so effortlessly!" Thomas continued, gesturing animatedly. "And when the director filmed kissing scenes and what not–"

Calm.

My dad abruptly dropped his fork, anger evident on his face.

"It's certainly something more than what the two of you have."

"Thomas!" Connie gasped, a horrified expression crossing her features.

Thomas took no notice to the rising tension and stared right at me. My hands clenched tightly together as I stared right back.

Don't let him get to you. Don't. Don't. Don't! My inner voice voice chanted, but I could feel myself slowly cracking.

"This puppy love you have with Adrian is quite juvenile, Macey. I understand that he's your.. Oh, what's the word?" He paused, looking up as if the answer was floating around with the dust particles in the air. "Ah, Childhood crush, but that was the old days. Don't you think he's a bit out of your league now, hmm?"

"Thomas!" Adrian shouted, slamming his palms on the table.

"What the hell is wrong with you?!" Kelly shouted, her chair screeching as she abruptly stood up.

Done with the conversation, my eyes burned with tears, and I shot up from my seat. I could hear Emma calling after me, but I ran up the stairs as quickly as I could with no reply.

My door shut loudly, and I leaned my back against hit, sliding down to the floor until I was sitting on the floor. The tears flowed freely now, but no sound came out as I silently cried into my folded arms.

How dare he! How could he just say that? Here in front of everyone.

It's true. I know that I can't live up to what Cara and all those other girls had with Adrian. It's obvious now. How could I think that this was going to work between us? What do I have that they don't have? They have so much more!

Rapid knocking came at my door.

"Macey?"

Adrian.

Talking to Adrian about this was the last thing I needed right now. I knew his promise was useless, anyways. It didn't surprise me that what started with a great night ended how it did. I was stupid enough to think we could go one night without talking or thinking about Adrian's career. It's a part of him now.

He will never just be Adrian. It's always going to be Adrian Chapmen, sensational heartthrob and successful actor.

Famous.

I ran my hands through my hair and tugged. Why does everything have to be so damn complicated!

He knocked again. "Mace?" The desperation in his tone made me lift my head from my knees.

Another knock.

"Macey..."

I didn't answer. Instead, I sat there like a statue. My limbs locked in their position, my mouth clamped shut and eyes staring directly at the red rose sitting on my bedside table.

Why couldn't things be like how it was on the boardwalk last night? Like nothing had happened. As if Adrian didn't disappear for four years and we were spending our weekend like we usually do: at the boardwalk.

I couldn't find it in me to respond, or to answer the door. What was there to say? I'm not even sure Adrian knew I had crush on him back then! He would always ignore everyone who would say the same statement. I doubt he dismissed it now.

Adrian's sigh was barely audible through the door, but just audible enough when I wasn't sniffling like someone with the cold.

After a few silent moments of me holding in my sniffles and Adrian keeping his mouth shut, he spoke.

"Mace, please don't push me away again," He pleaded quietly.

My mind flashed back to where I began to avoid him after the confrontation with the angry manager. His attempts to talk to me were blatantly disregarded. I always kept a good ten feet distance between us. That was until he cornered me at the animal shelter and left me no choice but to talk to him.

What else could I do when wedged between his well built body that resembled the exact wall I was pressed up against?

After talking about the incident with the spiders and his long wait to apologize to me, Adrian can't stand my being mad at him. Word from Brandon and Chase told me that he was beating himself up for it – figuratively speaking of course.

But it was Thanksgiving. My first one with him in a long time. I remembered the moments where he would randomly pop in my mind during these times of year. The sadness that washed over me because of how much I missed him was painfully overwhelming at the time.

Suddenly feeling like I was in those moments, I stood up and swung the door open. Adrian was leaning forward with his arms against the door frame. I only caught a quick glance of his grief-struck face before I jumped and wrapped my arms around him.

He reacted just as fast, hugging me to his chest with one hand stroking my hair. "I'm so sorry," he whispered. "I'm so, so sorry."

With all the things I had to say to him, only one sentence came out. "You promised," I whimpered. His arms tightened around me.

"I know." After a few seconds, he pulled away. His eyes scanned my face before looking up. I turned slightly to see what he was staring at.

The window.

"We're getting out of here," He said suddenly.

"Woah, what?" I croaked. Adrian pushed us in slightly before closing the door behind me. Then he walked briskly towards the window and pulled it open, letting a draft in from the cool night air.

Leave? We couldn't just leave! Everyone's downstairs, what are they going to think when someone comes up to find us, and we're not here when they do?

"Adrian, we can just leave," I told him in a distressed tone. My mom would kill me!

He turned around and caught my hands in his. "Mace, I need to be with you. Alone. Away from here," He added, turning back to the window.

One foot at a time, he stepped onto the window sill and held the the sides for support. Carefully, he stepped on the branch closest to him, testing it with his weight before putting his whole body on top, completely outside now.

I watched as he repeated the process of testing each branch and lowering himself onto it. Much to my horror, after he was just a few feet above the ground, he jumped.

"Alright, Mace," He called quietly when he landed safely. "Your turn."

Does he want me to take a trip to the hospital?

"Are you crazy?" I hissed. "I'm going to break my neck or some-thing!"

"Just do what I did," He answered as if climbing down from a two story house by a shady looking tree isn't a big deal.

Did Juliet have to do this? I don't think so.

"Adrian, I can't do this! I'm going to slip and fall if I do!"

"Don't worry," He shot me a charming smile. Why, hello there butterflies. Good to feel you again. "I'll catch you."

Even with his words, I stared at him with the highest amount of uncertainty.

"I'll catch you," He repeated, enunciating each word slowly that held a very strong promise.

If he says so.

I slowly stuck my foot out and tested the nearest branch. It creaked under the weight, but seemed stable enough.

Monkey see, Monkey do. I said in my head as I lowered myself closer to the ground. Adrian watched my every move, jumping forward when my foot would stumble. Luckily, I would regain my balance and continue my journey down. I was a quarter way down when I got the swing of things.

Test, step, down.

Test, step, down.

Test, step, down

Test, s–

"Oh, crap!" I cried when I lost my footing.

Test, slip, down.

It was a good thing I was wearing shorts underneath my dress.

I let a small shriek as I made my descent. A few branches stabbed me, snaps being heard as branches broke under my weight. In a split second, I shut my eyes and braced myself for impact. The solid collision knocked the breath out of me, my head knocking onto a hard object.

"Ouch."

Or figure.

I opened my eyes a crack to see Adrian groaning under my body weight. "Oh my god," I gasped, lifting myself with one elbow as I held his cheek with my other hand. "Are you okay?"

Adrian chuckled. "I told you I'd catch you."

Chapter 21

The entire ride was filled with complete silence. We managed to breakaway with no other struggles – you know, besides gracefully falling onto Adrian as I descended down an old tree in order to escape to a place I have no clue to where we're going – and slip away quickly.

Luckily, Adrian didn't bring his fancy car with him with the slightly higher amount of people, and we ended up making our escape with a regular looking family convertible.

It slightly satisfied my need for complete normalcy.

With the radio off, the only noise surrounding us was the light hum of the car as it advanced forward. It wasn't an uncomfortable silence, but there was a touch of tension in the air.

I let my eyes watch the passing scenery from outside the car window, while as Adrian kept his gaze focused on the road ahead. My phone was left behind, seeing as I didn't bring an necessities with me on this nighttime getaway.

Guilt lightly nudged my conscious as I thought of my everyone – excluding Thomas, who is probably only interested in Adrian's location that may lure paparazzi – and my hand flew to my necklace to fiddle with it out of habit.

It was Thanksgiving, and where was I? Away without either of our parents' knowledge. Emma and Kelly were going to flip shit, leaving them with Thomas all of a sudden.

"Adrian, I think we should go back," I suggested timidly, turning to face him. As much as I'm angry with Thomas' words, I didn't want to leave my family hanging. I'd rather endure his criticism than get in trouble for ditching Thanksgiving dinner because I got sensitive, and Adrian felt that he needed to 'talk.' Our couch is worthy place to have a talk!

Adrian spared me a quick glance before turning back to the road. "No. We need to talk." He said.

"What's wrong with talking at my house?" I questioned.

"I just need to be alone with you."

Is my room not an option? We could always result to locking ourselves in the bathroom, or sitting out in the backyard. "But – "

"Macey," He interrupted, "Please."

Something about his firm and unwavering tone had my mouth clamping shut instantly, and we were succumbed in complete and utter silence once again.

I took a deep breath upon seeing the beach front. It sat right next to the boardwalk, but not as many people were spending the holiday there. Without a word, Adrian opened the car door and stepped out, slamming it closed behind him. He gestured for me to do the same, and I did.

I stepped into the cool air and walked by his side. He reached for my hand and lead me down, slowly, to the sand covered ground.

Thoughts ran through my head as I tried to conjure up what Adrian wanted to talk about exactly. There were plenty of things to talk about between us. From Cara Pratt's banquet to what Thomas said about our ridiculous 'puppy love.'

My blood boiled at the thought. Though I know it shouldn't, his words had me rethinking everything between Adrian and I. Was everything between us really just a stupid little crush? Adrian's been my crush since we were kids. Maybe it's something that should fade and fade for good instead of coming back four years after he disappeared out of my life.

But it came back.

Adrian and I sat down a few feet away from the outline of damp sand. Adrian stretched his legs before him and stared out into the horizon. I slipped my boots and socks off and dug my toes through the soft, cold sand. Pulling my knees to my chest, I rested my chin on top and watched the tides rise and fall.

Sitting here on the beach with the sounds of the waves and distant noises filling my ears like a delightful tune created such a serene environment. It's a shame that we had to ruin the peace with topics that have been weighing down on us for a while now.

"What's going on between us?" I asked, my voice a bare whisper. Adrian stayed silent. And after a few moments of not getting a response, I spoke, " I mean, is Thomas right? Is all that's between us is puppy love?"

He still didn't answer. The only thing he was focused on was the waves ahead of him and the dark night sky that painted the horizon. The moon was in full view, it's ray of moonlight sprinkling the ripples of the water with it's delicate lighting.

Again, left with no response, I allowed a soft groan to leave my lips and let my forehead fall to my knees. This was certainly not how I imagined spending today. I expected a simple dinner filled with laughs and conversations about Kelly's wedding and teasing remarks from the men around the table who had a knack for mocking us women in a playful manner.

Not Thomas popping in to destroy that fantasy and replace it with drama, resulting to an awkward time at the beach where I was left to endure an uncomfortable time with Adrian, conversing through our relationship status that could not get anymore complicated.

"Say something," I mumbled dejectedly. "Don't just leave me hanging when you were the one that insisted on climbing down a tree, thinking I was falling to my doom, and then drag –"

"I like you, Macey."

"Me down to the beach and – wait." I lifted my head to meet his gaze. "What did you say?"

Adrian glanced over and held my stare, never wavering once. "I said I like you, Mace," He enunciated more slowly. "I like you a lot. I'm not going to lie."

"I-I..." Caught off by his blunt statement, I looked away, unsure of what to say. "Well I..."

"Do you like me back?" He asked cautiously, causing my head to whip towards his direction. What kind of question is that?

"Of course I do!" I shouted without a second thought. He raised an amused eyebrow at my quick response. Blood rushed to my cheeks as I realized that I should have approached that a little more subtly. "I mean, yeah. Yeah, I do," I scoffed lightly, making a face at my own stupidity as I turned away.

Idiot!

Adrian chuckled, and the sound of shuffling on the sand filled my ears before I was pulled into his warm embrace. His arms slipped around my waist, pulling me to his side and lying the both of us down side by side.

"It's not exactly bad news, Sweetheart, so don't feel embarrassed," He whispered into my ear, his breath tickling my neck. I smiled softly and relaxed into his arms, staring up at the dark blue sky. Well that bit was at least good to hear.

We fell into another round of silence, simply enjoying the moment while we were still living it. It was when thoughts of rushing back home and the urge to continue this conversation another day did Adrian finally speak. It wasn't something I wanted to hear, though.

"Did you really have a childhood crush on me?" He asked quietly, his calloused hand running up my arm lightly.

I sighed. I was going to have to face the music sooner or later. "Remember that paper in English that we had to do? The one where we passed it around so everyone could write something down about you?"

"Yeah."

"Do the words 'Then and now, you still have me crushing on you.' sound familiar?"

His eyes widened as he remembered the words. "That was you?" He asked, lifting his head to turn and look at me.

"Yeah." I smiled. "What we were writing was anonymous. I still hadn't given in to the fact that I had a crush on you to anyone back then, but I admitted it to that crappy piece of lined paper." A chuckle left my lips as I ran my hand through the soft sand.

Even in the state of denial, deep down inside I knew that my liking for Adrian hadn't completely faded. Most of it had when he left for LA, but it was never entirely gone. It was all in which I would accept the fact.

And I did. Now I was to have a heartfelt conversation about our feelings and relationship. Look where confessing got me!

"I thought it could've been anyone," He mused.

"Well now you know."

"Now I know. Just for the record, though, you guys were gushing over what I wrote." He said, a sense of cockiness in his voice.

My childhood crush.

"That was you?" I questioned loudly, raising an eyebrow at him.

"Yes, it was," He chuckled. "So now you know. I always thought you were kinda cute back then – and now, of course. But then there were other reasons why I thought you were attractive. Besides the basic sweet, funny, and beautiful, you were always so real with me, no matter what stage I was on back then. That's what I really love about you."

My cheeks grew warm with the string of compliments, and a smile spread across my face. It took me a moment for his words to sink in. I never knew he thought that about me. Being real was never an option because it came so naturally. Adrian and I have been friends for years; I never acted any different because I grew so accustomed to being myself. And really, that's all I was doing: being myself.

Suddenly, with that knowledge, all things that I found confusing made sense.

"Wait, wait," I exclaimed, jumping to a sitting position and turning to him. "Was I that girl you were talking about when things didn't work out with Cammie?"

"And every other girl." He nodded. Sitting up with me, my hand was enveloped in his large ones and his eyes was cast downwards, avoiding my stare. I almost sighed knowing that what he just said wasn't his final thought.

I knew whatever he had to say was something that he didn't. And I knew it was something I didn't want to hear.

"But?" I urged gently, giving his hand a squeeze.

"But..." Adrian lifted his eyes to mine reluctantly. "We be can't anything more at the moment."

The words came out pained. Even though I expected him to say something similar to this, the confession still made my heart stutter and ache. My face dropped down, and I kept my focus on the sand to hide my disappointment and, admittedly, my embarrassment.

Why did I think that there could be something?

A finger lifting my chin made me look back into Adrian's eyes. "Don't do that, Mace," He whispered. "You didn't let me finish."

The chances of us being together was proved nonexistent, what else was there to say? Confused on what else he had to say, I let him continue.

"Look," He sighed deeply. "I know a lot of things has changed since I came back. I'm not just another face passing through the halls, my parents aren't working part time jobs to scrape up money, and Emma's not that sassy teenager that didn't know the difference between looking good and looking like a flashy disco ball."

I nodded, already having known how their lives are now. Adrian's face can be identified by everyone who hasn't been living under a rock. Connie and Dave are living off of their children's income.

Sassy when need be, Kelly is an engaged women rocking the title of high fashion queen.

"And Thomas..." Shaking his head, a pained expression crossed his features. "Believe it or not, he's a good manager, and he know's best for my career. He made my dreams come true."

I wasn't going to deny that. Thomas, as much of a pain in the ass he is, was the one that landed Adrian his first movie. That movie started his acting career. Now he's living his dreams doing what he loves.

"We've got to give that guy credit, huh?" I chuckled, trying to lighten this conversation's mood.

"Yeah, we do." A brief smile touched Adrian's face before it dimmed down to a straight, serious line. "But he's not right about our relationship."

"He isn't?" I asked dumbly, backtracking the conversation when he said that we couldn't be anything more than what we are now.

The look Adrian sent me made me feel like I was the one who crushed the possiblities of there being an 'us.'

"No, he isn't," He said, almost immediately. "I told you, you had to let me finish. We can't be anything at the moment. That doesn't mean we can't down the road."

"What are you talking about?"

"All I'm saying is that we lay low for a while until we get our shit together," Adrian explained. "I don't want Thomas throwing a tantrum and causing an uproar with publicity. With Clara's banquet coming up..." His voice trailed off as he watched me carefully. "What's wrong?"

I ran my hand through my hair and looked away.

Trying to work out how we're suppose to be together isn't normal for a relationship. There shouldn't be barriers blocking our being together. Especially barriers that include factors of his career. Is being a couple really what's good for him? For the both of us? For his career?

I don't know where life is going to take me down the road, and whether or not Adrian will be a part of it, or just up and leave again. What's going to happen to us then if we become something more? I go off to college while Adrian leaves and continues living his dream?

I don't know if I could take being away from him again. I can't. I can't!

"Adrian." I shook my head. With my heart in my throat, I forced out the words that I never thought would say, "No. We can't be together. Not like this." Not having the guts to take in Adrian's expression, I stood up and began walking away.

I didn't hear anything at first – no footsteps, no sound of confusion. It came to me as more than a surprise when fingers wrapped around my wrist and pulled me backwards, twirling me around and colliding into Adrian's body. With my hands being restrained, my struggle was weak and worthless as Adrian kept me flush against him.

"Macey, wait," He begged, exasperation tinting his tone.

"No!" I shouted, halting my movements to stare him dead in the eyes. "It shouldn't be this complicated. We shouldn't have to be holding back. If you really wanted us to be together, it would have happened. But I care about you and your career, and with how things have been going lately, I'm sure as hell not good for it."

"I came back to do these things," Adrian argued, gripping my wrists tighter to the point where it was almost painful. None of that mattered as I listened to him yell in frustration. "I want to finish senior year, hang out with friends, celebrate holidays with your family like we use to. This is my chance to be in a real relationship with a real girl. I want to be with you, Macey, believe that."

"And what about after your 'break'?" I shot back. His leaving back then crushed me four years ago, and we had only been best friends. If we were to become something more now, I couldn't imagine how hard it will be when we have to go our separate ways at the end of graduation. It would hurt too much.

The whispered statement softened Adrian's features. His vice grip around my wrist were loosened, letting them fall limp to my side when he took my face in between his in a gentle and affectionate hold. I felt the roughness of his thumb skim across my cheek, gliding towards my hair and tucking it behind my ears. His forehead rested against mine, and I could feel my inner fight dying within me.

Just be with him!

It could be him, or it could be my brain malfunctioning with the lack of oxygen due to the close proximity that has me conjuring up delusions of Adrian being closer than before, almost to the point where lifting my head would connect our lips together.

Reality dawned on me then, causing the party of butterflies to throw the party of the century in my poor stomach, when Adrian's gaze flickered down to my lips before slowly, cautiously, brushing his own against mine.

Two seconds of shock.

Two seconds of nervousness.

Two long seconds of absolute courage.

"Don't give up on us," He whispered.

And the moment our lips met, I already made a decision.

Chapter 22

The rest of the week went in a daze, and before I knew it, school was back in play. After staying much longer than necessary at the beach – thanks to Adrian's ability to distract me for more than an hour with his amazing ability to kiss – we were able to return home.

The consequences weren't as harsh; not as harsh as the bone crushing hugs that I was enveloped in when I walked through the front door. Thomas was long gone – banned by my angry father and a very near-ready to kill Emma and Kelly. Suffice to say, I was touched by their extreme hate for Thomas that they would throw him out for my sensitivity. They objected, of course, claiming that what he said was rude and that I had every right to be angry.

The tension in the air was immediately crushed when my mom burst through the kitchen with a plate of pie.

The powers of pie were indescribable. Especially for my father.

I remained quiet through the rest of Thanksgiving dinner with the night on the beach replaying in my mind.

I wasn't going to give up on Adrian and I just yet. The way I felt when Adrian's lips met mine were a clear indication that I couldn't just let go of the feelings I had for him. The firm grip on my hips, soft moans, and gentle but urgent way his lips moved with mine was enough to drive me mad.

The toe-curling, butterfly rampage, spark flying moment was my cheesy first kiss on the beach, and I wasn't afraid to admit that I loved every minute of it.

Describing all this to the girls only made me squirm at their reactions.

"I can't believe this!" Amber screeched, falling back dramatically against the lockers with a dreamy look in her eye. "You two are so romantic," She gushed.

"I'll say," Dylan remarked. "You two are a walking cliché. Nothing more romantic than that."

I turned away from my locker to make a face at her. "Shut up, Dylan." I snapped lightly.

"Make out sessions, huh? One step closer to getting pregnant." Brynn sang teasingly, bumping her shoulder with mine.

"I am not getting pregnant!" I told her loudly. And, in my defense, there was only one make out session. So far...

I am a walking cliché, I thought distastefully.

"I never thought you would do something like this, Mace," Dylan mused.

My nose crinkled. "Do what?"

"You know." Dylan smirked at me, wiggling her eyebrows at me suggestively. "Friends with benefits."

"Dylan!" I squeaked, my face burning to a whole new temperature. I never thought about what was going on between Adrian and I as 'friends with benefits.' To think, I thought those people should just make themselves official rather than using each other for their own pleasure. Now I knew that some situations are different.

My situation just sounded ridiculous.

A complicated relationship with my superstar best friend that has feelings for me, but we can't be together because of his career. Now we're sneaking around because our hormones are so out of check with all this sexual tension that we kiss each other whenever we feel the need to.

Yeah, that's my reality.

Brynn's booming laughter floated down the hall and caught the attention of several students. Including a certain blonde.

Cammie's eyes narrowed down to cat-like size as she glanced over at us. I met her stare with a blank expression. Cammie has been blatantly ignoring us since the incident on Halloween, and I'd be lying if I said I didn't mind. In fact, I almost forgot all about her, and her suffocating perfume.

"Hey, Cammie." Brynn smirked her way. "Did you get all those stains out of your so called 'sexy' Halloween costume of yours? I bet it was a great addition, though."

Cammie bristled. "Whatever," She spat before swaying her hips dramatically down the hall.

"Brynn, just because Madrian is underway doesn't mean you can get all cocky with Cammie," Amber warned slowly, watching Cammie sashay herself down the hall.

"Madrian?" I coughed.

"Yeah," She said in a duh tone, "Macey and Adrian combined together makes Madrian."

"So, like Brangelina." Brynn wondered thoughtfully.

"We are not a couple." I answered flatly.

Dylan pointed a finger at me. "Yet."

I groaned.

"And anyways, Cammie's not a threat to us, now that Adrian's gone and admit his undying love for our dear friend." Brynn stood up straighter and crossed her arms across her chest defiantly.

Undying love. "You guys are impossible," I sighed in defeat.

"Why are they impossible?" A voice said from behind. A pair of arms snuck around my waist and pulled me into the familiar feel of someone's hard front. Judging by the smirks and wide smiles from the girls, I didn't need anymore confirmation on whom this person was.

"Well if it isn't the other half of this adorable relationship," Dylan said grandly. "On a scale of one to ten, how good of a kisser is Macey?"

Brandon and Chase appeared from behind and walked to the girl's with the same matching smirks. Adrian sighed deeply and leaned his mouth close to my ear.

"You can't keep anything from these girls, can you?" He mumbled lowly into my ear before ducking his head lower so he can nuzzle his face into the curve of my neck.

I elbowed him lightly. "They'd kill me if I didn't tell them you took my first kiss." I defended.

Suddenly, Adrian rose his head with an intense look in his eye. "Oh, I think I took more than just your first kiss." His voice dropped down to a low, husky voice that made shivers shoot down my spine.

Too bad I wasn't the only one who had ears.

Brandon and Chase let out into wild hollers, clapping each other on the back while the girls – including Dylan – squealed and giggled like a bunch of directions caught sight of Harry Styles naked.

I ripped away from Adrian's arms and turned, shoving him roughly backwards. That annoying smug smirk plastered onto his charming face made me even more annoyed.

"Screw you!" I shouted in embarrassment.

"So you are getting pregnant!" Brynn gasped so loud that several people turned to look at us. If I thought I was blushing hard before, my face was on fire now. Feeling flustered with all the attention, I sent my so called friends a harsh glare before speeding down the hall and though the front doors. I couldn't be anymore grateful that school was over.

Adrian's amused voice called out to me from a distance. "Macey!"

Rolling my eyes, I pushed the doors open and stepped out into the cool air. Just as I was a few feet away from the school, I was once again caught and pulled back into Adrian's muscular stomach.

A sharp squeal left my lips when my feet was lifted off the ground, and I was twirled around.

"Adrian, put me down!" I laughed. Adrian chuckled and stop his spinning cycle. The moment my feet touched the ground, I squirmed in his hold, trying to get out.

"Aww. Come on, Mace, don't be like that," Adrian begged me in a childish tone.

I huffed, pausing my movements to turn and look at him over my shoulder. "Asshole."

"Ouch." Almost too quick to process, Adrian had turned me around in his arms so I was facing him. His grip was firm as he pulled me flush against him, ducking his head low enough that our lips brushed when he spoke. "I think I deserve something to patch that wound in my heart that you caused with your hurtful insult."

My eyes fluttered shut at the slight contact, but I placed a hand on Adrian's chest and pulled back. Adrian frowned, and I smiled softly.

I shook my head. "Not here," I explained quietly.

Understanding dawned on him, and he nodded. Lacing my fingers with his, Adrian tugged me towards his car. He put the car in ignition before pulling out of the school parking lot and driving towards our destination. A soft smile touched my lips when Adrian reached across the divider and intertwined our fingers, resting our joined hands between us.

Adrian's large, luxurious house entered my line of vision. I haven't visited Adrian's house many times in the past. It still hadn't settled in my mind that Adrian now lives in this house instead of just a few blocks from mine.

"Is anyone home?" I asked as Adrian got his keys out and put it in the lock.

"Nah." He pushed the door open. "Everyone's out, like usual."

I nodded, automatically glancing around the luxurious inside of Adrian's house. "I'm still not used to this." I thought aloud.

Silently enclosing his hand around mine, I followed Adrian up the stairs. The tour he gave me all that while ago had disappeared into the farthest abyss of my mind, effectively not coming to mind when I tried to conjure up what the many rooms held.

Adrian stopped in front of one and gently nudged the small of my back for me to go first. "This is my room," He said.

My eyebrows traveled up my forehead. I've never seen his room before, and I was curious to see if his taste changed since the four years he's been gone.

Pushing the door open, I stepped inside and smiled at the sight before me. Any thoughts of expensive furniture and high class things dispersed when I looked around. His room was a mix of a normal teenager with a touch of Hollywood flare. It certainly didn't give the whole 'I'm a fucking rich actor, and I got loads of money to spend' vibe.

Clothes were littered across the floor and books and papers were scattered messily on top of his desk. A grand piano sat at the far end of the room beside the huge balcony that over looked the beach in the distance. A king sized bed that was semi-neatly made was located to the left side and the large flat screen TV hung directly across. The bathroom door was ajar, giving me a glance at the fancy bathroom that had products stacked on the counter top.

"You have a nice room," I commented, turning around to face Adrian. He smiled as he shut the door softly behind him.

"Yeah. Sorry if it's a bit messy."

I snorted. "You're a guy, Adrian. I didn't expect any different, even if you do have this awesome room."

Adrian hummed thoughtfully, reaching out hook an arm around my waist and slowly pull me towards him. "Why do I feel like you only like me for all the things I can offer?" He asked teasingly, pulling me close.

"You're delusional." Smirking up at him, I said, "I saw something in that scrawny idiot back in middle school."

Adrian's features softened at my words. His eyes flickered down to my lips and stayed there as he spoke. His breath brushed against my top lip, teasingly. "And I saw something in that shy nerd back in middle school."

I gaped at him. "I was not a – "

Adrian's lips met mine urgently, effectively cutting off my sentence before I could object of my nerd status that was obviously nonexistent. Turning us around, Adrian led us backwards until my back hit the door. He pushed against me, leading the kiss with his subtle lips in a fast pace. My hands traveled up his chest and shoulders, tangling themselves in his hair, tugging and pulling. His hand sliped beneath my shirt, his fingers brushing the bare skin with such a gentle caress that I moan into his mouth.

Before Thanksgiving, I wouldn't have any idea what kissing felt like, or how I was even suppose to. Now I knew that it came almost naturally for me, like breathing. I never felt anything like the way Adrian made me feel when we kissed. It was amazing, as if the intimate contact was enough to make me feel alive. Any stress or emotion I have just disappears; I don't have to think about anything else but the wonderful boy that has their arms wrapped around me.

What feels like hours of no oxygen suddenly returns to me when Adrian pulls away and travels down the length of my throat instead. His skilled lips pepper kisses everywhere he can, nipping and pulling the sensitive skin. My hand fists the fabric of his shirt, pulling him impossibly close. I rest my head back on the wall and try to catch my breath as he continues his assault on my neck.

Friends with benefits, she said. Why don't I like thinking that's the label on our relationship – even though it is true. This, kissing and being closer than best friends are suppose to be, this is exactly what friends with benefits mean. Adrian said we can't be official yet, but I can't help how I feel about the sneaking around. Like what we have is a forbidden romance.

We really are a walking cliché.

The sudden pain on my neck ripped me out of my thoughts and made me cry out in surprise.

"Ow!" I yelped, jerking away from Adrian. Did he just bite me? My hand flew to the sore part of my neck. I gave hin an incredulous look and exclaimed, "What the hell, Adrian?"

"You were analyzing things again, weren't you?" He sighed, leaning back to give me the look.

Oh.

"Yes," I admitted sheepishly.

Adrian groaned, prying my hand off my neck and softly pressing his lips against the injured spot. He pulled back after a moment and rested his forehead against mine.

"Well, don't," He says simply.

I give him a small smile. "Sorry."

Pulling out of his arms, I head towards the balcony. The winds were stronger than when we were last out in the open. My hair flew wildly to the side, and the breeze cooled down the increase of temperature that rose during my make out session with Adrian.

Adrian joined me, leaning against the railing and looking out towards the beach. We stayed silent for a while, just enjoying the fresh air.

"Can you do me a favor?" Adrian asked, breaking the silence.

I turned to him, curiously. Adrian doesn't ask for a lot of favors. "I guess." My response was weary.

I only became more weary when Adrian's face turned to one of discomfort. "Can you come with me to Cara's banquet on Saturday?"

"What?" I all but shouted. How could he even ask that of me with everything that was totally against the idea. All the famous people coming, the paparazzi swarming the event. And what about Thomas? Not to mention how awkward my attending the banquet will be when I watch Cara try to kiss up to Adrian and win his heart back. I would stick out like a sore thumb, and everyone will get the wrong idea.

There's too many cons that outweigh any pros - if there is any.

"It's not a good idea, Adrian." I shook my head.

"Macey, I know that you think it is and why, but it wouldn't be a big deal," Adrian argued. "There's nothing to lie about. I can tell everyone that you're my best friend, and that we're there just as friends. I don't even want to get involved with Cara, and Thomas could complain all he wants about my bringing you along, but I won't give a damn."

I wrapped my arms around myself and gave him a conflicted look. "I don't know, Adrian…" I trailed.

"Just two hours, and we'll leave," He pleaded. "That's all I'm asking."

I contemplated the idea in my mind. I knew that I would end up going with him because I didn't want to leave him in his time of need. He never asked for favors; I should at least give him this.

"Alright."

Chapter 23

"Turn."

Pivoting around on my heel, I heave a deep, exaggerated sigh that sounded like a simple dress up session was causing me actual pain.

It was.

So maybe not physical pain, but pain nonetheless. The banquet was tonight, and I could officially say that I was nervous as hell. Adrian assured me more than necessary that everything would turn out okay and that we would only be there for two hours max before we left, but we all know how it goes.

There's always that feeling. The uneasy churning of your stomach, the voice in your head that whispers constantly that something was going to go wrong. All the factors either foreshadow the storm to come, or diminish into thin air when all goes well.

But you don't know until you have to go through the event that has your mind going into overdrive. And from then on, you have to go through the most agonizing part of this whole thing.

Waiting.

Waiting for hours. Listening to the ticks of the clock as it counts down the time before it's time to find out if you were worrying for nothing, or that little voice in your head is going to say, "I told you so." And this, my dear friends, is why I'm close to throwing up my lunch into the toilet.

Now that my dramatic monologue is over...

"It's beautiful!" Came the excited shriek of Amber as she skipped into the room, clapping her hands with her eyes gleaming as excitement.

Currently, I stood in the middle of Kelly's extravagant bedroom as she forced me into dresses for tonight. She invited the girls to come over, thinking that would help come down the storm in my stomach, but also wanted to get to know the girls I've been closely acquainted with since her leaving Miami.

"I agree," Brynn chimed with a mouth full of food. I rolled my eyes, planting my hands on my hips as I stared down at the blonde from where I stood on a stool.

"Are you robbing the Chapmens' pantry?" I asked her.

"It's not robbing if we're a guest," she answered smartly, falling back into a white love seat with a bag full of chips.

Kelly laughed from behind me. I felt her nimble fingers pick at the dress that currently clung to my body. "It's absolutely fine, hun," she chuckled. Soon after, Dylan came in with a huge amount of various snacks and treats.

"Damn, it's like a movie theater snack bar down there," Dylan cried out, clearly impressed as she took a seat next to Brynn. She nodded at the dress. "You look sexy in that dress."

My eyes narrowed, despite the heating of my cheeks. She smiled cheekily at me and popped a handful of red skittles in her mouth.

Amber hopped onto her feet and came to inspect the dress in admiration. It was a simple white and black dress that clung to my body and complimented my curves. I tugged at the hem, turning and inspecting the dress with the full length mirror in front of me.

"Feeling sexy, Mace?" Brynn asked cheekily.

"Shut up!" I shouted lightly, grabbing a handful of skittles and throwing them at her and getting a scolding from Kelly.

"Yeah, shut up, Brynn. Like you wouldn't feel pretty in a dress like this," Amber defended.

"Why, thank you," Kelly said in a flattered tone. She paced around me in search for anything that would ruin the beautiful look that she spent hours trying to perfect. Once satisfied, she tugged me down the tiny stage and to her dresser. "I designed it a while back and thought I could jazz it up a bit. Seeing it on someone makes me reconsider," She mused.

"Glad to know I could make it work," I teased, taking a seat in front of the dresser.

"Is this the part where we get to torture her whole head?" Dylan asked eagerly, jumping up from her seat and rushing to my side. Knowing Kelly, I was sure to get a whole make-over in the two hours I had before the banquet. And knowing how much of a beauty queen she is, all of this cosmetic related work was going to leave me hurt.

Kelly grinned, almost sardonically, at me in the mirror and said, "Yup."

"Oh, joy," I grumbled.

Suddenly excited to see me in pain, Brynn jumped up from her seat and scurried to my side. Amber followed suit, looking forward to the process of dolling me up.

"When Adrian sees you tonight, he won't just see you as a sweetie," Kelly promised, winking as she fluffed my hair. I sighed out an uneasy response as they turned the chair so I couldn't look at myself and see what horrid things they were about to do to me.

This banquet better be worth the poking and tugging.

My fingers drummed rapidly against the armrests, feeling restless and losing the feeling in my butt. Another hard slap sent a jolt through my shoulders, a reprimand for moving while yet another person tinkered with my face.

"Macey, stop moving!" Amber whined as I felt pressure on my eyelid again. "I'm almost done applying eyeliner."

I groaned and gripped the seat. "What time is it?"

"Half past seven," A distracted Kelly replied. I jumped in my seat, opening my eyes in the process as I turned around to stare at Kelly in shock.

"Macey!" Amber shouted, exasperated at my sudden movement.

"Adrian said we were leaving at seven. It's thirty past!"

Kelly rolled her eyes and released a final curl from the curler. "Oh, relax, would you? He'll live. "Plus, we're already done. I held my breath as a mist of hairspray was applied to my brown locks. Dylan came holding a pair of black pumps, and I bent down to strap them on.

"I think this is worth the wait, don't you think?" Brynn asked, standing back with an intent look. The girls stood back as well, inspecting their work with admiration. Smiles graced their faces, and Kelly stepped up to pull me out of my seat and back to the mirror. Hands momentarily blinded my vision, and I groaned in protest.

"Is this necessary?" I asked. "We're only going to be there for two hours, so why do did you have to go through all this trouble to

-" Words failed me when the hands disappeared and a caught a glimpse of the girls' hard work.

My brown locks fell loose in big, soft curls down my shoulder. The light smoky eye across my eyelids brought out the glow in my eyes, and a pinkish-red lipstick painted my lips. The black strapped pumps added a few inches to my height, making me seem taller than my small figure actually claims to be. Courtesy to Kelly, a simple diamond necklace hung against my neck and glistened in the bright lightning.

"You guys," I breathed, smiling at my reflection. I'd be lying if I didn't feel insecure about going to the banquet with Adrian tonight. It didn't feel right to go with Adrian and be a part of his famous side. The most extravagant event I've been to was my cousin's wedding, and that was seven years ago. Everybody around me would be far from just normal – both in status and in looks. The host herself was some sort of Hollywood goddess. Though it was a bit shallow of me, dress up tonight made me feel like I could blend in with the crowd of the famous and talented. At least I could look the part of having more meaning than Adrian's plus one.

Kelly clasped her hands together and smiled widely. "Do you like it?" She asked, hopefulness lacing her tone.

"Like it? I love it!" I exclaimed, turning and opening my arms wide for a hug. Small cheers and laughs erupted from their mouths and they willing jumped into my embrace.

"Don't worry about tonight, alright?" Dylan said into my ear.

"Yeah," Amber chirped into my other ear. "It'll be fun."

"And you never know," I'm not even sure where Brynn spoke except that I could breathe in her skittle breath. "Maybe something will –"

"Don't."

Laughing, we stayed in our position for a moment before letting go and I headed downstairs with the girls trailing behind me like a group of lost duckinglings. The clicks of my heels and small chat from us girls were the only noise echoing through the whole house.

And then I heard Adrian's endless ranting.

"How long does it take to get ready for a stupid banquet?" His mumbled voice increased in volume with each step closer he took to the stairs. He then said in a louder voice, "Thomas, Macey and I will be there once the girls finish – " Him and his words halted when Adrian appeared from around the corner and saw us – me – standing at the front of the stairs.

"Wow, bro," Kelly chided disapprovingly. The smirk on face said anything but, though. "Thirty minutes past your said time and you're already complaining? I was expecting at least fifteen extra."

I couldn't help the the small smirk that slipped onto my face at Adrian's dumbfounded expression. Early today, he was doubting Kelly's professionalism in fashion and teased not to make me look like a tramp. Offended, Kelly remarked that I was nothing like those sluts he was involved with, whether I was dressed up or not, and bet she was going to get a dazed expression out of him.

Kelly obviously won that bet. Feeling smug, for both me and Kelly, I decided to play with him more.

Tossing my hair for dramatics, I slowly walked down the stairs and hoped that I looked somewhat sexy and not like a drunk prostitute. My eyes remained locked with Adrian's hazel eyes as I walked up to him. After a moment, his eyes left mine to trail down my body, lingering for longer than necessary. I tipped a finger under his chin and pushed his eyes back up to mine. It was all for show, but the quick glint of hunger and lust I caught in his eyes brought the butterflies out to play.

I rested my palms flat against his chest and felt the fast rate of Adrian's beating heart beneath the designer clothes. The extra inches from the heels brought my height to the point where I didn't have to stand on my toes to bring my mouth dangerously close to his ear.

Too bad what came out of my words were neither sexy nor seductive.

"You us five bucks," I whispered before pulling back. A bubbly laugh escaped my lips at Adrian's fallen face. I patted his cheek. "Oh, and you're going to have to put the hood up because I really don't want to mess my hair up after all the girls' work."

With that, I turned to the girls and said with a wave of my hand, "Have fun tonight." Light chuckles and giggles followed as I headed to the door.

I was instantly greeted with a strong gust of wind when I stepped outside. Dark outlines of clouds against the darkening sky was prominent, and the vague smell of rain hung in the air. Warmth enveloped my backside, and I looked behind me to see Adrian holding his jacket against my body.

"Sexy dress, but no matching coat?" he murmured in my ear.

I gripped the sides of the jacket and held it in place. "I didn't see you complaining."

"True…"

Shaking my head, the two of us walked quickly to the car. I gathered all the flying wisps of hair and held it in place while Adrian pulled the hood of his car closed. I breathed out a sigh of relief once we were no longer being assaulted by the wind. The blinking blue lights of the clock read that it was ten minutes before eight.

"We should get going," I said aloud, patting down the curls. I turned towards him when he didn't answer; his eyes were narrowed. "What?"

"You're such a fucking tease sometimes, you know that?" he said darkly. Suddenly, a hand wrapped around the back of my neck crashed my lips against his in a passionate kiss. A noise of surprise turned into a moan of pleasure, raising my hand to cup the side of his face. I let it go on for a few moments before pulling – rather reluctantly, may I add – away and settling in my seat.

Adrian groaned in protest and I scoffed, "The guy who was complaining of our lateness is putting off the time, so let's get going."

A frustrated growl left his lips as he started the car. "This damn banquet," he grumbled dejectedly.

All playfulness vanished the minute we drove out of Adrian's driveway. The farther we got from the house, the more I discovered how many times my body could fidget in a half hour ride. And for a split second, I thought all the movement was abnormal and that we should turn the car towards the hospital to get this checked out instead of going to the banquet.

Why did I even agree to this? I could have been dead set on letting Adrian go solo. Instead I let him coax me into being his date to this event. But this event will be the one that reveals to me how he actually is when living his Hollywood dream. Is he really this cocky but sweet Adrian Chapmen that everyone here welcomed with open arms, or is he the manwhore that Kelly makes him out to be with all the other sluts?

This night will tell me. The thought lowered my nervousness for a mere second before coming back and hitting me square in the face.

I stared at two raindrops racing their way down the window. What if Adrian is the latter? And worse, what is it that's going to prove to me that Adrian has two sides to him?

I was so engaged in my thoughts that I didn't realize we reached our destination until a warm hand wrapped around mine. Concern flooded Adrian's features, eyebrows furrowed as he stared at me. "You okay?" he asked quietly.

"I'm fine." I nodded.

His thumb brushed against the top of my hand. "I promise we'll only be here for two hours, tops, okay?" he said gently, as if he was afraid I was going to hijack his car and flee. I chuckled, nodding once again.

With a crooked grin, Adrian leaned in and pressed his lips to mine. There was nothing rushed about this kiss, despite being more than an hour late. Our lips moved in slow, synchronized movements that left me smiling when we pulled away.

"You look beautiful tonight, by the way," He mumbled, brushing a loose curl behind my ear. "You and the girls will get your five bucks."

I threw my head back in laughter, shaking my head as I turned away. "Let's just go," I giggled.

Considering it started to rain and I was left with no protection from the falling drops, Adrian rushed out of the car and ran to my side of the car. He took off his jacket once again and sheltered it over me as we made our way towards the entrance. My stomach twisted as I took in Adrian's actions. A true, sweet gentleman. Will he still be this way by the end of the night?

A couple of screams cut us off as we made it to the door. We whipped around to see a couple of, albeit, beautiful teenage girls running towards us with items in their hands.

"It's Adrian Chapmen!" The blonde one asked in an ear-splitting shriek. I cringed back slightly.

"Can we have your autograph, we're such a big fan!" The other shouted, her soaking red hair sticking to her forehead as she grinned widely at Adrian.

Adrian turned to me, "Go inside, okay? Give me a sec," he said. I nodded and after sparing the girls a split second to see their envious and curious glares, I scurried inside. Loud conversations and laughter filled the room, people standing around or seated around tables as they chatted happily. Girls in elegant dresses and men in sharp suits, their smiles blinding.

I twirled on my heel to see if the girls have stopped holding Adrian up, but when I did, a frown fluttered across my face. The fiery red head trailed her hand up and down Adrian's chest, smiling sweetly up at him. The blonde put up a seductive act, leaning against Adrian so she was pressed up against his side, fluttering her eyes. I almost laughed at how she looked like she was trying to get something out of her eye but didn't want to make it obvious.

But it was the way Adrian willingly let the girls close to him, his eyes wandering down their figures with his oh-so charming smile. The sinking feeling in my stomach only intensified as he made himself comfortable against the pole behind him and listened to the girls talk passionately about god knows what.

I was tempted to go out there and interrupt their little conversation, seeing as I felt completely uncomfortable and out of place just standing out in the open like an idiot. But I didn't. It's been a while since Adrian's gotten recognition and it felt wrong to pull away from whatever being known makes him feel. Plus, he doesn't seem to be in such a hurry to come inside with those two girls keeping him occupied.

Sighing, I slipped off Adrian's jacket and let it hang in my arms. I turned away from the sickening sight and turned towards the banquet. I wondered if I could just run off and hide in the bathroom for the rest of my remaining two hours, but the pent up awkwardness within me kept me rooted to the side, as if taking a step would make humiliate me in front of all these high-worthy people.

"Excuse me." The unfamiliar deep voice made me let out an embarrassing shriek of surprise. While in the process of whirling around to meet the owner of the voice, I was suddenly aware of their close proximity when my curly locks made contact with the person's face.

"Sorry, I –"

Too many people were rendering me speechless lately. This person, however, probably had the power to make every girl in this room drop their panties for him. Whether or not I would be a part of that statistic will remain unknown.

Ahem. . . Anyways.

Short dark hair, angular features, and a dazzling smile, this magnificently beautiful human being in front of me looked as if he belonged taped to a teenager's bedroom wall for them to stare at. If not, the "Sexiest Man Alive" cover magazine could fit just as well. Not that I'm insinuating here or anything. He was just really hot and brought out the inner fangirl in me. Now I could understand what kind of sick fantasies Brynn has about one direction.

Okay, not that far. But still.

It was not just the extreme looks of this man that made my mouth drop open wide enough for a seal to jump in, but it's the fact that I recognized him.

Heath Lawson was a young actor taking the movie world by storm. Amber and I were in Government class just the other day ogling over him as we watched his movie. He was much more interesting than the droning elf at the front of the classroom who didn't care when everyone tuned out her voice in exchange to busying themselves with technology. We took advantage of our time by rewatching his first movie, Trapped in Love.

Unlike most of the guys in the room, Heath wore a white blazer with a black bow tie which, admittedly, left me at awe at how adorable he looked.

"It's not big deal," he chuckled. That was one of the sexiest sounds ever. Oh my god, Macey. Get your head out of the damn gutter! It was a laugh! "Your hair is impossibly soft for a girl that looked as if she spent hours burning her hair to get those perfect curls."

About that statistic...

I'm so ashamed of myself, I thought, mentalling smacking myself for acting this way.

I laughed nervously and subconsciously touched the ends of my hair. And to think, I thought I needed to cut back in using heat products because I thought my hair was badly damaged. This guy begs to differ.

I willed myself to keep my stutter away. "Thank you."

Nailed it!

If that didn't make me break down in complete nervousness, then maybe sticking his hand out for me to shake would. "I don't think we've ever met before. I'm Heath Lawson, and you are?"

I hesitantly placed my palm in his and prayed to God that they weren't sweaty. "Macey Daniels. It's a pleasure to meet you."

Really, Mace, really?

I felt my cheeks heat up as Heath chuckled. He brought my hand up and pressed a small kiss to the row of my knuckles, his mesmerizing blue eyes never leaving mine. "I believe it's my pleasure, Macey."

Cue swooning here.

Suddenly, my hand was ripped out of Heath's as a familiar arm wrapped around my arm, pulling me away from Heath and behind his tall figure. Adrian stood glaring at Heath with eyes that looked ready to kill. Heath's confused expression was replaced with a mischievous smile when he looked at Adrian's fuming face.

"Aidy, buddy, it's been a while!" He exclaimed with mock excitement, smirking as he raised his arms for a hug. If anything, he was putting an invisible target on his internal organs by leaving his arms open like that.

"Heath," Adrian growled

Heath tsked, "Hostile. Not how I expected our joyous reunion."

"I was hoping to never have a reunion." Came Adrian's steely response. I raised an eyebrow at his bitterness. Where did this come from?

"Harsh."

"You've heard worse."

The two of them engaged in a heated staredown, both men daring each other to back down first. While as for me, I stood there watching the scene in front of me with a sense of confusion. Why did they look like they were ready to take an axe to the other's head and bury them at the nearest sandbox so they could dispose of their body as quick as possible?

Adrian was the one to speak first. "What were you doing talking to Macey?"

Heath smirked and shoved his hands into his dress pants. "Just as you said, Aidy. I was talking to Macey." His next words made Adrian twitch in anger. "A pretty girl should never be left alone, seeing as their date was too involved enjoying the company of other teenage girls."

"How do you know Macey is my date?" Adrian grounded out.

"Well, let's see…" Heath looked up, feigning deep concentration. "Maybe it's the protective grip you have on her right now, and the fact that I haven't said a word to annoy you yet and here you are, spitting out venomous words as if I've done harm to your family."

Registering the first part of Heath's words, Adrian loosened his vice grip and let go. I didn't hesitate as I walked between the two. I glared at Adrian and said, "Calm down, would you? Heath was just keeping me company while you took care of your fangirls."

His eyes narrowed. "Who's said are you on?" he asked.

"I'm not picking sides!" I exasperated, throwing my hands in the air and letting them fall limp at my sides. "Besides, you know I'm a big fan of Heath. The girls and I always watch his movies."

"Maybe now you know why I wasn't so thrilled with the fact," he grumbled.

That part was true. During a movie night when the guys (unfairly) lost the vote for what to watch that night, Adrian was noticeably rigid when Amber pulled out 'Trapped in Love.' The only way I got him to loosen up and stop snapping at us everytime we yelled out a compliment revolving Heath was when I snuggled up to him and kindly told him to shut up. It didn't work as effectively, but it was good enough at the time.

"Well it's nice to meet someone who could act so normal in front of a star like myself," Heath commented, nodding at me approvingly. It took a lot of self control to get myself to act as cool and composed as I did but hey, I'm not going to say anything.

"Maybe that's because her best friend is a star, too – a bigger one at that." Adrian responded cockily, wrapping an arm around my shoulders and pulling me to his side. I rolled my eyes.

"Alright, alright," Heath said, putting his hands up in a surrendering pose. "Put your claws back, kitty, I'm going to go sit down now. It was very nice to meet you, Macey."

I smiled and waved as Heath walked away. Once he was a few feet away, I slipped Adrian's arms off my shoulder and scowled at him. "What the hell is your problem? He wasn't assaulting me." I asked him angrily.

"He was flirting with you," he said hotly. "Heath is a complete ladies man, Mace. You don't know him like I do."

I laughed without humour. Who was he to judge after taking his sweet time give those girls his 'autograph.' Who knows what else he gave them when I wasn't looking. "That's rich coming from the guy who took thirty minutes to come back inside and join his date after having checking out your own fans."

Adrian opened his mouth to argue, but a voice I've come to hate reached my ears before he could.

"You two." I sighed audibly at the sound of Thomas' voice. Why was he here? Don't managers usually just make the agenda, not come along?

I crossed my arms as I turned to face Thomas. He huffed at the sight of me, and I raised an eyebrow, offended. Yeah, well I'm not so happy to see you to, so the feeling's mutual, buddy.

"Would you both just come and sit down. There are some important people here to see Adrian," Thomas ordered, gesturing with a hand. Adrian put a hand on the small of my back and lead me down as Thomas went ahead of us. As much as I loved meeting one of my favorite actors here, I wasn't so thrilled with everything else. This decision was proving to be even more worse with each passing minute.

"Adrian!" Someone bellowed. A man with thinning gray hair and a scruffy beard dressed in a tailor suit stood up and walked up to us. Adrian brushed past me to take the man in a friendly hug, patting each other on the back. Everyone else at the table stood up as well, besides a pretty young girl that looked to be the same age as Adrian and I. What movie have I seen her in?

Mostly everyone at the table were men, so each of them greeted Adrian with their own guy greetings. Adrian's smile softened as he glanced over at the girl.

She stared back at him with the same gentle expression. A giant smile erupted onto her face as she stood up and intertwined her fingers together.

"Hi, Adrian," she greeted, her voice as delicate as she looked.

"Kassie," he breathed, gazing at her with a fond expression. Never breaking eye contact, Adrian rounded the table and took Kassie in his arms. I was surprised when he picked her up and twirled her around, the both of them laughing happily. They didn't pull apart when Adrian said, "I missed you so much."

"I missed you, too!" she cried, burying her face in her shoulder.

I couldn't even describe the amount of awkwardness and jealousy that surged through me as I watched them. Kassie didn't seem familiar, but I could tell just by looking at her that she wasn't just a normal girl. Her designer halter dress was the definition of perfect as it fell down in ripples that represented the color a clear lake. Kassie's caramel brown hair was pulled back into an elegant ponytail with a few strands hanging out. Makeup didn't seem relevant with her flawless face.

I felt like a pimple-faced teenager next to this girl.

From the corner of my eye, I saw Thomas turn and try to hide the smirk that threatened to appear, but it was too late. I had already saw it.

Bastard.

I tried not to show any emotion as all the guests at the table smiled at the pair, and I even went out of the way of trying to tug the edge of my lips into one as well. I was sure it looked more like a grimace, though.

The ache in my chest didn't fade after Kassie and Adrian pulled away. "It's great to see you again, Kas," Adrian said.

"I know, I feel like I haven't seen you in so long! How's your break going?"

And from there it went.

Kassie and Adrian felt into a deep conversation about what's been going on in their lives. Apparently, Kassie has only been in commercials and that's why I didn't recognize her off the bat. After all, I usually change the channel when it's commercials before returning when the show comes back on. She was a friend of Cara's, and that's why she was here at the banquet. Though I have no idea how a girl as beautiful and sweet could be friends with someone like Cara.

The gentleman in the room sat down and listened as Adrian directed his stories to the rest of them. I was really reconsidering the bathroom thing. There was left over lasagna that was waiting for me at home, I didn't have to join everyone for dinner. I was about to attempt my getaway when the man with the bellowing voice pointed me out.

"And who's this lovely girl?" he asked, tilting his head to the side. He was probably trying to figure out where he's seen me before. Maybe he's seen me walking around the local supermarket, though I doubt he would be there in the first place. He was probably from LA.

Adrian's eyes flickered up to me and widened when he realized that I was still here. I kept the forced smile on my face and looked away from him, hurt that he was so caught up in his exhilarating stories to notice his date standing here silently. Now if only I could find out where the bathroom is.

Adrian stood up and wrapped an arm around my shoulder. The tensioning of my body when he did didn't go unnoticed by him, but he remained where he was. "Everyone, this is Macey. She's been my best friend since we were kids," Adrian explained, smiling down at me. I could almost hear Thomas' disgusted snort.

Besides getting the cold shoulder from him, everyone else at the table smiled politely. I was surprised when Kassie all of a sudden stood up and took me into a gentle hug. "It's nice to meet you," she said.

"It's nice to meet you, too," I answered, unintended confusion coating the words. When we pulled away, Adrian put a hand on Kassie's shoulder.

"She's a hugger," he explained, giving her a teasing smile.

Kassie rolled her eyes. "Bite me, Adrian."

"Well, if you say so."

"Adrian!" Kassie gasped and slapped Adrian's shoulder. He laughed in response before wrapping an arm around her and ruffling her elegant hair. "Oh my God, don't mess up my hair!" She squealed, trying to squirm her way out of his arms but failing miserably in the process. The weird ache in my chest was accompanied by a strong sense of anger while I watched the two mess around. Kassie seems more than welcome to keep Adrian busy, so why did Adrian have to invite me along?

"Alright, settle down," a man – probably in his mid thirties – said from across the table. He took a sip from his wine glass and shot them a pointed look. "This is a banquet, I expect you to act professionally. Just because you've been on break, Adrian, doesn't mean you can act like all those other rowdy teenagers."

An image of Brandon and Chase popped into my head. They were far from professional, but that's what made them fun. A pang inside of me wished I went with Kelly and the girls to the dance club that Dallas owned rather than here.

It was when Adrian and Kassie sat down that I realized that there was no seat available next to either of them. Neither of them noticed as they began another riveting conversation. The jolly man from before noticed and gestured for me to sit next to him.

"Come here, love," he said, patting the chair. I nodded in appreciation and kept my gaze low as I walked to my seat.

Everyone turned to their own small talk. I folded my hands together and observed the pristine silverware resting in front of me. Times like this were the ones where I wished the floor would open up and swallow me whole. The feeling of standing out while everyone went on with their lives was a feeling I really despised. I took the chance of glancing up at Kassie and Adrian. My eyes turned away when I saw Adrian's arm draped across Kassie's chair, their faces close as they talked animatedly.

I opted to twiddling my thumbs and trying not to make my fidgeting noticeable.

I don't know how long I spent circling my thumbs around each other. The overwhelming emotions building up inside of me was enough to consider the option of walking home in the pouring rain just so I could escape. I almost cried with relief when someone decided to break the growing twiddle thumb game time. Too bad it was thanks to a girl I was dreading to see.

Cara Pratt came strutting towards our table with such grace and confidence. Her classy white dress fell easily down to her knees and revealed heels that made me wonder how she kept her balance with shoes those high and skinny. Unlike Kassie, Cara wore her golden blonde hair pin straight in a length that brushed against her bare back.

Back to twiddling thumbs, it is.

"Adrian!" she exclaimed, opening her arms for a hug. Adrian stood up coolly and allowed Cara's lean arms to wrap around him. "It's great to see you again."

"Thank you, Cara, for inviting me tonight." The emotionless tone almost had me smiling. Almost. Greetings came from the men, and Kassie stood up to do that kiss-on-both-cheeks thing.

To be honest, I almost pissed my pants when Cara called me out. Really classy, Mace.

"And who's this?" Cara's voice became uptight and overly cheery, I tried not to wince when I looked up.

"Um…"

"Oh, that's just Macey. She came with me tonight."

Woah, hold the damn phone here. I didn't bother trying to hide the surprise on my face at Adrian's vague and dismissive reference to me. It may have not been a big deal to him, but that was a big blow considering what we've been through. As best friends and as… whatever the hell we were at the moment.

The older man who made the rowdy teenagers remark must have saw the resentment on my face because he took it upon himself to elaborate to Cara on who I really was. Respect your elders, kids. I was definitely respecting this one. Not that I'm calling him old. Definitely not old.

"She's Adrian's childhood best friend, if you will," he added, gesturing to Adrian.

Cara nodded slowly. Her eyes assessed me with a calculating look, a small smirk playing on her features. "Well it's very nice to meet Ardian's plus one tonight."

Well that hurt.

I gritted my teeth together and willed myself not to let the tears building up in my eyes fall. It's not what she said that hurt the most, but it was the fact that Adrian didn't come to my defense.

That's what hurt me the most.

The food was probably the highlight of my night. Adrian disregarded my existence while he kept up the conversation with Kassie. After Cara's remark and Adrian's ignorance to it, I began to count down the minutes of our two hours here. I was ready to just go home and bury myself under a pile of pillows and blankets. It was quite obvious that I was angry at my so called 'best friend,' and I was all on ignoring him and showing my hurt and frustration at him.

It was a half hour before eleven in the evening, and the announcement for why this banquet was being held in the first place was going to take place after desert. The red velvet cake did wonders on calming down the roaring waters inside of me. It wouldn't be long, though, before Adrian faced a real storm. And I'm not talking about the one going on outside.

The sound of a mic being tapped brought me out of my cake-induced trance. Cara stood at the front of the stage with a blinding smile that showed off her pearly whites. Kassie stood next to her on stage, looking rather shy and nervous.

"Welcome everyone," Cara spoke into the mic. "Thank you all for coming tonight." Applause erupted from the room for a moment before dying down and Cara spoke again. "You may all be wondering why I held a banquet tonight. But really, this is more of a celebration. For my dear friend Kassie is stepping out of the world commercials and into the real spotlight."

The two men next to me stood up suddenly and went to the stage. Arthur and Tom were their names. Tom, the jolly one, took the mic from Cara and spoke.

"Hello everyone. I'm sure all of you have heard about the movie production that will be taking place in just a few months. I, as the executive producer, and the director of this soon-to-be blockbuster movie, Arthur," He gestured to the rowdy teen referencer. "am proud to announce that Miss. Kassie Bell will be the star of the upcoming movie, 'Through the Eyes of Willow.'"

Cheers, hoots, and hollers filled the room. I even found myself clapping at the remarkable news. 'Through the Eyes of Willow' was said to be the next hit romance movie. Critics think that this will be Arthur's best work yet. Kassie seemed perfect for the main character, and she's exactly how I imagined the headstrong but gentle Willow to be.

The applause soon died down after Arthur and Tom talked more about the movie. Everyone returned to their own business once they finished. Multiple people went to congratulate Kassie. My butt had fallen asleep for having it glued to this chair for hours, barely even moving any part of my body besides my hands and head. I contemplated going up there to say congratulations too, but of course, I remained where I was and watched instead.

Jumping up from his seat, Adrian rushed to the side of the stage where Kassie was and enveloped her in a big hug. There was an uproar of hey's and hello's when Adrian made an appearance. Several girls squealed and pulled Adrian into a hug; guys coming to do one of those manly pat on the back hugs. He kept his arm around Kassie in the process. His eyes glowed as he talked to his old friends and acquaintances. I stood up to go join Adrian before I realized that I was really not needed. Not to mention that I didn't belong, and it would only make this night all the more embarrassing for me. As if I haven't been embarrassed enough.

I sighed and excused myself before going on that long awaited search for the bathroom. It just so happened to be right next to the stage where the group of people were celebrating. I stared at them for second, and realized that he Adrian wouldn't notice even if I waved a sign in his face and yodeled off key.

As expected, I slipped past them easily and walked down the hall to the bathroom. It was empty, thankfully, and I breathed in a sigh of relief, fancy soap entering my lungs. I carelessly threw my clutch on the counter after taking my phone out.

I dialed Amber and prayed that she would answer.

Ring one... Ring two... Ring Three...

"Hello?"

"Amber," I sighed, my voice coming out as a broken whisper. I leaned my back against the cool countertop and looked up in attempt to keep the tears at bay.

Loud music and voices filled the background. "Macey?" Amber shouted into the phone. "Hold on, let me go somewhere quiet ... Excuse me, excuse me... Exc –"

"Holy shit, move!" Dylan's voice yelled. I laughed lightly at her bluntness, a sad smile tugging at the ends of my lips. I really should've ditched.

After a few moments, the sound died down and Amber spoke again, "Mace, hey! How's the banquet going?"

"I want to leave," I replied straight to the point.

"What? Why?" Brynn's voice spoke.

I shook my head, looking towards the door just in case someone came in. "Let's just say I don't really belong here. And Adrian's not really helping me feel better, either."

"That little idiot," a voice muttered. Then Kelly spoke, "What did he do?"

From there I told them about Adrian's sweetness from the car to the ladies man after we got out. I told them about his hostile words to Heath (and promised to tell them more about meeting the hot actor), about his friendliness to Kassie, his plain and dismissive reference to Cara, and – more importantly – not coming to my defense when I was referred to someone of little value.

Telling the girls about Adrian ignoring my presence made it seem more real. I confirmed everything I thought was going to happen. He really did have another side of him. The Adrian I knew wouldn't let me feel so alone and out of place. The Adrian I knew wouldn't ignore me and refer to me as just a 'plus one.'

And the worst part? I don't know which side is the true Adrian.

"What was the point of me going with him?" I asked, staring at my own reflection. "He hasn't even talked to me all night."

Kelly growled through the other line. "That idiot. Go tell him that your two hours are up and give him what he deserves. It's pretty damn low of him to do that to you."

"I don't know, Kel." I frowned. "He doesn't seem to mind staying for longer than he said. He's probably having a grand time," I added sarcastically, referring to all the attention he's been giving Kassie. Thinking about how close we've been the past few weeks makes me feel like he's cheating on me. But that's not the case, now is it? I knew this was a bad idea in the first place. If Adrian wanted to really be with me, he would've asked to be official. Not sneak around like we're doing now. "I feel stupid for being jealous. It's not like we were serious!"

"With all the kissing and touching going on, I would think he wanted you to be his girlfriend." I could hear the frown in Amber's voice.

"Yeah," I answered quietly. "I thought that, too."

"This is exactly why you should tell him that your two hours are up," Kelly pushed.

I frowned. "Why?"

"Just do it!" she insisted.

"Alright," I complied hesitantly. I took a deep breath after hanging up the phone. I don't know why Kelly was so adamant on my asking Adrian to leave. But I wanted to leave anyways, so might as well get this over with. Mustering up the little courage I had left, I exited the bathroom.

The group had disassembled when I came out. I walked back to the table expecting to find Kassie and Adrian, but they weren't there either. Arthur and Tom were, though, but I got a negative response when I asked if they have seen Adrian or Kassie.

I wandered around the banquet a little in search for the two. Puffing out my cheeks, I huffed when I couldn't find either of them.

"Looking for someone?" I jumped at the voice, and turned to see Heath standing behind me, smirking.

"Have you seen Adrian or Kassie?" I asked.

"Oh, those two love birds?" Heath snorted. "They left after the big announcement. Something about going back to Kassie's hotel."

My stomach dropped. "W-What?" I stuttered. Did Adrian leave me here just so he could hook up with the next big thing?

"Yeah, they left just a few minutes ago," Heath said slowly.

I let those words process and fought back the tears. I couldn't believe it.

"It was really nice to meet you, Heath, I'm a really big fan," I told him before walking quickly outside. With tears blurring my vision, I pushed open the doors and stepped into the rain. I didn't care that it was pouring heavily outside. I had to know if what Heath said was true.

I really didn't want to believe it. I really didn't want to believe that my best friend would leave me at a banquet that I didn't want to come to in the first place to hook up with some other girl. I didn't want to believe that Adrian was that kind of guy.

But, apparently, he was. The spot where Adrian's car had been parked was now empty, a puddle of water in it's place. The overwhelming wave of sorrow and disbelief finally let the tears flow freely down my cheeks. I shook my head, letting a few sobs slip.

I took shelter again and took out my phone, thankful that no water could slip through the clutch. None of the girls answered when I called and my body began to shake with the droplets racing down my body. I couldn't go inside now. Adrian may have ditched me for the better deal, but I still had my dignity left.

Wrapping my arms around myself, I walked out into the rain once more, and kept on walking.

Chapter 24

In hindsight, walking home in the pouring rain was probably the worst ideas I've ever had through anger and disappointment. Drop after drop pounded down on me without stop, rolling down my skin and seeping through the fabric of my dress and bra and underwear. Not the greatest feeling. You know, feeling like you're taking a swim fully clothed and standing up?

I was fully convinced that, any moment now, I was going to slip and crack my head open with the aching heels that were becoming harder and harder to walk in through the multiple puddles flooding the cracks and dents in the ground. Let the blood run through the stream of water rushing down the side of the sidewalk and wash it down to the drains. If I don't die out here because of the dangers of nature or the oncoming flu that I was going to leave me close to heavens door for days – exaggeratedly speaking, of course – then I was surely going to collapse from fatigue and utter depression.

My tears that were disguised as just another drop of rain sliding down my cheeks had stopped, but the ache and betrayal was still fresh in my heart. It was not at all smart of me to walk willingly out into the cold, rainy evening where shadows lurking around a corner could jump me at any time. Not to mention I have no coat, no umbrella, and no transportation except the two body parts that were designed to allow me my own sort of way of moving from one place to another. I don't think using my legs – that currently have aching heels attached to their friends down below – as a way to bring me several miles back to my home was wise, either.

I mean, it was raining. Since when do I get this stupid to step out and disregard all common sense for my safety by walking out in this weather and into the night? I could have waited at the banquet and break the girls' phones with my many calls and texts, or I could have gone in and asked for a ride.

But both those options, though I hate to admit it, were blatantly ignored because I wanted to save myself from the embarrassment of being ditched by a boy who so strongly suggested that he cares about me, and savor my pride and dignity.

And now that I'm shivering in wet cold clothes down to my core, I realize how ridiculous I really am. Ridiculous for trusting Adrian and going to this banquet, and ridiculous for having a guy make me act out of painful emotions rather than conscious. You think you know better until something makes you forgot all of that. Adrian lead me on to believe that he wasn't that guy who let stardom get to his head and change whom he really is. He made me think that we could have get past our crushes and be something more.

Well I got news for him. Leaving me at a banquet that I highly refused to attend in the first place and driving off to hook up with the next big star of an upcoming movie contradicts all of that. I felt like an idiot sitting there and twiddling my thumbs while he talked it up with all those people, not even objecting to Cara's words or giving me any more meaning to him. He didn't need to add to the blow by abandoning me.

I huffed angrily at myself, stopping in the middle of the sidewalk and carelessly ripping the heels off my feet, not caring what could puncture me in the foot as I continued to walk. I should have let go of my feelings for Adrian. I didn't need this whole teenage drama! Letting go of whatever I felt wouldn't have brought on this whole 'I'm not good enough for him' feeling and the jealousy building up inside of me as I thought about God knows whatever those two are doing at Kassie's hotel.

These last few weeks were nothing to him. Thrown to the wind as he rejoiced with his Hollywood life and his old player ways.

I told you so, the voice whispered in my head.

Yes. It definitely told me so.

"Excuse me," someone said. A woman carrying an umbrella and a bag full of groceries stood looking at me with an expression of disbelief and concern. I know what she's thinking. I looked like the perfect picture of a young girl who just got abandoned by her boyfriend on the night of a special occasion, and now the girl was completely heartbroken as she walked home in the rain with a glum look on her face.

If I was thirteen and dumped at a school dance, then this would be the time where I would call my dad for him to come to his little girl's rescue. But my dad was working the graveyard shift tonight, so...

"Yes?" I asked, straightening my spine.

"You really shouldn't be walking out here this late at night. Especially with the rain," she told me, a frown settling on her lips. "Do you need to use my cellphone to call someone?"

I smiled at the lady's offer. "No, thank you," I answered, glad that someone was offering to help in my time of need. However, I did not want to waste anymore of her time. "I'm just going to meet my friend down the street, so she could take me home," I lied.

"All right, but do get home and try to warm up. You're sure to catch a cold soon," she said, frowning a bit.

I pushed through my miserable state and gave her the best convincing smile I could. "I will, thank you very much."

I waited until sound of her car faded behind the pitter patter of the rain. Quite reluctantly, I put my heels back on and walked as quickly and safely down the street and under the shelter of a chinese restaurant. There was no using of walking into any store while drenched with water, so I took out my phone again and called Amber again.

"Please, pick up," I whispered quietly to myself. The shivers made my body tremble uncontrollably, resembling the shaking of a chihuahua.

Five more unanswered calls later and all hope was drained away with the rest of the running water. My best friend ditched me for a booty call, it was late at night, nobody is answering my calls of help, and the rainy weather was increasing my chances of catching hypothermia.

I honestly felt the need to cry all over again.

Falling back against the cold cemented wall, I winced when my head fell defeatedly against it and came in contact with the hardness. I sunk down to my feet and leaned my back against the wall. New tears sprung to my eyes as an overwhelming feeling hit me like each rain drop pounding against the bare streets. Many of the stores around me were closed. Even so, I have a strong feeling that I would be kicked out of a store for dripping all over their floors.

I bit my lip harshly, wrapping an arm around me in desperate attempt to stop the shaking of my body while I held my phone out in front of me. My thumb seemed to slow with the temperature it was exposed to, moving at a snails pace as I scrolled through my contacts.

I hovered across Chase's number. At this point, I was in a deep state of distraught. Would he still be awake? Hell, if Chase doesn't answer then I will call my dad, work or not. I'm a popsicle in the making, as it is. I tapped Chase's number and brought the phone to my ear. My teeth chattered loudly as I listened to the rings.

I was just about to break into tears when at long last, Chase answered.

"Macey?" he responded groggily.

This time, I nearly cried out of relief. "C-Chase!" I croaked, slumping back against the wall.

"Not to rain on your parade," oh, very funny. "but, what's up? Everything okay?" he asked.

"I-I need you to p-pick m-me up," I told him, my voice stilly thick with emotion despite the stutter.

"What?" I heard some ruffling through the other line, and then a thud. He cursed quietly to himself. "Hold on, what's going on? Where are you?"

"Just p-please pick me up. I-I'll explain t-to you later, I c-can't –" My voice caught in my voice as another sob racked my body. I just wanted to get out of here. My emotions were going haywire, a pounding headache adding to my list of physical and emotional problems right now. All I could think of was how stupid I was.

Stupid, stupid, stupid!

"Okay, okay," Chase answered hurriedly. "I'm coming. Where are you?"

Pushing my emotions away, I quickly told Chase where I was. It was by sheer luck that he knew exactly where I was. Miami has been my home since I was born into this world, and it shamed me to know I had no idea where I stood in my own hometown. That's what I get for crying and walking with no conscious. All stores were closed and the idea of moving back out into the rain made me want to cry all over again.

I sunk down and rubbed the palms of my hands into my moist eyes. I needed to get a grip. The heartache from earlier only grew with each minute I spent out here. What an ass of a best friend he is!

A shuddering breath left my lips as I stared down at a single puddle on the concrete floor. It wasn't just the fact that he was my best friend and suddenly left without another girl. Friends ditch you at a party to go hook up with a random stranger all the time and they get over it. It's not the case here. Not completely, anyway.

It only made the hurt a thousand times stronger to get rid of the denial and face the reality of this situation. Adrian and I have been a hell lot more intimate than we should be. We admitted our feelings for each other – that there's more than just this puppy love. And the worst part? I didn't give up on us that time at the beach. All of what Adrian said we could have been was blocked by the worry of my ending up getting kicked to the curb for the better deal in the end.

It was pain I could have ignored, but I took the risk of getting hurt anyways. I guess it wasn't worth the risk after all.

The distant sound of a car coming pulled me out of my depressing thoughts. Two headlights shined through the darkness of the night, piercing through the droplets and giving me my own spotlight. I shakily stood up, my legs trembling from under me. The familiar dark paint of Chase's car came into a view. I don't think I've ever been so relieved to see that dork until now. It stopped a few feet away, and Chase jumped out no later than three seconds later.

"What the fuck are you doing out here?" Chase yelled through the loud pounding of the rain. I couldn't find it in me to explain, not until I could feel my body again. I took a step towards him and immediately stumbled. Chase ran up and caught me in his arms. My body sagged into his in relief, seeing his body was the only source of heat I've had in the last forty five minutes. "Shit, Macey! You're as cold as ice!" He swore, wrapping both his arms around me and tugging me to his car.

A few stumbles, slips, and colorful choice words later, Chase had managed to get me inside his car before he ran to the drivers side. I shivered hectically in the leather seat as Chase tore his hoodie over his head and pulled it over my own frigid body. The water seeped through the material, but with the slight warmth that it gave me, I couldn't care less. Chase turned the temperature knob and bumped up the heat full blast.

"God, Macey," he said, taking me in his arms. "You could have freezed out there. What were you doing out so late? None of the shops are open and, if you haven't noticed, there's a rainstorm outside."

"Way to state the obvious," I mumbled into his chest, not bothering to explain why I was outside in the first place. Chase understood and held me tightly, resting his chin on top of my head and rubbing up and down my arm. It got warmer and warmer inside the car, and the feeling in my body slowly returned.

I sniffled against Chase's chest and let my eyes flutter shut. Out of all the people who could have been here in my time of need, Chase left the comfort of his own home and drove in a rainstorm to come and get me. Not Kelly, not the girls, and definitely not Adrian.

Chase. My best friend from middle school whom I grew apart from since we entered high school. The same perverted idiot that started a food fight in eighth grade and poured spoiled milk down my shirt.

"Thank you." A whisper was all I could manage, but he heard me. I felt him shift, resting his cheek on the top of my head as he replied.

"No problem, Daniels."

The moment dragged. I stayed wrapped up in Chase's arms, stealing his body heat and taking in the warm air blowing through the vent. Soon, the trembling ceased, and my body defrosted itself, leaving a still hurting heart in its place. The slight dampening of Chase's shirt was not because of the rain still absorbed in my clothes. I felt tears well up in my eyes for another round, making me sniffle quietly.

"Adrian ditched me at the banquet to go hook up with another girl," I stated quietly.

"What?" The disbelief was clear in his voice, making me snort in agreement. Adrian lead everyone to believe that he had feelings for me, didn't he?

"That was only the icing on the cake," I muttered dejectedly. Chase listened as I told him the story of the banquet, from Adrian's flirtatiousness with his fangirls and the brushing off my presence pretty much the whole time. Chase had stiffened considerably since I started and his arms tightened around me to the point where it felt like he was trying to morph us into one body.

"That asshole." I felt him shake his head. "I can't believe he ditched you for a one night stand."

"There might be more," I sighed. "They seemed to really click earlier."

"Well, you two click."

I snorted.

"You still didn't have to walk out into the rain!" Chase cried. "Stupid." I breathed a laugh when he tapped my head in weak discipline. I pulled away and rested my head on his shoulder. Chase left an arm around my shoulder as he reached and turned down the temperature so it didn't seem like an in-car sauna.

"I don't think it's really safe to be driving right now." I frowned.

"It's not." He clicked his tongue. The windows were completely blurred with water. The front windshields swiped back and forth, feverishly trying to clear the drops blocking our vision of outside. I sighed and crossed my arms across my chest, sinking back into Chase.

The both of us jumped when a sudden ringtone filled the car. Chase fumbled in his pocket and took out his phone. "It's Amber."

My phone died somewhere after calling Chase. The level of gratitude that the device hadn't died on me before I called for help was beyond comprehendible. It irked me that the girls hadn't answered my (beyond several) calls after they knew my predicament with Adrian at the banquet.

Chase switched the phone to speaker and held it out between us. "How may I help you this lovely, stormy night, Amberkins?" I rolled my eyes. "I seem to be playing Prince Charming tonight. Shall I save you next?"

Amber's hysterical shout could have broken an eardrum. "Cut it out, Chase! Is Macey with you?" She shrieked, borderline hysteria.

"She is currently ruining my leather seats, so, yes, she is with me."

I frowned, turning to look at the streaks of wet coating the black leather seats of Chase's car. Oops. I'll just rob Adrian's wallet. Part one of never-forgiving-him.

I could almost hear see the relief on Amber's face. Then, Kelly spoke through the phone. "Let us talk to her."

"I'm right here," I drawled tiredly. "Thanks for answering your phones, guys, greatly appreciate your help."

"We're so sorry!" Amber shouted from the background.

"We got a little distracted. Dallas was showing us the controls on the DJ table," Brynn explained, a cringe in her voice.

"You guys are just as bad as Adrian," Chase tsked, playing the guilt card.

"About that. . ." I perked at Kelly's angered voice. "I may or may not have called Adrian."

"What?" I grabbed the phone from Chase. "Why would you do that?"

"Besides Kelly going off of her drunken state," Dylan started, "she went all batshit crazy on him. It was kind of amusing."

"Kelly," I groaned.

"Look, Adrian was supposed to make this one of the best nights of your life, not leave you to drown in rain and tears."

Chase made a face. "How was being dragged to some banquet going to be the highlight of their lives?"

Kelly sputtered over the phone as if she was trying to grab the answer from thin air. "I-I… Nothing! Look, tonight was supposed to be fun, okay?"

Oh, I'm sure. "So, what? You interrupted his 'happy fun time' with Kassie?" I retorted, Amber's words appearing in my memory. Who would have known that those words weren't meant for Adrian and I, but reserved for a girl who obviously has a history with Adrian – a pretty close one, may I add.

"I'm not sure. I hung up on him after yelling at him."

I suppressed the urge to slam my head on the dashboard repeatedly. How did Kelly even get drunk when they were at Dallas' dance club? Last time I checked, soda and water was the only beverages typed across the menus.

"Please tell me your home," I sighed. A throbbing headache was slowly wearing my already exhausted body to the breaking point. Though, I'm pretty sure I hit rock bottom more than once tonight.

"We're back at Kelly's," Brynn replied. "It was the closest."

"I don't think you guys should be driving very far, it seems really dangerous to be driving out in this weather," Amber told us, concerned.

Chase straightened up in his seat and leaned closer to the front window. He pressed his hand against the foggy glass and swiped back and forth. "I think we should head over there. It's getting pretty bad, and it's the closest place we could get to."

I didn't like the sound of that. A sinking feeling in my stomach rebelled against the idea of going to Adrian's house where he could come home late from his oh-so fun time with Kassie. What would he think about the giant slumber party going on in his house?

But, most importantly, as I sit here still soaking wet with the memories of tonight still sharp in my mind, the thought of seeing Adrian with a fresh wound in my heart makes me want to cry. I'm more into ignoring him for as long as I possibly can. Forgiving him is most definitely not on my to-do list.

"Macey, if he really is where you think he is, maybe he won't come home until tomorrow." The statement was like pouring salt on the wound. "We could head off by tomorrow."

I pressed my fingers to my temple and glanced out the window. "Just drive, Chase," I ordered quietly. A scorching hot bath and comfy blankets were calling to me. At least inanimate objects don't have the ability to break my heart.

The drive to the mansion was quite daunting. Treacherous claps of thunder boomed loudly, as if the sky was in an angry state and demanded to let itself be heard. Streaks of lightning racing across the night were visible through the rain attacking the blurry windows. Thick clouds blocked the biggest source of light in the sky, leaving the weak lamp post bulbs to vaguely outline the roads as we slowly drived down the wet pavement.

Chase leaned far out of his seat, squinting through the fast swipes of the windshield wipers as he tried to make out our location. The sick, sluggish feeling accompanied the fatigue and dispirited emotions coursing through my body. The dashboard clock read it was near one in the morning, and the cold-to-come was already a work in progress.

Arms crossed and eyes puffy from previous crying sessions, I sat limply in my seat with my head resting against the cool glass window and watched as multiple raindrops raced one another.

My whole demeanor perked at the sight of the mansion. There was nothing more I wanted but to bundle up in warm clothes and let myself drift off to sleep and escape all the overwhelming feelings that's been bothering me since I left the mansion all those hours ago.

For the first time in my life, there was a sense resentment as I stepped out into the rain again, chilly air and pelting rain attacking my legs and this time more-covered top once again. Together with Chase, the two of us made a break for the front door that suddenly swung open as we approached. Kelly, decked out in a hoodie and sweats, cried out when she saw me.

"Macey," she gasped in horror. "You look absolutely horrid!"

"Thanks," I responded with a trace of sarcasm. The warmth of the mansion welcomed us effortlessly and an instant wave of comfort washing over me. I hugged my arms closer to body, Chase's hoodie damp against my already wet body.

I need a warm bath. And some pain killers. And a remedy for heartbreaks.

That last one seems farfetched, unfortunately. It's a shame; there's a market for it.

"Goddamn, Adrian, why'd you have to screw up?" Chase muttered to himself as he wiped his arms free of raindrops.

"I'd like to know that, too." I didn't mean for it to come out the way it did. I wanted to be angry, completely and utterly pissed. I should have the desire to punch him in the family jewels and set Lulu off at him – though, I doubt she would do much harm.

But, no. It came out as a broken whisper. The simple but powerful action that brought traitorous tears to my eyes for the umpteenth time that night.

"Oh, Mace," Kelly whispered, pulling me into her tight embrace.

I sobbed quietly into her shoulder. "I feel so stupid. There was nothing going on between us; I have no right to act like a jealous girlfriend." I cried ashamedly.

"You have every right to feel this way!" Kelly retorted sharply. "He wouldn't be stringing you along if he didn't have feelings for you. I know he likes you, and that's what makes this even more ridiculous!"

"Macey!"

Brynn, Amber, and Dylan came running down the stairs all out of their party clothes and into whom I assumed were Kelly's pajamas. Without warning, all three of them attacked me into a much needed hug. It was the most benevolent gesture I've had in the last few hours. Besides getting rescued from my idiotic decision, of course.

"Are you okay?" Brynn asked.

"You're so wet," Dylan added with a slight cringe.

"This is all Adrian's fault!" Amber cried out vehemently. "That. . . T-That. . . Fudger."

Oh, Amber.

Chase wrinkled his nose. "Did you mean fucker?"

"Yes!"

He chuckled, shaking his head humourously. "Even at the worst times, you can't utter one bad word."

"This isn't about me," Amber huffed, crossing her arms and shooting Chase a half-hearted glare. Then, she turned to me. "Are you all right?"

"Not really," I mumbled, clutching my forehead as the headache pounded restlessly.

"Do you wanna talk about it?" Brynn asked tentatively.

I shook my head vigorously, heading towards the stairs. "Not at all. I'm going to shower."

"Use my bathroom. I'll leave some clothes out for you," Kelly called out softly. I replied with a simple thank you and sluggishly made my way up the stairs.

Arriving at Kelly bathroom, I was horrified by the reflection staring back at me. My brown hair was wildly tangled and matted around my head in clumps. Traces of makeup were smudged against my paler-than-normal skin, most washed off by the constant water running down my face and cheeks. Puffy and blood-shot, my eyelids felt heavy with exhaustion. A deep frown engraved the lower half of my face, my lips very much chapped from the cold.

My frown only deepened at the sight. I looked like shit because of a guy. A guy that was able to influence me to do something as stupid as walking deep into town with no way to protect me from a rainstorm.

Pathetic.

Shaking my head ashamedly at my reflection, I stripped down to nothing and stepped into the shower and let the warm droplets run down my body. But I knew, no matter how hot the temperature of this shower was, it may be able to heat my body back to normal, but it won't be able to heat the coldness in my heart.

A sweater and soft pajama pants lay folded at the foot of Kelly's bed, a pair of fuzzy red socks on top. I quickly threw those on – immensely grateful for the fuzzy socks – and decided to blowdry my hair to speed of the process of heading off to bed. I've had enough of getting wet for tonight.

In just a matter of ten minutes, I was warmly dressed and my hair was was dry. Fizzy, but dry nonetheless. Now, I was ready to drop dead into bed. The headache had ceased to a dull throb, but the running of my nose and scratchiness in my throat did nothing to ease my pain.

I was all for crashing in one of the guestrooms when I heard yelling from downstairs.

"I can't believe you had the actual nerve to leave Macey there!"

My heart sunk. It couldn't be…

"It's not what you think!" The voice snapped back angrily, and I felt my heart stutter painfully. He was back already? What happened to sneaking about before he comes home?

Slowly, I edged closer to the stairs and creeped down step by step as quietly as I could. Chase and the rest of the girls stood behind Kelly, glaring bitterly at said heartbreaker.

Adrian stood alone, his jacket gone and his tie loosened around his neck. His hair was unkempt, making me think of Kassie running her hands through it continuously. I scolded my heart for clenching painfully.

You shouldn't feel that way.

"You didn't even defend her back there," Kelly remarked, outraged. "You were too busy flirting with Kassie and your fangirls to notice your best friend was still there."

" I didn't do that. I was just catching up with everyone, Kelly!"

"That gave you no reason to abandon Macey at a banquet she didn't even want to go to."

Adrian let out a frustrated growl. "I told you it's not what you think."

"Whatever the hell your reasons are, you still left Macey out in the rain." Dylan snapped, taking a step forward. Amber grabbed her arm and gently tugged her back.

"Do you know how freezing she was when I had to pick her up in a goddamn rainstorm?" Chase asked, calmly. "If you wanted to go have a booty call –"

"It's not my fault Macey was stupid enough to go out in a fucking rainstorm, all right?" Adrian shouted, his tone so enraged and irritated beyond belief that it made everyone go dead silent.

In fact, it was so silent that everyone was able to hear the hurt gasp that unintentionally slipped through my lips.

Everyone snapped their heads in the direction of the noise. Each of their faces were blurry with the unshed tears, but I could see the dread flood Adrian's face as he caught sight of me.

"Macey. . ." He started, but I was already running up the stairs. "Macey, wait!"

I didn't listen. I pressed a hand against my mouth in attempt to hold back another sob as I quickly made my way towards the guest room next to Kelly's. A hand enclosed around my wrist before I could and pulled me back. I collided into a hard chest and a hand came up to cup my cheek.

I looked up at Adrian with angry eyes, my cheeks becoming wet with another round of tears. Only these tears I didn't reject the purpose of their appearance.

"Macey –"

No. I didn't want to hear his lies. I've had enough of his bullshit tonight. My heart thudded hard against my chest, and my mind was so erratic that any self-control flew out the window. So, I did the first thing that crossed through my mind.

I brought my hand up and slapped him across the face.

Absolute shock crossed his features as he stared at me. We've had fights before, but never before have I slapped him like I just did. And I honestly didn't care.

"Don't you dare," I spat, tearing myself away from him. Without a glance back, I slammed the door loudly and collapsed onto the bed covers, never ending tears running down my cheeks.

Pathetic.

Chapter 25

Can you imagine what has been playing through my mind as I lay here, staring at the ceiling?

Tiny, furious cavemen decide to sneak into your room at night with their giant wooden sticks slung over their shoulders. Bare-feet and as big as big foot, they begin to march into your ear and towards your brain. From there, they start to take out their personal anger onto your poor brain by taking multiple swings with no intention of stopping.

Now, add a horrible storm in your stomach, invisible corks being stuffed into both your nostrils, your whole body becoming a bunsen burner, jelly limbs, and the end result of a jackhammer on your heart, and that is the exact description on how I've been feeling since I pried my crusty eyes open the next morning.

I tried sitting up, and then the world beginning to spin uncontrollably forced me to establish a great bond with the bed I currently lie on. Other than that, the birds are chirping, the sun is shining, and loud arguing is going on in the hall! It's starting off to be a very lovely day, indeed.

Okay. Sarcasm aside, with the way I'm feeling, this bed will sooner or later become my death bed.

It took a herculean effort to haul myself in a sitting position, and even then I felt like I was going to pass out. I didn't realize I locked the door after my episode last night until light knocking was heard after shouting could no longer be heard.

I whimpered at the simple noise. Why can't the world shut up and leave me in my misery?

"Mace?" a voice called out gently. "Are you alright?"

"Are you alive is more the question you should be asking," someone said.

Opening my mouth up to shoo them off with a nasty remark, words fail me as a throaty cough almost has me hacking up a lung. Well, at least they got their answer. I could practically see the cringe using my x-ray vision that my ill state has given me. Right, so, no x-ray vision. But I'm almost sure they're cringing at my tuberculosis-like cough.

"Can you reach the door and unlock it?" Brynn asked through the door.

"Do you want me to faint as I try?"

Quick silence, and then, "Tell Kelly to go get the key before Macey dies in there," Amber ordered.

"I don't think that'll happen considering she's planning her own brother's death," Dylan replied casually. I stared blankly at the door, feeling a pang in my already broken heart. One of the tiny men must have moved on to jumping on the broken shards. Little bastard.

The girls' muttered words were muffled from the thick wood currently separating them from taking me to the nearby hospital. Well, my house, at least. The throbbing increased slightly as I fell back against the mountain of pillows. I breathed out a groan and squeezed my eyes shut. I knew standing out in the rain was going to come back and bite me in the ass, but I didn't know it was going to sink its teeth in deep and leave a huge mark.

The overbearing, sick feeling prevented me from any peaceful sleep; however, with all the crying and exhaustion of yesterday, I fell into a deep slumber. A slumber where I felt like I didn't slip off into dreamland in the first place and, instead, just stood at the other side of it, staring in like a moron rather than stepping into serenity.

"What are you going?" said a new voice. Chase.

"We're trying to get inside and save Macey from going to the light, Chase, would you like to help?" Dylan replied smartly.

Instead of snapping back at her, I could hear the smirk in Chase's voice as he said, "I'd love to."

I flopped my head to the side and kept my eyes on the door, half expecting Chase to crash through the door rather than going through a more civil way, which is asking Kelly for the key. Of course, they'll have to interrupt her evil planning...

There are negative factors, however, that make me want to a) stay here in my sick and depressing state; or b) throw myself in the car and floor it home. Weak and dying, I'd rather stay here. The thought of getting up and crawling down the tall flight of stairs isn't very appealing to me right now. In fact, I'm sure I'll throw up after taking a step. This bed is more than happy to keep me captive until I'm well enough to get back up on my feet. Connie has her day off today and rocks an amazing chicken soup recipe.

But, if I stay here, the chances of Adrian coming in to throw excuses my way is even more worse. Like, the little caveman recruiting even bulkier friends to come and break through my forehead kind of worse.

A clicking sound tugged me back to reality, much to my dismay. I watched in amazement as the door was pushed open and a triumphant looking Chase stood there with his chest puffed out and eyes glowing bright. A bobby pin was jammed into the golden lock.

Huh. Maybe he took the criminal way, then.

The triumphant smirk Chase had just five seconds ago twisted into one of disgust. "Woah, you look like crap."

My hero. How sweet.

Luckily, Dylan came from behind him and shoved him into the door as she walked past. Amber rushed to my side with a concerned look. Brynn was soon by my side and frowning down at my figure.

"Mace, you really don't look good," Brynn said gently, sitting at the edge of the bed. If I could, I'd probably shove her off the bed for stating the complete obvious. But since I don't have the energy, I narrow my eyes at all of them in a glare.

"Wow, thanks. I thought I looked like a princess today, but I guess I was wrong." My voice dripped with sarcasm, just like the runny nose I was starting to get. Chase noticed and handed me a tissue. All of us cringed as I blew all the contents out onto the one flimsy tissue. Chase, looking even more disgusted than ever, handed me the whole box of tissues and took a massive step back. I guess my Knight and Shining Armor from last night has hung up his gear.

Amber put the back of her hand on my forehead and gasped, "Macey, you're burning up!"

"I didn't notice."

Chase snorted from across the room. When did he get all the way over there? "You're so sarcastic when you're sick, Mace."

"Sorry," I murmured, hugging a pillow to my chest. Being awake for more than three hours and not taking care of my sick feelings is finally taking its toll on me. "I really don't feel good," I whimpered as my head pounded painfully. It only worsened at the loud knocking at the door.

I was surprised to see Oliver leaning his head inside the door. He grimaced as I let out another throaty cough. "Ooo," he drawled. "You don't look so well, kid."

I sighed.

"Yeah, she knows," Chase chimed oh-so helpfully.

"Well, I'm here by Connie's orders." Oliver stepped inside the room and walked to the side of the bed. He placed a hand over my forehead and frowned. It's not often that Oliver frowns. It makes him look more serious than he really is. He tsked as I turned away and coughed harshly into the covers. "I'm to take you downstairs. Kelly just finished ranting to Connie, and she's making her famous chicken soup. She wants to check up on you there."

"So, you know about last night?" I asked. He nodded and smiled softly.

"Kelly didn't go to bed until late into the morning because she was telling me about it. You know how she is, has to get that steam out of her." I smiled at the affectionate and humorous tone as he talked about Kelly. That only brought me back to Adrian's actions and how he dismissively referred to who I was. I think the fellow stomping on my heart brought a friend just now.

"He's not there, is he?" Dylan snarled distastefully.

"I don't think Macey wants to see him just yet, especially how she's feeling," Amber added, placing a comforting hand on my shoulder.

"I didn't see him when I came down. I'll just kick him out if he comes in the room, all right? You really need to get looked at." said Oliver, a stern, fatherly tone taking over. I nodded weakly.

Amber and Brynn stood at both sides of me and helped as I sat up. I pressed my hands against my head and shut my eyes as a dizzy feeling took over. Slowly but surely, I was taking each step at a time as I made my journey downstairs. Oliver looked about ready to scoop me up and take me down himself if not for my saying that he would get thrown up on if he tried. That convinced him enough, but he stayed close on our heels as the girls helped me down.

I was beyond lightheaded by the time I entered the kitchen. My butt landing on the kitchen stool acted as my anchor.

Don't throw up, don't throw up, please do not throw up. I chanted to myself as I gripped my head. Everything looks so expensive and pristine, vomit definitely won't be the best throw pillow.

"Oh, sweetie!" a voice exclaimed. Connie's cold fingers wrapped around my wrist and gently pried it from my head. Concern shone deeply in her eyes, she brought a hand up to my face and felt my cheeks and forehead. Murmuring to herself, she walked over to a nearby cabinet and shuffled through until she pulled out a black pouch. From that pouch, Connie took out a thermometer and plopped it under my mouth. "Keep that in your mouth for a minute, okay?"

I nodded and held the the object in place in my mouth. It was then Kelly abruptly entered the kitchen from the back door, thoroughly looking pissed. All looks of anger disappeared when she saw me looking as sick as a dog. "Oh, Jesus," she breathed, dropping her bag on the floor and coming to my side. Kelly was officially added to the list of people who have touched and felt my warmer than normal skin with a look of utmost worry. I almost felt the need to tell them to stop worrying about me, since this was all my fault in the first place.

Since when do I allow myself to go, "Hey, how about I go stand in the middle of nowhere in the pouring rain for an hour?"

Will I do it again? I think not. One time, and one time only. This will definitely not become a daily thing. I will prefer warm, fuzzy socks and oversized sweaters anytime.

"You shouldn't be out of bed," she said, frowning.

"Sorry, honey, I just needed to check on her. Thought I would cook her up some chicken soup before sending her off to rest. I didn't think it would be this bad of a flu."

"Obviously, it's much worse," Oliver said, patting my head. "I have 911 on speed dial. Click number one, and there you go!"

Everyone turned to look at Oliver. I even pulled my head up from its comfortable position of my arms. Although looking very much confused, Kelly tried not to laugh as she said, "Babe, why do you have 911 on speed dial? It's only three numbers."

He shrugged, coming to wrap his arms around her. "You could never be too careful," he said simply, kissing the top of her head.

The light chuckles from Oliver's words alleviated the tension that's been weighing down on us like an elephant trying to squeeze his big butt into a tiny can. But, as the back door opened once more, that tension came back and landed on me with full force, the puny, tinfoil can flattening with the insurmountable weight.

Because there, standing at the doorway with wide smiles and joyous laughter flowing out of their mouths, was Adrian and Kassie. Kassie leaned comfortably against Adrian's side, her hand resting against his hand that rested on her shoulder as he kept an arm around her. She looked up at him admiringly, and Adrian returned that look effortlessly.

It didn't help that Adrian was currently shirtless, hair dripping with water droplets' and a tower slung over his other shoulder. Kassie's thin throw-over was able to show the midnight blue bikini beneath. Adrian had gone swimming with Kassie as I slept in his guestroom.

Rest in peace, my precious heart. The shattered pieces have now turned into dust, just like it does in the cartoons.

Poof.

And to make matters worse than it already is (though, it's quite unbeatable already. Anymore problems and Oliver best be calling that number on speed dial number one) Thomas decided to join the happy party of two, trailing behind the duo with a wide grin on his face. Setting his eyes on us, the Cheshire cat was shining through his impossibly huge smile.

Adrian, however, stiffened as his eyes met mine, the smile vanishing as quickly as my heart did. I tried not to show any emotions as I stared at him. Obviously, a few people didn't have the same plan as me. None of the girls has met Kassie, but it didn't take long for them to figure out who it is.

"Oh, fantastic," Brynn drawled sardonically, parking herself in the seat next to me and dropping her chin on the palm of her hand.

Chase whistled, albeit looking impressed by Kassie's gorgeous looks. I almost wanted to throw up on him. Almost. "Look what the superstar brought in," he chimed, raising an eyebrow.

"Um." Kassie, looking a bit uncomfortable, stopped and shifted her eyes between all the unknown people. Well, except for me. Her eyes lit up when she caught my eye but was soon put out as she noticed I wasn't in the best shape. "Hi, Macey. Are you okay? You don't look too well." She frowned and assessed my pale features.

I forced a smile, ignoring the alarmed looking Adrian. I tried not to make a scene and make my cold seem as bad as it looks. I mean, it's just a cold right? A really bad, stomach-wrenching cold, but a cold nonetheless. Unfortunately for me, another nasty cough left me abruptly. I turned away, grabbing hold of the thermometer and coughing into my elbow.

"I-I'm fine," I choked out, waving my hand carelessly in the air. "Just a cold, that's all."

"You don't seem fine," Kassie commented, concerned. At least she was kind. Hopefully, that won't change as she goes through with living life as a star.

The need to cough only increased, so I sealed my lips shut and gave her a tiny smile instead. Oliver came to my side and took the thermometer in his hands. The look on his face said anything but good news.

"What's wrong?" Adrian asked, pulling his arm away from Kassie and rushing towards Oliver. "Is it bad?"

Oliver looked at me and put a hand on my forehead, shaking his own head in the process. "No wonder you're so warm. It's a hundred three degrees right now."

"What?" Adrian shouted. He tore the thermometer away from Oliver and held it close to his fact, as if Oliver was incapable reading it and he needed to be the one to make the final decision. His eyes held regret as he looked up at me. I dismissed it. "Macey," he breathed.

My hand twitched when he placed a hand on my forehead. I so badly wanted to slap him again, push him away and laugh in his face. If he says it wasn't what it looked like, he sure isn't helping his side of the story. I'm sure I'm not the only one with that thought.

Brynn pushed Adrian's hand away from and stood in front of me in a defensive stance. She narrowed her eyes, almost predatorily. "I don't know why you didn't see it coming. You were the one who put her in this position, anyways."

A flash of annoyance crossed Adrian's features, and he scowled. "I didn't do anything," he sneered, crossing his arms and matching Brynn's stance. "I'm not the one –"

"Who was stupid enough to walk into the rain, I know," I muttered, turning in my stool and away from him. I didn't need to look at him to know he was looking at me with dread, just as he did last night. It didn't affect me at all. He's done and said enough to get the message clear.

"Macey –"

"Don't," I snapped harshly, putting both my hands up and shutting my eyes. The caveman were starting to go all out now as my head pounded painfully.

The impatient sigh across the counter made my lips purse in anger. "Do not take your anger out on Adrian, Macey. It was your decision that you walked out into the middle of nowhere during a storm; this has nothing to do with Adrian."

"Stay out of this, Thomas," Kelly growled, scowling. "Adrian left with no word to Macey, at all."

"And that gives her the great opportunity of walking out into the rain and freeze while she could have stayed at the banquet and gotten a ride like someone in their right mind would do."

My hands clenched tightly against my forehead. The sound of his voice always annoyed me. Hearing it criticize me to the extent of my stupidity in front of several people only makes my headache worse.

"Thomas, do not start right now," Connie warned.

"All I am saying is –"

"Thomas." Oliver's loud, sharp tone made everyone flinch. Thomas shut his mouth with an audible click.

"Why are you even here?" Dylan asked with a disgusted tone. "If we knew you'd be coming, we would have been out of here by dawn."

"For your information," Thomas started, looking at Dylan in annoyance. "I am here to take Kassie and Adrian out to lunch downtown. Arthur and Tom will be there to discuss Kassie's new role. Adrian wants to take Kassie out for a tour of Miami after," he finished, grinning quite too smugly for my liking. Another wave of jealousy rattled the empty spot where my heart should be.

It's great to know that after our fight last night and knowing I was going to end up getting sick by all the rain, he arranges plans to hang out with Kassie as I lie sick in bed, coughing out a lung and writhing in pain.

"So not helping your case right now, dude," Chase whispered disapprovingly at Adrian. I scoffed. He hasn't made any attempt on setting things right besides saying the same useless words over and over again. And initiating that I'm stupid. Like I don't already know and feel even more stupid for my level of stupidity.

Stupid.

I growled quietly, squeezing my eyes shut tighter.

"Did I miss something?" The hesitance in Kassie's voice made me look at her. Extremely uncomfortable now, there was a hint of guiltiness in her eyes as she observed the scene in front of her. My shoulders hunched forward.

Kassie was a naturally sweet-hearted girl and was now being hated because of my sensitivity and jealous actions. I made the decision last night that whatever was going on between Adrian and I wasn't serious enough to continue on with, especially with a better option on the table. They're from the same world. Their passion for acting only makes their bond stronger, and I'm the obstacle getting in their way. I may have the right to think that I was cheated on, but in reality, that's not the case. And I won't allow it to, either.

Smiling as brightly as I could, I said to Kassie, "It's nothing, Kassie. Just stayed out in the rain too long and the consequences are catching up with me. Go have fun with Adrian today, Miami is a great place to visit. If you'll excuse me." Willing myself to stay upright, I stood on my feet and pushed past everyone and out the kitchen. Chicken soup or not, I wanted to go home. This thought only had me groaning when someone gripped my wrist.

"Macey, wait," Adrian demanded softly. I sighed irritably and pulled my wrist free, looking at him tiredly. The look of despair grabbed my attention. His features were tight, regret and pain swimming in his eyes. I could tell he hated this, my ignoring him and want for distance. He wanted to explain, but I didn't have the heart – or stomach – to hear whatever he has to say. Besides, he seems to have a fun day planned with Kassie. No need to hold him back because I'm pushing through a cold.

"You should go get ready," I say. "Kassie's waiting for you. You don't want to keep her waiting."

"But, I really need to explain –"

"There's nothing to say!" I snap. Then, sighing, I continue, "Stay away from me, Adrian. I don't want to hear what you have to say right now."

"How do you expect me to fix things if you won't hear me out?" his voice rose, suddenly angry.

"Hear what?" I match his tone. "How you totally ignored me last night? How you suddenly ditch me to go hook up with Kassie? How you keep pointing out how much of an idiot I am when I already know I am one? I don't want to hear it!

"It's not what you think!"

"That's all you have been saying since last night!" I yell, pushing at his chest.

A tinge of red painted his cheeks as he flushed in rage. Suddenly, he was standing directly in front of me with narrowed eyes.

"Macey, I didn't cheat on you, and even if I did happen to do something with Kassie, we're not even more than friends with benefits right now."

It was like he slapped in me the face this time. This whole endeavor made it seem like the Adrian I knew before the banquet had vanished and was replaced with this completely new stranger. Because I know, my Adrian would never say what this Adrian just spat in my face. The words hurt. They hurt like hell, piercing right through me and making my chest constrict painfully. I don't even know who he is anymore.

"You're right," I said coldly. "I have no right to feel like we were actually more than that, because we're not. One night of feeling like the Superstar you are and you're a completely different person. You said you were the same Adrian from when we were kids, but obviously that was all fake. You're exactly who I was afraid you would be." He flinched at the harshness of my words. I knew what I was going to say were going to be a whole lot worse.

"I never should have gave us a chance."

The house was strangely silent besides my erratic breathing. All the anger on Adrian's face had dissipated, replaced with a great deal of sadness, shock, and remorse. I paid no attention to the evident guilt I saw. Shouting and snapping words was no good on my soar throat, and the heat of the moment was causing the dizziness to hit me full force. My stomach rolled and crashed. Turning away, I inhaled and exhaled deeply as I tried to calm myself.

"Macey, are you –"

Whatever he was going to say was cut off when I abruptly slapped a hand over my mouth and made a dash for the nearest bathroom. The door collided with the wall as I pushed the door open with an excess amount of strength. Shouts of concern could be heard from behind me, which I blatantly ignored when I collapsed on my knees in front of the toilet and disposed everything from my stomach.

Footsteps were heard over my – much to my disgust – loud puking noises. Soon, my hair was gathered away from my face while I continued. A hand ran smoothingly along the line of my back, calming me as I came to a halt a few moments later. I only had a chance to let out a shaky breath before I started to cough fervently.

Oh, sweet Jesus. Why couldn't I have thrown up the caveman along with my dinner? Maybe then I wouldn't feel like they had set atomic bombs up in there.

I sit back on my knees, feeling the cool tile beneath the palm of my hand. Lungs still in my body, I took a moment to sit and breathe. I knew people stood at the doorway, and I know Connie was currently playing the mother roll as she stroked my hair. What embarrassed me the most was that Kassie and Thomas stood there as well, Thomas finally not showing his jackass smile at a girl who's close to death's doorstep. Like I wasn't feeling self conscious before in front of them, the last thing I needed was to puke my insides out in front of them.

I closed my eyes, embarrassed and tired. "I want to go home," I whispered.

"Sweetie, you're not in the condition to be moving. You should be in bed," Connie told me gently.

Shaking my head, I knew that wouldn't be an option. I'll feel even worse if I stay here. Maybe not physically, but I'll be an emotional rollercoaster that just keeps going down. "Just take me home." I ordered weakly. My knees wobbled unsteadily, and I gripped the corner of the counter and pulled myself up.

"I can take you home," Adrian offered, stepping forward. To say I was appalled was an understatement.

Dylan made a noise of objection. "Oh, no! You've done enough, thank you very much."

For a minute there, it looked as though he wanted to finally put his foot down and take control of the situation, demand what he really wanted to do. The end result only made me shake my head. For one glance at Kassie, and Thomas' challenging raise of the eyebrow, had Adrian tucking his tail between his legs and backing down again. Typical.

"We'll take you home," Amber murmured. "We should get going anyways."

"Are you sure?" Kelly pushed once more. She was trying to right her brother's wrongs by taking care of me, and I appreciated that. But only Adrian had the power to explain his side of the story and prove to me why I should give into his reasoning. My being sick isn't fully his fault; I had to take responsibility on staying out in the rain for too long. There is, however, more to the story than just being ditched.

"I'm sure." I nodded. Connie agreed, saying that it's best if I were to be home with my family as I couldn't even return last night. After saying that she would pack up some of her chicken soup for me to go, everyone was ushered out of the bathroom so I could clean up. The taste of vomit lingered in my mouth, so I grabbed a spare toothbrush and brushed vigorously until I foamed at the mouth, resembling a rabid animal going mad.

I returned to the kitchen feeling slightly better than I did before I had a meeting with the toilet. The girls stood with their stuff, Chase shoving a piece of fresh toast into his mouth. Kassie, Adrian, and Thomas were already gone. Sighing, I dropped back onto the stool.

"He sure doesn't seem to be in a hurry for your forgiveness," Brynn commented, taking a sip of apple juice.

"Too busy with Kassie." Chase shrugged. "I mean, she is kinda –" He stopped upon seeing the looks on our faces. He cleared his throat and shoved more food into his mouth.

"It doesn't matter." I coughed a little and dismissed the comment. It wasn't a lie, after all. I glanced at Connie, noticing how she kept silent as we verbally beat down her own son. I never thought that I would be angering her with how we've been acting. I can hear the cavemen chiding me now.

"Alrighty." Connie placed a container filled with her soup made in heaven on the counter. "All done, and make sure to drink a lot of water, as well as getting plenty of rest. I'm going to make sure Adrian doesn't come to bother you, even when it seems you have a lot to talk about."

I fidgeted in my seat. Intertwining my fingers, I looked down and allowed myself to wince as I said, "I'm sorry if this made you angry, Connie. I didn't mean to get you involved in this."

Connie pursed her lips before placing a hand on Oliver's shoulder. "Can you take everyone out into the living room while I talk to Macey?" she asked him.

Being the doting son-in-law that he is, Oliver obliged politely. "Of course." Everyone quickly swarmed out of the kitchen; the girls murmuring to themselves, Chase shoving food in his mouth, and Oliver tugging Kelly out with his arm around her waist.

Feeling uncomfortable around Connie was not common. She was the one who took care of me when my parents and Emma were unable to. Nights of mine and Adrian's rascal years often involved Connie watching over us and making sure we didn't cause too much trouble. Almost everyone has to have that one person who seems to fit the perfect position of 'second mom.'

Well, Connie's mine. She's one of the closest people I would go to if I needed motherly guidance if my mom couldn't provide it. Like, a godmother, or my mother from another family.

Sitting here, twiddling my fingers the way I did last night, I felt like the elephant decided to come back and return to his original position. The fat thing, crushing us with his fat ass on our heads, suffocating us mercilessly. Could you imagine the smell if it were true? Its weight wouldn't be the only thing suffocating you.

"I'm sorry, Connie," I said, unsure of what to say.

"This isn't your fault. Well, partly. Adrian never should have left you at the banquet last night; it was wrong. I know what kind of scenarios may have been running through your mind when you found out, but I can assure you, Macey," Connie took my hands in hers. I noted the extreme softness of her skin and wondered if mine were as baby butt smooth in comparison to hers. "Adrian does care about you," she finished in that assuring, motherly tone she's nailed through years of practice.

"It doesn't seem like it," I grumble. "It's like he was a completely different person. And earlier, what he said to me is something Adrian would have never said to me back then. It hurt, Connie."

"You have to understand that Adrian's been through a lot of changes to be where he is now. Adrian's been dreaming of becoming an actor since he was in diapers, and he was able to make it come true. But, there were some things that had to be done for him to accomplish that. It's just how the Hollywood life goes."

"Being an ass is one of those things?" I asked, a bit snarky. I felt my cheeks flush at my bluntness. "I-I mean. . . That's not what I meant," was my lame save.

Connie laughed. "I understand what you mean. All the fame has influenced how he is sometimes, but he's still our Adrian. He's still the guy that took you to the boardwalk almost every weekend. Kassie is a form of fame that brings out that influence. Adrian acts on instinct. Being famous, anything you do could grab the attention of the media and ruin everything you've been working hard for. Kassie and the banquet is a form of that fame that influences his actions. Think of it as those people, Kassie, Thomas, Cara, Arthur, Tom and whoever you met that night, being a camera lens. Adrian has the urge to put a front for the camera, and if he slips up, he thinks he's ruined the reputation he's built for himself.

"It's why we came back to Miami. Adrian was tired of always trying to make sure he did everything possible to keep living his dream. He was tired of letting people and the camera influence him. It's not something he wanted to do at the moment. The pressure was unbearable. With you, Macey, he doesn't need to do that, because he knows that you don't look at him the paparazzi or his fans do. One thing they didn't like and they would go on a judging rampage all over the media. This is the whole point of his break. To be let out off his leash and do whatever teenage boys do: Be reckless and free. Sometimes, though, they can be too reckless." A puff of air left her lips as she rested her chin and shook her head with a 'What are you gonna do?" look.

I stared at the granite countertop, letting the words process in my mind. I wouldn't go on one of Adrian's fan websites or movie trailer links on Youtube and start bashing on him when he did something stupid like haters tend to do. I didn't plan on sending the juicy details to a gossip magazine or radio segment when I got home like the paparazzi. I'll stay mad at him, slap him across the face (granted, I kind of cringe at the thought) and make him beg for forgiveness, but never go to the lengths of stopping what he loves to do.

"I understand," I said quietly.

"Good." Connie smiled and came around to pull me into a light embrace. "Do keep in mind that having you so angry with him is killing him slowly. You know how he can't have his Sweetheart mad at him for too long," she whispered in my ear, causing a blush to form on my cheeks.

Chicken soup can't heal a broken heart, but Connie sure was gifted with patching it up a bit.

Returning home later that day was a great relief. Mom and dad both had no work to attend today, making them waiting anxiously at the door with a slightly fuming Emma. Walking through the door and being attacked with hugs and apologies made me feel like I ran away from home because of the hatred I had for them. It turns out Emma went berserk with the news and dumped it on our parents the moment they walked in.

Surprisingly, dad made a comment I never thought I would hear from him. The one every protective father says for his little princess when they get hurt. My mom looked appalled when he actually went upstairs and brought down the case that held his gun inside. Emma and I found it quite hilarious and, despite my sickly state and her murderous attitude, we ended up collapsing onto the couch in a fit of uncontrollable laughter. Dad's gun was now safely packed back in its original place.

Mom did her job of taking care of me upstairs and making sure I had everything I needed. Medicine was taken, chicken soup had long been eaten, and I was still snoozing peacefully under the covers of my own bed with Lulu at the foot of my bed. Apparently, my exhaustion was more than I gave it credit more. Because the moment my head hit the pillow, I was out cold.

Before Adrian left for Los Angeles, the both of us had an ongoing and unofficial tradition. Adrian knows how I like to be as comfy as I can possibly be during my recovery period, and this involves taking out out my childhood bear and snuggling with it until I'm better. Well, since Emma was (and, sometimes, still is) an evil sister, back then, she had snuck it into one of the boxes during a garage sale as revenge for something stupid, like always throwing my bowl of mush in her face when I didn't want it. I kind of see where she's coming from when I look back, but that's not the point. Out of all the stuffed animals I had back then, she ended up getting my Daisy bear sold to the kid across the street.

Unfortunately for little me, I got sick on my birthday without the comfort of my Daisy. Adrian and I were already on the road to best friends by that time, so he ended up saving all his allowance to buy me a new bear in which I loved even more than Daisy.

That wasn't his only time, though.

Adrian begun to get me a bear each time I got sick. It wasn't often that I got sick. I wasn't the one who is present at school for one day and then gets sick for the next four days. It was a handful of times a year that I would become so ill that I felt the need for a bear to hug as I went through the motions. Big or small, Adrian got me a bear each and every time I got sick.

As much as I appreciated the thought, I told him to quit it. He was wasting his money by getting me a bear when I keep using the one he gave me all those years ago. As we got older, I grew out of the comfort bear stage and fought through the cold like a big girl. If anything, I just used one of my pillows to hug to my chest. Even then, Adrian continued with his tradition.

Most those bears were donated as Christmas gifts to the less fortunate, but I always kept Mikey – the first bear he ever got me. It sat in my closet with the other sentimental things I collected over the years. I also kept Steve, the little Koala Adrian won for me at the boardwalk the night before he left.

A fury coat coat brushed against my face, a light weight being wedged against my side. Lulu came two years after Adrian's leave, and she preferred to sleep with me on the bed. Knowing it was her, I put my arm around her and continued on with my peaceful sleep.

I woke to my clock reading five in the morning. My eyelids drooped closed again, knowing it was way too early to wake up. My body shivered at the cold temperature of my room. Why is it so cold? Quiet snorting came from behind me, and the shake of Lulu's collar chimed through my room. I felt and breathed her panting breath more than heard it. Dog breath hit the side of my face and made me cough and gag at the stench.

"Lulu," I whined quietly, pushing her face away. She made a noise. Then, I felt her pawing against the fluffy pillow I was hugging to my chest. "Lulu, no," I commanded her again. Receiving disobedience again, I willed my eyes to open as far as they could as I glared at the puppy in front of me. She whimpered, staring down at what I was holding.

You would think after all the nights she's slept in here with me that she would be used to my pillows and covers by now. Apparently, that's not the case. Huffing, I nudged her backwards before hugging the pillow closer to my chest and burying my face in it. The unfamiliar smell made my eyes crack open again.

Wait.

Gasping, my arms unwound from the object as I sat up quickly in alarm. I blinked away the sleepiness blocking my vision until I got a clear image of what I was snuggling with. What I saw was definitely a surprise.

It was a bear.

A bear I've never seen before.

Adrian.

I grasped for any memories of last night. My eyes snapped to Lulu like I expected her to explain to me what happened last night. She grunted at me. Frowning, I took the bear in my arms and held it out in front of me, collapsing back onto the mattress.

It was cute, I'll admit. The bear was soft and silky with a single touch, its tan red fur brushing through my fingers with a feather like touch. A red little rose was held against the bear's chest with his arms wrapped around. Along with its left paw, a white ribbon tied neatly against the green stem of the rose read the words: 'I love you.'

Light billowing of my curtains drew my attention to the window, and the puzzle pieces fell into place as I saw the slightly ajar window that let in the early morning air and increased the chill in my room.

In my line of vision, a small card perked itself on my bedside table. Two simple words in a handwriting I'll always be able to identify.

I'm sorry.

Chapter 26

I knew that letting the girls know about Adrian's nighttime delivery wasn't going to compare to any reactions they've had in the past when I received some kind of sweet gesture. I almost predicted the exact way they were going to handle this and, honestly, I shouldn't have expected any less.

I sat on top of my bed, not at all fazed by the way each of them were reacting. Dylan and Brynn have been spewing out threats since they walked in and saw the bear sitting on my bed, along with the two word note. Always one to handle situations with her head rather than her emotions, Amber has taken it upon herself to try and save the innocent stuffed animal from their evil clutches.

"Dylan, honestly. Put the bear down."

The girl in action scowled at Amber's pleading demand. "I'm going to do it," Dylan warned. "I'm going to throw this thing out the window."

"What good will that do?" Amber argued in return.

Her nose scrunched as she considered it. "Can I rip its head off instead, then?"

It was safe to say that neither of the girls were swayed anymore than I was. It was sweet that he remembered our bear giving tradition, but it wasn't enough of an apology after what happened. I was still suffering from the aftereffects of that night, both physically and emotionally.

"Well . . . When you think about it," Brynn began as she tore the bear from Dylan's angry vice grip, "I think it'd be better if you ripped its head off or something. Dropping it from Macey's window means it's just going to end up in the front yard. At least this way you can do some harm. Getting it dirty won't exactly make the statement you're looking for."

"Oh, come on, guys," Amber piped once more, trying and failing to save the thing from the hands of two girls whose judgement was clouded with anger and disgust.

Brynn snorted and handed the bear back to Dylan, who proceeded to pull at the arms. "You come on, Amber. This is the best Adrian can do after how he treated her? A stupid, sappy bear that says 'I love you' and a lame I'm sorry note?"

"The guy sure knows how to express his love and affection," Dylan added in a drawl. "It's going to take a whole lot more than a couple bucks spent to win Macey's forgiveness back." She turned to me with narrowed eyes. "You better not forgive him so easily, Mace."

It was my turn to snort. "The bear's cute and all, but he's an idiot if he thinks it'll win me back." I turned away as I recalled all the hurtful things that he said and done that brought us to where we were now. Completely disregarding me at the banquet before abandoning me all together to be with Kassie, his calling me stupid and degrading what we had for nothing more than just friends with benefits. Even if we weren't officially together in a relationship, the way he threw those words at me were demeaning when you factor in our feelings.

Filling the resentment for him boil up inside me once again, I scowled heatedly at the stupid excuse of a sorry. The card was still sitting on my bedside table; Dylan had nearly ripped it up if it weren't for her wanting to throw it at Adrian's face and let it fall like confetti. He couldn't even apologize to my face and instead chose to write it out in words that weren't given when I was conscious.

Brynn directed her finger at me. "See that? Adrian better be on his knees, pouring his heart and soul out. We're not going to take this."

"I doubt that would be a good idea. His feelings are confusing as hell now that he said loud and clear that he thought they were nothing more than friends with benefits, yet he kisses and holds her like she's the one," Dylan remarked. Having those words come out of someone else's mouth really harshened the reality of the fact. I rested my forehead down on my knees, groaning.

"I don't ever wanna see him again," I grumbled, feeling my chest tighten with humiliation and anger.

Amber's face twisted in sympathy. "I don't blame you," she sighed, sitting beside me on the bed. "Don't think that I'm taking his side. While I'm not going to go make threats of twisting Adrian's internal organs …" We looked at Dylan, who so vividly and dramatically laid out her whole plan before us not long after we all gathered in my room.

"I'm just really pissed at him," she replied in defense to our pointed looks.

"I'm also mad at what he did to you. We were there to see it, after all," Amber continued. "He abandoned you at a banquet he persuaded you to go to, then went on to ignore your existence while you were there. Then he practically destroys all his admitted feelings for you by saying that there was nothing more going on. I don't think you should forgive him that easily."

Each statement was a blow to the gut. "Trust me, I won't," I told them firmly.

Adrian wasn't going to be let off the hook that easily, no matter what he tried to drop off in my room next. I don't care what its cost or sentimental value is. A couple of gifts aren't going to move me. I'm not even sure if he'll be able to move me with words. And besides, the least he could do is try to make it up to me when I'm awake. His so called romantic gesture made me feel like I had an Edward creepily watching me while I sleep.

A rip tore through the room like a scream through the hair, startling me from my thoughts as I realized just how serious Dylan was about doing damage to the bear.

I scrambled towards her. "Dylan, cut it out already," I ordered, taking it away from her. There was a significantly large rip where the arm connected to the body; fluff jutted out of the fabric and hung limply from the wound. I sighed and delicately placed it on the bed, then turned towards the girls with my shoulders back.

"Let's get out of here," I suggested. "I'm not going to stay here and sulk about this, and you guys aren't going to stay here with me and plan out anymore evil plans. Why don't we go to the studio and dance like we own the damn place?" Dancing has always been an effective remedy. I could use a little spotlight routine to perk me up.

Amber laughed. "I actually own the place," she said. "And I think that would be a great idea, Mace."

"I'm in. Adrian doesn't know what he's missing – blowing off a girl who can dance so well that any guy would be turned on," Brynn boasted. Ignoring my unamused expression, she linked her arms with mine and proceeded to pull me to my closet.

A total change of plans was laid down by Emma after she saw me coming down the stairs. I was to take it easy for the day. Although I was feeling better after my day's rest, I had to opt out in joining the girls dance around. It would be a better idea if I didn't jump right into sweat-inducing dances when I still break out into the occasional cold sweat.

Being the only attendee for an audience of one wasn't too bad, anyway. It was up to the rest of them to spice up my sitting and watching so that all of us could take our minds off of this boy drama. They had nothing planned and winged everything they did. Spontaneous, random fun made for the best times, after all.

Their spotlight dance transformed into a compilation of epic fails, chalking up their performance to one of complete hilarity. All of this then led up to weird free styles along old songs we used to jam out to in middle school. Some songs remained a guilty pleasure, just as Brynn's love for One Direction, according to her, will live on until her forties. It won't be playing in the car radio, but lyrics will come back to her like sweet teenage memories if they're ever played.

Eventually, Amber went off to rummage in a storage closet at one point before returning with two long jump ropes, eliminating the desire to dance, and replacing it with us putting our double dutch skills to the test.

It were times like these where I couldn't have been anymore grateful to have such wonderful friends there to pick me up from my sorrows.

"Tapping out already?" Brynn teased as Dylan tiredly collapsed onto the floor. Brynn proved to be the most skilled out of all of us and looked as if she could keep going until the sun falls and rises. Her stamina was incredible.

Completely worn to the bone with exhaustion, she said, "I'm tapping out for the rest of my life. You've got to be a super human to keep going for as long as you have."

"Switch out with me then," Amber said, which was fruitless when Dylan was unable to pull her limbs up off the floor.

"Death by double dutch. I didn't think you'd go out that way, Dyl," I laughed and quit my job as the rope twirler. It's a real tiring arm exercise if you do it for a while. Plus adding in the common weakness that comes with being sick, I might as well have participated in all the dances with how tired and sweaty I was.

"Wow, you all bailed on me. Thanks," Brynn scoffed as Amber and I joined Dylan on the floor, who was spread out eagle style on the hardwood floor.

"Hello?"

The abrupt call coming from outside the dance room stole a startled squeak or shout from all of us. Knowing that the studio was closed and was supposed to be empty, cautious, wide eyed glances were exchanged before we realized that it was just Lucile.

"Amber!" her mom shouted. The sound of her rapid footsteps became increasingly louder.

"We're in the dance room, Mom," she called in reply, getting to her feet. Lucile came in and released a breath.

"Thank goodness you girls are here. None of you have been answering your phones!" she chastised, searching the room for our bags. They were all piled together at the far end of the room. With the constant music streaming from the speakers, any phone calls that were made while we were here were drowned out.

Amber flushed and went to retrieve her phone. "Oh." she gasped, turning to us, "I've got calls from Connie, Emma, Kelly, and your mom, Mace."

"We've been trying to contact all of you for the past hour," Lucile explained, scrolling through her phone before putting it up to her ear. I quickly went to check my notifications and cringed at how many people tried to contact me while we were here. Even Adrian called. Twice.

"Yes, they're still here at the studio," Lucile began to speak. She gestured for me to take her phone. Kelly was on the line.

"What's going on?" I asked, slightly worried with how frantic everyone tried to contact us. They should've known we would come here of all places, especially since Emma was aware of our whereabouts. Have we really been here that long?

Kelly cut to the chase, saying, "You need to come over. Right now."

The urgency in her voice threw me off guard for a moment. "Is someone hurt? What happened?" I asked again.

At those words, Brynn stole the phone and put it on speaker just in time for Kelly's response. "Nobody's hurt, but there's someone here who really wants to speak to you."

My anxiety level dropped to a flat line. "If it's Adrian then I'd rather not," I replied bitterly. It was still too early to see him, despite his trying to mend things with the teddy bear.

Kelly hesitated for a second and then said,"It's not Adrian, but it's about him and more. Kassie wants to talk to you alone."

Dylan was by my side in an instant. "That's it?" she exclaimed, taking possession of the phone. "She's a big part of this drama fiasco. You guys went out of your way to contact us just so she can have one on one time with Macey? What does she want?"

"Look, girls," Kelly sighed heavily, making me frown. "There was a big meeting that happened earlier with Kassie, Adrian, Tom, and Arthur. It's not my place to say what it was about, but Kassie really wants to speak to you, Macey."

A meeting? What could they be talking about that required Tom and Arthur to be there?

The side of me that still held hatred for Kassie suggested that they were discussing plans to make them the new power couple. The majority of me was still thinking realistically, signing the idea off as ridiculous. I won't know until I head over there, right?

Kassie was a sweet girl, from what I know. I have nothing over her except the jealousy and accusations from the night of the banquet. She wasn't the one I was mad at right now, and the least I could do was hear her out on what she wanted to say. If anything, I'll only be walking into her trying to do damage control.

"Is Adrian there, too?" I asked with a sigh. The girls knew my decision by that sentence alone. Amber's worried look was a severe contrast to Dylan and Brynn's murderous what the hell are you doing look.

"He's not here. He . . . kind of ran off after the meeting," Kelly stated slowly.

"Some meeting, huh?" It must've been pretty big if Kassie's all of a sudden requesting to have a word with me while Adrian goes off on his own.

"I'd definitely say that. Just come quick, okay? Kassie's been waiting."

I noted the graveness in her voice and hung up the phone with my stomach in knots.

If the idea of having to meet with Kassie didn't put me off enough, Thomas greeting me at the door made me want to shut the door on his face and drive away. He already looked as if he was already irritated at me, which was probably his natural face to pull since he didn't like me in the slightest. I didn't need any of his sassy, smug manager jabs right now.

"Finally you're here," he drawled, opening the door. Fortunately, Kelly was just behind him and readily pushed him to the side before taking my arm.

"Sorry to spring this on you all of a sudden. How are you feeling?" she asked, raising the back of her hand to my forehead.

"I'm fine," I assured her. "But what's with Kassie wanting to speak to me? What happened at this meeting?"

Her smile dimmed as she dropped her hand. "It accomplished to create a lot of confliction. Remember that when Kassie explains everything to you."

She led me out to the back porch where Kassie sat in one of the patio chairs. She looked just as beautiful dressed casual than when she dressed formal, yet she still had that air of elegance that made me instinctively straighten my posture.

She stood as I approached and offered me a genuine smile. "Hi," she greeted.

"Hey," I said, the initial awkwardness of being in her presence finally sinking in. To make it worse, Thomas then came out to join us and continued to take a seat. Oh, God. He wasn't going to sit in on this, was he?

It seemed that Kassie was as confused as I was. "Um, Thomas? What are you doing?"

He folded his hands together and said, "Well, I believe that I should be here to offer some professional advice. There's a lot riding on this conversation, you know?"

My eyes widened.

Kassie's frown twisted into a scowl. "I'd rather not have advice tainted with bias. I've heard enough from you today, Thomas. I'd like to talk to Macey alone."

"Adrian said you were free to go home, so why don't you go do that?" Kelly piped, aiming a dirty glare at him.

With everyone pitting against him, Thomas intelligently chose not to pick a fight with us ladies. He merely sighed and stood. "Fine," he caved. "But remember what the main objective is, will you?"

"I'll do as I so wish, no matter what you tell me the objective is," Kassie said firmly. "Now, leave."

Grudgingly following her orders, Kelly clasped her hands together and mustered a satisfied yet anxious smile of her own. "All right. I'll leave you two to talk. Oliver and I will be inside making dinner. You two are welcome to stay for dinner if you'd like."

As the door slid shut behind her, Kassie gestured for me to take a seat. "So I'm sorry that our first meeting wasn't a great one. Or the second one, at that." She grimaced as she thought back on it, and I did, too. She did see me puking in the toilet after my huge argument with Adrian.

"It must've been uncomfortable for you to stand there and watch," I said, not knowing what else to say. Yes, it was Adrian that I had a grudge against right now, but I did put possible false accusations on this girl. Kinda makes me seem like the bad guy here.

"That was a pretty tense morning," Kassie admitted, "but I don't blame you for the way you acted. I'm really sorry I stole Adrian away from you that night and that you had to walk home. He said that he would let you know that he left."

But he never did, I thought bitterly, then shook my head. "My getting sick wasn't anyone else's fault but my own. It was pouring that night, yet I still made the stupid decision to walk out despite that."

Clearly I wasn't in the state to be thinking straight if I thought I could walk all the way home in such bad weather. I was just so angry at Adrian for the way he treated me, and him abandoning me without a warning was the last shove that threw me off the cliff.

"Nothing happened that night, by the way," Kassie said hesitantly, as if she was nervous I wouldn't believe her. All the ridiculous things I'd conjured up in my mind about what this was going to be about vanished an instant, bringing humiliation rushing forward in the form of a warm blush. Of course I allowed my irrational self to jump to conclusions. "That's actually what I wanted to talk to you about, besides some other things. You remember at the banquet where it was announced that I would be starring in the new film, Through the Eyes of Willow?"

I nodded. "Of course. I didn't get to give you my congrats. The movie's expected to be a really great hit, especially with Tom and Arthur in charge."

It was such a big step going from commercials directly to the big screens; however, it could definitely be a game changer for a person's career. Adrian got his big break playing the brotherly figure of a main character after being in nothing more than small characters in random shows. Since then he's created quite a reputation as an actor and a Hollywood hunk.

"Adrian's been a really close friend of mine for maybe three years now, so he was really excited when he found out that I got the roll and was working with Arthur and Tom. I told him that I had the script back at my hotel and he wanted to go check it out. I wasn't aware that he never told you that we'd be leaving as you weren't there when we decided to leave. I figured he'd at least send you a text," she explained with an apologetic frown.

Right, so Kassie has proven that she shouldn't be under any of Dylan or Brynn's death threats.

"When I swung by here later that morning, Adrian was in a pretty bad mood since Kelly forbid him from seeing you, since you were still asleep and not feeling well. After we went for a swim and you left the house, Arthur and Tom joined us for lunch. I'd made some joking comment about the possibility of Adrian being casted alongside me in the movie, but I didn't think they'd taken me seriously. They said why not."

I rested my arms on the table and leaned forward. "They wanted to cast Adrian on the movie, too?"

She gave an affirmative nod and said, "Adrian brushed it off as a passing comment and didn't think much about it after lunch, but then we were called to a meeting today. Arthur and Tom gave it some thought over the past few days and thought Adrian would be a really great fit for my love interest." At the last two words, Kassie put her hands up and shook her head. I caught the light blush of her cheeks. "We're close, but not that close. There's more reasons as to why they think he'd be able to take on this roll."

Adrian was offered a new roll? But that would mean ...

"And what did he say?" I asked. I bit my lip and braced myself for the answer.

Judging by the expression on her face, she probably guessed what I was thinking. To take on this roll meant that Adrian would have to give up his little break. He'd have to drop out of school and move back to Los Angeles. Filming would take him all over the place.

He'd also have to leave you again.

Momentarily, the anger I felt for him dimmed until there was nothing more but a sad ache in my chest. An ache that grew prominent at the thought of losing Adrian just as I got him back.

"That's the thing," Kassie began, "Adrian looked as if he was considering it until he said that he couldn't just leave his break. It's only been a few months since he decided he wanted to move back here and he had planned to stay until graduation. Arthur and Tom understood, but were pretty disappointed. They said they'd leave the spot open for a little while just in case he wanted to change his mind. Adrian left after they did, but Thomas wanted to see if he could get Adrian to change his mind. That's why he wanted me to talk to you, but I just wanted get you on board with everything that's happening."

"Adrian had planned to stay until graduation," I murmured, my eyes dropping down to hands, "but that doesn't mean there couldn't be a change of plans."

A movie opportunity like this wouldn't be one that's lost forever. Adrian could, without a doubt, land more rolls within the span of his career.

But I knew Adrian. I knew my best friend.

Giving life to a character and personifying all its flaws, its characteristics; bringing the audience on the journey of this character and making them feel a myriad of emotions within a time span of a few hours; seeing the outcome of months of hard work and having it payoff – this was Adrian's passion. The life he dreamed of when we were kids and he took me out to the backyard with a camera and had me film his mock audition, or created silly screenplays for me to do with him.

If Adrian was considering it like Kassie said, then deep down he knows what he wants. There's just things that are holding him back, and I don't think completing high school was the reason why. He won't admit what he's truly feeling until you really sit and talk with him.

It was then that I declined Kelly's invitation for dinner and said a temporary farewell to Kassie. Neither of them had to guess where I was off to, all they needed to know was that I wasn't going home right away.

I guess Adrian and I were going to have a much more serious conversation than just making up. The hours ahead of me were going to be just as crazy as the storm I walked into a few nights ago.

Chapter 27

"Come find me, sweetheart."

Buried beneath the swarm of text messages I was receiving from the girls and my sister, that text sent from Adrian were the only words I was concerned about at the moment. If he'd taken off so quickly after the meeting, he must've went off to think on his own. I would've, too, if I had an overbearing manager hovering around, and who's persistent into getting what he wants all the time. Nobody had a clue as to where he ran off to, but I hoped that my inkling was correct. And this text was an invitation to take it.

Putting all my trust in one assumption, I turned my phone off and began to drive. I had already made a decision about what I wanted to do the minute after I drove away from Adrian's house. Everyone had mixed opinions on what I should do, but my mind was set.

The sun was nearing its complete descent as I arrived at my destination. The fading rays left a warm orange tint to the sky as it hid behind the sea's horizon. In the distance, the lights lining the entire boardwalk lit up, shining nice and bright as if some stars were out early to play. Removing my sandals, I left my feet bare and exposed as I walked onto the sand in search for a superstar in disguise. I headed east, farther from the boardwalk, farther from their bright stars, until I could no longer hear the faint laughter and conversations that mingled with the waves washing upon shore. By the time I spotted a familiar green hoodie with an old baseball cap on, I could hear nothing more than my own footsteps and the the ocean's tides.

My feet stopped on their own accord, as if my body was physically giving me a moment to pause long enough for me to know that things were drastically going to change from here on out once I sat down beside him.

This conversation was not going to be an easy one to have, but I knew my best friend.

I knew the subtle habits, hated foods, preferred fashion choices, his flaws and his quirks and everything that made him my Adrian. And you know what? My Adrian would not be Adrian without his drive to live on his passion. He thrived on passion, used it as fuel and motivation to get things done and make things happen. Coming home to Miami on a break only put him back where he was four years ago. Although he's no longer a face that so easily blended into the crowd, the Adrian then and now would never turn down amazing opportunities for him.

He came here to try and catch a break, but maybe a short breather was all he needed.

Neither of us spoke as I sat down on the sand beside him. With his face seemingly blank and neutral, his eyes said otherwise. I knew in that moment that he'd been sitting here in thought for a very long while, and that he was nowhere near a conclusion. It's that exact reason I found myself bracing myself for the inevitable results of this talk.

I pulled my knees to my chest and rested my cheek on top, saying with a voice just loud enough to hear over the water, "Do you want to do this movie?"

Straight to the point, that's how we're going to do this. His gaze never left the horizon as he drew in a breath. "Mace, you know I can't go do it. Production starts in just a few months and I'll still be in school."

"That's not what I asked you," I said. "I asked if you want to do it, not if you're available to do it."

"I'm not going to do it, if that's what you're going to try and make me do," Adrian replied, this time with a drawl in his words. "Sure it's a cool opportunity, but I'm not going to -"

"And why not?" I interrupted.

Accusation lit eyes as he finally looked at me with narrowed slits. "Do you want me to go? Is that what's going to happen here, you're going to tell me to go because you're still mad at me about Kassie?"

Is he kidding me right now?

"You idiot," I snapped, straightening with a scowl. "This isn't about me and jealousy, Adrian. Forget that for a moment and answer me truthfully, will you? What the hell kept you from taking the job when I know you want to do it?"

"It doesn't matter if I want to, I can't do it."

That right there was all I needed. He didn't deny that he wanted this, he just admitted there were things holding him back. And that's what I was here to find out.

"Why?" I continued to push. "Tell me why you can't do it. What's holding you back?"

A moment of hesitation. The fire in his eyes dimmed down, and he replied, "School, for one thing. It's been almost three months since school started, am I expected to just drop out?"

I shrugged, knowing that signing up for public school would be his first argument. It was nice getting to experience going to school with him again, but I highly doubt that attending high school for a year was the sole purpose why he couldn't take this movie roll.

"You can sure as hell drop out of school. I'm sure everyone will understand why you did it, and you're at an age where you can drop out anyway," I said with an eye roll.

His jaw locked at my valid point, but he was armed ready with additional reasons. "Okay. Well, it's more than school. What about Brandon and Chase and the rest of the girls. And is my family just supposed to up and move with me after they settled into the house?"

"Knowing your friends and family as well as you do, don't you think they'll respect and support any decision you make? I'm sure they wouldn't want to be the anchor keeping you from furthering your career," I said, believing with all that was in me that Brandon and the gang would be nothing less than psyched for Adrian. Sure, they'll be pretty bummed that he's leaving, but what kind of friends wouldn't cheer on their friend when he's been offered an opportunity like this? As for Connie and Dave, there's no way those two wouldn't do the same for their son. Doesn't he realize how much support that's behind him on this?

The conflictions returned as I shot him down. He scowled and said, "If I didn't know any better, you're actually encouraging me to go."

But I actually was. I wasn't the only one who didn't want to feel like I was anchoring him here.

With a sigh, I reached over and shook him by the shoulder, as if rattling him a bit would make him see this situation better. "Don't you get how happy I am for all that you've accomplished in a matter of four years? Or how extremely proud I am to know that my childhood best friend is the main lead in a movie everyone is in line to see? You're an international heartthrob. A rising star hopping from one big movie to the other. That was the dream, wasn't it? The reasons we found ourselves outside in the backyard with a camera and hand written scripts?"

"You're not going to fool me with anymore of your crap reasoning," I surged on, turning my body so I can look at him. "You used to dream about being casted for such an amazing roll, and I hardly doubt school and friends and family are the reason you would turn away. You're being put in the same situation you were four years ago, and you took the opportunity. You know each and every one of us would support you to the end with this, just as we did back then, so what's the real reason you told Arthur you wouldn't do this?"

My words were enough to shoot down any other arguments he had in mind. The two biggest excuses I knew he would use was school and loved ones. But for someone who can easily drop school and had immense support behind him, there was definitely something more holding him back.

He still looked reluctant to tell me. "Why does it seem like you're here to force me to go?" he asked, rewording the same question he asked me just moments ago.

"I'm not trying to get rid of you because I'm still angry about what you did, which I still am." Adrian nodded, as if he expected that the bear wouldn't sway me. "I'm not going to force you to go either, but I'm here to tell you to follow what you really want to do. I know you want this, yet you won't tell me the real reason as to why you won't take this."

"The real reason?" He shoved his hands through his hair with a groan. "I already told you the reason and the reason is the friends I've made in such a short time. It doesn't feel right leaving so soon after I just got here. It's like I'm turning back on my word on you and on everyone, cutting our time short to do all these fun stuff. As much as I want to take this roll, it feels too early to leave you guys."

I couldn't help but smile, one that came out a bit wistful. No matter how mad he might've made everyone, he still put his friends before his career. I still stood by my previous rebuttal, but it died on my tongue as Adrian blurted out, "And what about us?"

I sucked in a breath. "Us?"

"I might've screwed everything up when I said we're nothing more than friends with benefits but, dammit, Macey, I hope you know that wasn't true. You mean so much more to me than that, and I'm sorry for how I treated you."

I looked away. Whether his apology managed to move me or not, it wouldn't change anything.

Right now, I was thinking about the future. Let's say Adrian did stay for the year, but when we all leave for college after graduation, he will end up leaving for California, anyway. Being together long distance will only be further complicated given the success in his career. Could we really make it given all that?

I squeezed my eyes shut as I said in a weak voice, "Adrian …"

"I'm sorry," he said again with earnesty, "I'm sorry for how I've been treating you, but I -"

"Adrian," I interrupted, shaking my head. His mouth tightened, and we both knew what I was going to say. I took his hand, squeezing firmly, and pressed a kiss to the back of it. "You were right, saying that right now isn't a good time to be with you. And whether or not you decide to leave isn't going to change that. I can't, Adrian … I can't be with you, not now."

It was difficult, trying to say words that I've been trying to swallow. It did not just hurt him, but it hurt me, too. This was all physically painful, with a strong anche blooming within my chest as I watched recognition and disappointment mix together on Adrian's face. But the complications and indecisions that came with our possible relationship were hurting us more than benefiting us, and I knew, truly, that I couldn't be with him. Our circumstances hindered so much.

"Listen," I continued, pressing my free hand to his cheek, "whatever you choose to do, and no matter what label is put on us, it's not going to change the fact that I will be there on the opening premiere of your movie. I'm your best friend before everything and anything else, who's going to support you in whatever you do. Always."

"I know that," he murmured. He closed his eyes to hide the emotions in his eyes, yet when he opened them a moment later, they were filled with only resolve. "I love you, Macey. That's not going to change no matter what."

"I love you, too. Back then, right now, and in the future. That's not going to change."

I wrapped my arms around his waist, and he slid his arm around my shoulders. I smiled at the familiarity. I realized in that moment that this - just sitting and enjoying each other's company was enough for me. Friendly not romantic, I was okay leaving us the way we were.

Sometimes, a crush may just be a crush. Not all of them can transform into something more, but for some it may become something much more different than how one wants it to be. Adrian and I will always be best friends before romantic interests, and that's the one thing that we'll hold close to us. It's the foundation our friendship has left that will always strengthen our bond, no matter the miles.

"Hey." With an encouraging smile, I repeated the same thing I told him back when he was buzzing over his first role: "Go get 'em, superstar."

The buzz still lived. "I will," he said.

Epilogue

Trying to tiptoe around your friends in the darkness proved to be a lot harder than I thought. It was like a game of avoid the lava and my friends' bodies were the lava spread out across the living room floor. They were all fast asleep, though I wouldn't be too surprised if either of them were awake considering how loud Chase was snoring near the couch. My reasons for being up at four in the morning, however, wasn't the tremulous snoring. It was the digital clock reminding me of how close we were to morning, and how close I was to losing my best friend.

Yesterday was Adrian's last night here in Miami, and in just two hours he'll be leaving for California.

Was it selfish of me, I thought to myself as I concentrated on not stepping on anybody's legs, to wish that time had gone slower, just so I could have him around for a little longer?

Safely making it across without waking anybody up, I carefully removed a spare blanket from the arm of a couch and wrapped it around myself, protecting myself from the early morning cold. Adrian was fast asleep on that couch, and after a spare glance at his peaceful face, I padded upstairs to my room.

Just hours before, dread and happiness were battling it out in my stomach. The whole gang got together one last time, each of them probably filled with the same feelings I was. Emma was having her own night with Kelly and Oliver, as they would be heading to LA with Adrian for a little while as moral support. With my parents at work, I had the house to myself and was opened my doors to my friends so that we can spend Adrian's final hours together.

There'd been much anticipation for the day's festivities; however, the whole reason they were happening in the first place brought an onslaught of hidden depression that neither of us expressed.

That feeling lingered and worsened throughout the day. Well, for me, at least.

It was always at the back of my brain as joy became the blaring emotion, brought out by the gigantic stacks of pancakes in the morning, the unpredicted dance party at lunch, and the all around night fun we had at the beach before returning back to my place.

The fun was supposed to continue till daybreak when we would drive Adrian to the airport off with only good feels spurring us through our exhaustion. We should've known that the energy burned throughout the day would tire us to the core.

Nonetheless, we'd stayed up for as long as our bodies allowed it. But then the girls crashed by midnight and the guys followed two hours after. I alone was the only one who didn't knock out. My complete and utter exhaustion payed no heed. My mind was too busy. My chest was somewhat hurting. My stomach had butterflies that weren't the ones I wanted.

I sat by the window and drew the curtains open, sighing. There was no streaks of light in the sky yet. I knew, though, that the second I saw just a hint, it would heighten how I was currently feeling. I didn't need a clock to tell me how close I was to losing him, it was written in the skies.

Outside my closed door, Lulu's nails tapping against the floor as she neared caught my attention. I quickly went to open the door for her, hoping my friends were deep enough sleepers not to notice her footsteps, and froze as Adrian stood before me. Lulu brushed past my leg as she entered.

Of all people to be a light sleeper . . .

I didn't know what to say. "Um, morning?" tumbled out of my mouth.

Though his hair was disheveled with sleep, his eyes said other-wise. He looked just as awake as I was.

His mouth quirked up into a half smile. "Not tired either, huh?"

Believe me, I am, is what I really wanted to say, but I refrained and shrugged instead. "Did I wake you up when I left the living room?"

"No." He was careful to keep his voice low even as he shut the door behind him. "I was awake when you got up."

"How come you're still awake?"

"Ah, well same to you, too, sweetheart," he said, sitting by the window. "So, since we're both apparently up, let's trade a penny for our thoughts, yeah?"

I joined him on the seat and pulled my knees up to my chest to give him some room. I was rather reluctant to trade thoughts, but I think we both knew why the other one was up.

"What time is it?" I asked.

"Time to spend some quality time with my best friend before I leave her."

I cocked my head. "Is this the type of quick, smooth talk answers that get girls to fall at your feet and do as you wish? Not gonna work on me."

He shrugged with a smirk, a classic Adrian response. "It'll be a lot easier for you to deny me over the phone."

"You'll have barely any time to contact me," I retorted and almost winced at the bitterness in my voice. It was too late to cover it up, so I looked away.

That was the thing, wasn't it? In the back of my head, I'm truly afraid that this loss of contact will dissipate our close friendship. It happened the first time he left and it wouldn't be too surprising for it to happen again. But no matter how much I wish he'd stay around for a bit more, that wouldn't stop me for giving him my complete and utter support. It's easy to see how excited Adrian is to be getting back out there after his break.

I've noticed that he's tried censoring his excitement for the sake of being considerate, which was a kind but unnecessary gesture. As sad as it is to see him go, I wasn't kidding around when I said he had my full support. I'd listen to him talk about his job for hours if it came down to it. Acting has been a dream of his ever since he was a kid – something he's shared with me through the skits and homemade films we videotaped in our backyard, sets we'd set up around the house, improv sessions at the park. So it was an incredible thing to see him climb up from humble beginnings to grand success.

Even so, this wouldn't make losing him any easier.

"Mace ..." he began softly, but I stopped him with a shake of my head.

"I didn't mean to say it like that, and I don't want this to end on a bad note. Yesterday was a lot of fun and that's what I want to think back on in terms of your last day."

I was half-expecting to find a mass of people from school gathered at my front door for some kind of party. Everyone knew that Adrian would be dropping out in order to pursue the roll. Suffice to say, his last day was kind of a big deal. Adrian was showered with goodbyes and good lucks from the student body, many of whom come to recognize him as a regular guy. His leaving only reminded them just how big of a deal he really was. With the principal announcing over the intercom how grateful we all were to have him join us this school year and everyone was wishing him the best of luck, it was one hell of a send off.

Fortunately, things went to according to plan and I didn't have to host a massive goodbye party. I'd choose our close knit kind of party anyday. A lot of nice memories were made, I didn't want to ruin that by having a last minute cry on Adrian's shoulder a few hours before he was leaving. It all seemed contradictory, in a way, yet it was understandable.

Happy but sad. Wanting him to go but wanting him to stay.

My thoughts weren't doing much to keep the tears at bay. Soon, I found myself wrapped tightly in his strong arms, my face pressed against his shoulder, and fresh tears seeping onto his shirt.

"I'm just really going to miss you," I managed to say, my words sounding almost like an incoherent whimper.

"And you think I won't miss you?" he said, stroking back my hair. "Leaving Miami. . . It means I'm leaving a lot behind. This is my home. This is where my friends are. This is where you are. And, look." As he gently pulled away, I was forced to meet his eyes. It held firm determination in them, and even more so as he said, "I promise it won't be like the first time. I will keep contact. I'll come home."

Now initially, that promise would've done wonders to comfort me. But the thing about promises is that it holds exactly what you want to hear at that moment, and a person can promise you whatever you desire just to provide you with ease. It's only temporary until that promise is broken. It always smart to remember how easily a promise can be broken as it was made.

"Please don't do that," I said. "It'll only make it worse when you don't keep it. Don't promise me things."

Adrian shook his head firmly. "But –"

"No," I said again. I didn't want that disappointment.

He pressed his lips together. "Fine, then I'll make that promise to myself. That way, I won't be breaking it to anyone but me. But just know that I fully plan to keep this promise, which I'm making to me, Adrian Chapman."

"But also," said a new voice that came muffled through the door. "You could totally make that promise to me, because I'd totally get on a plane to come kick your ass if you don't come back and visit us."

The door opened to reveal Chase giving Adrian the look. The others, all decked out in their pajamas, stood behind him, sharing the same expression.

Adrian laughed. "Man, I give you full permission to give me a good whoop if I let myself get carried away with all this Hollywood stuff."

"Hell yeah I will." Chase grinned, cracking his knuckles for good measure. "Gotta keep you humble, you know?" He turned and slapped Brandon on the stomach, saying, "Help me out when it happens, okay?"

"No doubt," Brandon answered, throwing his arm around Brynn. Unlike Adrian and I, their relationship was still going strong. "The girls can come, too."

Dylan glared at him. "This is your warning, Adrian. Get a big head and we'll beat it down until you come to your senses."

Amber grimaced and put her hands up. "I don't think I'll beat him."

"I will," Dylan snorted.

Adrian smiled at each one of them. "Deal."

By the time strokes of color in the sky became painted with sunset orange, the seven of us had taken advantage of the extra time we've been given by waking early, and it was time to bring Adrian to the airport.

The Chapman family and Daniels family arrived at my place early so we could all go together. Saying goodbye at the airport felt like a repeat of our goodbye four years ago, just with twice the crowd and triple the emotion.

Knowing I couldn't hide my tears for the life of me, I let them fall and laughed as I did. Brynn and Amber were doing the same, and the three of us made quite a blubbering mess.

"Aw, come on now," Brandon hushed, never one for dealing with tears.

Dylan gathered us into a group hug. There was a crack in her own voice as she said, "Yeah or you'll make Chase cry. Just look at him."

He scowled at her, but didn't have the heart to tease any of us. Soon, I found myself surrounded by bodies as I was pressed into the center of a group hug by even the guys.

Amber, who sounded right next to me, whimpered and said, "We're going to miss you Adrian."

Adrian's voice came from behind me. "I'm going to miss you guys, too. And whether or not you believe me, I'm going to keep that promise I made to myself. There's no way I – or you guys, for that matter – will allow me not come to home once in awhile."

"Yeah," Brandon snorted, "or we'll come for you. Don't think we won't beat your fancy ass, all right?"

As the group dispersed on a much lighter note, Connie announced that it was time for them to head in. We gave our individual hugs. My heart clenched as I said goodbye to Connie and Dave, then when Kelly gave me a bone crushing hug.

"We'll be back in around three weeks after things settle down, okay?" she said as Oliver stepped in for a side hug. Then Adrian came up and held me for the longest time.

"I know you didn't make that promise to me," I murmured, "but I really hope you keep it."

His arms tightened. "I will, sweetheart," he said, and kissed me one last time. It was the first time he'd done it since that day on the beach when he made his final decision. I had a feeling that this kiss held some unspoken words; it'd have to wait until later down the road.

Although the line between was blurred, Adrian was my best friend before he was my first love, and what went down between us was for the best. Maybe there could be something in the future, but I was focused on the now.

The pain in my chest would linger for a while. Chase was the first to speak as he and his family disappeared into the airport. "Don't worry guys, we'll see him soon enough."

Amber sniffled and wiped her nose with her sleeve. "When?"

I smiled. "We'll see him on screen on the night his movie premieres, obviously," I said, wrapping an arm around her neck. "And you know what? We're going to be the most proud people there."

But the thing is, we already were.